A VERY PRIVATE HIGH SCHOOL

Mar Preston

A VERY PRIVATE HIGH SCHOOL

Mar Preston

Pertinacity Press, 2015

ॐ

Mar Preston
A Very Private High School/Preston – 1st edition

ISBN-13: 978-0-9844952-5-2

ISBN-10: 0-9844952-5-8

ACKNOWLEDGEMENTS

I am grateful to the Santa Monica Police Department and in particular, Lieutenant Richard Lewis who has been kind enough to answer many impertinent questions about the department. The Citizen Academy program was my introduction to police work, and Santa Monicans for Renters Rights my first taste of grassroots politics. Both have become abiding passions. I ask the Department to overlook any procedural mistakes or omissions. I try really hard to get it right.

My thanks also go to Sergeant Derek Pacifico of the San Bernardino County Sheriff's Office. Sergeant Pacifico gave me a foundation on police procedure and has been a personal inspiration. I am also grateful to Sergeant Mark Brown of the Kern County Sheriff's Department for a view into the inner workings of rural policing.

My editor, Jenny Jensen, was a collaborator and invaluable critic in delving into the heart of this book and helping me to make it as good as it could be. I marvel at her skills. Special thanks to proofreader Mary Goss. It is nearly impossible to find errors in your own work. There is a tendency to be so involved in the content that your mind overlooks inaccuracies in typos and the finer subtleties of grammatical structure.

A story told to me by Abby and Jeremy Arnold was the spark for this book. I wish that their story of a private high school had ended so neatly.

I thank my BFF's Gita Nelson and Leslie Bricker for agonizing with me every step of the way. They support me and provide comfort in ways they hardly realize.

The Phoebe Windsor Academy is a star among the glitterati of Southern California's exclusive private schools. Perched on ten acres in the old industrial section of the storied beach community of Santa Monica, the campus, with its leafy trees and lush grounds, has provided the best academic record money can buy for the third, fourth, and now fifth generation of the sons and daughters of Southern California's rich and powerful - as well as the striving upwardly mobile. The Academy also boasts a commendable roster of scholarship students who have gone on to achievements far grander than their background would predict.

Senator Bailey Ralston, Craig Knight, CEO of Kensington Industries, Michelle Philpot of the trendy fashion empire, Jules Greenhood, VP of Engineering of Lockheed-Martin's jet division, Hannah Beals of the multi-million dollar .coms, not to mention Rhys and Caroline Kensington, descendants of the founder, represent a fraction of the successful alumni.

Steeped in the caring, nearly one-on-one atmosphere of the cramped, damp classrooms, the students consider the Windsor Academy as the best time in their lives. Alumni take pride in the decaying 1940's bungalows; wifi is available, instruction is cutting- edge technology and the students and alums proud, nearly smug, about their institution. Funky is the new Ivy League; a little deprivation on amenities adds to the cachet. From this endearingly shabby campus, Phoebe Windsor Academy sends forth the best Southern California, and particularly Santa Monica, has to offer.

Old Mr. Kensington, as he was fondly known, set up the institution to honor the memory of his wife, Phoebe Windsor, a life-long educational advocate. Funded by the Kensington Trust with the oversight of a stellar board of directors, the school is poised to continue its coveted educational tradition well into the 21st century.

California Style Magazine, July 2015 issue

The threats to the Academy began when Leonard Bricker, current Chair of the Board, was jogging on a balmy summer night along 26th Street. A speeding car ended the life of a tidy man of rigid beliefs, personal discipline, and solid sense of responsibility.

1

Sunday, August 1, 10:30 p.m.

Mason caught the report of a traffic fatality on the radio as he was headed home after dropping his daughter Haley at her mother's house. The weekend had been refreshing and he was hoping his high spirits would linger. But there was nothing to go home to, and he probably wouldn't sleep anyway, so he got off the Santa Monica Freeway at the Bundy exit and turned north heading into the industrial section of Santa Monica. Traffic fatality. What poor bastard had been alive, tooling along, going somewhere, thinking his own thoughts, and then was suddenly dead?

This particular fatality wouldn't be his case. Ahead the red and blue light bars on the patrol units strobed near the 26th Street exit from the Bergamot Arts Station, the big lights already set up to illuminate the scene. Mason turned the engine off, and sat a moment watching.

Deputies were already moving bystanders on. The looky-loos had begun to drift away. Car doors slammed.

He got out and walked toward the scene, expecting to see two vehicles which had pranged into each other. Incidents involving cars and people had grown a lot more important to him lately.

No collision. The victim must have been a pedestrian. Only police and emergency vehicles. A two-ton vehicle versus the carapace of the human body made of bones, tendons, and muscle. No contest. Traffic was blocked off. Mason moved through the phalanx of cops, faces turning to glance at him. Somebody said, "Hey Dave," and there was a slap on the back.

Chuck Palmer, the traffic investigator, was directing the show. Under the glare of the high-intensity lights, Chuck's big square teeth shone with a yellow sodium glow. The crinkles at the corners of his eyes faded in the light and he looked hard and grim. Mason stood at the edge just watching. The coroner's death investigator was there, and they were about to roll the victim. At this point in his career Mason had seen a couple of hundred dead bodies, dead by one misadventure or another, mostly just plain died-dead, but the sight still affected him. The widely-spaced streetlights sent out pools of illumination in the deep darkness that lay between them. The surroundings were bathed in a liquid coating of darkness. A slight breeze shook the trees with a shiver of something late night and secretive.

A white-haired man in jogging pants and a white T-shirt lay crumpled in an unnatural fold at the base of one of the eucalyptus trees lining the street. He'd hit the tree hard with a shoulder that had taken the force of the impact. A clavicle tenting the material of the T-shirt was covered in blood that still glistened in the big lights. So it hadn't happened all that long ago. The blunt force injuries would probably be internal, so there wouldn't be all that much blood.

"Got an ID?" Mason said to one of Palmer's team.

"Yeah, lives a few blocks away. This one's going high profile. He was a big executive at Kensington Industries."

The paramedic assisted the coroner's investigator, Ruthie Grimsby. Mason's heart jumped a little seeing her breezy small figure. Ruthie was fun and he remembered her from a case he'd worked a few months ago. He also remembered a photo of her and what she called her two kids, a pair of Irish wolfhounds sitting next to her on a couch, dwarfing her.

"Easy, easy, guys, I want him in one piece," she said quickly, looking over her shoulder and spotting Mason.

"Hey, handsome," she said. "What're you doing here?"

"Caught the report," he said, stepping back a bit. "I'm just on my way home."

"Hey, hang out a while. We'll have coffee."

"How are your wolfhounds?" Mason said to give himself time before answering Ruthie who was looking at him, her head cocked waiting for his answer. He knew asking about the huge dogs would distract her.

"Beautiful," she said, her face creasing with pleasure.

"Maybe, Ruthie. Long as it's not too late. I gotta get up in the morning." Mason knew from experience all the measuring, and documenting the scene with digital and video would take hours. Any outdoor scene had its own complications, especially in the darkness. In Santa Monica just over the past year, traffic collisions involving impaired drivers/riders added up to about one hundred collisions, leading to three deaths and twenty-eight injuries.

Palmer and one of his guys bent beside the body, now turned on its back, the head tilted, mouth open, eyes showing white. Palmer stood up, glanced at Mason, and screwed up his face in deep thought. He left the body to the coroner's investigator and walked a few feet away into the roadway, looking for skid marks, acceleration marks, anything to determine how some vehicle and this old man had intersected.

Palmer was muttering to himself, hunkered down again beside the body.

Mason told Ruthie he'd call her, knowing he wouldn't. He was working a rash of car jackings involving high-end autos taken late at night from idiots leaving bars drunk and flashing around a lot of money. Some of the jacked cars were transported to Mexico. Getting a line on where they were going hadn't been easy, and he was still working the streets along with the Auto Theft detail. His street informants were cagey, and he didn't trust any of the intel he was getting. The jackings became his case when a theft had become an assault.

And it had become personal when he'd made the mistake of getting too involved, even though it wasn't his case. Not that he'd crossed the line, but he thought about Andy Klepper way too much. He and Andy had tomcatted around years ago when they were both single. A cop, a firefighter: rivals, compatriots, and pals who knew the dark side of Santa Monica. Marriage and children had headed them in separate directions.

A bungled carjacking had left Andy Klepper with a head injury that made him confused and combative. First he'd lost his accounting job at California Chicken, and in an incident he didn't even remember, he hit his wife Judy so hard he'd broken her shoulder. A formerly happy marriage had turned sad and precarious and there were the three little kids. The jackers wanted the Klepper's new Camry and they just took it, leaving Andy Klepper gazing out into a world he couldn't comprehend. The situation Judy had been left in haunted Mason. He couldn't even bear thinking about the kids. Samantha was his daughter Haley's age. Every time he thought about the car jackers, he cursed to himself. On his own, he monitored all the 415 disturbance calls to the condo on Idaho Street asking for help in getting Andy calmed down. He visited as often as he could make himself go.

Friday morning he slid into a booth at Huston's where a bunch of the detectives from the Santa Monica Police Department met to bullshit and kick around cases. Fredericks, who was assigned to him when he had a big case, was there in her drab beige suit. She dressed in beige in an attempt to tame down the impact of her orange-red frizzy hair. Not much could dampen her high-voltage personality. He liked working with Fredericks, even though she was annoying. He'd found himself telling her things as they worked out next to each other in the gym at the station. Things about Ginger and their breakup that he meant to keep private just slipped out when she was running on the treadmill next to his. He had to talk to somebody; it was always easier talking to a woman, even Fredericks who could never be accused of playing her femininity.

Chuck Palmer, the investigator who'd been in charge of the hit-and-run fatality last Sunday was there as well, back to his usual self, looking refreshed and boyish.

"So what have you got so far, Chuck, on the hit and run?" Mason said, acknowledging the other detectives with a smile and taking a seat next to Palmer. "Is this one going to break easy?"

Chuck ran a hand through thick, sandy hair. "Ah, who knows? The victim's one of the good guys, and all his friends want to help us. So it's not like chasing down some banger, getting witnesses to roll over. You realize how many cases I already got?"

Mason put on a mournful face and swiped a finger under his eyes as though he was wiping away tears. "Poor, pitiful, pathetic you."

"Mason, you didn't used to be an asshole."

"Yeah, I was." Mason felt bad for a second, but then thought about his own caseload.

"Saw your old girlfriend last week," Palmer said. "The commie."

"She still out there declaring war on capitalism?" Mason tried not to show interest in any news involving Ginger. It was too painful. She reminded him of having fun and feeling alive.

"Even now when she's got the rich boyfriend."

"Oh yeah? Who's that?" he said despite himself. He knew it was inevitable after the last six months.

"Rhys Kensington, heir to the Kensington fortune."

This was no surprise to Mason. Kensington had been after Ginger for years. Shadowing her was easy as Ginger's best friend was his sister Caroline. "Well, good luck to him. She's a handful."

"Word says she's got a job at that school, the one my victim was involved in, that private high school."

"The Phoebe Windsor Academy?" Mason stopped stirring his coffee.

One of the other detectives from Property Crime waved his arm in the air signaling for the waitress. Fredericks bounced up and went to the coffee station and brought back the pot and poured a refill for all of them at the table. The waitress glared at her.

"Hey, I could see you were busy," she hollered over her shoulder at the waitress as she took the pot back to the coffee station.

Palmer got to his feet and threw bills on the table. "We got a witness down the street who used to see Bricker every night. Bricker would be running more or less in the middle of the street and then he'd get over to the curb when there was a car coming. When we got some good daylight, we could see the acceleration marks where the car speeded up to hit him. Besides that there were no fresh skid marks. This might not have been an accident. I gotta run my numbers, do some thinking. But hey, we've got a good lead. The right headlight bezel, that thing that keeps the headlight in place, came off and we found it. It's got a part number in it."

"So what's that mean? You can trace it back," Mason asked, leaning back at the waitress brought him his breakfast. He smiled up at her.

"Well, it won't take us right up to the front door, but we're a ways down the road once we track that down with the manufacturer. How you doing with the carjackings?"

"I've got a young guy on the job a year and, man he loves cars. A real motorhead. Talk the ears right off your head."

"Oh yeah, what's his name?" Palmer said.

"Trevor Robinson. You know him?"

"Know him? He's willing to move in with me, do the dishes, and walk the dog for a spot on my team."

Back in the cubicle farm that passed for a squad room at the Public Safety Building, Mason regarded his old friend and longtime partner. Delgado was already looking as though he'd just been dragged through hell by the ankles, having trailed his tie through a plate of huevos rancheros at breakfast. Delgado refused to buy new suits because he said he might take retirement at any time. His mother-in-law had run out of money, and it was now either take her in again, or let her go to an even more terrible nursing home that dealt with Alzheimer's victims. Delgado didn't seem all that upset about working beyond his retirement date; the veteran detective loved the chase and capture as much as he did. Mason figured lack of stress would kill him.

One black hush puppy propped on the edge of his desk, Delgado tipped his chair back reading field reports and making notes. He gave his pen an amazed look and shook it to get it writing again. Sensing Mason looking at him, he lifted his arms and laced his fingers behind his head.

"This kid?" Mason said. "Robinson? He's smart, but just coming up on a year on patrol. He gave me a line on two guys who started up a new car lot down on Lincoln near Venice."

Delgado humphed and went back to reading. Then he looked up again. "Why don't you make it up with Ginger? I saw she left you a message. I don't think it would be all that hard."

"Yeah, we talked for about three seconds. She just wanted a phone number."

"She couldn't call Information? Sure that's all she wanted?"

"Why don't you butt out? I got somebody on the line that would be a lot easier to deal with than Ginger."

"Just sayin'. Judy Klepper came by again. I told her you'd call her later."

Judy Klepper was his old firefighter pal's wife, both of them now the victims of the carjackers who had taken their Camry. Mason couldn't face calling her yet so he thought about Ginger instead, slumping into his chair and calling up his email. It was a lie about finding somebody else. He kept running into nice women. They were all over the place. He and Ginger were at an impasse, and nothing about the issue had changed. Why talk to her?

In the meantime he was doing pickup basketball with guys in their twenties to get rid of an incipient gut.

His legs ached for days afterward, but it passed the evenings. He was glad that he had a couple of court appearances that didn't require any thinking. Just yes sir, no sir, I was there sir, that's my signature sir. Working with an Assistant District Attorney he'd come to like, they'd put together a case against a rapist slimeball that was rock hard. It did him good to see that some of the fuck-weasels he arrested actually made it to court and had a long bus ride to prison afterward. This guy would have sold his grandmother's coochie. See how he liked to be raped. Mason shot the cuffs of his best suit and gathered his notebooks, preparing to walk over to the courthouse next door.

2

Ginger McNair spotted Venetia Sorensen, the headmistress of Windsor Academy, and technically, her new boss. She'd heard the stories about Sorensen. Among the grey suits in the colorless boardroom, Venetia glittered like a strobe light in a club at midnight. Of course, she would be at the special board meeting following Leonard Bricker's death. She loomed over a smaller man twinkling, talking and talking and talking, her body in eager, graceful animation. Like a dancer, she flung her arms out, bracelets jangling, long neck arched. Watching her, Ginger recalled long-ago ballet classes. Her first real heartbreak in life was the discovery she had the wrong feet for a ballet dancer. And then she got too tall. Sigh.

Ginger watched Sorensen work the room, spinning from one board member to another looking for information and assurance, her skirts swirling around her.

Sorensen had been headmistress of the school for three years, ever since her father had died. With a genius for promotion and publicity, she had positioned the school almost at the height of Los Angeles' private high school community. Not quite Crossroads and Westlake School, but close. Or so it was said. Every year she took out a full page ad in the *Los Angeles Times* trumpeting the high SAT scores and the number of students who went on to Ivy League Schools.

Ginger was trying to like her. She had been contracted to raise money for the school and handle their public relations. The Windsor Academy was the special project of Kensington Industries, set up by Caroline and Rhys's grandfather and named after his wife, their grandmother Phoebe Windsor. Rhys and Caroline Kensington had urged her to attend today's meeting to deal with Leonard Bricker's death.

Venetia fluttered her fingers at Ginger as she approached, holding an intent conversation with one of the Kensington Industries executives who sat on the board of the Windsor Academy Foundation. The board members, mostly men, were filtering into the conference room at the Industries' prime location in Santa Monica's industrial section. The area had long ago morphed from light manufacturing to post production houses and CGI studios.

Venetia broke off her conversation, turned and saw Ginger. Coming closer, Ginger was hit by a wave of Opium that almost buckled her knees.

"Oh, Ginger, isn't it awful about Leonard?" Venetia favored tops that clung to her small breasts and full skirts that were either very short or very long. They were cinched in at the waist so that they swirled around her. She looked good, very good, for a woman in her forties. The air around her buzzed with a flamboyant energy.

"First Harry died and now Leonard Bricker," she said breathlessly, her eyes huge with excitement. Her hair was a flyaway, silver spiked cut above a chiseled face with bright blue eyes.

"Who do you think will be the next chair of the board?" she said, lowering her voice confidentially.

"Venetia, I'm new here. I'm still trying to understand everything."

Ginger made her face blank and tried to forget all the stories she'd heard about Sorensen—the hirings, the firings, the meltowns, the bitchery, the promises, the betrayals. The rumors about her large and various sexual appetites. She was going to get along with her new boss, no matter what. Jobs in her field were not plentiful; still, she'd still thought long and hard about taking on a contract funded by her boyfriend, Rhys Kensington. Sick of networking and sending out resumes she had signed the generous contract, knowing it wasn't a good idea to involve business and pleasure.

"Well, I'm just so glad you're here to help me," Venetia gushed. "I just know you and I are going to be besties."

"Besties?"

"You know, best friends? We have so much in common." Sorensen was tanned with the appearance of the windblown worshipper of extreme outdoor sports.

"Hunh?" Ginger said in surprise. "Well, sure. I guess. You know what would really help me are those financials I sent you an email about. I need to prepare a donor packet so we can jump on raising major donations. Donors are generous people, but they're smart about money and they want to see the facts and figures."

"I can't think about that now. Poor Leonard." Sorensen wiped away sudden tears with a very pretty handkerchief.

Ginger hadn't seen a lacy handkerchief in quite a while. Venetia Sorensen must be one of those people who could go from euphoria to tears in a nanosecond. "You must have been close."

"Oh, you can't imagine. Next week, I promise. It's just been crazy with the new semester beginning, students, ensuring tuition is paid up." She reached forward and rubbed the fabric of Ginger's red sweater between her fingers. "Cashmere. Nice. Where'd you get it?"

"Um, I forget." She knew perfectly well. Caroline Kensington did a periodic closet purge and Ginger wasn't too proud to accept rejects.

"Can't have too many cashmere sweaters. Let me see the label." Fortunately, Ginger saw Rhys waving over Venetia's shoulder and jerked away from her prying fingers. The nerve of her, looking for the label. "Rhys is calling us in. We should go."

Rhys Kensington, the Vice-Chair of the Foundation Board, had taken a chair at the head of the long mahogany conference table as Ginger came in. He had pursued her it seemed forever, even during the time she had been involved with Dave Mason and all his cop business.

⚜

So this was the fundraiser Rhys Kensington was shoving down her throat. Venetia Sorensen took in the tall confident woman at Kensington's side, the one said to be Caroline Kensington's best friend. Okay, she was pretty. Good hair. Trim.

Venetia sniffed and put a smile on her face. She could handle her.

⚜

The attention centered on Rhys as it always did. Rhys Kensington put a large square hand over Ginger's as she took a seat next to him. Rhys smiled, his fine features looking strained. He watched the headmistress of the Windsor School squeeze a chair into the table between two candidates who would be rivals for the now vacant seat of chair.

"I want you all to know Ginger McNair who will be working with Venetia to implement a development plan to put the Academy on a self-sustaining financial footing. She knows Santa Monica and many people in Santa

Monica know and admire her." Rhys smiled and put a hand on her shoulder. "Especially me, as Ginger has come to share a special place in my life. Please welcome her." There was a polite spatter of applause. Venetia Sorensen's applause and incandescent smile was the most enthusiastic.

"Thanks for your welcome. I'm looking forward to getting to know all of you," Ginger said, wishing that the implication wasn't that she got the job solely because she was his girlfriend. The hand that remained on her shoulder conveyed authority and ownership.

"But in the meantime, we have things to discuss regarding filling Leonard's position as chair." He turned to Venetia. "This is a Foundation executive session, Venetia. May I ask that you excuse yourself?"

"Oh certainly. Sure. Sure." Venetia jumped up and her red and silver skirt swirled around her. "I really wanted to be here just to share my condolences with all of you. Leonard was just the best, just the best. You all know that." A tear slid down her cheek. She hugged a clipboard close to her chest and stumbled as she made her way to the door.

"Yes, well," Rhys said uneasily. There was some foot-shuffling and clearing of throats as she swirled out of the room. A few of the women board members exchanged glances.

There were interruptions from staff and every time the door opened, Ginger heard the whoosh of a copier just outside the door and smelled the tang of the toner cartridge. People had liked Leonard Bricker well enough, she gathered, but was he as beloved as Venetia Sorensen suggested with her tears and dramatic exit? She tuned Rhys out and instead noticed the way he took command, comparing him to Dave Mason. She jerked herself back from exploring that blind alley.

Rhys took a phone call and turned his back to talk on his cellphone. When he resumed the meeting, his brow was furrowed and his voice serious. "That was the police. They're calling Leonard's death a vehicular homicide. That means somebody ran him down deliberately…"

There was a rapid buzz of speculation and alarm. Several of the board members sitting around the table looked at each other.

"It must be some drunk. It's gotta be," Keats Sefter interrupted with all the authority of his position as Legal Counsel of Kensington Industries. "Who would kill Leonard? It must have been an accident. I'll make that clear to the police. I have friends there."

"Wait until the police contact you," Rhys said. "They want us to stay available. We also have friends there too if it comes to that."

Ginger poured herself a fizzy glass of Perrier, knowing how Dave Mason and the rest of the force regarded civilian interference.

She also knew that Rhys Kensington was no fan of Detective Dave Mason.

Venetia Sorensen was waiting outside the door after the meeting broke up. She pulled Rhys close for a whispered conversation. Ginger and Caroline edged around them in the hallway. Caroline snorted, and shot a glance at Ginger.

"Venetia's always working it," Caroline huffed. Caroline cultivated the chiseled, thin, androgynous look, relishing masculine outfits that had people wondering about her sexuality.

"You don't like her?" Ginger said.

"I get tired of her always trying to one up me. She basically hates me because I was born rich. I can't help that. She started calling Leonard *uncle* when she heard Rhys and I do it. But to us he was family. Her? Just show-boating."

Ginger felt Rhys next to her and then an arm across her shoulders. Rhys Kensington was pale-complexioned like his sister, of medium height and had a few pounds too many on his slight frame. His startling basso profundo voice rumbled with authority, and he had that indefinable quality of charisma.

"I just talked to the police again. This is a mess, on top of what else is going on." He gave a sideways glance at his sister that Ginger caught. He checked a slip of paper on which he'd made notes. "A Chuck Palmer from the police? You know him?" He said to Ginger.

"Not really. I just know he's the traffic investigator. He's a detective who's trained in aspects of crime involving vehicles of any kind." If this was a vehicular homicide, she wouldn't have to deal with Mason as the lead investigator–and that was a relief.

"He was asking me questions about Harry's death, the old chair of the board. Sounds like they're implying his death is suspicious, if that's what I think is going on."

"But," Ginger protested, "didn't he have a heart attack? Think, two people serving as chair of the board of the school die within two months of each other? Wouldn't you be suspicious if you were a cop?"

3

Santa Monica wasn't the murder capital of the world, so Mason worked a lot of other cases, mostly major violent crimes. He'd pretty much seen the gamut of ways people thought up to avoid being a working stiff with a boring 9 to 5 job. Currently he was living in the world of carjackings, which led him to the universe of car theft, which touched on the recent vehicular homicide. Friday was winding down and Mason hoped it stayed quiet until the end of his shift. His phone vibrated on his belt and he looked down to read the caller's name. The Dentist. He ignored it, thinking that the tooth that had flared up again could wait. It wasn't that bad anymore. Leaning back in his chair, he pulled out the new phone he'd been issued and studied the instructions on importing his contacts. He'd worked through the setup three times, doing everything exactly the way the instructions read and still no success.

He looked up to see Trevor Robinson at the entrance to the cubicle farm given over to the two teams working Major Violent Crimes. There was something smart, something goofy, something innocent, about the rookie patrol officer. Light glittered off his glasses and he had a way of holding his head as though sniffing the air. Robinson was polite and endearing and seemed to have no awe of rank. He liked everybody, and it seemed everybody liked him, even Fredericks who smiled every time she saw him. Yet Mason had heard he could bring in his quota of bad guys and celebrities all cuffed up.

Mason looked up at him from under his eyebrows and tossed him the phone. "Import my contacts, would you?"

"Sure." Robinson entered the cubicle and sat down in Mason's visitor's chair. He took the phone, worked it effortlessly and handed it back, making Mason feel about 90 years old. "There you go."

"Why are you here, Robinson?" Mason said impatiently.

"We get briefings at roll call, all that on your carjackings, sir? I've been working Beat 2 down in the south of the city, right? I noticed this new used car lot that sprung up like a mushroom on Lincoln Boulevard. That takes major money, and I notice there's way too much traffic going in and out there for a new car lot. I've been watching the place, just casual like while I'm patrolling, and I get a tip from one of my guys on the street to watch the owner. I hear he shows up at this bar in town with his posse around midnight. How'd you like to meet me there and I'll point him out to you?"

"Can't you just shoot me a photo?"

"Well, I suppose I could but..." Robinson paused. "Did you know I'm working on a screenplay about the life of a detective, sir? I'm taking a class at UCLA Extension in scriptwriting. Maybe we could talk about it."

Mason grinned. "Well, here you see the exciting life of a detective sitting at his desk reading a stack of reports. This is pretty much how exciting it is most of the time. Then I get to do paperwork and talk on the phone."

"Yeah, well, I was hoping you could tell me about that Chechen gang you arrested."

Mason laughed out loud. "Robinson, there's guys here who'd talk your head off with all their war stories. Ask Fredericks. She's got stories."

Robinson skidded the chair back. "Oh, man, I'm scared of her."

"That's smart. If you're really sure you got something..." He stood up and straightened a photo of his daughter in her soccer outfit. He could hardly afford to ignore a lead even if it went nowhere. Delgado was hardly the one to take to a hipster bar. Maybe he wasn't either.

"This is where the young wolf cubs go to howl nowadays, is it?" Mason asked. He thought about the empty evening ahead. "Oh what the hell, yeah, okay. Why midnight?"

"That's when him and his posse show up. During the day I don't know where you'd catch him. I just see him once in a while, and you know how some people just look wrong."

He'd seen it a million times in the TV cop dramas he watched once in a while for a laugh. The detectives had all the bright ideas. The uniforms just bumbled around like Keystone cops tracking fiber and hairs through the crime scene and screwing up the take-down. But the uniforms were out on the streets every day. They were the ones who saw who hung with whom, which skanky old ho was passed from one banger to an-other, whose kids were truant because nobody cared. They saw guys they knew looking over their shoulders in nice neighborhoods wearing uniforms and carrying clipboards going from door to door trying doorknobs.

One of these days when he had time Mason figured he'd roll with Robinson just to see him in action. New guys often tried to prove how tough and unfeeling they were. Robinson was different. In Santa Monica uni-formed officers worked a car alone, so he must have mas-tered the bag of tricks that would take a suspect down. Mason suspected that he just persuaded the dirtbags to put their hands behind their backs in these nice hand-cuffs and come along quietly and they'd have coffee at the station and talk this whole thing over.

That night Mason met Robinson at the bar located in the basement of an old Victorian house on a busy corner in the Ocean Park section of the city. Lights flashing. Stepping inside, the noise was like an assault, shouted conversations, music from the band, laughter, like a party in progress. The music, harsh enough to strip paint, rose and fell at an edgy pitch that reflected the smiles of those on the prowl. The frenzy on the dance floor was Dionysian; few people partnered up, the rest twerking to their own beat. Mason looked around without appearing to, his attention drifting past a skinny girl with a shrill manic laugh. She was feinting and darting among other dancers, annoying people. Anybody with claustrophobia would be twitching being in this shoulder to shoulder crowd. No point in trying to talk. In the back under a moose head, people were lounging watching a Turner Classic movie. Somehow he muscled his way to the bar, got a drink, and paid for it.

A buzzer rang and Mason looked around. A short, fat Asian guy, bobbing on his toes and grinning, became the center of attention. The girl with the manic laugh pushed in next to him, screeching "Zombie Nightshade. Zombie Nightshade." A video popped up on the screen behind the bar, which a moment before had been playing ESPN. It showed a guy drinking a yellow concoction in a big glass. Mason leaned down to scream in her ear. "What's going on?"

She looked up at him, dismissed him as old and stupid. "He's gonna drink another Zombie Nightshade."

Okay, he was old and stupid. "What's that?"

"Just watch," she giggled.

Robinson crowded in next to him. "It's five or six shots of pure liquor, including 151, bourbon, and tequila. No mixers. They call it Instant Blackout. Watch the guy."

His Adam's apple bobbed as the drink went down his gullet. His knees sagged and everybody laughed. "Gimme another one. I can take it." Party monster.

The bartender in the tight white T-shirt had one ready. "This is your last one, man. We only serve two Zombie Nightshades."

Robinson pulled Mason back. "Watch out. He might puke."

Mason couldn't pull his eyes away, imagining the impact of ten shots of liquor in two minutes. Binge drinking horror.

The bartender leaned across the bar to scream at Mason. "People run in the bathroom and hurl in the sinks, all over the place. Disgusting. Sometimes they just go outside and lie on the sidewalk."

Mason turned to Robinson. "Does ABC know about this?' Alcohol, Beverage Control supposedly regulated this kind of thing.

Robinson just shrugged. "Hey, people do it all over the city, sir."

Mason didn't want to see what happened next. He and Robinson pushed through the crowd at the bar and went back to standing at the edge watching the dancing. The music was giving Mason a brain tumor headache. He was at the point where he was willing to chew his own ears off to make the noise stop. Robinson was rubbing the palms of his hands on his pants, watching the action, looking too cool for school. The menu offered fried mac and cheese balls but that was a little much, even for Mason.

He scream-talked at Robinson. "You see him?"

"He just came in." Robinson gestured with his chin at a man wearing a black and white French fisherman's sweater molded to a tall, elegant body. He wore sunglasses and an air of arrogance, his hand on the ass of a pregnant woman standing next to him. She was shouting at a man shorter than she was in an amiable fashion, cradling her heavy belly outlined in a tight, white T-shirt that showed her belly button had popped. Her companion had a squat compact body and wore a black leather jacket. Mason didn't recognize any of them. Sunglasses, tattoos, and gold jewelry was the favored look.

"The guy in the sweater is Vlad Yurkov."

Mason nodded, memorizing their faces. "Russian?"

Robinson nodded. "People say he's Russian."

"The woman?"

"That's his wife or girlfriend. I don't know her name."

"Okay, let's get out of here." He was done. "Get some photos."

"Nah, I want to stay awhile."

"You aren't planning anything stupid, are you?" Mason cocked his head back and looked at him hard.

Robinson gave him his goofy grin. "Nah, I just wanna get laid, sir. I'm off tomorrow."

4

"Doris!" Venetia Sorensen sailed into her office, the parrot on her shoulder, and barked out a sharp reprimand. As if there wasn't enough to deal with.

"What?" Her assistant, Doris Arnold, swiveled around in her chair in a corner of Sorensen's office. She looked up from her laptop computer dwarfed by the spread of her fat thighs.

"You're wearing those awful sweats again. I asked you. In fact, I told you. Can you not do one thing to please me?" She pinched the shoulder of the grey sweats between two manicured fingernails. "Did you buy these in a thrift shop?" Gazing into her assistant's homely face drove her to madness. So much to do, plus having to look at Doris Arnold's hangdog face, the grey leggings and the T-shirt that failed to cover her hanging belly and buttocks.

"Venetia, you don't know how busy I am between the school and taking care of my sister."

"I don't care. Go home and change, or just go home. Work at home today. I don't care. Just get out of my sight." Everything about the woman was misery and medicine smells and obligations and bad life decisions. "I have problems too, you know." Venetia allowed Petrovich to climb down her arm and into the huge cage occupying much of her office.

Doris Arnold heaved herself up out of the chair using the arms like an old lady. "So what did they say about Mr. Bricker?" she asked. She shrank away from the parrot.

"Nothing," Venetia snapped. "I'll tell you later. Email me." Petrovich had flown with long turquoise wings onto a perch beside her desk.

"Petrovich, kiss mommy. Kiss mommy. Beautiful. Beautiful."

On her first day of work the headmistress greeted Ginger with much less enthusiasm than she had shown in Rhys and Caroline Kensington's company. She led Ginger into the kitchen in the Administration cottage.

"You can work here," she said. "We're very crowded as you know." Except when she was cooing into the face of the parrot, Venetia talked fast, as if conversation cost money.

Ginger gazed around the long, narrow room, trying to keep her face from showing dismay. Off to the left was a sink. The counter held a microwave, a coffee maker, tea kettle, and hot plate. Storage cupboards lined the other walls.

"I'll make the best of it then," she said, setting her laptop down on the table that held napkins and paper plates. She could imagine what her work space would be like at lunch time.

"Maybe Rhys could give you an office in the Kensington Industries complex," Sorensen said and sailed out of the room with a smirk.

Ginger could hardly complain; every inch of the school's premises was crowded. Enrollment was limited because of space. Sports activities were off campus and expensive to organize and run. That was why she'd been hired—to raise money to build a new campus. And she would not be asking Rhys for any special favors. She remembered she needed Venetia to sign a tax form and hurried out the door of the kitchen to catch up with her.

Ginger was a little too far behind her to call out and get her attention, but she caught up with her as Venetia entered her corner office and paused riffling through a stack of mail. She seemed unaware of Ginger just behind her.

Ginger and Doris exchanged a glance, hearing Venetia muttering, "It's too much. Leonard's death. The bills. The deadlines. The students. Their insufferable parents. Oh my darling, Petrovich," she cooed. "Give

Mommy a kiss. Kiss mommy. Kiss mommy." Venetia grabbed the door of her inner office.

"I want an answer, Venetia. Come back. You have to give me an answer." Arnold's voice had a faint wheeze.

"I don't have to give you anything," Venetia yelled back at her, leaving Ginger standing in front of Doris Arnold. "Do what I told you. That's all you have to do." She slammed the door so hard that Ginger jumped.

"Well," Ginger said lightly to Doris, "Sounds like it's not a good time. How 'bout I come back later?"

"If you like…" Everything about Doris Arnold was drab, thin gray hair, pale sweater with pills, stretched out rayon pants, SAS orthopedic shoes. "Don't pay any attention to Dr. Sorensen. It's the stress, you know."

"Oh, I know how responsibilities can get to you."

"She works so hard, you know."

"I can see that. So then, can I get graduation statistics from you for the last three years?"

Arnold frowned. "Oh, Venetia wouldn't like that. I'll ask her though." The phone rang and she picked it up and began talking to a parent. "No, no. The entire year's tuition is due."

This might be a long conversation so she waved good-bye to Arnold's unsmiling face and continued down the hall to the office she shared with the sink and kitchen cupboards. Did Sorensen treat parents and students with the contempt she treated her assistant? She had asked around about the headmistress amongst her pals in city government and the education community. One of her friends on the Women's Commission confided that Sorensen never sponsored any proposals or worked on anything, but she was always there for photo ops, and the first one to second the motion to be sure her name appeared often in the minutes. It was obvious she was going to be a real treat to work with.

She opened up her laptop and set it up on the flimsy table. She did have a window that looked out over the well-kept lawn in the middle of the three school buildings.

The school was located in the once light industrial section of the city next to the Kensington Industries headquarters. One old white clapboard cottages housed the administration offices and two tiny classrooms. Three other small cottages were devoted to classrooms and a rudimentary lunch room called the *cafe*. Efforts had been made to disguise the aging condition of the campus: bougainvillea tumbled down trellises at the doorways in a waterfall of magenta blossoms.

The kitchen was stuffy and Ginger went to the window, which had an old-fashioned sash. It slid up stiffly, bringing in a hint of jasmine on the fresh air. Then she heard Sorensen faintly.

"Yes, I know. So Leonard's dead," Venetia said. "Are you getting calls yet? You need to work on Dennison, Ailetcher, Monty, and Betty Ann. That will give you a majority of the directors."

Shamelessly, Ginger listened, concentrating everything to hear.

"Rhys Kensington doesn't want the job." Venetia's staccato delivery.

Silence. Ginger eased the window higher.

"Thought all he did was pro bono for that fancy outfit that gave him a job. He hardly needs the money," Venetia snorted. "So we need to swing both Kensingtons over to your side. That's if Monty doesn't cave. I think he looks sick. Somebody told me it's his heart. He's fat. I hate gross fat people."

Wow. Who's she talking to? Does she talk to everybody like this?

"We need you at the head of the board. Remember, we both need you to have that job. Okay, we'll both be working it. I gotta go."

Ginger stepped back from the window quickly and sat down in her chair lacing her fingers behind her head, thinking about the headmistress. Moments later Venetia swirled into the kitchen to rinse her coffee cup at the sink. She was humming, the parrot on her shoulder. He flew towards Ginger with great sudden wings. She couldn't help it and put up her hands in alarm. The bird roosted on the back of a chair next to hers at the table and screeched in her face.

"Oh, don't be scared," Venetia said. "He only bites if you get too close, don't you, Petrovich darling?"

Up close the bird was beautiful, with iridescent turquoise plumage, an orange breast, and soulless black, unblinking eyes.

"How does he tell you you're too close?" Ginger said, pressing her back to the chair away from him. The parrot slid closer. "That must hurt if he bites," she said, regarding the lengthy bone-colored beak. "Don't you worry about liability?"

"Oh, he's no trouble. The students love him," Sorensen said, unconcerned, as she stabbed buttons on the microwave.

Ginger kept one eye on the bird as it paced back and forth along her chair back on long, scaly talons. The bird tilted its head at an impossible angle, watching her. Tentatively she reached toward him. He skittered a few inches closer.

"Just in case," Sorensen said. She walked over and bent to hold out an arm for Petrovich to perch on. She set him on her shoulder.

"Hey, while you're here," Ginger said. She reached for the list of questions she'd kept handy for the moment she got Sorensen alone. "I don't see your C.V. posted anywhere on our website. Can you shoot me a copy?"

"Oh, that thing. My resume is so outdated, it would take too much time to put all the new stuff in. Time I just don't have." She took her Cup of Soup out of the microwave. "Soon though. Soon. Come with Mommy, Petrovich." She left in a swirl of gauzy skirts around her long legs. Big white smile over her shoulder for Ginger. The parrot gave Ginger another look and flew after Sorensen.

"Wow, he likes me." She snorted with amusement.

5

Mason ran into Chuck Palmer at the vending machine on the first floor of the station and asked him how the Bricker fatality case was developing. He knew the country–and maybe the whole world– was in the midst of an epidemic of hit-and- run vehicular homicides. Other than that it involved Ginger McNair, he wouldn't have taken an interest in the Bricker fatality. While he and Ginger had agreed to end it six months ago, it didn't mean he'd stopped thinking about her.

"I've got something. Remember the trim piece that we found at the scene of the Bricker fatality?" Palmer was sandy-haired and bouncy.

"Kind of. Remind me." Mason had other cases on his mind, other victims, other crimes, other dead bodies that haunted him.

"The headlight broke and the chrome bezel broke off. We got the make of the car off the camera near

Bergamot Station. So we know he's driving a 2003 white Toyota Corolla. Yeah, I know there's a lot of them on the road. Headlights are fragile. But the bezel gives me a part number. Here's how it works: you need the VIN, the Vehicle Information Number, right? The first few letters indicate the year, make and model. The last numbers are the sequence off vehicles produced. With the headlight trim part linked to a specific vehicle, and that just came through, we've got everything but the sequence of production."

"Yeah, and…." Mason didn't quite get it. He leaned up against the soda machine.

"So I access DMV and ask for all the registrations with the same year, make and models registered in Southern California. That's where it gets tricky. As this is an old car, a lot of them are off the road. But I still came up with eight thousand 2003 Toyota Corollas."

"That's great. But still 8000 of them."

"You figure that's the end of it? Hardly. I got ways I can go with this. I'll get him."

"Soon?"

"Maybe." Palmer yawned so hard Mason heard his jaw pop. He rubbed at it, making Mason think about the aching tooth on the lower left side of his jaw.

"Kids. No sleep. I'm still interviewing all the artistic types at Bergamot Station down the street looking for somebody hanging around prior to the killing. Artists notice things like color, shape, things out of synch, so I'm hopeful. Daytime Bergamot Station is full of artists, technical people, sales staff, and all the art lovers. At night not so much. Nobody saw nuthin', which probably means that whoever was driving looked like he fit in."

"But Bricker was well known around town, wasn't he? That should make it easier. Not like chasing down some asshole gangbanger."

Palmer raised his eyebrows, drained half his Coke. "Easy? Oh yeah." He gave Mason a punch on the arm as he left.

Mason had heard people talking about eHarmony for years and had reluctantly signed up. He didn't have much hope, but there was one woman who seemed to want to try him out. Until the last moment he meant to cancel, but what the hell. The woman turned out to look somewhat like her online photo. He had said only that he worked for the City of Santa Monica, which was true, nothing about being a cop. Sometimes it was a turn on for women; other times not. It was an okay evening, not great.

They stopped for a quiet drink after dinner at Shutters on the Beach. A three-member combo was playing a slow tune and people were dancing. Ginger had pushed him into taking dancing lessons and Mason was capable of a mean tango and pretty good foxtrot and waltz. He got up and shoved this woman around the floor. She was game, but she was no dancer. After she'd stepped on his toes too many times, she asked him if they could please sit down. That was the trouble with partner dancing. You needed a partner who knew the same steps you did. He wondered if Rhys Kensington could do the tango.

Probably.

There was nothing completely weird about this woman at least. She worked in Human Relations for a legal firm—civil not criminal lawyers. She didn't have seventeen cats, belong to a megachurch, or complain about her old boyfriends. He couldn't help comparing though. Ginger could make even a trip to the grocery store fun. She was generally in a good mood and light-hearted. He couldn't say he'd had fun with this woman, who wasn't bad looking. On the way home, he realized he'd probably not been that much fun either.

He zoned out in front of *30 Rock* when he got home, roused himself at midnight to stumble off the couch and into bed.

So much for the single life. He missed having a dog to talk to.

At 3:00 a.m. a smoke alarm somewhere in his condo started chirping. He tried to ignore it and go back to sleep and couldn't. Dragging out the stepladder, he bumbled around with the alarm in the kitchen where he thought the noise was coming from. That wasn't it. He then went from room to room, finally locating the sonofabitch alarm in the back bedroom where his daughter Haley slept when she visited. Then he couldn't go back to sleep. A memory roared through him of this happening when his dog had been alive and he and Diana were married and Haley was just a baby. His old dog had figured since Dave was up, it was fun time. He missed old Buddy. He stuffed the emotions down and rearranged his game face.

Today Mason was schlumping around trying to fill up an empty Sunday. He'd made himself get up, ignore his email, get dressed as though he had places on go, and drove to the Santa Monica Farmers' market. The whole city was there: middle-easterners bargaining for the choicest heirloom tomatoes, shoving chefs with tall white hats out of the way, tired campesinos who'd been up since the middle of the night to drive to trendy Westside LA to sell fresh produce, honey, fish, bread, and pastries.

At 6'4" Mason was usually able to scan the tops of heads in every crowd. He couldn't help but look for pickpockets, and watch the dead-eyed homeless, the recent runaways amidst the crowd of fashionistas dressed in leggings and hoodies. The street cop in him never died. That was the dealbreaker with Ginger. She wanted him to move up the ranks, take him away from any danger that might happen on the street. There had been a shootout on a routine felony pickup down in Sunset Park that nobody had any warning about. The scumbucket's buddy had been under the car and came out shooting. Mason's arm had been grazed and Ginger had gone crazy.

She had finally walked away and apparently had dumped him for a rich lawyer, that Kensington guy with the funny first name. Who named somebody Rice? She could have picked the usual reasons for a cop girlfriend dump: he was never around, he'd missed one too many birthdays or parties, said the wrong thing at one of her liberal cocktail fundraising parties, locked eyes with some guy he'd busted. But it was more than that and they reached the edge when neither would relent. Yet he'd tried hard, harder with Ginger than anybody in his life, including his ex-wife Diana and the mother of his adored little girl. Haley cried when he told her Ginger wouldn't be around any longer. She told him he was stupid to let Ginger go and sulked the rest of the day they had together. He'd found out that she and Ginger had recently spent a weekend together camping. He tried to pump Haley for information but Haley had gone tight-lipped.

The day yawned in front of him. He was getting used to being alone, and not liking it much. It wasn't his weekend to pick up Haley way the hell out in the far eastern edge of the Greater Los Angeles sprawl where she lived with her mother and Harvey the Comic Book artist. Harvey made a shitload of money and they talked about moving back into the city from Rancho Cucamonga but it hadn't happened yet.

Mason's phone began vibrating. It was supervising sergeant, Joe York.

"Mason, get your cop ass in here. I've got something for you."

"What's up, sir?" Mason said,

"I'm on hold with Citibank. If I cut you off, call me back. My credit card's been highjacked. Bastard thieves," he growled. "Listen, I got a call from the Monsignor over at the big Catholic Church. One of his parishioners is on his back so he calls us. Her sister has gone missing. Missing Persons looked into it and didn't find anything, but now the missing female's car shows up and it's a blood-stained mess so that's you. Get Delgado in and check it out. Gotta go."

So far Mason's jackers hadn't killed anybody. Now the stakes were amped up.

He and Delgado were up next on the wheel for major violent crimes. Homicide was rare in Santa Monica, but violent crimes weren't. Look at what had happened to the Klepper family. He owed Judy Klepper a call and dreaded it. It had been a few weeks since he gone over there to say hello to Andy. Nothing new to report. Judy seemed to feel that if he took lunch or went home at the end of the day he wasn't doing his job looking for their carjackers. It wasn't said directly but it was there. The rash of new carjackings Mason was working were a worry to everyone in the community, especially the business and travel industry.

He checked out a curvy free spirit wearing tie dye in the crowd, dragging behind her a grocery cart filled with fruits and vegetables. Didn't women eat pizza anymore? Next time he'd find one who did. When he started looking. On the way out of the Farmers' Market heading back to the station, he bought a few apples he probably wouldn't eat, and some cake disguised as muffins that he knew he would.

"Here's the Missing Persons report," Sgt. York said, stretching across his cluttered desk. "I told them I'd be taking it off their hands as a special favor to the Monsignor. Your kid Robinson was the one who found the car."

Mason paged through the report quickly. "Robinson, huh? We were just beginning to get somewhere on the Klepper thing," he objected. "Can't one of the other teams…" Mason made a few pro forma moans and groans, but he was glad to have something to do to fill the rest of the weekend.

"Figure it out," York said, waving him away. "I gotta take care of this deal with my credit card. You know how long I been on the phone?" The wall facing Mason was taken up with bowling trophies and police awards. York picked up the phone again, straightening a pile of paperwork on his desk. York had a round head, sloping shoulders, and short, thick neck. He wasn't good at what he did because he was pretty. He was also the station champ at eating raw jalapeño peppers.

Mason called the Monsignor to tell him they were on it. There was no reason for the Monsignor to know the car had been found with a blood-stained passenger seat.

He called Delgado. "Hey, buddy. We're up."

"Ah, shit. I promised the wife I'd… Look, I put in for this time off. She's gonna be pissed."

"Yeah, I know. I'll meet you at the beach parking lot." No wonder people involved with cops got tired of it.

Mason checked through the file for information on the missing person, a Doris Arnold. A uniform had done a welfare check at the request of her sister after she'd been gone 48 hours. Doris Arnold lived in a granny flat in the backyard of one of the stately old places above Montana Avenue. The sister had given the Missing Persons team door keys to the place, and their report stated there was no sign of any disturbance, but her car was gone. Doris Arnold was her sister's sole support, other than a small disability check she received from the State.

Mason's eyes narrowed when he caught the name of her employer: the missing woman was an administrative assistant at the Windsor Academy. Mason's eyebrows rose in surprise.

Hmmph. He remembered the hit and run fatality Palmer was working on with the Kensington connection. Ginger worked there now as well.

The first thing to do was take a look at the car, call forensics in to process the scene, and then get the car towed into the station where they could work it over. He called the sister, a Loretta Swinson, and set up an appointment for later, dodging her questions. On his way to the parking lot in the basement, he paused to read the writeup of a bicyclist convicted of assault with a deadly weapon, a bicycle which had collided with a pedestrian in a crosswalk. This was the downside of making Santa Monica a bicycle-friendly city. Now there were green bicycle lanes and pedi-cabs clogging up the streets, making the traffic even worse.

While he waited for Delgado to get there, he familiarized himself with the facts of the case. The Kensington Industries connection was probably nothing. The conglomerate was a big deal in Santa Monica. Plaques all over town celebrated KI's support of good causes, especially the schools. He took the elevator down to the basement motor pool because his knees hurt today, and got into the black Crown Vic assigned to him. He was sitting behind the wheel with the door open reading the file when Delgado drove in. Delgado parked, and came over to get in the vehicle, looking not more than usually disheveled. And pissed off at being called in. He'd missed a strip of grizzled beard shaving under his chin, and was stuffing his arms into a wrinkled, shit-brown jacket that had been flung into the back seat of his car.

"You look like you're working undercover on the homeless detail."

"What? What?" Today he wore a golf shirt with a red stain over the front that looked like dried taco sauce, but resembled blood.

Mason went Pffft, then handed him the file and started up the vehicle, driving out onto 4th Street and across the overpass that spanned the Santa Monica Freeway, the I-10 that began in the east and led onto a brief glimpse of the ocean before the condos began along the Pacific Coast Highway.

Delgado began reading and looked up to comment, "Missing Persons did a fair amount of work for it being active only a couple of days." He paged through reports taken from the sister, the employer, neighbors, and the usual backgrounders. "So she kept to herself and lived quietly. The sister doesn't seem to think she had many friends. Oh man, this sounds like work."

Mason thought of how many people he ran into who had no friends. Wasn't America supposed to be the friendliest country in the world?

Santa Monica had quite a shine on it today. Late summer and it was another ho-hum perfect day in the Mediterranean climate that kept Santa Monica cool except during the worst heat waves. The city was seventy-percent renters, even now in the declining days of rent control. All the renters nowadays seemed to be young, well-paid technocrats. They all wanted to live up close and personal with each other in what was called Silicon Beach to maintain the hot buzz of the downtown that brought the tourists in by the millions. Mason remembered growing up in Santa Monica when it was old people occupying the city's housing stock, street after street of apartments in mid-city, and big houses and money in the north end of the city. Over the years the apartment owner lobby and their lawyers and politicians had defanged the rent control laws. The old people had slowly disappeared or died off—and rents had risen. Oh, how they had risen.

Delgado ploughed through the file as they drove north to one of the pay lots where Arnold's car had been found. On a hot day the beach threw out a smell of kelp and brine. Robinson, the eager rookie who had found the vehicle was there waiting for them. Mason felt tired just watching him. Had he ever had all that energy? Robinson was just busting to tell them everything he knew.

"I was cruising the parking lots checking on things and I happened to notice the driver's side window was busted out. I got out and looked, saw the blood on the seat, and called it in."

"And you didn't tramp all around the car to see what's what?" Mason asked.

"Hey, I know better than that," Robinson grinned. He had a smile that showed a lot of gum, the nice pink gums the dentist told Mason he should have.

Mason and Delgado stood with Robinson well away from Arnold's old Subaru waiting for the forensic specialists to get there. The white truck pulled up and the two silent forensic specialists began unloading their wares.

"Okay, let's get out of the way and let them do their thing. Thanks, Robinson. You can go now. Write me up a report, okay?"

"You want me to get the camera footage from the pay kiosk over there? It could be this one or that one," the patrol officer said, pointing to the little white shack where visitors paid the fees to park.

"Nah, we'll take care of it. You go enjoy your day."

"I didn't have anything much planned. I could come back after my shift. You're sure about it, sir?"

"Yeah, yeah."

"Wonder if it's those carjackers, sir? You think?"

"I don't think anything yet."

"They drove it here and dumped it, and maybe the body is someplace else?"

Mason turned as a sea gull wheeled in and parked itself beside the car out in the sand. "Maybe. You can take off now, Robinson."

Reluctantly Robinson left, walking slow to give Mason plenty of time to call him back.

Delgado grinned. "You got a fan club. Maybe you should be the next Officer Friendly."

"Nah, I wanna be McGruff, the Crime Dog, and wear a trench coat and scare the kiddies."

Poor Doris Arnold was probably lying dead somewhere and he was fooling around. He was glad her sister couldn't hear him.

"I'll put you in for a transfer to play McGruff then, Mason. I'm going over to the kiosk now to line up the camera feed. Probably the last 48 hours, huh?"

"That should do it. Then we go see the sister."

All the parking lots had cameras, color during the day, and black and white at night, which enhanced the images. The sun felt good on Mason's back, another ordinary, beautiful California day. This might be the worst drought in California's recorded history, but it sure made for good beach weather. A pretty woman wearing a gauzy white tunic over blue leggings was walking three barking pit bulls on a leash. Mason smiled at her and she smiled back, pulling the dogs closer. Behind him were the white sails of boats scudding across Santa Monica bay. A family carrying a plastic cooler passed, the young mother holding a Down Syndrome child by the hand. The boy flapped his hand and smiled at him with such sweetness that Mason smiled and waved back. The pavement was hot in the sunshine and beautiful young people with white zinc on their noses were tossing breadcrumbs in the grass, a volleyball game going on the sand. Gulls wheeled in from all directions shrieking. The day was suddenly filled with ordinary goodness, sweeping the malevolence away.

Mason walked over to the parking kiosk. Delgado was already there with the guard in the kiosk playing the footage back to make sure it actually worked before he had him email the file to the station. They found Arnold's car on the screen in the crowded kiosk without too much trouble and went back to the station to watch the event unfold. The car had driven through at 2:20 a.m. Mason's expectations dimmed as he watched. The Subaru had a slightly tinted windshield and a reflective top border across the top. The interior lighting and exterior street lighting obscured what the camera picked up. He saw the vehicle drive in, the driver looking down as though searching for something on the passenger seat when he punched the button to issue the ticket. He watched a hand wearing a glove feed in the bills. The driver wore a baseball cap with a long bill and a big scarf around the neck pulled up to the chin. Long sleeves.

Delgado came in behind him and watched over his shoulder as Mason froze the best frame. "Shit," he said in his broken glass voice.

"Right. You can tell he's human and that's about it."

6

They drove over to the sister's apartment just north of Wilshire Boulevard, kicking around a few ideas, primarily whether this was the work of their merry little band of carjackers. The sister, Loretta Swinson, edged the door of her apartment open as Mason and Delgado came up the walk in front of one of the old dingbats, newly painted in beige with brown trim. The dingbats were old housing stock built in the 50's and 60's. Dingbats were inexpensive to build, boxy, two- story apartment houses with an overhang sheltering street-level parking, usually in the rear. Here the over-hang was in front, the stairs leading to the second floor running up the side of the building. There were no real slums in Santa Monica, despite the age of much of the housing stock.

Swinson's building had the usual jade plants, a Jupiter's beard, and a couple of spindly ficus trees. A

Latina scooted past them down the cement walk, scolding a little boy she was leading by the hand. Mason looked up the stairs at the landing where a small woman with greying, uncombed hair wearing a brown velour workout suit beckoned to them. He was aware they looked like cops. He introduced himself and Delgado when they got to the top of the stairs. Mrs. Loretta Swinson, Doris Arnold's sister, was a little brown hen of a woman, all fluttery feathers and darting movements, and head bobs of agreement. Swinson hobbled in front of them into an apartment filled with too much furniture, the home of someone who couldn't bear to part with anything.

"My sister would never have disappeared without mailing my rent check," she began in an urgent tone. "Doris was always so thoughtful. I've missed a doctor's appointment as well and this makes me so scared for her," she said, her blue eyes wide, her fingers fluttering at the zip on her warm up top.

Mason edged her back into the living room and took a seat on a worn brocade couch. The place smelled of furniture polish, a good clean smell. Swinson perched on the edge, looking back and forth between him and Delgado. "I just can't believe something terrible hasn't happened to her," she said, a tissue held to her nose. She shook her head and a few tears flew off her soft cheeks.

"I realize this is terrible news to you. Give us a chance though before you think the worst," Mason said. There was always hope at this stage. Despite the blood.

"You just don't know. You can't imagine. Never hurt anyone. They just love Doris over at Saint Monica's. She's one of the Monsignor's favorites."

Mason hated to give her the bad news. "We've found something in the meantime. Your sister's car has been located. A green 1999 Subaru. Right? Everything matches to the details we have on file with the DMV. This is your sister's car."

"But what about Doris?" Swinson's face caved in as though she'd just taken a punch. "Where was the car found?"

"On one of the beach parking lots."

"She never went to the beach." Loretta Swinson's mouth opened in shock. "Then where's Doris? Where is she? What happened to her?"

"We don't know," Mason said. "Do you know if she was taking a trip somewhere? Had any plans for the weekend?"

"She wouldn't just leave me…something terrible has happened. I just knew it. She wouldn't leave me like this." She slumped back against the couch, breathing hard.

"I should also tell you that there's a substance that resembles blood on the driver's seat of the car. And the driver's side window has been smashed."

"But that means…."

"Before you get carried away, remember it could just mean she had a nosebleed. Things like that happen." Mason felt stupid even saying it. He thought of Andy Klepper, the victim of carjackers he hadn't found yet. It was far more likely Arnold had surrendered that blood unwillingly.

"Can you tell us a little more about your sister? When was the last time you saw her? Let's start there."

Loretta Swinson sagged into herself. "I already told them everything. She was at some do they were having for the Academy, a Silent Auction that the parents and alumni put on to raise money. I showed those young fellows who came from the police the receipt. Doris brought me those cookies that I like from Trader Joe's and my prescription from the pharmacy. I saved you the receipts. Both of them have the time printed on it." She drew out two receipt slips she'd been using as a bookmark in her Bible and handed them to Mason.

"Here, put them in here." He pulled out an evidence envelope and held it open for her to drop them in. He handed the bag to Delgado who began filling out the evidence slip.

"She probably came over pretty soon after she left the fundraiser because she was bringing me ice cream," Swinson said quickly.

"She got here when?"

"About 8:30, I guess. She just stayed long enough to put the ice cream away and chat a minute. It was a big event and she was tired. But she said she was going right home. Right home." Swinson repeated it as though saying it twice made everything more real and she had more control over it.

"Was she meeting anyone?"

"No." She began to cry again. "She was tired. They'd had one of their parties at the school and she'd stayed behind to clean up. That's so like Doris. Everything was just so ordinary. If I'd known…"

"She didn't leave anything with you, in case anything happened to her?" Delgado asked.

"Like what?" Swinson looked puzzled.

"It could be anything. Key to a safe deposit box? A password? A bank book?"

Swinson continued shaking her head. "She didn't leave anything."

Before she gave into the grief, Delgado leaned forward and said, "Do you have any ideas what might have happened to her?"

"Well, no. Nobody we know…" she trailed off. "We're just not the kind of people something like this happens to." She fingered her Bible and gave a gasping breath. "Her employer, Dr. Sorensen called me on Tuesday. Doris hadn't shown up for work on Monday or Tuesday and she just thought…Well, I can't imagine what she thought because it wasn't like Doris not go to work for two days."

The doorbell rang just as Delgado was getting ready to say something. Swinson hobbled to the door. She opened it and Mason saw a grey-haired woman with a sensible old lady haircut crowd past her with a casserole dish, wearing an expression of horrified pity. Going missing would be big stuff in this set.

"Oh, you have company," she said. The visitor wore a long skirt made of fluffy stuff and a black World Wildlife

T-shirt. "We thought you shouldn't be alone. Monsignor told us we should come over and make sure you had everything you needed."

Swinson turned pink and her hands fluttered to her face. "Oh, yes. Oh, well, these gentlemen are the police."

Mason and Delgado stood up. "Hi, I'm Billie. We were at the Program Committee meeting and the secretary came in and told us. Monsignor is very concerned about you."

Swinson took the casserole dish and stood there, as though waiting for instructions. She held herself stiffly, her shoulders hunched up around her ears. When she turned her head to look at him, her whole body rotated as one piece.

"Billie, how about you take that," Mason pointed at the dish, "in the kitchen and wait there for us?"

"Oh, I want Billie to be here," Swinson twittered, her hand on her friend's arm. "I'd just feel so much better. I don't have any secrets from her. And she knows Doris. They all do at the Church."

"I'll stay with you, Loretta." Billie took that as the signal to flump down in a much cat-scratched wing chair opposite Mason and Delgado who were sitting on the couch.

"How you doing, Loretta?" Billie said.

"Well, I'm just devastated. They found Doris's car and there was blood in it, but they didn't find Doris. You can imagine..."

"Oh, my God." Billie came over to hunch down and hug Loretta in an awkward embrace. This set off a storm of tears. Mason and Delgado looked at each other and waited it out. The interview circumstances weren't ideal, but this was early in the investigation and the broader the perspective they got on the victim, the better.

"Okay then," Mason interrupted after a bit. "Can you tell me more about your sister?"

Both women looked at each other. "I don't think I've seen you at church, have I, Detective Mason? How about you Mr. Delgado, are you a Catholic?"

"Yes, ma'am, my wife and I attend our parish out in the Valley."

"Oh, that's nice. That's so nice."

Loretta Swinson had more to say. "Dr. Sorensen asked me about a deposit for the bank. Apparently Doris had it when she left the Silent Auction but it never got deposited. She didn't say it but I know she thinks that Doris had something to do with that, but I can't believe that. Doris is as honest as the day is long."

"How much was it?"

"Twenty-seven thousand dollars and something else. I can't remember."

"That's a lot of money," Mason said, surprised. A whole new line of investigation sprang open. "We'll be talking to her next. And your sister didn't mention this money? Or making a bank deposit?"

Swinson shook her head and reached for the box of tissues. She blew her nose and mopped at her eyes. "No, nothing."

"Did your sister have a man in her life? A special friend, you know?"

"Oh, no. Not for many years now. She put so much into her job. And then there's me. She did all the shopping for both of us. All the errands. All my doctor's appointments. It's a lot, you know. I don't know what I'm going to do." Her eyes filled with tears again.

"Don't you worry, Loretta," Billie said. "We'll figure it out. We are just praying to the Lord to give you boys a big clue so you can catch the perp."

Mason caught Delgado's grin, which instantly disappeared, replaced by his cop face.

"Did your sister routinely handle money, big deposits like that?"

"Oh no, all that was done with computers. She was very smart about computers. Did you know her purse was gone? Those other young fellows who came around from the police told me they went in her apartment and they didn't find it? Did you find her purse? Or her cellphone?"

They hadn't. Swinson went on and on. Everything was nice and lovely and sweet, obscuring the fact that she was all twisted up and tormented by pain, her movements small and pinched. Both she and her visitor grew pink-faced with excitement when a phone call came in from Saint Monica's saying that the Monsignor might, just might, be over later to pray with them. Billie was joined by two other worthy-looking women from the parish bringing a nice salad and some nice brownies for lunch. More tears: very little more information.

7

Ginger put a smile on her face and took a few hurried steps to catch up with Venetia Sorensen in the hall outside her office. Sorensen turned to her, her face tight, prepared.

"What now?"

"Could I have an hour of your time later today? We have a lot of things to implement and I'd..."

"I'm really busy," Sorensen snapped. "And my assistant hasn't shown up for two days." Sorensen was as tall as Ginger, the two of them that new crop of women raised on vitamins and hormone-enhanced beef. Both of them knew how to use their height to an advantage.

Ginger braced herself, "I'd like to try out some ideas that will really benefit you and the school."

"Can't we do this by email? Just send me things," Sorensen said impatiently. "It is a bad time. I'm sure you'll understand." Venetia dropped her face, and looked away. "I'm pretty broken up over Leonard's death. He meant a lot to me."

"Yes, I can imagine. Well, not really. I guess I can't imagine." Sorensen kept her hand on the doorknob. The beautiful green and yellow parrot shrieked a greeting to Ginger from its perch on her shoulder. The invitation to come in and sit down was not forthcoming.

"Okay. I'd like to go over your graduation and grades stats too. They're so outstanding we can work up some stories on that alone, comparisons with other private schools. How about roughing out some plans for the fundraiser we started talking about?"

Sorensen interrupted her, running a hand through her hair and looking away. "I just don't have the time now. So many cash flow problems."

"Oh?" Ginger said. "Cash flow problems?"

"How about we do an Alumni Dinner here in Santa Monica somewhere?"

"I like doing dinners," Ginger said enthusiastically. "We need at least six months lead time though. You have a good list of donors I could work from? I need that to get started."

"Oh, a donor list. Not really," Venetia said, "Doris had all that stuff on her laptop and you may not know it yet, but Doris has disappeared along with all our records."

"Oh." Ginger didn't know what to say to that.

Venetia put her head in her hands as though she were exhausted. She passed a hand over her forehead and seemed to shudder. She looked up under her eyebrows at Ginger. "It takes so much effort to just keep the school going that I couldn't face doing anything about raising money until now. Leonard and I had been making the first beginnings."

"Oh, I didn't know that," Ginger said. "Well, could I see anything you've got on paper?"

"It wasn't formal," Sorensen said. "We were just talking." She was already dismissing Ginger. She took the parrot off her shoulder and its talons curled around her forearm. "Kiss mommy, Petrovich. Kiss mommy."

"Have you thought about setting a financial goal for the dinner?" Ginger said, before she lost her chance, and before that alarming bird flew toward her. "If I had some idea of that, I could start planning."

"How about $200,000?" Sorensen seemed to just pull that figure out of the air.

"That seems doable from what I can see. But I do need to see where the school stands right now in terms of revenues and expenses. And put together a donor list." She put enthusiasm into her voice. "So let's set up a meeting schedule then? Caroline Kensington will be sitting in on these meetings. She and I have done a lot of fundraisers and events, and we work really well together."

Venetia made a show of pulling out her iPad and punching away at it. She looked up. "How about Wednesday mornings from 10 until noon?"

Ginger made a note on a lined yellow pad. "That's fine. What I can do in the meantime is start working on the publicity material. Could you find some time to post on social media? All the other schools do. And your website needs work."

"Yes, yes, I know. But we're focused on education here," Sorensen said dismissively, "not pretty pictures to hand out to parents. Besides there's always a waiting list for new students and it never seemed very important to work on recruitment."

"You're fortunate. Most private schools are always working on recruitment."

"You know that for sure?" Sorensen tilted her head with a superior smile.

"Well, it's what I hear."

"Let me be the expert then."

Sorensen yanked at the door of her office and Ginger saw through the open doorway a handsome man wearing a black leather jacket, a black golf shirt, sunglasses and jeans, sitting wide-legged in a visitor's chair. He gave Sorensen a long, slow look and then smiled, coming to his feet languidly and holding out his arms. He did *not* look like a parent.

Sorensen seemed galvanized, hissing at him like a snake. "How did you get in here? I told you never to come here."

"Baby, baby." He gestured lazily toward the French doors opening out onto the deck outside.

Sorensen seemed to remember Ginger was standing there taking it all in. She steamed through the doorway and slammed it in Ginger's face.

Whew! I wonder who that was. The man's smile reminded her of the wolf in bedtime stories. Something about the insouciant way he'd risen to his feet and the slow smile suggested he and Venetia knew each other very well. Full of speculations, Ginger walked across the quad to a corner table where she spread out her things in the student lunchroom. Venetia had given her so-called office in the staff lunch room away to a new part-time teacher. There was nowhere else to work. A student with buds in his ears gave her a disinterested smile as she sat down and went back to banging on his tablet. There were notices that the entire year's tuition was due this week. Why would she be having cash flow problems?

The dietician the school had hired to serve the needs of its many students who seemed to have dietary restrictions was poring over her notebook to keep track of who was vegan, the gluten-free kids, the no carbs, the peanut allergy, the kosher kids, and the pescetarians.

"No, no, we can't do this here," Venetia protested, as Vlad Yurkov pulled her on top of him where he sat in the visitor's chair in her office. Petrovich, who didn't like Vlad, screamed from his perch.

"Get that thing out of here," he growled.

"Petrovich stays. Wait, wait, let me lock the door." Venetia jumped up. It had been three days and she was hungry for him. Hungrier and hotter and crazier. He saw it in her adrenaline junky smile, felt it on her. She saw him when she saw him, with no promises when she'd see him again. Anytime she could grab him was the perfect time. She ran to the door and locked it.

He was ready for her and she sank down on him.

"Vlad, Vlad, my Impaler," she sighed.

Afterwards, Venetia pulled herself away from him and perched on the couch, sated for the time being, but always unsatisfied. She fought to keep it contained, to set her jaw, steel her spine, not let him know.

"I saw your wife the other day. A real cow."

"Hey, she's pregnant." His face went dark and she knew she should stop herself right there.

"Pregnant women shouldn't wear leggings. Leggings are a privilege, not a right. Her ass is three feet wide. Fat women who wear leggings look ridiculous."

"You be nice," he warned her. "My wife is good woman." He got up and pulled on his black leather jacket, preparing to leave.

Defiantly she stared at him. "But dull, stupid, boring. Am I dull or stupid or boring, Vlad?"

He sucked his teeth and eyed her with disdain. "Sometimes you are very stupid woman."

Then he was gone.

Delgado was testifying in a court case, which left Mason the chance to go through Palmer's book on the vehicular homicide. The connection between Bricker and the missing (and probably dead) Doris Arnold was the Phoebe

Windsor Academy. Two cases of foul play connected to the Academy was too much to call coincidence. He did his best not to dwell on the fact that he would likely run into Ginger as part of the investigation. He couldn't decide if this was a good thing or a bad thing, so he didn't think about it. Clearing a place on the desk that took up most of his grey-upholstered cubicle, he spread everything out, hoping the phone wouldn't ring for a few minutes while he read through it chronologically.

Leonard Bricker, by all reports, was an upstanding John Q. Public. His wife had suddenly died a few months ago, just as tickets had been booked on a round-the-world cruise. He read Palmer's report on an interview with Bricker's daughter and her husband who flew in from Missouri to deal with her father's estate, now that both her parents were dead. Neither of them had been able to supply a motive for his hit-and-run death. What interested him was the tone of antagonism in the son-in-law's interview. But how unusual was that? Maybe there was another side to Bricker's story.

They'd done the initial on Arnold's sister, next was her employer, and her few friends. His email box held a report of Arnold's credit card receipts and phone records, which he downloaded and printed. He was waiting for the forensics report from the team who had towed the victim's car into one of the two examination bays in the basement of the station.

He made a few notes, and when he looked up, Delgado was there leaning over the top of his cubicle.

He was wearing a yellow shirt, his shit-brown suit, and a mustard-colored tie. Quite natty this morning, if you didn't notice the frayed shirt cuff and stained tie.

"Ready to hit the school?" Delgado said.

"Yeah, let's roll," Mason said. They made desultory conversation on the drive over, the light at every intersection turning red as they drove along Wilshire Boulevard, one of the main thoroughfares bisecting the city from downtown Los Angeles all the way to the ocean.

"Jesus, the traffic," Delgado complained and launched into his usual tirade on the unchecked growth of the city.

The traffic was a constant in Santa Monica, along with the tourists. Was this what it was like to live in Paris or Rome, other cities that everybody wanted to visit? Didn't they have traffic too? Mason didn't bother to argue anymore. What was the eastern part of the city going to be like once the new light rail line was finally extended to Santa Monica? And on and on.

He had never been to the Phoebe Windsor Academy before, although he'd driven down the street with its edgy, angled Leggo-like architecture that maximized small lots. They passed the Kensington Industries building, and the grassy lots next to it, a surprising empty space in a city built out to the edges. There was only one way to build now in Santa Monica, and that was up. The no growth and slow growth factions warred with the developers over every square foot. They turned into a driveway next to two small white clapboard cottages with blue roofs and trim that faced the streets. Between the buildings was an emerald green lawn, and behind them in the corners of the lot, two similar clapboard cottages. Five acres of woodland lay behind them, open to joggers and dog walkers.

"I can see why they want to expand," Mason said aloud to end Delgado's rant. "The parents certainly aren't buying in for the fancy campus amenities and art programs like Crossroads School has."

They parked in a lot behind the cottage and walked across the grassy quad towards the building near the street with a sign that said Administration. Pretty flowerbeds edged the walkway. A few students sitting on the grass nodded as they passed. Above them the sky was the blue of tourist posters with wisps of clouds blowing slowly towards the ocean.

No one challenged them as they walked up a few steps to a deck and followed a sign that directed them to the headmistress' office. The sound of adolescents in a classroom having a good time was loud. The place had a musty smell of old wood and lath and plaster construction. Doors were open along the corridor showing students and classrooms and a teacher at a computer or at a whiteboard. He and Delgado looked at each other in surprise. Mason knew what Delgado was thinking; anybody could walk right in here.

They heard a loud scream and turned to look at each other, eyes alert. The scream came again, this time more of a squawk.

"It's a bird," Mason said.

A tall, willowy woman charged down the hall and frowned on seeing them. Wind and sun-burned, she wore a swirly cotton skirt that flowed around long legs and a red turtle-neck sweater that looked expensive. Her hair was short and silver spiked. That and the long, iridescent parrot perched on her shoulder gave her an arty look. Her Michelle Obama arms were bare.

"You must be the police. I thought you'd be coming. Well, you look like police. Am I wrong?"

Mason smiled back. "Detectives Mason and Delgado. We're looking for Venetia Sorenson."

"Well, that's me. Please come into my office. I'm really glad to see you."

They followed her back into a large square room that looked more like a living room than an office with a huge parrot cage near the window. Sorensen opened the door of the cage and the bird climbed off her shoulder onto her hand. She slid him into the cage onto a perch.

"Petrovich loves visitors," Sorensen said, beckoning them over to the wire bird cage. "Say hello but don't get close. He was my mother's bird. I grew up with him. He'll probably outlive me." She stuck her face close to the bird which bobbed up and down. "Kiss mommy, kiss mommy, Petro. Kiss, kiss."

Mason had heard that parrots were loud, messy, and they bit. There was a streak of shit on Sorensen's shoulder that she seemed unaware of, or indifferent to.

"He's beautiful," Mason said with genuine admiration. His long green plumage and turquoise head seemed to glow. Still he and Delgado kept well back. They talked parrots while they got a read on Sorensen. She had left the cage door open and the parrot flew out onto a roost next to her desk and hung upside down looking at them with its head twisted around sideways.

"He comes in with me every day. He'd tear the house apart if I left him alone."

They took seats facing her on a long, black leather sofa.

"So I thought you'd never get here," Sorensen said. "Have you found Doris?"

"No. We're still trying to get a sense of her and where she might have gone."

Her eyes filled with tears. "I'm so worried."

"This must be hard for you."

"You mean first Leonard and now Doris? You bet it's hard on me. I've lost two critical people in my life." She got up and walked about the room, touching things, as though reassuring herself everything else was still there. Her skirts swished around her. "And the work still goes on. Doris and I have worked really closely together over the years, you know. You've seen her sister?"

"Yes, we just came from there," Mason said.

"Poor woman. I don't know what's going to happen to her. It's going to be awful unless Doris comes back soon. Rheumatoid arthritis, you know. Loretta's more crippled up all the time."

Delgado shifted to the details of Arnold's employment history while Mason watched. Sometimes they did it that way. They were so attuned to each other they didn't always plan out an interview beforehand. Arnold had worked for Sorensen's father for fourteen years prior to Venetia's taking over the school. She did the routine administrative work of a fifty-student school, which employed ten teachers, and supervised the outsourced workers. Janitorial work was contracted out, along with tax accounting, and some of the other business operations, and the van drivers that took the students to off campus arts and sports programs. They also employed a dietician and catering service for the school lunchroom.

"You mind if I take a look at her office?" Mason said. He noticed how chilly Sorensen kept her office was yet she was wearing a dress with bare arms. and lowered neckline. Lots of money spent on artwork and furnishings.

"She didn't really have an office per se," Venetia explained, rising to her feet. "We try to make the most of every dollar here so she did a lot of work at home. Still I could depend on her to be here at 7:30, especially on Mondays. She'd always be here if I needed her. Sometimes she worked over there." She smiled, pointing to a small round table in the corner of her office. "Doris didn't like Petrovich. Said his talking gave her a headache. I suppose he gets noisy at times but I'm used to it. Everybody loves him."

Mason could understand the headache. He frowned to concentrate over the squawks of the parrot. "And her computer is at home then?" Arnold's laptop, purse, and cellphone had not been found. Nor had the night deposit bag.

"She carried it back and forth. A laptop, you know. We met every day at some point and went over things."

"Looks like you're a real outdoors person," Mason said easily over his shoulder as he stood, jingling the change in his pocket while examining the wall of photographs of kids in graduation regalia. Sorensen with a group of young people on the top of mountain peaks and diving expeditions. He was just making conversation. Sorensen shaking the hands of politicians. Sorensen standing next to a helicopter, holding skis on the top of a mountain. Another in a paragliding harness.

"I keep fit." She regarded a slim arm and turned her wrist to make the forearm muscles ripple and dance. "I was a competitive marathoner years ago."

"You ever try out for the Olympics?" he said.

"I got into competition too late for that."

Ah, some tension there. She had frozen right up in front of him. "So again, Ms. Sorensen," he began.

"It's actually Dr. Sorensen," she said stiffly. "I worked very hard to get my doctorate and it's useful with students and parents."

Okay. He pulled out his tablet to refresh himself, but he had the facts pretty well memorized. "I just checked the other investigator's reports and they noted that you'd called and left Ms. Arnold messages on Monday and Tuesday asking why she wasn't at work. And then you called her sister late Tuesday to check on her."

"Yes, that's right. Monday we had a very heavy schedule and I wasn't pleased that she didn't come in. She did a lot of work at home and sometimes she got sulky, so I figured we'd check in during the day. I didn't like it, but I wasn't really worried. Then when I didn't reach her again on Tuesday that *was* unusual. I called Loretta and learned that she'd gone ahead and reported her missing. I thought she was over-reacting, but I guess I was wrong. Oh, we talked on Monday but I'd said, don't worry, don't worry. You know the things you say. I mean we were talking about Doris. She's a little church mouse. I hate to say it but she's kind of a colorless person. I mean, you have to know her. She wouldn't go anywhere without telling her sister. And she has this job here and I think that means a lot to her. I meant to call her sister earlier on Tuesday but I got busy and I forgot. I was angry with Doris at that point. There were things I needed her for."

"But then you learned a bank deposit hadn't been made?"

"Yes, Doris did all the banking and so forth but I needed to write a big check so I went into the account to check the balance and the money wasn't there. At first I thought she'd deposited it in another account, but I called the bank and they told me the bank deposit wasn't there. That was when I really got the wind up."

"My notes say the money came in from a Silent Auction. So it surely wouldn't be cash, would it? Checks?"

She interrupted him. "Mostly credit card slips. That's the funny thing. The money wouldn't have been any use to her. There was only $872 in cash."

"That's still a lot of money to some people," Mason said. "Was anything taken from other accounts? She has access to all the accounts?"

"Not a cent. Believe me, I went over everything carefully with the bank. You know, that money means an awful lot to us. It was my idea and I worked hard to raise it."

"We'll do our best to get it back," Mason said without much assurance that was true. "What kind of security do you have here? I notice we came on campus without anyone stopping us."

"I always thought it was safe living in Santa Monica."

Did she mean this seriously, Mason wondered. "There's crime everywhere, even in rich neighborhoods, Dr. Sorensen. Thieves go to where the money is. Why rob poor people?"

She looked hard at him and shrugged. "We don't keep any money here."

"Lots of nice cars out in the lot."

"Many of our students come from well off families, that's true, but not all. We have a number of scholarship students as well."

Mason made a note to check with the beat patrol on car thefts, property crime at the school and in the area. "We'll put you on increased patrol surveillance here. You might see more cars in the neighborhood for a while until we figure this out."

"You ever think of hiring private security?" Delgado said in his raspy voice. He'd had a tumor removed long ago that had scarred his vocal cords.

"We try to keep costs down as much as possible, plus we've never had any problems until now."

Mason decided to advance the pace of the interview. "There's been a new development. Ms. Arnold's car has been found at one of the beach parking lots in Santa Monica with the driver's side window smashed in and blood on the driver's seat."

"Blood? Where's Doris then?"

"There's no trace of Ms. Arnold. We are looking at her disappearance as very suspicious."

"That can't be," Venetia Sorensen said, rising to her feet. "That's just crazy! What's going on here?"

8

Ginger McNair stared at an email on the screen of her laptop, as if she stared hard enough new meanings might appear. She read the email response from Venetia Sorensen again, her face slowly flushing, anger rising. To do her job she had to familiarize herself with the school's financials. From the email that she just read, the headmistress of the Phoebe Windsor School felt the financials were none of her business.

Oh really? We'll see about that. Ginger rose to her feet, grabbing her notes, and started down the hall to her office. Sorensen was all over her, gushing and complimentary, when Rhys or his sister was present, but Ginger was hardly a stranger to hypocrisy in the public relations field. Sorensen was still over the top with her enthusiasms and dislikes. She loved, simply loved the Kardashians. One day she'd told Ginger she thought women who didn't use their blinkers when driving ought to be put in jail. Jail? This was the woman she was dealing with.

She knocked on the door of Venetia Sorensen's closed office, and it was jerked open by Venetia, on her face a displeased scowl. Behind Venetia sat Dave Mason and Art Delgado. Mason's mouth fell open. Ginger felt her body turn to stone.

There was a beat of silence, the parrot's scream, then Sorensen demanded, "Can this wait? I'm busy. "

"Yes, but I would like to see you when you're finished here." Seeing Mason had thrown Ginger off her stride. "Dave, how are... Hi, Art."

Mason got up from the couch and approached Ginger and Sorensen standing at the door. Delgado just sat there on the couch, watching them. "Actually we're nearly done here," Mason said, walking toward the door. "I'll be in touch, Dr. Sorensen."

"Hello, Ginger," Delgado said, with a lazy wave. "You go ahead, Dave. Take your time. I'll finish up."

The parrot flew out of its cage and landed on Ginger's shoulder, nuzzling her hair. Sorensen held out a hand and beckoned to the bird who stepped onto her arm.

"He likes you. How nice," Sorensen said acidly, returning him to his cage and slamming the door.

Mason cleared his throat and started over, saying to Ginger who was standing there looking as surprised as he was. "I wonder if we could talk a minute?" he said.

"Well, sure." What did he want, Ginger thought wildly? They'd had a few brief phone calls following their breakup regarding belongings left behind and incidentals, but the interactions had only pointed up the sharp boundaries between them that neither could cross.

Mason started to shake his head, a smile? Then he followed her out into the hall where she turned into an empty conference room. The short walk seemed endless. Silence throbbed like an ache between them. He sat down in a wooden chair at the opposite end of the table. She waited for him to begin, fingering the scar across her cheek, which she did when she was nervous.

"It turns out Dr. Sorensen's assistant has disappeared under rather strange circumstances and we're doing interviews with the staff and everybody connected with the school."

"Doris? Disappeared? Really?" So this was all business? Okay.

"I don't know that I have much to say about Doris." She sat down, smoothed her hands over her skirt and tried to breathe slowly. It was hard to look at him, and as yet he hadn't looked her in the eye.

"I hear you've been hired as a fundraiser here."

"The school needs to raise money to start a capital building campaign. That's what I do."

"And they asked you…" Mason said, looking at his iPad open on the table in front of him to give himself somewhere else to look than her indigo-blue eyes.

"You know all this, Dave. I have contacts with big money. I know people."

"Sorry, that was clumsy. I know why they'd want you."

"If Doris Arnold has disappeared, something damn funny is going on here. They told us Leonard's death wasn't an accident. I don't have any idea about what's happening if that's what you're hoping. I just started here."

"I hoped you might have an angle on things, that's true," Mason said, drawing his phone out from its belt holster as though checking it to avoid looking at her.

"I haven't been around long enough and Sorensen isn't exactly my buddy." She couldn't help remembering disappointments in their relationship as she looked at him. The good things too.

"Sure, okay. So what can you tell me about Doris Arnold? You knew her?"

"Hardly at all," Ginger said. "I only had a few brief interactions with Doris. She wasn't real chatty."

"Okay. Can you tell me about the way things are set up here? How it's funded and so forth. I'm learning it's not exactly altruism to set up a family foundation."

Ginger had seen both Mason and Delgado pretending to be just dumb cops, which was a good ploy in investigations. She settled in the chair, trying to relax in his presence. The relationship was over and done with. She couldn't imagine how they could ever be just friends after everything that had happened. But she missed him. She missed him a lot.

"No, it isn't," she said, making her voice colorless. "There are enormous income and estate tax benefits. But on the other hand, the Academy has quite a number of scholarship students. And their record of kids being admitted to first-rate colleges is well-known." She hoped he wouldn't ask her how many because she didn't know. Another one of the details she couldn't pin Venetia Sorenson down on.

"And directors of the foundation are paid?"

"Well, yes, sometimes. There's a great deal of work and responsibility involved in being a director of the foundation. Oversight on expenses, for example, meetings, fundraising." She tried not to sound defensive.

"I suppose," he said agreeably. "The directors are executives from Kensington Industries. Isn't that unusual? Isn't there usually more representation from the community?"

Ginger shrugged. "It is unusual but that's the way old Mr. Kensington set it up, so that the family and KI could maintain control. There are community people on the Advisory Board but they don't vote." She rattled off the names of the high profile people everybody in the big money circles in Santa Monica knew.

"Sure, sure," he said, holding her eyes for the first time.

She noticed the scar on his jawline, remembered the way he smelled. Spicy. "...and I'm looking for another job, something permanent. I'm sick and tired of scuffling, going from contract to contract. And I'll bet you know that salary for directors is not uncommon. Are you just fishing?"

"You know how investigations work, Ginger," he said with a grin, using her name for the first time.

"Whatever I'm being paid is certainly not enough money for me to murder Leonard Bricker and disappear Doris Arnold," she said with a strained laugh.

Mason leaned forward, hunching his heavy shoulders. "I know that. Something's going on though. You're in here. Got any leads for us? There must be competition for whoever is going to be named chair of the board."

"People love power. There's perks, I suppose. Prestige for sure." She relaxed enough to let her back touch the chair.

"If there's that much money in the trust, why does the school have to do any fundraising?"

"Old Mr. Kensington wanted the school to be self-supporting eventually, and the time is coming for that to start to happen. He also put in a provision that a permanent campus should be built on this property and the lots next door. These cottages were only meant to be temporary, but it's been decades now, and the City is pushing them to do something. If they don't build, the money could revert to the foundation and eventually to Kensington Industries. Some could even go to the University of Southern California. It's complicated. The Academy has a long way to go toward being self-supporting and I suppose, there's a lot of contention right now on the board about different directions this could take. I've heard rumors even that some of the directors want to close the school."

"Close it to save money?"

"That's right."

"Big enough issue to get Leonard Bricker killed?"

"I don't see how. I wouldn't think so," she said honestly, "but you know people. There's pressure on me, and I guess all the directors, to generate income from donors. And do it quick. Caroline and Rhys are completely against closure, but they're not a majority."

"That's interesting. So not everybody's agreed on this?"

"What do you think? People!" She raised upturned palms and shrugged.

The door opened and Delgado looked in and gave her a big smile. He and Ginger liked each other and she and Delgado's wife Maria had gotten close.

"People is what's wrong with the world. Isn't that what you used to say, Ginger?" Delgado said with a smile of welcome.

She smiled back at him. Delgado was easy to like, unless you got crossways with him.

"Yup, I still say it. People is pigs." Then she went serious. "I haven't been around here that long or know that much, Dave." This time her laugh sounded more natural.

"Let us know if you come up with something," Mason said, standing up.

"I sure will," she said, standing up as well. She put a hand on Delgado's arm. "How's Maria? How are the kids?" She and Delgado fell into an easy conversation while Mason took out his smartphone. He turned his back on them and made a call. Ginger knew him so well she could interpret his posture. She was having an effect on him as well.

"I don't know anything about Doris Arnold, Art. I mean absolutely nothing. She was one of those people you just didn't notice. I heard her and Venetia arguing a few times, but that could mean anything. I know she hated that bird. She told me it gave her allergies." Chatting with Delgado all the way into the hall, Mason caught up with them and gave her shoulder a little squeeze as he passed.

Okay. That was that. Her heart started beating normally again. At the same time a great wave of sadness swept through her.

Neither Mason nor Art said anything about meeting Ginger as they drove back to the station. Mason knew it was inevitable he'd run into her but he hadn't looked forward to it. When he'd met Ginger she'd been running a local election campaign fending off a downtown casino development proposal; then she'd worked as a fundraiser for the California Democratic Party setting up events and big ticket fundraisers. Primarily she drank tea with rich old ladies charming them for donations. A run of bad luck and the bad economy meant Ginger and a whole lot of other people hadn't followed a straight-ahead career path. Since they'd parted months ago, her Dad had Mason and Ginger's brother Art over for barbeques once in a while, but Ginger was only mentioned in passing, and Mason was too proud to just plain ask about her. That was the problem between them: too much pride to be the one to make the first move.

Now she was dating that asshole lawyer, Rhys Kensington, who'd been after her for years. He thought he'd seen them once crossing Pacific Coast Highway turning into the Jonathan Club at the Shore in Kensington's yellow 1956 Porsche 911E, the convertible model. Back when he'd been with Ginger, he'd seen the way Kensington looked at her. He disliked Kensington with a heat that he found quite pleasant. The guy had a big house over on 25th Street, about as close to Brentwood as you could get while still living in Santa Monica. And a place at the beach, of course. Mason watched the papers, eager to read that the place had been burgled or had burned down.

They found Doris Arnold's address and checked on the closest neighbors. They were all out working at high-paying jobs somewhere. Latinas, with little kids howling and clinging to their legs, answered the doors up and down the streets.

La senora no en casa.

The neighborhood was laid out on large lots on a leafy street of bungalows interspersed with second-story renovations and McMansions. Nobody was home at the big house on Princeton Street in whose backyard Arnold occupied a granny flat. Big dogs barked behind high wooden fences on both sides of the alley as Mason and Delgado went around the block and entered through the back gate with a key given to them by Arnold's sister. Doris Arnold lived simply. There was one big room and a small bedroom and bathroom, everything neat and dusted. No dishes in the sink, the counters bare. There were religious pictures up on the walls and a collection of Hummel and Lladró figurines. No laptop on which Sorensen said all the school business records were kept. One two-drawer filing cabinet contained the elements of Arnold's life, and a section where her sister's medical bills and records were filed. No airline ticket. Old tax returns, warranties, keepsakes. No suicide note. Bed made up. Perishables rotting in the refrigerator.

Her living space didn't offer up any leads or any clues to where Doris Arnold might have gone, and not surprisingly they didn't find the $27,000 in credit card receipts. Or the $872 in cash.

9

Ginger settled herself in the so-called campus café to make calls while it was quiet, nodding to the harried-looking dietician. Dealing with difficult donors and volunteers was part of the job and this morning she was working the phones to assemble a fundraising committee. Finding a place to work at the school was a problem. If there were only a few students in the lunchroom, she could make calls from there.

Rock posters interspersed with motivational slogans, bulletins on tests, sports equipment for sale, and upcoming concert events. On the counter across the room was a microwave thickly spattered with pizza, and a vending machine that sold high salt/fat/sugar snacks, the despair of the dietician. Six of the very coolest teenagers were drinking coffee and goofing around. There wasn't an actual textbook in sight. All of them looked up at Ginger as she invaded their sanctuary. They had no other place to go because it was cool and rainy outside. Neither did she.

She gave them a smile, "Sorry, guys, I don't have an office. My job here is to raise some money for new buildings. I bet we'd all like to see that."

"Sounds great," one of them said languidly. Without curiosity, he dismissed her and went back to talking to his friends. Money was uninteresting, unless you needed it.

She tried to work but seethed with resentment and frustration over Sorensen until lunchtime arrived and she could explode with Caroline Kensington. She was still thinking about the handsome, languid man with the accent who had been waiting for Sorensen in her office. It was easier on her than thinking of the interview with Mason. She drove to Ocean Avenue and actually found a parking place. Sitting down at a sidewalk table in a long-time site of excellent cuisine and celebrity watching, she waited for her best friend. The air around them buzzed with privilege.

Caroline shook out her napkin and picked up her water glass, looking around. A shoal of Japanese tourists streamed out of a bus and passed them, laden with high-tech camera equipment. "Why are you taking Venetia so personally?" Caroline said. "She's always been secretive and hard to get along with, except with parents and kids. And the most important part of her job is to get along with them. Not you."

"But I can't get any hard information out of her. I've caught her out in lies. She swore up and down she gave me financials and I know damn well she didn't. She doesn't listen. Half the stuff I tell her is gone in the next minute. It's so frustrating, dammit."

Both of them sat back as their salads arrived. Caroline examined a tiny spot on her red silk blouse, and then wet a finger and smoothed an eyebrow. "It's the start of the semester. She's trying to get in every cent of money in tuition she can right now. There's the Doris thing."

"Oh, big crocodile tears over Doris and Mr. Bricker, boo hoo. I don't think she gives a damn, really."

"Give her a week or so. There must be other things you can do in the meantime."

"I guess I am taking this personally. I've gotten along with narcissists like her before. Half the big executives I've worked with are sociopaths. I thoroughly dislike the woman," Ginger said bitterly.

"Hey, remember Betsy McIver?"

Ginger grinned. "Yeah. Remember that day she got the new Mercedes and we were standing on the steps of the Broad Theater watching her park?"

Caroline gave Ginger a little arm bump. "She finally gets it next to the curb and she pulls forward and bashes the car in front and then she jerks it into reverse and ploughs into the car behind her and she just grins and waves at us? She thinks she's just so cute and charming."

"Thank God, you're not like that."

"I know lots of rich people who would murder their relatives over a gift card to Sears. We're lucky they give us anything. So forget about Venetia. She's worried about Doris, and she's in the middle of trying to hire someone."

"It's hard to feel sorry for her."

"Well, I wouldn't go that far," Caroline laughed. She pushed away from the table, their salads finished. Ginger got up, reaching for her purse.

"I know how to get along with people," Ginger assured her. She leaned forward in full gossip mode, eyes shining. "By the way, there was a guy waiting for her in her office. How could I forget? Very, very dashing, with some kind of European accent. Very rich guy, dangerous looking. I had this sneaking suspicion she was a lesbian until then."

Caroline grinned wickedly. She enjoyed dishing the dirt as much as Ginger did. "Really? That's not what I heard. I heard she likes being one among many. And that she likes bad boys."

"This was definitely a bad boy."

They paid for lunch, and the valet brought Caroline's Prius. Ginger got in and strapped on her seat belt. Caroline drove too fast, jack-rabbiting from every red light, soft-voiced curses at the clusters of tourists who wanted to jaywalk between the long blocks in a fever to spend their money.

"You think Doris took that bank deposit?" Ginger said to keep herself from thinking she was going to die at any moment driving with Caroline.

"I don't know what to think. The whole thing is too bizarre."

"You just like Venetia because she sucks up to you. Keep your eyes on the road, please. And why are you making that face at me?"

"Sucks up to me? Hardly. And who says I like her? I think she's vulgar and awful, but she gets the job done. The school is a good thing, even if we need to subsidize it. I don't want to see it closed."

"But how do you know she's telling you the truth?"

"What are you saying?" Caroline narrowed her eyes and looked at her sharply.

Ginger said stubbornly, "I don't trust her. Where does she get the money to live like she does? And besides that, you know grades in private schools are really inflated. I found this file where she'd done some follow-ups. You add them up and there were more graduates going to Ivy Leagues than she ever had enrolled here. It's all showbiz, all her stats. Manufactured."

Caroline looked dubious. "Rhys said something one time and Venetia bit his head off. She said all the private schools do it."

"Do you believe that?"

"I don't know. Maybe. Yeah."

Ginger sat back in her seat in disbelief. "Isn't there a state oversight agency that's supposed to monitor private schools?"

"I think so. Venetia always said everything was fine."

Ginger flew forward and put her hands on the dashboard. "For God's sake, watch those bicycles. I found this memo when I was snooping around. Leonard Bricker wanted to bring in a new audit firm. He was asking questions too."

"Ginger, why are you looking for trouble?"

"Don't you think there's already trouble, for heaven's sake? What about Doris?"

"Will you please just let it be for now? I hope we can get a lane in the pool. I feel like swimming my head off." Together they entered the YMCA on 6th Street.

"Oh God, I forgot," Caroline shrieked. "It's afternoon. The pool's infested with children. Why do we have to come here?"

"Because it's the gym I can afford," Ginger said.

"I don't know why you won't let me buy you a membership at my gym," Caroline said over her shoulder as Ginger marched ahead of her.

Ginger shook her head. Neither Caroline nor her brother seemed to have any conception that most people didn't buy whatever they wanted. Or do whatever they liked.

"You know Rhys wants children, don't you?" Caroline said with a sly smile.

"You think he hasn't made that clear to me?" Ginger said with more acerbity than she had intended. At least Mason had been subtle about it. Once Mason had lightly poked her on the arm and said, "You're not getting any younger, babe."

While they were at the Windsor Academy, Mason, Fredericks, and Delgado interviewed the teachers. Ten teachers were employed: all but two as part-timers. The first teacher they had a sit down with was a Harold Foster. The guy was wearing his hair short and brushed up from the sides on the top to form a little crest, like a mini, mini Mohawk. He had a very precise way of speaking and gave off an air of annoyance on being told Arnold was missing and so was the money.

"This pisses me off that the money we worked so hard for gets stolen. Me and the other teachers hustled everybody we knew to get donations to bid on for the Silent Auction. She took off with it, didn't she?"

"We don't know that yet. You think that's what it's about then?"

"Well, don't you?" Harold Foster shifted uneasily in his chair. They could tell he didn't like cops.

"What do you think happened to her?"

Foster shrugged. "The whole thing's depressing. This is confidential, huh? Whatever I say?"

"Not if you tell me something that goes in the case we take to court. What do you mean?" Delgado said.

Foster hitched the chair forward and put his elbows on the table. "I mean, you don't tell Venetia everything I say." A frown pinched his narrow face.

"No. We don't do that. What do you want to tell me?"

"Oh, just about working here, that's all. The pay's for shit but the kids are great. They're all really smart and want to learn and it's a kick to teach them, but the administration is lousy. Venetia's always watching us, always crying poor. Always pushing us to inflate grades. Every single kid has to be an academic star."

"Really?" Mason said.

"Nobody can get less than an A and some of these kids are just average. She was talking about a staff pay cut, so me and the teachers got together and did this Silent Auction and while $27,000 isn't a big deal, it would help a lot. At least she said it would. But it's impossible to get straight answers from her. And now the money's gone. That's depressing after all that work." He sighed.

"You don't think she had anything to do with that, do you?"

"Venetia? I wouldn't think that's her style, no. It's just funny, that's all. I mean $27,000 isn't going to save the school. I hear she's hired a fundraiser though. We're supposed to meet this lady and brainstorm later today. On our own time, I might add."

"I thought the Academy had a big endowment," Mason said, flipping through his notes.

"I don't think it's an endowment exactly. It's supported by a foundation but hey, I just teach math and science here. Until I get a better gig."

"Things have changed," Mason said. "We have evidence that indicates it may be more than just a disappearance. Ms. Arnold's car was found with a considerable amount of blood in the passenger seat."

"So somebody knocked her on the head and took off with the loot? Oh, c'mon, man, you gotta be kidding…" Foster laughed. "Doris?"

"What was she like? I'm trying to get a picture of her."

Foster rubbed his face. "She was like a nothing. She had no conversation, no charm—a nothing. We never talked about anything but business. If you made a joke or said something personal, her face just went blank. And she could be a real bitch. She fought with Venetia all the time."

Mason sat back, surprised. "What about?"

"Venetia was always losing paperwork, cancelling appointments, taking off without telling her. The parrot gave her the itch. Stuff like that."

"Anything in particular you remember? Anything different lately?"

Foster thought about it, tapping a nervous foot. "Not that I can recall. Everybody's tense wondering if we're going to have jobs or not. It gets pretty crazy around here sometimes."

"What do you mean?"

"Oh, Madame the French teacher has regular meltdowns. Everybody here has problems, but nothing to do with the school and certainly not Doris."

Mason considered his notes. "I don't think I need to put you through this, but where were you last Thursday?"

Foster slapped the top of his laptop down and started unplugging it. "You really want an alibi from me? Me?"

"Save me the time. I've got paperwork too."

"I had dinner with my parents in the Palisades," Foster said, scribbling down a name and phone number and handing it to Mason. "It was a fix up. Some guy my Dad knows at work. He's finally come around to me being gay, and just to show he's okay with it, he keeps trying to fix me up. I come out and he discovers suddenly he knows a lot of gays. Funny, huh? They'll back me up."

"So how was the fix up?" Mason smiled.

Foster rolled his eyes. It made Mason think about his own dating life.

The next teacher ushered into the utilitarian classroom where Mason and Delgado were doing interviews was a tidy little French woman in her 30's. This was the one Foster had referred to as Madame, the French teacher. Her name was Marie-Claire Guzel. As she sat down, she looked at the watch on a black ribbon on her narrow wrist.

"This won't take long, will it? I need to pick up my children." She adjusted the silk scarf at her neck.

"No, not long. Tell us about your work here. You teach French, don't you?"

She blew out a Gallic puff of air. "And Spanish, and once in a while I have a private student in Italian."

Mason shook his head. "Wow, three languages and English."

"Oh, that's not so much really. It's only in America…," she said, trailing off. "Well, it's different here."

"I suppose. Well, tell me what it's like teaching at Windsor Academy."

"I need this job, so I'm hoping I can tell you this in confidence? You see, Venetia likes to hire people who have immigration problems because we're cheap and she can hold the green card over us," she said bluntly. "My husband is from Turkmenistan. You can imagine what it's like for us."

"Oh. How long have you been working here?"

"Two years too long."

"So were you part of this Silent Auction on Monday night?"

"Briefly. My children are small so my time is limited, which Venetia always tries to make me feel guilty about. She's always finding ways to get the teachers to work more but there's never any extra pay. She told us that if we didn't raise money our hours would be cut."

"So when was the last time you saw Doris Arnold?"

"I had to leave around seven o'clock, and I just wasn't paying attention other than watching the clock. I heard the auction closed around eight and people were impatient to pick up the items they had bid on and go home. Doris and Venetia were collecting money. The students were boxing up items that didn't sell. Jane Siegel was making a fuss about her rose bushes when I left."

"You didn't see anybody who didn't belong around the place, did you? Somebody who might have followed Ms. Arnold when she left with the money?"

She shook her head in puzzlement. "No, just us. A lot of the parents I know. At least the ones who try to help the school."

"Was everybody aware that Ms. Arnold was collecting the money to take to the bank?"

"No. Not that I know of. I didn't know that. I didn't find that out until I got to work this morning and the other teachers were talking. You think that's why she hasn't come back?"

"It's too soon to say. Do you know of anyone who didn't like her?"

Again the eyebrow went up. "Nobody liked her. She was an unpleasant woman to deal with. She made a lot of mistakes in our pay slips and the accounting for tuition. Venetia always covered for her. The parents complained too. Venetia made it clear she was here to stay no matter what. I had some glorious battles with Doris trying to get my pay straightened out."

"Anybody that you think really didn't like her?"

The teacher thought, twisting the scarf at her neck. French women and their scarves. "There was this one student who used to set her off. But I'm not sure I should say anything. We have discipline problems with him. Many of our kids come from homes where there's marital discord and violence."

Mason flashed on an incident not that long ago where a twenty-three-year-old similar to the one Guzel was describing had shot his father and brother and set the house on fire, then carjacked a ride to Santa Monica College shooting up a Big Blue Bus and an SUV on the way to a shooting rampage in the college library. There were a lot of kids with those kinds of problems, and nobody said a thing until they went off the rails.

"Things happen when nobody speaks up. You know that, Ms. Guzel."

"Yes. I know that. But you don't want to speak up unless you know something for sure and I don't. And I don't want to get involved there." She shook her head. "Nobody specifically," she insisted.

"No?" He didn't believe her. Her eyes had darted to the ceiling, avoiding his look.

"If somebody had just spoken up about this kid in that incident over at the College, maybe five people would be alive today." He let that reverberate in the air, but she didn't bite.

"Let me think about this," she said finally.

"If you come up with anything else would you let us know?"

He and Delgado said all the usual et ceteras, standing up and moving her towards the door. She smelled good. He'd heard French women never got fat. Wonder how that was.

The next teacher, an anorexic-looking woman, Mary Lou Masterman, stated she was only at the Academy because she couldn't get a regulation City Unified teaching job since she was the sole caregiver for a husband who'd had a stroke at the age of thirty-eight. Presumably she was around his age, but she looked much older, careworn and slow-moving, eyes ringed with the violet bruises that told of sleepless nights.

Masterman was the only one who had anything pleasant to say about her employer and spoke of her gratitude to Venetia for giving her the opportunity to design her courses online so that she didn't have to be in the classroom. She flicked away a fly that was buzzing around in the still air. "Of course that means that Venetia could crowd in a few more students and free up a classroom too. The kids love this high tech stuff anyway. I did all the course setup on my own, so the software didn't cost her anything and the kids could come to my house for counseling and so forth." She smiled and flexed her feet in sandals. They were worn at the heels and the straw material was coming off. "Probably the whole deal is illegal somehow, but it's a win-win for both of us."

"And Doris Arnold?"

"Never figured her out. The two of them bickered and fought all the time. I know that much. Doris made a lot of mistakes. It felt to me like passive-aggressive stuff. You know how that works?"

Mason thought of a guy in the property office passed over for promotion many times. The police union was a good thing, but sometimes...

"Sorensen ever threaten to fire her?"

The teacher bit her lip, leaned her head back and gazed at the ceiling. "Not that I ever heard and that's peculiar, isn't it, when you think about it? I felt for Doris because I know what it's like to be a caregiver, always living on the edge of catastrophe, and I knew what she did to keep her sister out of assisted living. But why would Sorensen tell me her problems with Doris?" She turned away and looked out the window. "Venetia plays me like the Sleeping Dog, I know that. Long as I get those kids through Advanced Placement Math and Calculus, I can do whatever I like. We all heard Doris took off with the proceeds of the Silent Auction. You haven't found the money, have you?"

"It's early days yet," Delgado said. "And we don't know that for sure."

"It makes sense to me. I'd almost kill for that much money. Know what I'd do? I'd hire this nice old gal I know who does respite care for my husband. I'd book myself into the Holiday Inn and I'd sleep for a week straight. Then I'd take him and we'd go and sit on the beach in Santa Barbara and watch the waves till the money was gone. That's what I'd do." She stood up.

"But I didn't kill her. You know that, don't you? I'm too busy to kill anybody. She's probably dead by now anyway. Poor woman. Poor sister who's left all alone. Doris and I used to talk. I know what her life was like. Maybe she's gone someplace to sleep for a week."

Another teacher confirmed that Sorensen got the maximum work (and unpaid overtime) for the minimum pay from her teaching staff. No benefits, no job security. Fredericks had much the same answers from the other teachers.

Welcome to the modern workplace.

10

Mason and Delgado headed back to the station after the interviews. Delgado slammed the door of the black Crown Vic and sat back to make himself comfortable, reaching for the bag of Doritos he'd stashed.

"So how'd it go when you saw Ginger this morning?" he asked as they shoved through traffic on Wilshire Boulevard.

Mason turned to him, frowning. "Okay. It went fine. It's over between us. Why?"

Delgado grinned. "Just sayin'."

Mason noticed his sly look, or what Delgado figured was a sly look. Delgado and his wife Maria liked Ginger. She was fun; she was good for Mason, they thought. They didn't know how difficult she could be with all her dippy liberal ideas. But it wasn't as if she was all talk. She actually put herself out to help people.

First thing Mason did on returning to the station was to connect with Palmer, the Traffic Investigator, and see what he'd been able to put together about Bricker's hit-and-run. Maybe he could provide the link to the disappearance of the Academy's administrator.

Palmer leaned back in his chair, linking his fingers behind his head. "Me and my guys are working this and I'll tell you it's going to take time," he admitted with his big, cheerful grin.

"There must be lots of cameras around there," Mason said, leaning over the wall of Palmer's cubicle.

"Not as many as you'd think."

Mason humphed to himself. "What did the backgrounders on Bricker turn up?"

"Victim was a big donor to Saint Monica's Church here in town. Hey, you want me to investigate Saint Monica's next? The Monsignor?" He and Mason shared a grin. "Bricker was a retired company executive and family friend of the Kensington's. You know the family's a big noise in town."

"What's your theory of the case?"

Palmer shrugged. "Me and my guys have been kicking it around. Who wants his job at Kensington? He got a paycheck of $100,000 a year as Chair of the Board. His check was a little bigger than the other officers of the board, but regular directors make $75,000 a year—and that's on top of their salary working for the manufacturing side of the company. I got more questions than answers at this point. Anyway, are you just here to give me grief or what?"

"I'm here again because we just picked up a missing person case," Mason said, twirling his pen between his fingers, and then getting up to pace outside Palmer's cubicle decorated with photos of his boys playing baseball. "That missing person case that came in on Monday is the administrative assistant at the Windsor Academy."

Palmer's eyes narrowed. "Now that is very interesting. This is the vehicle we just picked up?"

"Robinson reported it and he figured it looked like blood in the passenger seat."

"Robinson? Man, is he eager."

"Yeah, a year on patrol and he's ready to move up."

Palmer laughed. "Knows it all by now, does he?" He stood up, jamming his phone into his pocket. "I gotta go check on this. More work. Yeah, all's I need is more work." He began sweeping papers off his desk into a drawer and locking it.

Mason watched him. "This happens just when I was thinking there was a cool breeze blowing over the Bricker case. I was thinking we have to kick in a few doors over at Saint Monica's to get things going."

Palmer gave a short laugh, wiped his hand across his face and slapped his pockets to make sure he had everything before he left. He was almost out the door now.

"Hey, anybody mentioned the push to make the Academy self-supporting?" Mason said, walking with him to the door. "Like suddenly there's a need to set up a capital building campaign?"

Palmer shook his head and paused. "What's a capital building campaign?"

Mason only knew because Ginger had told him. "That's a campaign to raise money to replace those old bungalow-type classrooms with fancy new buildings. Like suddenly the school has an incentive to bring in big money."

Palmer's eyebrows met in a vee of suspicion. "Money is always interesting."

"Apparently they have to build according to the terms of the way the trust is set up. Bricker was backing the side that feels it costs too much to build in Santa Monica, and they should just close the school. The Kensingtons and one other guy on the board were against it. They wanted to keep it open. Bricker was pushing for a vote."

"Here's our motive then." He was gone, leaving Mason to kick around the idea of who benefited from Doris Arnold's death. Fredericks was working Arnold's financials. She left behind a lot of misery in the case of her sister and no big brokerage account they could find.

He thought about Laura Fredericks, sliding his key card to enter the Special Operations office where the detective and probation officers worked. She had a dozen annoying mannerisms, talked too loud and fast and sometimes made him crazy with all her martial arts stuff, but he liked her and he could talk to her. She'd been flirty with him when news that he was on his own again had got around. He'd always known she had a crush on him because of the way her red-head complexion pinkened when he stood close. Even her flame-red hair seemed to glitter when they were crushed together in an elevator or as training partners in krav maga, the Israeli martial art the department promoted.

Fredericks knew what the job was and the stink it filled your head with. Ginger knew it too from growing up in a law enforcement family. He'd always watched himself to monitor the way his head was filling up and might overflow in a way that wasn't right. Like the night with the tango instructor when it all came to a boil, the last night he'd spent with Ginger.

Venetia Sorensen was worried, gazing at herself in the mirror in her office, approving of what she saw. She seldom had self-doubts, but she hadn't heard from Vlad since his brief visit in her office, so she allowed herself to wonder if she'd gone too far about his cow of a wife. After all, she was offering him herself. He couldn't possibly care about that woman? He just wanted a son. All men wanted sons. The wife wanted to play happy families and Vlad was hardly the type.

Once their deal had gone through she was sure she could get him to dump the wife. She'd even live with him in Moscow. It didn't sound so bad there. Money could be made. Whatever he had now, and it was considerable, she could make it better. He would see. Russia was a great place if you were rich, and she was determined to be rich.

She stroked a hand down her cheek, smiled at herself, and swished her long skirt around her narrow hips.

"Come, Petrovich. Kiss mommy."

11

Mason and Delgado had an early morning appointment with the Peabodys, the parents who made the rear garden of their McMansion available for the Silent Auction. Mason crammed a 7-11 muffin in his mouth as they drove over and scalded himself on the coffee. Both parents worked in downtown Los Angeles and insisted they had to be on the road by 8 a.m. The early morning meeting was a major concession. They refused to meet during the work day. It had to be 7:00 a.m. or else.

The front door opened into a foyer thirty feet tall. Mason felt vaguely threatened by an art piece chandelier. He glanced upward at the arrangement of springs and bolts that looked as though they were liable to go off and stab downward at any moment. He was glad when Ms. Peabody–no, they were corrected, it was Jane Siegel, not Peabody–who led them into a large room that seemed to occupy the entire first floor of the house built out of what appeared to be concrete. A Latina in a maid's uniform was bustling away in the back where the kitchen lay. One sheet of continuous glass brought in a view of gardens beyond the kitchen to a fence teeming with purple bougainvillea. The house resembled a large, clean box. The walls were painted a glossy white. Mason found himself squinting.

Business-suited and brisk, Jane Siegel sat them down on an arrangement of couches that looked comfortable but weren't. She chatted away, saying her husband Jason would be down soon, sneaking looks at her watch. She sat her iPad next to her. Mason perched on the edge of a chair. Jason Peabody breezed into the room, sleek as a seal, carrying the scent of a fresh shower with expensive lotions and pomades. Peabody wore hipster glasses and a suit that looked way too expensive for Mason to even consider envying. Both were in their forties, trim and tanned.

The carpeting was thick and white, the couch and chairs done up in shades of beige canvas, with throw pillows in beige and white shades. On the glass coffee table Siegel fussed with a stack of decorator magazines. There were no knickknacks other than two silver-framed family photos with blue skies taken on white sand beaches and ski slopes. The niceties were barely out of the way before Jason Peabody took control.

"I don't know how you found out, but let's set that aside for now. Of course we're suing. They've left us no choice."

Mason put up his hands in a stop position. "Wait a minute. We're here to talk about the night of the Silent Auction. You may not know this, but Doris Arnold is missing under very suspicious circumstances along with the proceeds of the Silent Auction."

Jane Siegel blew out a puff of air. Her eyebrows rose. She exchanged a glance with her husband. Jason Peabody gave a snorting laugh of astonishment that looked entirely genuine to Mason.

"She must have been robbed then," he said.

"That's something we've been looking at. She's very involved in caring for her sister who has serious health issues. It's unlikely she'd leave her to fend for herself."

"You're sure about this? I gotta question it because it seems so unreal," Peabody said looking back and forth between Mason and Delgado. "The money's gone. Did she clean out the bank accounts at the school as well?"

"No. The only funds missing are the $27,000 collected that night. $872 in cash."

Peabody got to his feet, frowning. He walked around behind the couch where his wife sat and put his hand on her shoulders. He took the opportunity to straighten the collar of a blouse that lay under her suit jacket. Jane Siegel turned, reached up and slapped his hand with a hot, annoyed look.

"We have nothing to do with this," Peabody said. He shook his head in disbelief.

"And we have no reason to think that you did. But we need to know more about that night. Can you just take us through it step by step?"

Jason Peabody took center stage. "Doris and a couple of other parents and teachers arrived around four o'clock along with the caterer and they started setting up. The parents put up tables to display the Silent Auction items. I got home about 5:30 maybe. You, Jane?"

"A little after you. People started coming around six o'clock. I'm trying to recall even seeing Doris," she said looking at the ceiling to try to remember. "Venetia was the one you noticed and she was all over the place hustling people to bid on the items. She had organized a program and got some alums to speak--and Jason, you gave the pitch, didn't you?"

"I did. And it all broke up around 8:00. I had a deal that was coming to a head, so I was in and out of my office here taking calls. You were around more than I was, Jane."

"My attention was on the roses actually. We paid a fortune to put in the landscaping and honestly, people are so careless. Then there was that Romero kid." Her eyes darted to her husband. "I don't trust him and I was watching him all night. Our daughter Melody and he... well, Melody is so naïve. Romero's one of the scholarship students from the inner city."

"Actually, darling, they're from West L.A., hardly inner city," Peabody said.

"You know what I mean. You do the best you can, don't you?" she said, imploring Mason's understanding. Delgado grunted to convey sympathy. It had to be terrible dealing with the Romero kid her daughter liked.

"So there must have been somebody taking money, a cash box, somebody with a square, something like that."

"Sure," Jason Peabody said. "They had a little setup where people could check out, pay what they'd bid and then the parent volunteers put the item in a little gift bag. Again, I wasn't really paying attention."

"According to Dr. Sorensen, the proceeds were given to Doris," Delgado said, "and she put them in a night deposit bag and was supposed to drop it in the slot at the bank on her way home. Problem is the deposit was never made and no one's seen her since."

"That's what you said," Jane Siegel repeated, shaking her head, "but what we're more concerned about is the suit against the Foundation. The school has to stay open. Like the banks? It's too big to fail. I mean I'm terribly sorry about Doris but maybe she snapped. You'll find her, I'm sure. Somebody like her always comes back. But we should talk about the suit. Are you aware then of the details of the issue?"

Mason shook his head. "If there's something else going on, you're going to have to tell us about it." He didn't like having things sprung on him. He glanced at Delgado and knew he was thinking the same thing. They liked being in control.

"Our backs are against the wall. KI wants to close the school. You knew that, I suppose?"

Mason nodded. "We heard something."

Peabody hitched forward on the couch. "They say the Academy is under-performing as an asset and they need to close it to support the value of Kensington Industries stock. Even though the trust was set up to run at a deficit and ask tuition of only sixty per cent of the students. This school is an essential progressive, developmental model of education that you're not going to find anywhere else. Do you appreciate that?"

"Sure."

"In terms of college prep it's a jewel on the Westside and has been for more than fifty years. I went there myself."

"More than forty per cent of the students get free tuition to provide a good education to bright students," Jane Siegel stuck in. "It's the only school our daughter has ever felt comfortable with—because it's so small for one thing, and she's made friends there. A lot of other parents feel the same. You can't imagine what it's like with a difficult child."

Mason had seen a few *difficult* children of rich parents in his time. Siegel's smartphone rang and she answered it, turning away slightly to carry on a muttered conversation.

Jason Peabody was anxious to tell his story. "We've tried and tried to work with the Foundation officers, but there's no further options after our last request for mediation. Along with several attorneys among the parents, one a judge, we're crafting a suit. We decided to give up dealing with the trustees and just go ahead and file."

Siegel interrupted her husband, "They've been stalling us by not responding to letters or emails, or we get answers but they're nothing to do with our questions, and getting financials out of Sorensen is a lost cause. Nobody can decide if it's poor record keeping or incompetence or what!" she exploded with frustration. "So for weeks we've been laying the groundwork for the filing, researching other schools with educators, lawyers, accountants."

"What would this mean?" Delgado asked, trying to work it out, just as Mason was doing.

"We're asking for a forensic audit for one thing, to get a look at revenue and expenses just to see what the financial situation is," Siegel said, her voice rising. "And an injunction to stop any school closure."

Just then a dark-haired waif of a girl appeared at the bottom of the staircase to the second floor. She twisted one foot behind her other leg and wound herself around the newel post. "Daddy, Maria's car won't start. She's all upset. You have to take me to school," she whined.

"Sure, honey. Oh, Jesus," Peabody said. "Look at the time. The traffic. Look fellas, sorry about this." He leaped to his feet, grabbing his briefcase, reaching out to shake Mason's hand, then Delgado's. He touched his wife on the shoulder and she frowned at him, then he breezed out the door.

"This is complex. We need names, a timeline, a lot more detail than this—the perspective of a lawyer." Mason said in alarm.

"I'm a lawyer," Jane Siegel snapped. "Sit down."

Mason sat down. Jane Siegel slumped back against the itchy fabric of the hard couch, looking as though she was waiting for him to give her something else to be annoyed about.

"Surely the board is aware of the financial situation with the Academy?" Delgado asked.

"You'd think, wouldn't you? Things go on with family foundations you wouldn't believe. With nonprofits everywhere. The board?" She made a rude noise, pursing her lips. "Don't you follow the news?"

"I've got enough trouble keeping up with law enforcement legislation, Ms.

Siegel. So does Dr. Sorensen know about this?"

Siegel's smartphone rang again and she answered it, sounding curt and angry.

"Dr.?" she snorted, finishing the call. "From some diploma mill. Venetia? Did you know her real first name is Sandra? She's trying to play both ends against the middle to save her cushy job. Her father built that school and built its reputation. Not her." Siegel jumped to her feet and paced around, adjusting with a finger a huge white painting with a narrow beige strip.

"Venetia was always in the background until five years ago when her father died. She was a competitive long-distance runner, and always taking time off for training and races all over the place. I don't know if she ever won anything. Her parents supported her."

"And your competitors for students would be Crossroads and Windward School?" Mason said, naming the private schools in Santa Monica that made the news and had very fancy properties and amenities.

"Of course, but we have our own niche." She jumped to her feet. "Look, I have to go. Whatever revenues there are isn't easy to determine. But we were all aware that provisions of the trust are going to kick in, hence the fundraising efforts. We've got somebody good now, I heard. I'll email you later with names of the parents working on the filing. Venetia can give you the sign in sheet for the people that turned up at the party, the donors, all that. Email me with any other questions you have." She was herding them out the door.

Mason and Delgado grinned at each other, standing on the sweeping front steps of the McMansion.

"What a piece of work!" Delgado said, shaking his head.

He and Mason walked down the flagstone pathway lined by cheery beds of impatiens and bright orange California poppies bobbing in the flower-scented breeze. North of Montana a canopy of trees shaded the big houses and double lots. The air was quiet with just the birds gossiping in the trees and the swish of a Mercedes going by on pavement where no potholes were allowed. Mason got in the driver's side of the vehicle and looked over at Delgado who was juggling his phone and tablet, catching up on his emails.

"Notice we never heard word one about this from Sorensen," Mason said.

12

Nobody had seen Doris Arnold after she'd left the home of the Peabodys. Knock and talks at doors in the neighborhood of Arnold's granny flat or around the Peabodys didn't turn up anybody who'd talked to her after she'd left her sister's that night. Where did she go?

They sat in the car, kicking it around as a city garbage truck chugged by, breaking the well-bred tranquility of the neighborhood. Mason and Delgado speculated that somebody knew she had cash and receipts from the Auction and took her down after she left her sister's place. Or she ran into somebody. Was it the ring of carjackers that had been operating in Santa Monica? It was all questions without answers.

"So her life was all church and noble self-sacrifice for her sister?" Mason asked Delgado.

"Why not?"

"Is anybody that saintly nowadays? C'mon?"

"Yeah, I think they are. Let's go. I'm hungry," Delgado growled.

"Thought you were on a diet?"

"Just drive. Hit Chez Jays."

In the end Mason figured nobody really knew anybody. And more important, where was her car last seen before it ended up in the beach parking lot? Who drove it there? Cameras were placed all over the city now. He could put Fredericks on it. She'd hate it though.

There were other leads to follow up. Doris Arnold had one bank account that Fredericks had already pawed through and was still hunting. The difficulty came when they asked Venetia Sorensen to send access to the Academy accounts. It was phone tag back and forth. Mason finally nailed her down. They wanted to check that Arnold had not been siphoning off funds before her disappearance. It was a reasonable request and they were surprised when Sorensen put up roadblocks. First she said their accounting records were customized and she would need to explain everything and it would take too much time. She couldn't meet because she had a string of interviews with people to fill Arnold's place, plus a school to run.

"We have an online backup service for all our work, but it looks like Doris cancelled it six months ago," Sorensen wailed. "We don't have any backups. I can't believe she'd do this to me. I've got stuff on my computer that might help but...without her laptop," Sorensen broke off and Mason could hear a sob and a nose blown. "We have nothing other than the current month. How could she do this to me?" she repeated in a thick voice.

"Where are the paper backups? Your invoices, etc. etc." Mason said, his voice hard.

"I just can't talk now. I have too much to do." She hung up on him.

Mason ambled down the hall to Economic Crimes to see Wozinski who was buried in a welter of white-collar crime documentation. "Sorensen? This woman's been in business all these years and she doesn't have backups? No paper backups either. She can't find the storage place. Says the backup service was cancelled. People! How can there be no backups? You believe this?" He helped himself to a handful of goldfish crackers from the bag on Wozinski's desk.

Wozinski listened, his head on one side, his glasses slipping down his nose. "I don't believe it."

13

Venetia congratulated herself. That went well, she thought, rubbing her hands together and checking her reflection in the mirror. She had always been able to summon tears, or laughter at a moment's notice. Disposable emotions were useful, she found.

Of course, she couldn't put the police off forever but all she needed was another couple of weeks. She had it all scheduled out.

Arnold's personal account had a balance of $458.16. She was paid a very, very good salary, Mason noticed going through Frederick's report. Where did all her money go?

"All her money was spent on things for her sister," Fredericks commented.

Mason had noticed Loretta had treated herself to red acrylic fingernails the last time he'd seen her. What women did to make themselves feel better always surprised him.

"No unusual deposits of more than a thousand dollars, no charges for airline tickets or hotel stays. Nothing's been charged on her card in five days," Fredericks said, leaning close to point something out.

"Are there other accounts you just haven't found yet, you think?"

"It's looking unlikely at this point. She's probably dead anyway."

"So young to be so cynical," Mason said, standing up.

The disappearance of Doris Arnold played out low priority. Without a body it wasn't a homicide and Mason was working other cases where the family and the brass were hounding him every day. People like Judy and Andy Klepper whose lives had been ruined in a carjacking. In the meantime he talked with Palmer about the rash of thefts of catalytic converters. Arnold's car hadn't been touched, Palmer told him, but that didn't mean Mason still didn't have a pile of reports to work through on the catalytic converters. He planned to spend a few hours working his street informants for some link between these thefts and carjackings. They all tied together in some way that he just hadn't figured out yet.

Catalytic converters were required by federal and state law as part of the emissions system. What made them valuable was that they could be made of platinum, palladium, rhodium, or even gold. Thieves could turn the parts in for $200. Recyclers were known to extract thousands in precious metals from each converter. It was a good living for a nimble-fingered thief.

The department had two forensic bays that looked and smelled like an auto body shop where vehicles under examination were towed. The space was utilitarian: metal desk, metal chairs, metal files, and the smell of oil and burnt air. Mason found Palmer there. The Traffic Investigator was watching one of the specialists removing the back quarter panel of a gleaming black SUV Escalade, probably looking for drugs. Arnold's green Subaru with the window missing in the driver's side lay partially disassembled in the other bay.

"Why is the Bricker investigation taking so long?" Mason said impatiently.

"DMV is backed up for one thing. I got on my knees and begged which got me a little ways up the line," Bricker replied. "I kept waiting and waiting. They said they sent it." He turned away to answer a question from one of the technicians.

"No results though," he said, looking back at Mason. "Why not?"

"They transposed two numbers."

"Oh, for God's sake," Mason said, disgusted. He knew it happened, but he didn't have to like it.

"Hey, Mason. Did you think I was just standing around doing nothing? DMV's working with the best technology 2005 has to offer. The State's hard up, didn't you hear? They said they'd call me back by the end of the day."

On the way back to his cubicle, the Public Information Officer ran into him in the hallway. "KI has offered a reward for information on the death of Leonard Bricker. It's all over TV."

The news gave him a headache.

Heading to the conference room, Mason passed Lieutenant Ross in the hall as Ross was heading to a budget meeting. Being a cop wasn't all crime fighting and nabbing bad guys. The command structure of the Department were responsible for administration, grant writing, and liaising with other law enforcement agencies. It was work that held no appeal for Mason, even though the pay was better. Ginger had nagged the ears off him about moving up until he'd finally told her to shut up about it. That hadn't helped their relationship any. Every time he thought about advancement he reminded himself that he liked the street; but sooner or later, he'd probably put in for it. Child support and a mortgage were pushing him in that direction.

Ross gave him a curt nod. Mason wondered how his new romance was going. Ross had shocked everybody by leaving his wife and family and taking up with the Irish clerk in the property office who collected blue smurfs. A thought Mason discarded flitted through his head about calling a woman he kind of liked who worked in the court house next door. Everybody else was getting laid.

He made his way down the corridor of cubicles, nodding at detectives on the phone, letting the buzz energize him. The old bulls were pretty much the same, except that nothing smelled like nicotine any more. He set his tablet on his desk and sank into the chair in his cubicle, flicking his screen on to catch up on emails, hoping there was one from his daughter. While he scrolled through departmental directives, he called Chuck Palmer.

"Palmer," the Traffic Investigator answered, snapping it out into the phone so fast and hard it caught Mason by surprise.

"It's Dave Mason, Chuck. Wanted to have a minute with you. When's a good time?"

"Not now. Not ever it feels like." Then a long sigh. "My daughter is throwing up and the wife is about ready to go home to her mother's and leave the kids behind, and oh shit. My truck got sideswiped and my son didn't make the volleyball team." Long sigh. "I hate to tell you, but we're stalled in the water on the Bricker case, if that's what you're calling about. Feels like the whole world is killing itself by car."

"I guess you heard I'm still working this carjacking deal," Mason said, interrupting before Palmer ramped it up to a full-blown whine. "You know this guy in the photos I sent? I got an ID on him."

"This the guy Robinson likes for the car jackings?"

"Yeah, but he's new to me," Mason said. "A Russian by the name of Vlad Yurkov. He's a player. You know him from the photos I sent?"

"Nope. Always somebody new wanting to piss in the punch bowl. Let me know what you get. What do you make of this Kensington deal?"

"I've got a lead or two still to follow down," Mason said, shifting through papers on his desk, "and I'm still working the timeline for Arnold's last seen appearance, pulling in backgrounders, you know. The routine. Say, you mind if I interview Bricker's daughter and son-in-law again? I've got a follow-up for him. He's a financial guy and I'd like to get this trust thing filled in a bit."

"Help yourself. Do it quick because I think they're leaving town today. Go. Go."

Mason wanted to save more critical interviews for a time when Delgado would be available. He peeled off a Post It from his screen reminding himself of the dentist appointment. He got himself in for checkups, but anytime work had to be done he agonized. Dry mouth, squeamish stomach, clammy hands. He knew he could have gotten sympathy from Ginger who shared his creeping dread of dental work.

Move it, Mason. Move it. Because of traffic congestion, there was no quick way to get through the city, even for a cop. Leonard Bricker had lived over on the eastern side of the city in an old leafy neighborhood of small bungalows from the '50s and '60s, interspersed by homes rebuilt into two and three-story behemoths that came within five inches of the lot line. These McMansions and the city planning department were Delgado's Rant Number 37. No cop nowadays could afford to buy a house in Santa Monica anyway.

A walkway up to the home Leonard Bricker had shared with his wife was lined with big bushes with pink flowers. Ginger would have known the name of them and had probably told Mason any number of times. While he could almost memorize a crime scene, the name of flowers drifted straight through the empty space in his head, and out his right ear.

Bekins moving boxes were stacked next to the front door. Bill Davis, the son-in-law, opened the door as Mason had just lifted his hand to knock. "Come in, come in. You found the place."

Mason smiled inwardly at the thought of getting lost in Santa Monica. After more than a decade on the job he could have recited the names of the buildings occupying every four corners of the eight-square-mile city, and named the residents of a surprising number of homes and apartments on every street. Street cops got to know these things without trying, and there was a lot of street cop still left in Mason. Lot of intersections, landmarks like the Third Street Promenade, he remembered by who got shot there and died, people in the store who got robbed: bizarre things like the spot on Olympic where a body fell out of the back of a coroner's van.

Davis led Mason into a house that was bigger on the inside than it looked from the street. White rectangles on the walls showed where pictures had once hung. Side chairs were stacked and wrapped with tape and shipping labels. *Estate Sale Tomorrow* signs were stacked high.

"Yeah, we were going to leave today, but the wife, she…anyway, we're still working on it," Davis said, gesturing to the back of the house. "Let's go in the kitchen, okay?"

Mason followed Davis past a living room, noticing the athletic bounce in his walk, the way the muscles in his calves moved. Big guy.

"So what can I tell you? I watch *Law and Order*. I know how it goes."

"Oh, good," Mason said with an easy smile. One of those. "So give me a picture of your father-in-law then. Let's start there. What was he like?"

"Probably the last person I figure would ever get murdered for one thing. Glad the wife isn't here. If I tell you things, it's not gonna get back to her, is it?"

"Depends, all depends. You watch *Law and Order.* You know how it goes."

"Nobody's saying it was an accident, right?"

"Somebody took a run at him. Any idea who it was?"

Davis shrugged, then grinned. "Beats me. He was to the right of Karl Rove and worshipped at the shrine of Ayn Rand. So tight that if he opened his wallet moths flew out. We got into a mess one time buying too much stuff and my wife asked him for a $5000 loan. Her Dad's rich, or mostly rich. Smart investor. He said no. She didn't speak to him for a month or let him see the kids. That did it. He offered us a loan--at 6% interest. Real family feeling. He was always saying 'If you don't listen to me how do you expect to learn anything?' How do you like that? Made me feel like chopped meat." At this Davis got up and went to the counter. He took a couple of mugs out of the cupboard and set one in front of Mason. Then he looked up as a crash came from the back of the house.

"The estate sale people, I guess."

"Something else has happened over there at the Academy that's connected to Kensington Industries and the trust. The administrator of the school has disappeared under suspicious circumstances."

"No shit." Davis' eyebrows went up in a look of surprise. He dropped some Fig Newtons on a plate.

"No shit. I need to understand the trust and what all the caginess and whispers are about over there."

Davis laughed and sat down at the table again. "I'm surprised they've been able to hold the lid on it this long. Meredith wouldn't tell you, but I will because you're going to find out anyway and it will make KI look bad." Davis opened the fridge door and got some ersatz creamer to pour into the coffee. He doctored up his coffee and shoved the creamer and bowl of fake sugar packets across the table at Mason.

"So?" Mason said, "What's going to bust open?"

"The trustees of Windsor Academy, and remember Leonard was one of them, are also the trustees and working executives at Kensington Industries. The loyalty of the trustees, as they have admitted, is to KI and secondarily to the school. The Academy is set up as a nonprofit, exempt from taxes, right? Kensington Industries is very much for profit. Would you say there's a conflict of interest there? I'd say so."

"Is that legal?" Mason took a sip from his coffee.

"You bet. Welcome to the shadow world of nonprofits. You see, the trust owns 59% of Kensington Industries. The rest is owned by stockholders and while the company is doing well, like stockholders everywhere, they want maximum profits. What's happening is that the trustees are looking for a way to close the school, and dump an asset that's not performing."

He gave Mason a big grin. "Leonard was pushing for closure. But the legal eagles are all over the place about it, and now they're calling in consultants to see how they can break the trust without breaking the bank doing it. It's a big deal. Leonard's being taken out of the loop throws an oar in sideways. Whoever's going to replace him as Chair of the Foundation is going to be pushed for the decision-making vote."

"And does the headmistress go along with this?" Mason said, doctoring up his own coffee with a hit of the creamer.

"I don't really know. I wouldn't think she'd like being thrown out of a job." He got up to look out the window. "But she'd find something. She's one that's always going to land on her feet. But I hear things about her..."

This was a new line of inquiry to check out. They heard the side door slam.

"Ah, here's Meredith now," Davis said. "Don't say anything, will you?"

Mason grinned. He stood up just as a toddler in shorts ran into the room shrieking and buried his jammy face in his Dad's lap, squirming with the joy of being alive. "Daddy, Daddy."

Mason's heart turned over remembering Haley at that age. Meredith Adams, a bedraggled-looking, overweight woman, looked as if she'd been digging through dusty boxes in the garage. He introduced himself and she gave a sigh of weariness. He could tell she just wanted to say "What?" and skip all the niceties. But she restrained herself and stood with her back to him, pulling out a drawer in the kitchen cabinets, unloading a drawer of dishtowels, and placing them in a cardboard box at her feet labeled Goodwill.

"You want to know if my father had any enemies, I suppose?" she said over her shoulder. "That's what the other cops kept asking. Well, he didn't. He was a good man. He did a ministry at Saint Monica's for low-income kids. If he wasn't at the church, he…" She turned to face him. "I know you want to find dirt on him, to blame him somehow, but there *is* no dirt. He was a good man." Her face was red. Tears glittered in her eyes. "I wish you'd just leave us alone."

"But you know we can't, Mrs. Adams. You want to find out who did this, don't you?"

"I don't care. What does it matter? My Dad is dead."

Adams got to his feet and came to stand behind his wife and put his arms around her. "She hasn't slept for two days, and I'm trying to get her to lie down for a few hours. We've got so much to do today before the sale tomorrow. You mind coming back later? I don't think there's anything more to say really. The other guys were with her for hours."

"Sure, I'll come back if I need to, but here's something to think about in the meantime. Doris Arnold from the Windsor Academy is missing. She's the assistant to the headmistress. It's too much of a coincidence—two people from Windsor."

Meredith Adam's shoulders rose under her ears, and she hunched her back and drew in a deep breath, spinning around to rage at Mason.

"I don't know anything about that. There's nothing to find. You're just trying to make my dad look guilty of something. He didn't do anything," she shrieked, spittle flying. "It wasn't his idea, what's happening. My father was smart. If he said closing the Academy was a good idea, it was."

Mason pretended this was new information. "Closing the Academy?"

"Nobody told you about that?"

"It wasn't anywhere in the notes," he said truthfully.

"That surprises me. They're usually a bunch of old ladies gossiping over the back fence."

"And you knew about it? He talked to you about it?"

"I have an MBA from Wharton. That comes as such a surprise to you?" Her mouth twisted nastily.

"No, no," Mason said hurriedly, waving a hand in the air. "Of course, not." But it did, meeting her there amidst the turmoil and confusion. He'd pegged her for a Daddy's Girl housewife.

"And Doris Arnold?"

Her brow creased. "Who is that again?"

"She's the assistant to the headmistress."

"Oh, her. That's just coincidence. They had nothing to do with each other. I don't know anything about her."

Just then an Asian woman came in wearing stained sweats and a headband pulling her hair into a cockatoo's crest. "Okay, Mrs. Adams. We have to make some final decisions here."

Meredith Adams looked between her and Mason. She made brief introductions. This was the Estate Sale planner.

"If you could just bear with me a little longer, Mrs. Adams..." Mason said.

"I really can't. We have one day to do this. We're booked to fly home tomorrow and this has taken a lot more time than we thought it would."

Mason could feel the hysteria rising off her like steam.

The estate planner shifted her weight from foot to foot impatiently and scratched the cockatiel's crest of hair with her pen. Mason was close enough to hear her mutter, "Not my fault."

14

Venetia Sorensen left the school for an appointment with Paget, the Treasurer of the Phoebe Windsor Academy. Vlad appeared suddenly, as he always did, rapping at the window of her BMW. The day brightened and Venetia stirred in the seat of her car, rubbing her thighs together, feeling the rushing throb of being close to him. She clicked the door open and he swung into the seat beside her, smelling of expensive cologne and his own scent that she tried to breathe up and store.

"So you have money?" he said.

Without consideration of who might be watching Venetia flung herself across the seat, reaching for his mouth. "I told you. It will take more time."

"Ten days more. Then must be done."

He moved away, denying himself. No, no. She felt the gun in his waistband and it thrilled her, along with his foreign, exotic scent.

"You tell me you have problem with this woman so I take care of it for you. Now you say you have no money? You want to live like rich woman? Yes?"

"Yes," Venetia said desperately, feeling her control slip away. "Where is she? What happened to her? I can't keep a lid on this."

He grinned at her.

"This has all gotten so bizarre!" Venetia said wildly.

He reared back in the seat, further removing himself from her hands. That she couldn't stand. "You want to play games with me? You like funny sex games? Scare yourself? You like to fuck my guys? Fuck me? Live like rich bitch playing games?"

"Yes, yes, please don't," Venetia said.

"Games over. You find money. Ten days you have."

How could she get both; the sex and the big money score from Vlad's operation?

Delgado had gone back to interview the French teacher at the Academy, and his soulful brown eyes had gotten from her the name of the student who had had repeated run-ins with Doris Arnold. An interview had been set up, but before Sorensen would let them talk to the kid, she warned them. "His father is a doctor and one of the doctor's best friends is a lawyer. The lawyer's in the room with him along with his father. You're wasting your time. This kid had nothing to do with Doris' taking off."

"So you think she just took off with the money then?" Mason said. "Wasn't a robbery? What about the car?"

"I don't know what happened to her, but if she just took off for a vacation I'm going to be very unhappy with her." She opened the door of her office, introduced them all around, and then slammed out of the room.

Mason had expected some slouch-shouldered, sullen, pimply adolescent. Chase Reynolds and his father were cut from the same mold. Both were preppy, blonde, and sure of themselves. The lawyer he'd seen around court before. They gave each other curt nods.

The lawyer blah, blah, blahed about what questions Chase Reynolds, Jr. would answer and what he wouldn't. The kid smirked, another professional smiler. He was wearing a white shirt with a tie and pressed chinos. Child actor good looks, eyes as large and clear as a lemur's.

The lawyer let off a further five or six thousand words while Mason waited for him to shut the fuck up. They hadn't been expecting much and that's what they got. Mason read between the lines and decided that Arnold got into it with the kid because Reynolds enjoyed antagonizing her. She was impotent to do anything about him, and he knew it. The arrogance that towered over the room made Mason's teeth itch, but he couldn't see how the kid could relate to Doris Arnold's disappearance. But still... he'd check him out.

Fredericks came into the viewing room at the station, a work out towel over the shoulder of her beige suit, dragging her heavy gym bag. She was pissed at Mason because he had her watching camera footage from the parking lot on the beach where Arnold's car had been found. What lay ahead was thousands of hours of footage from all over town. Fredericks was on the short side but bulked up with weight training. Cameras caught a decent image of a driver at the kiosk where the ticket was issued, but not if a driver was wearing a cap with a bill, rubbing his face with a hand wearing a glove, and kept the face averted. Theoretically a camera kept track of anyone walking from the slot where he parked his car at the beach, but the cameras were placed on light poles and anyone with eyes in his head could detour around them. Frederick had freeze- framed and printed the best shots, which showed someone tall holding the right shoulder forward, a gym bag held close against the chest, the head wearing a white ball cap. The face was angled down into the chest. The other hand was jammed into the pocket of a long black coat. Under the coat were legs in what looked like black jeans, thick-soled dark shoes on the feet.

"He was watching the cameras," Mason said over her shoulder, skidding his chair closer. He caught a light, astringent scent from her frizz of red curls.

"Man or woman? What do you think? I think it's a man," he said.

"The limp though. You don't really get a good sense of the gait. Like whether it's a man or woman."

"The limp's a fake," Mason observed, hitching his chair forward.

"Yeah." Fredericks pursed her lips, focused on the screen. One finger tapped the desk impatiently. "Real smart. Those crime shows teach you everything you need to know."

"Hey, I learned something myself from *Criminal Minds* the other night."

"You watch that?" she boomed. Everything was loud with Fredericks.

"I keep hoping they'll put me on TV someday to celebrate my brilliant detectiveness."

"You wish." She turned back to the screen. The image began to move. The figure continued to look down, clutching the bag to his chest. Then it was gone.

"Hey!" Mason said in surprise.

Fredericks turned to grin at him. "All's I can figure is he ducked down between cars and crawled between those two RVs." She flipped from one screen to another showing the parking lot from a different angle.

"There. There," Mason pointed.

The video rolled and she went silent, but Mason could hear her breathing. The time stamp said 12:20 a.m. He leaned forward in his chair as if to make the image come in clearer.

"Keep watching."

The figure they'd been watching emerged and crab-walked toward the dark at the edge of the lot.

"He's gone."

Mason got up and kicked a chair in annoyance. That helped.

❧

Mason caught up with Palmer in the gym at the station. "Did you know that there was a push to close Kensington Academy? Bricker's daughter told me the school was failing."

Palmer shrugged. "Everybody says they're one of the top schools. Why would they do that?" He wiped away sweat from his face with a small towel.

"But what would it have to do with Doris Arnold?"

Palmer grinned. "One less person on payroll."

"Be serious."

"Seriously then, I don't know."

"Let's find out." Mason looked at his watch.

"Aw, Dave. I want to go home. When I'm done here I'm off the clock."

"Since when are we off the clock?"

"Just because you got nobody to go home to doesn't mean I don't."

That stung. "C'mon, it's only 5:45. We might catch her there."

He couldn't persuade Palmer, so he went without him. Delgado was attending a training session on new surveillance equipment. He pulled into the parking lot at the rear of Windsor Academy to see a surly looking teenage boy climb into a Range Rover. The father wrenched off his tie, snarled at the kid, and peeled out of the lot. Sorensen would hardly leave until the last student had gone so she could close the place down and lock the doors. However, all the lights were off and the drapes in Sorensen's office were drawn. Walking around to the front of the old cottage building, he knocked on her office window from the outside. The parrot was quiet. He could practically hear her breathing with that sixth sense he'd developed over the years. She was inside watching him as he knocked at the entrance. He knew it.

She didn't answer and he finally went away, at least to the billiard bar on Wilshire where he looked in on the action for a while before he went home. The players were way too good for him. He would fill the evening reading the new manual on the emergency disaster plan the Lieutenant wanted comments on by Monday. Then stay up until stupid o'clock watching hockey on ESPN. Another action-filled day in the exciting life of a homicide detective to update Robinson on for his script. At least this weekend he was seeing his daughter and had thought up some fun stuff they could do together.

Sorensen watched the tall, good-looking cop leave through a gap in the curtains. He scared her. She grabbed her prepaid cellphone, hit some numbers, and waited impatiently.

"What?" he answered.

"Hey, you. A little respect here," Sorensen said.

"I don't like this at all. I heard about Doris."

"That she took off?" She could hear him wheezing. Fat.

"What's that about?"

"The money's nothing. Nobody would kill somebody for $800. No."

"You're not traveling in the right circles. People get killed for five bucks."

He wheezed into the phone. "The cops will be all over this."

"They've been here. I can handle them." She could feel him waver.

"So what happened to her then? You've gotta know something."

"I think she just snapped, with Leonard breathing down our neck. If she lost her job..."

"You threatened her?"

"Of course not. Leonard thought her salary was way out of line and wanted to fire her and get somebody cheaper. I guess she heard about that, but never in a million years did it occur to me that she'd do anything to him."

"Really? You think she killed him? You think that Doris...You think she took off with the money too?"

"You didn't really know her. She was hard as nails. A demanding, greedy woman," she insisted.

"Sure didn't look it."

"You didn't know her, did you? The thing with her sister was weird. You know they slept together in the same bed until Doris got that place a year ago."

"Oh, c'mon, Venetia."

"Anyway, forget Doris. What's going on over at KI? Is there a date set for the election of the new chair?"

"Be patient. That's small potatoes right now with the other thing looming."

"Hurry it up. I've got commitments."

15

Mason schlumped into work on Monday morning without his usual jaunty step after a weekend with his daughter. Haley was in a grouchy mood that foreshadowed the sulkiness of adolescence. She still hadn't forgiven him for taking Ginger out of her life, Ginger her BFF. Nothing suited her. Daddy was to blame for everything.

He and Delgado sat down to debate which one to hit first: Sorensen or Doug Paget, the treasurer of the board at the Windsor Academy. The previous board chair was a good old boy, a serious golfer who dropped in occasionally to chat with Venetia and order the fine wines and cuisine that was served at board meetings. Nothing fishy about his death. They still hadn't figured out how Bricker, or Arnold, or any of this connected. First there was the hit and run on Bricker. Did it have anything to do with his personal affairs, or did it connect to

Kensington? Then what did the disappearance of Doris Arnold have to do with anything? They had to tell a story connecting all the dots that made sense to the Sarge and the Lieutenant of Operations. New dots on the screen made the Kensington picture scatter in a way that now didn't make any sense at all. That was the way it was in investigations, hoping to find the needle in the haystack to sew it all together.

The same was true for the string of carjackings that would not connect no matter how Mason tried to string the dots together. There must be somebody running it, but his street informants hadn't picked anything up about the Yurkov operation. The Yurkov crew was new in town and nobody was talking yet. The setup looked legit. He had businesses all over town, dry cleaner's, printing operations, car washes—and a string of criminal associates in the Hollywood Russian community. Mason was on the phone to different agencies pooling information and resources but nothing was cracking open.

He made an appointment for later that afternoon with the huffy personal assistant who worked for Doug Paget at KI. Did she think he sat around all day eating donuts, reading guns and ammo magazines, just waiting for a chance to talk to Paget?

"Let's hit Sorensen first," Delgado said.

"Good," Mason said, settling in for the drive over to the Windsor Academy. "That woman's cobra smile gives me the creeps."

"She looks okay to me. I think it was the assistant who was up to something and took off."

Mason just snorted at that, looking out the window. They were both alphas. It wasn't surprising they disagreed.

They cornered Sorensen between two of the small cottages, talking to students who were sitting around in the shade on a scrap of lawn, working smartphones and iPads. Seeing them, Sorensen pulled the two detectives around the corner of the building where an old swamp cooler chugged away. She tilted her head in a question as soon as they were out of hearing of the students. "Is there anything new on Doris?"

"No, that's not why we're here," Mason said, making his voice hard. "We're following up on new information. Why didn't you tell us there are plans to close the school?"

"Oh, that." She waved it away. "Just rumors. There's always rumors. Who did you hear that from? Jane Siegel? She can huff and puff all she likes. She gets upset about something concerning her precious daughter and immediately she's going to sue somebody. Anybody. She was going to sue the vendor who supplies the soft drink machines here because he wouldn't provide Green Smoothies, which is apparently what her anorexic daughter lives on."

Mason was surprised to see the venom show in Sorensen's face. He always made sure his own face was presented to the world in a wooden, noncommittal expression.

"It sounded a little more serious than that."

"Please," she said urgently. "Do you think I wouldn't know the provisions of the trust? Please. That's why we have Rhys Kensington's girlfriend here who's supposed to be raising money. At least that's what she says she's doing. But it looks to me like she's just having fun before she gets him to marry her."

Mason didn't like that. "So then you aren't worried about meeting big financial obligations to keep the school open?"

"Of course not. We provide for these things with a capital reserve account. And the fundraiser is setting my plan in motion. Honestly, Detective Mason. Do I strike you as naïve? The Academy is my life, a legacy from my father. It has a position in the community. I couldn't possibly let it fail. The alums would never let me."

Mason nodded. "Right. And it pays your own bills as well. Okay. We'll be in touch."

"Wait. Have you found Doris? I thought that's why you were here. Isn't there any news?"

"Not yet. But we will."

They left, walking across the grassy quad toward the parking lot in the rear of the property. Lotta nice cars back there. "You buy it?" Delgado said to Mason.

"In this job? I wouldn't buy my dear old mother telling me she baked chocolate chip cookies if I saw her take them out of the oven. You?"

"I donno," Delgado said, brushing back his widow's peak. "Maybe. Yeah, she's got a lot to lose if the school closes. Who wants to go looking for a new job for one thing?"

Mason made a note to ask Paget about her salary. They'd noticed Doris Arnold made really good money, more than he did. That was worth a follow-up. "Why didn't she tell us what was going on?"

"Mason, you dreamer, when did anybody ever tell us the whole truth?"

Mason shrugged, casting a surreptitious eye over the grounds, not sure if he was relieved or disappointed not to catch a glimpse of Ginger.

They drove back through Palisades Park, down the California Incline to the Pacific Coast Highway that gave visitors a brief glimpse of the blue Pacific before the Pier and the Ferris Wheel and baby roller coaster.

"What the hell's this?" Delgado groused, pointing at a circle of people on the beach a hundred feet away from the roadway on the sand.

"Didn't you know it was International Peace Day—and just to make things more exciting it's Heal the Bay's Coastal Cleanup Day. Some yoga place is forming a human peace circle of healing and sound meditation. Don't you read the bulletins?"

"Stop the car," Delgado snorted. "They're expecting me."

Mason laughed out loud, his first laugh of the day.

The carjacking investigation had fallen by the wayside and Mason was getting pressure on it, so for now Doris Arnold would have to stay missing. Pricey cars and people with money in their pocket would always be a target for thieves. The department was also taking heat from the activist Neighborhood Associations in Santa Monica. On TV, cops got to work one case at a time. Mason snorted every time he saw that. They were still waiting on the lab for reports on Arnold's car and keeping up with the reports and paperwork a major case generated. Delgado had insurance companies and car owners on his back with calls and emails that needed to be returned. The insurance companies were jacking up the rates and nobody liked that.

He thought of Trevor Robinson, the kid with the unashamed eagerness, and his big, white Chiclet teeth. Teeth. That led to thoughts of dentists so he stopped thinking about it.

"Carjacking in progress at the mall." Mason heard Fredericks yelling from down the row of cubicles. Everything Fredericks said was loud, a holdover from being in a family with five brothers.

"Let's go," she hollered at him. "We got a seventy-year-old woman shopping at Bloomingdale's. I guess they thought she'd give up the car without a fight and she didn't."

She skidded into the passenger seat beside him. Mason hit lights and siren and watched the traffic make a half-hearted attempt to let them scream by. There was always some blond in a big Escalade talking on her cellphone who sat in the middle of the street and wondered what all the fuss was about. "Get over, you stupid bitch," Fredericks hollered out the window. Mason grabbed her arm while she was reaching for the bullhorn.

"Finally some action," she grinned at him, "I was so sick of working those jewelry store robberies and I'm goin' blind watching camera footage."

The mall was being renovated with construction work tying up Colorado Boulevard. They parked in front of the exit on Colorado and took off running up to the third floor. Mason's longer step barely kept him in front of Fredericks as they hit the stairs to burst out on the 3rd floor. A crowd of excited bystanders, all of them talking at once, greeted them.

A group of young kids who looked like Iranian students stepped all over each other telling him what they'd seen. Mason selected one of them, a boy with dancing black eyes and a techie haircut.

"Yeah," he said, "we sorta saw the tail end. Two men jumped this lady." He pointed to a white-haired matron who lay unmoving on the cement, her arm at an angle that physiology did not allow. "They held her down and cut a Rolex watch and other jewelry right off her arm," he stammered with excitement.

"And what we were doing while this was happening?" The radio was crackling with police chatter. He heard Fredericks yelling at somebody to get a description from behind him. An LAPD Air unit circled overhead.

One of the girls screamed at him. "We were parking the car, cop. Don't blame us. We were the ones who called you."

The boy next to her pushed her back behind him. "The lady was screaming. The one in the ball cap pried her car keys out of her hand and tried to get away in her car." He pointed to a late model Toyota SUV parked crooked, the driver's side door open.

"Tell us what they looked like," Mason said, expecting nothing. To his surprise, the girl gave a good description. The boy said it looked like they thought they'd just grab her jewelry and drive off in her car."

"Stupid," Mason grunted. It was too crowded to flee from the mall parking lot at the best of times, especially in a vehicle.

"And where did they go?" he said, eyeing the crowd. A uniform on bike patrol wheeled in beside him, listening on his chest mic. Mason turned to him. Delgado appeared, looking winded.

"They split up. We've got eyes on one in the Promenade. The other one ran into Tongva Park, scaled the fence and we're onto him."

"Nasty," Fredericks said, joining the others who were watching the paramedics bustling the old woman with blood in her hair onto a backboard and into the back of an ambulance. The one eye that Mason could see was blinking rapidly. Her hand worked spasmodically and the paramedic tucked it under the blanket and then patted it with a quiet word to the old lady.

SMPD was out in force: Delgado, Palmer the Traffic Investigator, and Gomez and Wilson who worked Auto Theft. The scene became well-organized pandemonium, trying to evacuate the parking structure into already deadlocked downtown traffic along Colorado, Broadway and the popular Third Street Promenade. The Promenade brought shoppers from all over the world and they were all there today, eager for a look. Held back by patrol officers, the crowd pressed as close as they could get to the action, standing in doorways, buzzing with excitement, and clucking their tongues at how awful it was. Some were trying to be helpful; others just wanted their faces on TV. Mason was lead on the car jackings so he became command, issuing brisk radio orders, listening hard. Fredericks was directing the roping off of the crime scene, trying to keep people back.

A report came through that one of the jackers was hit by a bus as he ran across Broadway and 4th against the light. The bus had clipped him and flung him hard against a row of parked cars. An ambulance had just roared off with him.

"How many jackings that make now this month?" Gomez asked Delgado, sucking his teeth and standing around watching.

"Five. Three during daylight hours, like this one."

"Guess you better do something, huh?" Gomez sneered.

"Somebody's been playing way too much *Grand Theft Auto*," Delgado said. "I wouldn't want any of you guys to break a fingernail tryin', Gomez." Delgado turned his back on him.

"Let's see you make an actual effort for once, Delgado," Gomez said to Delgado's back as he walked away. Oh yeah? Mason looked between them wondering what was going on.

Hours later they met back at the station to start the pissing contest as to which team was going to take the lead. The Downtown Bicycle detail was still patrolling the area in conjunction with officers in vehicles looking for the guy that got away, melting into the crowd of tourists. The mall was riddled with cameras, but no one had yet come forward with a shot. They got various other descriptions of him: he was tall; no, he was short: he was wearing a T-shirt and a ball cap. The consensus was that he was a white male, probably young. One witness said he had "mean, slitty eyes." That description would help a lot, especially if the case went to court.

Everybody was pissed off by the time they'd assembled in the conference room back at the station to strategize interviewing the one guy they'd nailed–unfortunately he was unconscious.

Delgado was just back from St Johns' ER with a fingerprint ID on the unconscious jacker who had been hit by a bus. It had taken charm and bluster and more than a few connections to get a thumbprint off the patient to run through Department of Motor Vehicles.

"Okay," Delgado announced, "He's in surgery right now. Name's Raymond Anthony Hayder. Know him?" He looked around. Nobody answered. "Okay."

"Check Hayder's known associates. Start getting names," Delgado said. Mason started making notes.

"Hey, Delgado, back off," Gomez said. "This is my case." Gomez was all 'roided up, with trapezoid muscles that almost met his ears, his head shaved, a prognathous jaw. Stereotype cop with attitude permanently stuck on the *Asshole* setting. Mid-forties, stuck in rank, with a file of citizen complaints.

"Hey, yourself, Gomez. I'm not looking for extra work, but it's a jacking, not auto theft. Me and Mason are working these jackings, putting together a file. We got a tip on new guys in town. Russian named Yurkov on Lincoln."

"Yurkov's our operation. We had them first," Gomez objected.

"Then why haven't we heard about this until now?" Delgado shouted.

Sgt. York walked into the conference room to see Gomez and Delgado nose to nose now, testosterone fumes in the air. He took in the situation, looking back and forth between them. Both Gomez and Delgado eased back in their chairs at the long table.

"Listen up, girls. This isn't high school. I want Delgado and Mason on this. Nothing personal, Gomez, but it's more Major Violent Crimes now than Auto Theft. And I'm seeing linkages here. We have to hit these jackings hard with everything we've got. This has gotta stop."

"Hunh," Delgado grunted, taking the chair beside Mason. The chair protested under his weight.

Sgt. York set a stack of printouts down on the table between Mason and Delgado.

"You'll all get a piece of this. Pool resources here, figure it out and get it stopped. There's talk of a Task Force. This is getting too big for one department." He exchanged hard looks with all of them and strode out of the room, whistling.

"So, okay," Mason said into the vacuum of silence in the room. "I'm lead on the jackings. What do you guys know before we start interviewing Hayder? Let's put together a file on him. If he's in surgery now, we probably won't get a whack at him until tomorrow."

Gomez blew his nose using a roll of toilet paper left on the conference room table. He examined the contents, shifted his ass in the chair and exchanged a look with his partner. "We've been building a case on Yurkov, and now we have to give you everything and you take all the credit," Gomez grumbled.

"You heard the Sarge," Delgado said. "He knows you're gonna give us your book. C'mon, man. We're supposed to work this together."

"Okay. Okay. I don't get credit and I'm grieving this with the union," Gomez said.

"Oh, c'mon, get real, man."

"Hey, what's the deal with you two?" Mason said, puzzled.

Gomez looked away and Mason studied the cross-hatch of wrinkles above his collar arranging themselves in new wrinkles. Delgado got up from the table and beckoned to Mason. Mason followed him to the door-way and out in the hall.

"One too many citizen complaints. Problems with women," Delgado said quietly. "They've got Wilson rid-ing with him. Wilson's on him like a dirty shirt."

Mason nodded and they came into the room and took seats at the table.

"Look, I said okay, didn't I? We'll give you our book." Gomez trumpeted a huge sneeze and blew his nose again.

His partner, Jack Wilson, who had nothing to say until now, skidded his chair forward to the table and opened his mouth. "We got two solid leads on this. One takes us in the direction of a guy named Milan Cheslowski and his posse. The other lead is Vlad Yurkov and he operates with a guy named Yuri Kozlov. They opened up a new car lot down on Lincoln. Let me start with Yurkov."

Mason sat back. Two Russians, the car lot on Lincoln. Ah, yes.

Gomez couldn't stand it. He interrupted, grabbing the file back from Delgado, flipping through it. "Yurkov, yeah. Owns an auto body shop and a whole bunch of other businesses. Lots of rumors he's into something big and we're just waiting for him to make a move. But he's smart. You'll never touch him, but you might work up the chain pulling in one of his crews. We've been working with the Auto Theft detail out in the San Gabriel Valley, and you want us to blow the operation now," he said resentfully. "We can link one of his guys to a Lexus up on Montana last Saturday night. The guys out in the Valley went to one of Yurkov's businesses and found a Honda motorcycle reported stolen from here, along with parts to a Toyota Tundra out of Lake Elsinore, and a partially stripped Ford Ranger truck that was in the process of being body-swapped with another Ford Ranger truck. So we got him good, but it's in his wife's name. Everything's in one of his relative's names. He manages to keep about five layers between anything on the street and himself."

"So this slimesucker at St. John's is one of his boys?" Delgado asked. Mason was scribbling notes, trying to keep it all straight.

"Nah, never saw him before, judging from his DMV headshot. But that says nothing. My mother's picture makes her look like a felon. We don't know who this guy belongs to. Shit."

"So what's the deal then, Gomez?" Delgado looked directly at him. Gomez shrugged.

"Ah, Gomez is just pissed because he's hot for one of the people with the Auto Theft Interdiction Detail out there," Gomez's partner said with a grin.

"Me and her are gettin' married," Gomez said, crossing big beefy arms over his chest.

"Oh, blow it out your ass, Gomez. You're dreaming. She threw you a pity fuck, that's all."

"I'm givin' her a ring," Gomez insisted, his face turning dark, fists clenching. His temper coiled inside him, a snake ready to strike.

"Shut up, both of you," Delgado growled. "What's wrong with you, Gomez? We got work here. Do your dreaming on your own time. What about the other lead?" he said, addressing Gomez's partner.

Gomez got up from the table with a jerk and walked over to the coffee set up on a table at the side of the room.

"Hayder might be, just might be connected to the Cheslowski ring. Or maybe not. They've been all over them back in Cincinnati for years. They're behind a number of local criminal activities, including drug dealing, but the two of them are just plain slippery. The cops there are able to cripple them once in a while, but they've never been able to bring charges that stick. Informants are disappeared or killed," he shrugged. "Undercover never got anywhere near them, and nobody's been able to get enough information to put them out of business. They were just delighted when the two of them left town and showed up here. Deeeelighted."

"Cheslowski's news to me," Delgado said.

"You working the chop shops?" Mason asked, his eye on Gomez. He was the kind of guy who never sat still long. He tapped his fingers on things and paced, subterranean energy bubbling to the surface. He liked guns and machines, loved tools of any kind. And he had an obsession over this woman on the Auto Theft detail. Unpredictable.

"Sure. But there's new ones springing up all the time, guy working in his backyard with a big fence around it. They get pit bulls and the dogs bark. It usually pisses off one of the neighbors and somebody calls it in. If patrol's got anything on the ball they tip us. We're working them.

Because jackers are only interested in high-end vehicles, it means well-paid, well-off asshole owners who have connections," Wilson said.

Gomez interrupted him…"And all these assholes know their rights and by God they're going to grind them in your face." He got up and stamped across the room again for coffee.

Wilson gave Mason a shrug. "What's in it for your average jacker or car thief?"

"What we hear," Gomez answered, "is $4,000 to $8,000 for a stolen car by street-level fences, and they sell them up the chain to higher-level fences. They put out an order for a particular car and the crew goes out to pull it in."

"You got any idea where they're going?" Delgado said.

"The cars there's a specific order for, lots of them go through the port at Long Beach on containers. We got other agencies sniffing around too."

Gomez came back to the table, stirring a cup of coffee that had been on the burner several hours by now. He actually drank it. He must be in love.

"The car thefts are all late model luxury cars," Wilson said, "like the Lexus with the anti-theft devices, which rules out your average car thief. Unless they try and take it with keys in it like they did with the old lady. But what we've got here is a bunch of bad guys with the knowledge and equipment needed to bypass the security they put on these new ignitions."

"Like what?" Mason said.

"Well, like for instance, on cars equipped with RF transmitters inside the key. The RF transmitter ID has to match the security module and the engine computer. So, not only does the physical key cut have to match, the RF transmitter has to match as well."

"So how do they get around that?"

"Some of these guys establish relationships with car dealers and get multiple car keys cut directly from the dealer themselves."

"Oh, shit," he said, thinking of Santa Monica Boulevard lined with car dealerships. He actually knew people over there. Everybody was nagging at him to trade in his old Jeep.

16

Ginger was feeling the rising thrill of accomplishment. Alumni loved the Phoebe Windsor Academy and no one had ever approached them with a well-thought-out program for raising support for the school until Ginger came along. Even with the sketchy financial picture she'd been able to put together, within a week she'd assembled a high-power fundraising committee who didn't blanch at the idea of giving $10,000 to buy a table of ten at the alumni dinner held at one of the nicest venues in the city. Some of the potential donors she already knew from serving on other good-cause boards throughout the city. With that, plus placing a story about the school's shabby chic image in *Los Angeles* magazine and approving a new concept for the website, she was on a roll. The board was pleased. She felt frisky and buoyant. Venetia gave her a grudging nod when she saw the magazine piece and said she could have done better—if only she had the time.

The FedEx guy had just humped in four boxes to a corner of the cafeteria. Ginger ripped open the first box, which contained the fundraising dinner program. Her eyes widened and her breath caught. She scrambled to open a second and third box and compared the program with the invitation and dinner handout. She marched into Venetia's office and opened the door without knocking.

Venetia looked up at her. "What?"

"What is this?" She flung the invitation and program down on Venetia's desk. "It's unusable. I won't send it out. The school colors for fifty years have been blue and gold. Not red and purple. It's garish and not even good design. It's a waste of thousands of dollars."

"You think your boyfriend can't afford it?" Venetia said, rising to her feet. "It's what I like and some of the members of the board agree with me. We hired our own designer."

"All this time I've been showing you designs and layouts? You've been saying to go ahead with whatever I liked." Ginger ran her hand over the top of her head to keep it from flying off. "You're too busy to look over proofs or even answer emails but you're not too busy to cook up your own scheme behind my back."

A wave of anger hit her and she turned to look out the window as a way to control it. The air between them was crackling and keen. Just then Petrovich swooped from his perch next to Venetia's desk to land on Ginger's shoulder. She leaned her head to nuzzle him automatically as he bobbed up and down, his squawks breaking the opposition.

"We're not using this, Venetia, and that's final. It's amateur-looking and would make the school look ridiculous."

"We'll see," Venetia said, jutting her chin out, her face dark with rage.

"No, on this one you lose. I let you choose your own caterer and menu even though it amped up the price of each plate by $20."

"You wanted a rubber chicken dinner," Venetia objected. "Donors expect…"

"How would you know what donors expect? This is your first rodeo. This dinner is supposed to make money. And it's not going to with…." The name of the keynote speaker caught her eye on the program. She picked it up off Venetia's desk and her sudden movement caused Petrovich to fly off, then land again on her shoulder. "I can't believe you did this. You know this guy is a gun nut. That's all he talks about. He gives speeches for the NRA."

"I like him."

"What did you tell him you were going to pay him?"

"He gets twenty thousand, but he's going to do a pre-dinner cocktail party for free. I negotiated his fee down by the way."

Any sense of control fled Ginger. "You can cancel him. Our donor base is the liberal LA Westside."

"How would you know?' Venetia stood up. "Come, Petrovich." Petrovich stayed where he was on Ginger's shoulder

"Because while you've been wasting your time pretending you're so busy running the school, I've been talking to donors. This one I win, Venetia. You can cancel any further sabotage plans you had. And take your damn parrot." She raised her arm in a violent shrug and Petrovich flew off.

It was satisfying to slam the door behind her.

Mason took a call from Delgado as he was heading into work the next day, waiting at a light on 7th Street. Delgado was chuckling.

"Man, you're gonna love this." Delgado burst into a belly laugh.

"What?" Mason said sourly.

"Kensington got his ass carjacked. His pretty yellow Porsche is gone."

"No shit. Where? Did he get hurt?" A smile of *schadenfreude* lit Mason's face.

"Nah. It was at the Shell station just before you get on the freeway."

Mason pulled over by the curb. He knew it was stupid and juvenile and still couldn't stop laughing.

"Hey, buddy, get a grip. The whole station's gone APE. They want you over there. I'm headed out now."

APE: Acute Political Emergency. DEFCON 3. By the time Mason got to the Shell station in the mess of traffic near the entrance of the freeway, the commotion was still going on. Two patrol cars had pulled in nose to nose near the pumps. The area next to the pumps was roped off with crime scene tape. Kensington was wearing a charcoal grey suit and pale blue shirt, the knot in his tie yanked askew, his eyes wild, hair disheveled. The leather in his custom-made shoes would have paid Mason's mortgage for two months. Mason put on his cop face. Kensington's head whipped around when he stepped out of his vehicle. A cut on Kensington's forehead had dripped blood down his face. He was holding his elbow funny and had his hand wrapped in a handkerchief. Blood was soaking through. He was still shaking. He turned away from the uniformed officer who was trying to take his story when Mason walked over.

"What's next, Detective Mason? I'm asking you. First Leonard Bricker and then Venetia's assistant and now me. When are you going to do something about this?"

"Easy, easy. Tell me what happened here." Mason made his tone calm and soothing.

"I don't care about the car but that bastard took my dog! My dog was in the back seat. I'm afraid for her. Never mind the car."

Only a rich guy could say a car worth $100K didn't matter. Then Mason saw that standing next to Kensington was the mayor of Santa Monica, whom Mason knew slightly. They gave each other a nod of greeting.

"I was talking to the mayor here while I was filling the tank and I saw something out of the corner of my eye." Kensington was almost hyperventilating. "Some kid in a t-shirt and jeans and ball cap was coming up beside my car—fast. I saw him open the door, get in and hit the gas. The keys were in it. I tried to grab him but my hand got caught by the mirror. He hit me with the fender. Look!"

Mason looked down and saw the rip in Kensington's suit coat, blood soaking through at hip level.

"You were damn lucky," he said. "We need to get you some medical attention before you pass out."

"No, no, I'm fine," Kensington insisted. "This can wait. What about my dog?"

"Give me a minute, sir," Mason said. He held up a finger and took the patrol officer aside.

"Did you call the paramedics?" he asked Officer Miller, a man who looked thin and stringy yet was their krav maga expert and trainer.

"Sure. APB on the car. BOLO on the dog just in case he was dumped."

"How did the mayor get his nose in on it?" Mason said.

"He was talking to Kensington standing on the other side of the pumps while Kensington was filling the tank. Keys in the ignition, nobody there. Made it sweet and easy for the jacker." He smiled. "Nice Porsche. I've seen it around before."

Mason smiled. "How about you canvass these people here. See about security cameras."

"Will do, sir."

Mason turned back to Kensington and the mayor. The mayor was ready to run his mouth, but a look from Kensington stopped him.

"Did he have a weapon?" Mason asked Kensington, noticing how white and pasty his face was.

"Oh Jesus, now you're really scaring me. I didn't see one." Kensington turned in a circle whipping his head back and forth. "My hip is really starting to hurt. If he hurts my dog, I'm going to kill him. I'll kill him."

"We need you to sit down until the ambulance gets here. I don't want you passing out." In the distance Mason could hear the sirens. He looked around at the crowd of onlookers. Cars were still pulling in off the street looking to gas up. The other patrol officer was trying to direct them away and keep witnesses in one place. The looky-loos had assembled in force, willing to be late for work for a little excitement.

Mason sensed Delgado by his side. He looked around at him.

"This is going to create one almighty stink," he said to Mason in low tones. He looked around for reporters. "I called the Public Information Officer. He's on his way."

"Yup, big stink." Mason stepped over to Kensington, who was still going on about his dog. "What kind of dog was it?"

The paramedics spilled out of the ambulance and Mason held an arm aloft pointing at Kensington, who was having trouble staying on his feet.

"A medium-sized black dog. I got her from the pound. Sort of a lab-Schipperke mix. Her name is Lily," he said stuttering with excitement. "Get my dog. Never mind the car."

It made Mason like him better that he didn't have a high-priced dog from a breeder.

Ginger banged hard on the door of the condo Caroline Kensington owned overlooking Santa Monica Bay. Caroline yanked open the door. Ginger breezed past her holding aloft the offending red-and-purple program and invitation.

"You should look before you open the door. What if I'd been the Axe Murderer?"

Caroline took the invitation from her, scanning it, then reading more carefully. She looked up with a snort of a laugh. "Are you serious?"

"That viper's doing an end run around me. You didn't think I did this, did you? This is something Sorensen cooked up with her buddy Paget at KI."

Caroline sank down on a brocaded wing chair in the living room. Ginger took the one facing her. Caroline scrutinized the invitation and program, then flung them down on the coffee table in front of her. "Don't worry. This isn't going out."

"Thank you."

Ginger stopped breathing hard with tension and took a call from Rhys. She listened hard.

"What?" Caroline said, picking up something from her face, which showed alarm.

Ginger stuffed the phone in her purse. "Let's go. It's Rhys. He's been carjacked and taken to the hospital."

Mason was at St. John's Hospital in an ER room with Kensington. A portable X-Ray had just been wheeled out of the room with pictures of Kensington's hip and elbow. He was still white but calmer now that he'd been given a shot for the pain. "I know you think I'm a pussy to be scared. Big tough cop like you," he said wearily to Mason.

"Actually, I don't. What happened to you would have scared anybody," Mason said sincerely.

Rhys gave him a skeptical look just as the door burst open and Ginger and Caroline Kensington streamed in. Mason went alert seeing Ginger. Their eyes locked. Caroline rushed over to her brother, patting his feet and talking frantically to assure herself he was okay.

Mason touched Kensington on the shoulder and interrupted the flow, "Think I got what I needed here. We'll be in touch." He didn't want to see Ginger throw herself on Kensington if that's what she was planning to do. He gave her a smile as he passed her on the way to the door.

Kensington called after him. "Thanks, Dave."

For what, Mason wondered. They still had a long way to go.

Mason and Delgado dodged the station lobby, which was mobbed by journalists and all the town politicos howling about Rhys Kensington's carjacking. The animal activists were incensed about the dog. The mayor's political buddies were hitting the blogosphere with diatribes about police incompetence and Wild West Silicon Beach. Mason slid into his chair and wheeled it around to gaze out the window onto a view of the Santa Monica freeway. He expected at any moment to be yanked off as lead on the carjacking team. Maybe he'd end up handing out samples and wearing a hairnet at Costco. In the meantime he coordinated the search for Kensington's car and his dog, hitting every animal place in the surrounding cities.

Delgado came in with a smile and read notes off his tablet. "This guy Yurkov and his posse. The Auto Theft detail out in the San Gabriel Valley are surveilling an auto body shop Yurkov's got out there. They might have a finger on him but it doesn't mean he's not in the jacking business too. Hear they took office space over in the business park on Ocean. There's money behind him. Big ambitions to diversify their scuzzy little outfit."

"And the new guys in town from Cincinnati? Cheslowski and his associate?" Mason said, rubbing his cheek where a hard lump had appeared on his jaw.

"No connection, but we're watching them. So far they're keeping their noses clean. I'm working with Gomez and Wilson."

"And the guy in the hospital?"

"He died."

"No kidding. Oh, well. He still left us a slime trail to follow."

Kensington's dog was found unharmed later that morning, weaving in and out of traffic on Olympic Boulevard and picked up by Animal Control. The publicity value of returning the dog to Kensington was maximized by having a good-looking Community Relations person delivering the dog in person accompanied by feel-good journalists with cameras. Kensington had already been discharged from the hospital. Mason was not invited to be in on the happy occasion, though he caught the clip of local news later where the dog and Kensington were reunited. Kensington opened the door of his Tudor near Brentwood and the dog frisked around him, jumping in the air, licking his face. Kensington sank to his knees and hugged the dog. Tears ran down his cheeks. Heart-warming, Mason thought cynically.

The rest of the day was writing reports, and reading Wilson and Gomez' book on Yurkov. Maybe he should have kept track for Robinson about an exciting day in the life of a detective.

17

Dead bodies were rarely discovered during working hours. It was always at night, at the end of a horrible day, raining, or in the 50's, which in Santa Monica passed for a polar vortex.

A battered station wagon with two frantic old people had pulled into the cul de sac at the end of Euclid off Michigan just beside the freeway. Rain was spattering down wetting the sidewalks, which everyone welcomed in the middle of a drought. A blown tire flapped on the passenger side. When they got out to look at the tire and find the spare, the wife had glimpsed a large bundle wound with plastic sheeting. A faint stink rising from under the pile of fallen palm fronds and gardener waste had piqued her curiosity. Bored with holding the flashlight for her husband who was changing the tire, she took a closer look through the gate of a chain-link fence and then freaked. Neighbors heard her screaming and called the police.

The freeway had bisected and destroyed Santa Monica's black community in the 1960s, and now a ceaseless stream of traffic passed by overhead, looming over a short block of small bungalows and apartment buildings with tidy yards. The embankment fell away ending at a chain-link-fenced enclosure. The fence ran ten feet out from the bottom of the steep freeway embankment.

Ruthie, one of Mason's favorite coroner's death investigators, wasn't working today. Much as he enjoyed the banter with her, Mason was just as glad she wasn't there. It was time for him to quit flirting around and ask her out, or leave her alone. Anyway, she had these wolfhounds that were as big as she was. He was 6'4" and she was 5'2" and they'd look ridiculous together, unlike himself and Ginger. Tango with her?

The fire guys were there, EMT, forensics, everybody was in on it. Mason and Delgado shared a comradely moment, staring down at the body wrapped in a plastic drop sheet. The first swarm of flies buzzed over the corpse, even in the cool of evening. The forensics techs moved in to document the scene. When the wrapping on the bundle had been partially unpeeled, the facial features were still distinguishable. One of the uniforms who had been first on scene spotted the resemblance, remembering the morning briefing. She made the match to Missing Person reports and photos posted in the station.

"It's the Arnold woman, your missing person." She scratched her ear and then walked back to her vehicle, shaking her head.

Mason cursed softly, thinking about telling Arnold's sister. He didn't need another Judy Klepper in his life. He couldn't bear to meet Andy Klepper's eyes who wandered toward him then skidded off towards the wall.

"You notice the padlock on the gate?" Delgado said, out of breath, squatting beside him.

"Yeah, it wouldn't take long to park the car, snip the padlock, and dump the body. How fresh you figure she is?" Mason said, easing down next to the body exactly where the coroner's investigator pointed.

"Couple weeks. I donno yet." The investigator, a new guy this time, raised his head and looked around. "Not many streetlights, but I'll bet there's lots of dogwalkers in this neighborhood. Ask around."

Mason already had Fredericks out with uniformed officers doing the neighborhood canvass. Fredericks was charged up with the excitement of a new case and had gone bopping off ready to take somebody on. The technical work showed a few yellow nylon fibers buried in the victim's neck and a crescent of a broken fingernail. This took hours to determine and would take days to verify. The finding pointed to strangling with a nylon cord cutting deep into the skin of her neck. But nothing was certain until the coroner's guy said it. She'd bled some from the nose, mouth, and ears, but not a lot. There was always hope for fingerprints on the plastic drop cloth. That looked new. Criminals were getting smarter–except the ones that weren't. The drop cloth made it look planned. Or suggested somebody who'd done this before.

Most murders solved themselves quickly. It was the husband in the back bedroom sobbing, the transient giving off waves of alcohol fumes, or the kid running away with a gun too big for his hand. Not this one. Mason prepared himself for the long nights ahead, snatched meals, and fitful sleep, added to what was already on his plate.

After the body was taken away they had the unpleasant task of making the death notification. They found Loretta Swinson, Arnold's sister, home in her apartment, her face falling into ruin seeing them at the door. Her worst fears had come true, leaving her staring alone into the future.

"Finding whoever did this, will it make me feel better about losing Doris?" she asked through her tears.

"Yes, it will," Mason lied. Even a trial on Court TV and a public hanging on the Third Street Promenade would never make Loretta Swinson's life better again. Or Judy Klepper who was living with a violent stranger, a victim of a carjacking.

Mason and Delgado hit the Windsor Academy to catch Sorensen's reaction to her assistant's murder. They took Montana Avenue, one of the city's elite shopping districts and waited at the red light on 17th Street. Rolling towards them was a red double-decker bus, the recorded soundtrack reciting a lot of celebrity fluff facts: who got engaged here, lived here, shopped here.

Mason was trying to read a bulletin, talk to Fredericks on his cellphone, and drive all at the same time, setting a great example for the citizens. They found Sorensen in her office with Ginger. Mason's eyes clung to Ginger's face, her alarm at seeing him. Then her face went expressionless, and once again he was left wondering. He had read a press release she'd put out from the school smoothing over Rhys Kensington's carjacking.

"It's about Ms. Arnold."

Sorensen beckoned the parrot to her. He stared at her, unwinking.

"What?"

Ginger's eyes went to Mason. "You want me to leave?"

"You can stay," Mason said.

"What about Doris? Have you found her? Where is she?" Sorensen said, leaning forward at her desk.

"We found her here in Santa Monica. She was murdered," Mason said, watching her carefully.

Venetia Sorensen took in the news of her assistant's murder by standing up behind her desk and throwing her arms in the air. In alarm Petrovich flew from his perch and landed on her shoulder. "But...but, how? I don't believe it," she said in a strained voice. "She can't be." Sorensen began striding around the room, straightening a painting, her brow furrowed. "This is just terrible. I thought, well, I just thought she..."

"Thought what?"

"That she just snapped under all the stress of..." Again she broke off and went to her desk, for a moment staring out the window then ruffling through papers. She rotated her shoulders, bent forward, then clasped her hands behind her and raised them high. "When?"

"We'll know more about that later after the autopsy."

"How then?" She swung around to face them. The cords in her neck stood out. "Tell me."

"It looks as though she was strangled."

At this Sorensen sank down at her desk her head in her arms. Mason was observing her from the side and thought he saw her mouth curve into a tight smile. Ginger looked at Mason, locked eyes with him and then gazed up at the ceiling, her face troubled.

"It's possible she was killed the same night as the Silent Auction. We need alibis from everyone for that weekend. Where did you go after the party broke up?"

"Home. I was very tired. I had no idea this was going to happen."

"Alone?"

"Yes, alone," she snapped. "Why would I kill her? We've been through this."

Delgado stepped in. "See, we know you had a lot of arguments with her."

"That doesn't mean I killed her!" Sorensen shouted. "If you don't have anything new to ask me I'd like you to leave now."

"Okay then. We'll be back. Get your financial records ready for a forensic examination."

"But I've explained to you. We have…I have a school to run…"

※

Venetia flung the handkerchief aside and pounced on the phone the moment they were out the door. She hit fast dial. "You bad boy," she cooed. "The cops were just here about Doris. You had me guessing, didn't you?"

"I told you I would take care of it and I did."

"Yourself?"

"You don't have to know that."

"Did you have anything to do with Kensington's Porsche? That was pretty close to home."

"That was business. I found a buyer."

Venetia smiled as she hung up the phone. It was a relief to be free of that unsightly creature and at no risk to herself. Kensington's car…well, business is business.

※

"That's one cold woman," Mason said, reflecting on Sorensen's reaction to the news. They were grabbing a quick lunch at McDonald's. The Lieutenant wanted a progress report on the case, the anticipation of which had turned his stomach sour. "Sure she said all the right things, but it was just off."

"Maybe that's just the way she is," Delgado said. "You've seen all kinds of different reactions to grief. Know I have."

"Yeah, but…"

"You and your yeah buts."

"Still…," Mason said, looking at the door where a crowd of City Hall employees had just come in. He didn't have any energy left to be social.

If Doris Arnold had money stashed away they couldn't find it and it was not without looking. No way was the Sarge going to give them one of the Economic Crimes investigators. So while they waited for forensics and the autopsy results to come through, Mason decided to kick in some doors at the top level of Kensington Industries. The business occupied a modest old-fashioned stucco building painted grey with accents of tasteful colors. Old man Kensington had bought several adjacent double lots where the new Phoebe Windsor Academy would some-day be built. Hibiscus bushes with showy yellow blossoms and flowerbeds with marigolds and impatiens gave off a skunky smell. The lobby of Kensington Industries was updated with a lot of glass-and-chrome furniture. Like every industrial building it had a water feature off to the side in an atrium, which pretended to be a rain forest. Behind a sheet of glass sat a starved-down beauty who informed them that Craig Knight, the CEO was unavailable. He would be in meetings all day. Mason and Delgado gave each other a look.

Delgado growled at her. "You tell him we're here and we want to see him right away." He gave her his card and handed over the one Mason flipped him. Instead of making a phone call, she looked at them doubtfully and took both cards, swaying gracefully on high heels through double doors. Mason was tired and didn't want to fool around with a show of executive self-importance. He expected they would have to wait, but that didn't happen. The beauty showed them into a corner office of Kensington Industries, an office with a view of Silicon Beach Santa Monica.

The location must have taken a real uptick in price recently with the coming of the Subway to the Sea that was inching its way to the ocean. Kensington Industries had been in the city since the early 60s and the founder whose pictures graced the hallways had been shrewd. He'd made one fortune in rubber gloves for the medical industry and another fortune in twist ties. Maybe at one time these goods had been manufactured nearby but no longer. The land was too expensive here.

Craig Knight, the CEO of Kensington Industries, appeared backing into the room talking on a cellphone, carrying a tablet opened up with a mug of coffee balanced on top of it. He presented himself, milking the entrance, making sure every eye in the room was on him. He stopped at the edge of the table, ignoring Mason and Delgado, and sat his coffee cup down on the table, raising two fingers asking their patience while he continued his conversation. Millions were mentioned. Beijing. Berlin. He talked very loud, barking out instructions to somebody on the other end.

Mason looked at Delgado and sighed. They watched while Knight took off his suit coat and laid it carefully on a chair he pulled out from a mahogany table, smoothing out the wrinkles. Finally Knight turned and greeted them with a hearty, two-handed handshake and apologies. A big white smile with a whole lot of nothing behind it. Over in the corner he had a standing desk where he put his laptop. He had a treadmill he walked on while working on his tablet.

"I know it's weird," Knight said, calling attention to his standing desk, "but I have a bad back. No good for me to sit all day."

They kicked the subject of the standing desk around for a while making small talk to get a bead on him. Delgado seemed genuinely interested in the desk treadmill idea, but that was a talent he had—looking interested. Mason let his eyes roam around the room, letting Delgado talk, taking in all the artifacts of business success on display.

"So what can I tell you, gentlemen?" Knight said, tall, silver-haired, and confident. "We've heard, of course, about the murder of one of the Academy employees. So sad, really," he said, one eye on the screen of his laptop.

"And there's Leonard Bricker as well," Delgado pointed out. "Another death, a deliberate hit-and-run.

I know you've had meetings with our traffic investigator. I understand Bricker's appointment followed closely on the death of the previous chair of the board of the Academy."

Knight gave a spluttering laugh. "You surely can't think Ed Clark's death was a murder. He had a heart attack and died in his wife's arms over at St. John's Hospital. I mean, surely..."

Delgado let the laugh float in the air, fixing him with the cop stare down. They had eliminated Clark's death as being foul play, but all the same it was good to get a reaction.

Knight leaned forward to show earnestness, giving them his full attention. "There have been upsets here at KI, it's true, but we've been very cooperative with Detective Palmer about Leonard's death. I don't know what else we can tell you about this. Your people have interviewed everyone here. Exhaustively, I might add. And KI is entirely separate from the Windsor Academy. I don't think I'd recognize Doris Arnold if I saw her in the street."

"Tell us about the trust and the Academy."

Knight turned on a dime. Now he was comfortable. "Well," he said expansively, "the trust was set up to support the Academy. Then came the crash in 2007 that we are only beginning to climb out of. The trust fund portfolio has dwindled and no one has made a secret of that. The headmistress, Dr. Sorensen, is well aware there's a stepped-up timetable to reduce operating costs by ten percent this year, or fundraise the equivalent. I believe she has been writing grants and looking for sponsors. She has known this for some time and has been acting very responsibly on it."

"But closing the Academy altogether is not on the table?"

"Not that I'm aware of," Knight said. "I'm not sure the education community would allow it," he laughed. "They have very well-placed alums who'd fight us for sentimental reasons."

Mason could hear Delgado thinking about whether to spring the information they'd gained from the Peabodys about the threatened school closure and their lawsuit. Knight couldn't possibly think he could keep that contained, but maybe the suit hadn't been filed yet.

After a weighted silence, Delgado tapped his chin. "You're aware that some $27,000, the proceeds of the Silent Auction are missing."

"Yes, I was told that. Was Ms. Arnold robbed?"

"The money is still missing. No action on the credit cards, though."

Knight threw up his hands with a smug bark of a laugh. "Then surely that's the motive for her murder. Who benefits from her death? Don't they say look at who benefits? Least the crime shows I watch say that."

"Oh, we watch them too. So far we can't see how anyone benefits from either Mr. Bricker's or Ms. Arnold's death. We were hoping you could help us out with that."

"I don't know what to tell you. We're saddened here. Leonard Bricker was well liked, and while none of us had a personal relationship with Ms. Arnold, it's a terrible upset at the Academy. Dr. Sorensen is devastated. The students are troubled. The parents don't like this adverse publicity. A lot of good-paying jobs are dependent on Kensington Industries' good name. Then there's Mr. Kensington's carjacking and injury. This isn't good. What can we do to help you?" He was all civic openness and cooperation now.

"So there's no basis to the story that the Academy has been threatened with closure?"

"I don't see what that would have to do with Doris Arnold. We are always considering options, sure. But by the drift of your questions, I'm getting the picture that you think these deaths are related and the origin is here." He tilted his head to the left and then to the right and then back again, raising his eyebrows, as if he had truly given consideration to some wacky theory that was just crazy enough to be true.

"It's something we're looking at."

"We run a business here, a very successful one I might add." He ran a hand down his tie and shot his French cuffs.

"Did Leonard Bricker have an office here after he retired? A computer? Some sort of clerical help that he'd use in his duties as Chair of the Academy foundation?"

"No. Absolutely not." These overeducated, confident bastards stirred up Mason's *lesser than* feelings from having completed a police science degree part-time at a commuter college. He'd read up on the execs over at Kensington Industries before they'd come. Knight was Harvard and Wharton Business School. Ginger's fund-raising stuff with big donors had given her an ease with wealth that he envied. He knew he was being unreasonable and that hating this guy for no reason at all made him likely to make mistakes.

Nothing more came of the interview other than the sight of Knight tap dancing, pirouetting around the issues. Doug Paget, the treasurer of the Academy and Chief Financial Officer of KI was next.

18

Paget was short, bald, and porky with a thin, grey moustache that grew over his lower lip. Mason always wondered what a moustache like that was hiding. He had a mentholated smell about him. Paget's office was a shrine to the game of golf. He greeted them uneasily with a cold handshake and a nervous habit of scratching his head.

"Gentlemen, sit down, please." He led them to a couch and took a chair opposite. "I don't know what I can tell you."

The technique was to small talk for a bit to get a read on what was normal behavior for Paget, then start asking questions they thought might shake him a little. Delgado knew more about golf than Mason, so he did the heavy lifting while Mason watched. Mason finally interrupted. Bad Cop today.

"They tell us that you're a candidate for Chair of the Board of the Academy to replace Mr. Bricker."

"A number of people are up for consideration, not just me," Paget gulped, his Adam's apple bobbing in a long neck.

"But you are Treasurer now. You handle the financials for the Academy?"

"I've been doing that for many years. We all take an interest in the school."

"So then you have a lot of interaction with Doris Arnold?"

"Well, yes, I did. But almost entirely by email. We seldom met."

"And you know the proceeds of the Silent Auction are missing?"

"Of course. That's really unfortunate. It makes it seem as though Doris stole the money and I'm very surprised to hear that."

"Why? She fits the profile. Medical expenses for her sister. They had been living together until recently when she took on the expense of separate living quarters."

"Yes, but her salary is commensurate with these expenses," Paget maintained. He was beginning to sweat.

"Oh?" Delgado said.

"I hadn't really thought about it that way. Then why would she be killed?"

"That's the question, isn't it? See, we pencil and papered it out. Ms. Arnold had some pretty heavy debts, credit card debt over $22,000, expenses for her sister she couldn't claim on her taxes, back taxes. She was living beyond her means."

"I didn't know that. I guess that explains her stealing the proceeds of the Silent Auction. That's very sad she felt she was driven to that. If she'd said anything to any of us, we might have found a way to help her. Sad, really."

"The money is still missing actually. It was mostly credit card receipts. Only $872 in cash."

"Oh. We've been so busy here lately. I haven't had time to check the details."

"Isn't that your job? Details? To liaise with the school?"

"Yes, but…as I say we've had a number of issues to handle here lately."

"Like closing the school down?"

"That's very iffy and hard to do according to the provisions of the trust."

"Would you be in favor of closing the school? I understand your son attends Kensington Academy."

"My son is a good student. He would be accepted anywhere." They could see the white around his eyes now.

"Who do you think killed her?"

"I have no idea. I can't imagine. Really I can't."

"So you'd vote to close the school then?" Delgado said, circling back.

"There are so many considerations, Mr. Delgado. I don't know how I'd vote just yet." He stood up. "I must go. We have an important customer from China arriving today. You can always call me," he said, handing them a business card. "Email's probably better though."

"Sure, sure," Delgado said, standing up as well. "One last question."

"Oh, like Colombo?" Paget smiled.

"Yes, just like Colombo. "You have regular audits for the Academy?"

"Yes, of course we do. What are you suggesting?"

"Not suggesting anything. We'll be in touch."

On the way out to the car, Delgado turned to him. "What got up your ass with Knight?"

"I don't know. I just didn't like the guy," Mason said, knowing that sounded adolescent.

"So what? Of all the asswipes we deal with, you didn't like the guy. Jesus, Mason. Listen to yourself."

"Just something about him…"

"You got a bug up your ass about rich people."

"Knight's not rich," Mason said, slamming the door of the Crown Vic.

"You know what I mean. We've been working together long enough that I know all your shit, Mason. Your mind snapped shut like a bear trap before we even met the guy."

"You notice the entrance he made? There's something hinky going on there," Mason said, looking out the window at another new hole in the ground feasted on by the developers.

"I'm not saying there isn't. Paget is the one I'm going to start digging on now. But we take them apart brick by brick and then build our case back up again. I'll start on the alibis for both of them. You better get your head together."

"Let's see what forensics has for us on Arnold's scene," Mason said, gunning the engine hard as though he could get away from Delgado. "Paget," he muttered.

"Oh yeah, Paget," Delgado answered.

"You know what happened with that ridiculous print job Venetia came up with. I feel as though I'm wasting your money and my time with her," Ginger McNair explained to Rhys as they leaned on the railing, waiting for a table at 41 Ocean Bar, a members-only club directly opposite the Santa Monica Pier. "She stonewalls me. We have an appointment to meet and she cancels five minutes before I get there. I set up another appointment and she cancels that too."

Rhys humphed, then shrugged. "Nobody ever said she was easy to work with, Ginger. She's a pain. Always has been. That parrot drives me insane. How do you put up with it?"

Ginger shrugged it off. "I like him. Apparently I'm one of the few people he likes, and that's another reason Venetia doesn't like me. She's so concerned about her father's legacy, that he was such a great man, that the school means so much to her. But I sure don't see it. If the parents could hear some of the things she says about them…" She broke off. "Hey, look. There's Venetia with that guy I saw in her office." She pointed.

The dark man with the black leather jacket and sunglasses was bending Venetia back over the hood of a foreign-looking car. They were kissing. He broke away to take a hit on a cigarette he held in his hand then blew the smoke slowly into her mouth. She was laughing, shrieking in mock protest, wearing a long white tube dress. Her silver hair shimmered against the tall man dressed in black.

A short compact man also wearing black leather and gold jewelry glanced between them and the traffic. Ginger then caught sight of two big men in leather jackets wearing sunglasses across the street who kept a careful eye on the pair who were twisting sinuously against each other.

"Are those bodyguards?" Her voice rose high and excited. "Rhys, those are bodyguards. Who is that guy she's with?"

"Oh forget Venetia," he said, pulling her away. "They're not bodyguards. Don't be silly."

Ginger took one last look over her shoulder. She was certain it was Venetia and the man she'd seen in her office.

Rhys kept talking. "Pay attention to me. Venetia thinks she's the only one who can do anything right, and unless she's on the premises everything is going to fall apart. I just want you to be happy, you know that?"

Ginger pulled her hand away from his, still thinking of Venetia.

"You don't have to work at all, with her or anybody else, if you'd marry me. Let me spoil you. I know you've always wanted to see Tuscany. We could take a house there. Fiji? Norway?"

Ginger squeezed her face together and sighed, shaking her head. "Not now, Rhys, please. If you think she would get along with somebody else, I'd be glad to step aside. I had a call about an event planning job yesterday anyway."

He reached for her hand again. "No, please. Stay with it. Forget another job. Look, things have been so miserable for you, let me add to your salary. It's the least Caroline and I can do."

"No, that's not it, Rhys! What you're paying me now is embarrassing."

"I'll talk to Venetia then."

"Rhys, I don't want you to do that. I can handle this myself." She looked through the windows to the grey, choppy ocean. "But there's something big going on, isn't there, over at KI? It's not business as usual, is it?"

He twisted his mouth and tilted his head back as though debating whether to tell her something. Finally he put his arm around her and pulled her closer.

"Yes. The Trust is heavily invested in Kensington Industries and owns fifty-nine per cent of the stock in the company. The trust states that the School has to pick up more of the costs the way my grandfather wanted it to happen and Venetia is being pushed hard. She's increased tuition, and we've hired you."

"Yes, I know all that." The duck confit appetizer arrived. Rhys pushed his plate away.

"But the price of the stock is going down because the business climate is just plain bad. If the trust's stake of 59 percent falls below 50 percent, an outsider could take control of the company. That's what's going on."

"You think that's going to happen?"

"A lot of things could happen. We have a lot more competitors than when my grandfather started the business. Things are very uncertain. But don't worry about it. I'd tell you if it was important to your work."

Ginger stared at Rhys Kensington, trusting him, feeling she knew him to the core. Nobody had ever wanted her as much as he had. She hadn't cared for him especially when she and Caroline had first become friends. He was too tame, too conservative, too vanilla. She liked people with edges and angles and strong opinions. He hadn't changed to please her; he'd just made himself inevitable. He became the one she turned to when her car broke down, or when she had an ear ache or a car insurance question. Rhys just swept problems away. Like the day he said he heard a funny noise in her old Audi. He asked her for the keys and when she got it back, it ran like new and had new tires. Then along came Mason. It sounded whiny if she complained about piddly life problems to him. During the time of her relationship with Mason, Rhys had drifted into the background, but

Ginger still called him up or went to dinner with him just to stay in touch. And besides that, he was likeable. And who didn't like being adored?

She had been certain that she and Mason would somehow get back together, but the mechanics of it didn't work. A stiff-necked pride prevented her from calling him. He'd called once and caught her by surprise just as she'd walked in the door after a long day and was too tired to be flirty and approachable. And time went by. She called him and Fredericks answered his desk phone. Snort! Fredericks. There was Rhys. Love had been a word that hadn't been much used between her and Mason. She had been careful, remembering past relationships where she'd fallen in love and out of love too fast, too hard. The *love* word had been hard to say.

And then Mason was truly gone. It had taken six months, but eventually Ginger had opened her heart to Rhys, and allowed him in her bed. He was a good man who wanted to turn himself inside out and give her everything he had, and she knew it.

The only thing was–he smoked. Ginger's mother had died when she was nine, of lung cancer. Smoking was a bogeyman growing up, and the smell of cigarettes that clung to Rhys was an irritant. She tried to tell herself smoking was such a little thing, but it wasn't. And sometimes he drank too much.

19

Venetia Sorenson and Doug Paget met at 8:00 a.m. at Denny's on the corner of Lincoln and Colorado. She and Paget were meeting there because she figured that no one she knew ever went to Denny's.

"What do you hear?" she said, sliding into a booth at the back opposite Doug Paget. He wore a grey Mr. Rogers sweater. Beads appeared on his forehead. He mopped at them with a wad of paper napkins and threw them down on the table.

"I think I've got the votes for chair," he said, looking around for the waitress.

"You think? All this effort and you just think you're in. You assured me…"

"Yeah, well. The police are all over the place."

"Tell me something I don't know," Sorensen snapped.

"Who do you think killed Doris? I mean, Jesus, this is awful. First Leonard and now her…"

"I don't know and it doesn't matter..."

"Doesn't matter!" Paget's eyebrows shot up into his receding hairline. "What the hell is going on?"

"It was a robbery. That's all."

"But what about Leonard?"

"A coincidence."

The waitress appeared with a coffee pot. Venetia looked up at her and said, "High octane. Him too."

"I'll be jumpy."

"You need to be on your game today. You need caffeine."

"Look, I'm not so sure even if I'm chair I can keep the school open."

"Let me remind you. Your son Evan is no student. But we've got him looking good on paper. I stepped in and gave his grades an extra boost and rewrote some of the notes in his file. He's applying for colleges now and if you want him to get into anything better than some forklift operator course, you make it happen. Your job is to keep the gravy train rolling. Got it?"

Doug Paget huffed and puffed as he tore the tops off yellow and blue packets of fake sugar and poured them into his coffee.

Venetia was pleased that Vlad Yurkov had been willing to kill for her. Venetia and Vlad sounded so good together, lovers and partners—Venetia and Vlad. The mirror told her why he wanted her, of course. Discipline, that's what it took. Discipline. Any woman in her 40's could look 29 if she had discipline. And a willingness to take risks.

But risks had to be managed. She needed to deflect attention away from herself. She could shift the police radar onto Vlad, or whoever had dealt with Doris, but the time wasn't nearly ripe for that.

Patience. Planning. Just a little longer.

The Watch Commander raised Mason from a sound sleep where he was dreaming he'd just swooped in on the net, throwing up a tall rooster tail of ice and scored a hat trick, three goals in one game. He came into consciousness, almost smiling, remembering his hockey days of glory. He snatched for the phone.

12:03 a.m. "Yeah, Mason," he said in a froggy voice.

"We've got a report of an attack on a woman in your Kensington case."

"Who?" he said, thinking instantly of Ginger.

"Says she's the headmistress of the Academy. Sorensen? Somebody was waiting for her outside her garage. She scared him off."

"Okay. Gimme an address. You call Delgado?"

"Thought you could go over first and take a report and see what's what. You're lead on the Arnold murder and this is maybe connected."

"Yeah. Got uniforms there?"

"Sure. Your kid happened to be first on scene."

"My kid?"

"Yeah, Robinson."

"Oh, man, he'll love that," Mason grunted. "Sherlock Holmes will have it all detected by the time I get there."

Actually Mason was glad it was Robinson with his big Saint Bernard puppy ways. He had a way with people and that was the biggest part of police work. He edged out of the parking lot behind his two-bedroom condo on the corner of 7th and San Vicente, heading east up San Vicente. Sorensen's address was right on the edge of Santa Monica where the houses got bigger and fancier as Santa Monica ended and Brentwood began. He'd picked up that Sorensen lived in the house her father had left her, one of the lesser grand houses on 23rd Street. All the lights were on in the mock Tudor surrounded by pines. If there'd been any big excitement there, it was all over now. There were two patrol units with the light bars off. This wasn't a neighborhood where you wanted to disturb the neighbors at 12:18 a.m. Robinson must have been watching for him. Mason found a parking place, got out of the car and was headed to the door when Robinson bounded toward him.

"Hello, Detective Mason. Great to see you." Robinson's uniform was immaculate, his face glowing with gee whiz excitement.

Mason felt tired just looking at him. "What's going on?" he said, looking up at the big house.

"The lady, a Ms. Venetia Sorensen, said she heard noises outside by the garage, a kind of thumping sound

197

and went out to look. She says she surprised an intruder trying to break into the garage. He saw her and came at her real fast and she got back in the house and locked the door on him. Hurt herself getting in the door. I looked around. Nobody there. That's it."

"She hurt bad?"

"Nah, I wouldn't say that. I was going to call the EMTs, but she said no. Watch Commander told me to give it a few minutes until you got here, so I did, and here you are."

Well, golly, here I am, Mason thought. I sure wish I was as glad to see me sometimes. "Let's go talk to her."

"You want me to stay then?"

"Yeah, you know the deal." Mason expected Robinson to jump in the air and click his heels. He knocked on the door and it was immediately swung open by Venetia Sorensen in a tight black workout outfit showing a lean, sinewy body. She was pressing a blood-stained white towel to her forehead.

"Oh, Detective Mason, come in. Come in, officer." She stood back and led them into a living room off the entryway. The place had the look of decorator chic, no expenses spared.

"Sorry to hear about this, Dr. Sorensen. Do you need us to call the paramedics?"

"Oh, this is nothing." She removed the towel and Mason saw a scrape on her forehead that was not bleeding badly.

"Okay, but if you change your mind…Why don't you tell me what happened?"

"He just scared me. Seeing the gun and everything."

"Gun? Here, let's sit down. Why don't you start from the beginning?"

"I was reading, catching up on paperwork. Since Doris's gone, my days are really long. Poor Doris," she sighed dramatically. "I heard something. Then I heard it again so I got up and looked out the kitchen window at the garage in back."

"What time was this?"

"About half an hour ago, I think. I didn't really look."

"911 call came in at 11:40, sir," Robinson said helpfully.

Sorensen darted him a look, then dismissed him. She turned her attention back to Mason. "I opened the back door and stepped out onto the deck when I saw a shadow move beside the garage."

"Let's go take a look," Mason said.

Sorensen led them through the house, opened the back door off a designer kitchen and flipped a light switch. She looked puzzled.

"That's funny. I realize now the light outside didn't come on when I saw the man back there. That's why it was so dark," she said in a surprised tone. She reached up to touch the bulb in the fixture.

Mason stopped her hand. "Leave it for now, would you? We'll have somebody look at it."

"This is all so crazy," she said. She turned away. "I don't know what's going on here lately."

Mason walked to the edge of the redwood deck that framed the back from one side to the other. In the moonlight he saw lawn and flowerbeds, a couple of Adirondack chairs, a garage constructed of the same material as the house occupying a third of the back yard. She came and stood next to him and Robinson, her hand on the doorframe as though ready to run.

"Where did you see him? Are you sure it was a man?"

"Absolutely. But I couldn't tell at first. With all that's going on here I've gotten suspicious of everybody. You think I'm going to walk out in my backyard at midnight when I see a man in the shadows? Hardly."

"So what did you do then?"

"I just stood there in shock. And suddenly he rushed at me. I don't know how he did it but he was at the bottom of the stairs here coming at me, and he had a gun."

"What kind of gun?"

"I don't know. I hate guns. Horrible things."

"Okay. We'll get back to that later. Did he say anything?"

She tilted her head, thinking. "I think he growled."

"Growled?"

"I know that sounds crazy. But everything's crazy. He came at me so fast I stepped back and lost my balance and I must have hit my head somehow on the door frame."

Mason looked around. It would be better in daylight. He'd get the crew out there and go over the place.

"Then I somehow got the door open and got inside and locked the door. I just crouched down behind the sink there and waited…"

"Waited?"

"Waited for him to shoot me through the door or come bursting in or something. I was really scared. Then I crawled out of the kitchen where there's a phone and called you." She gestured them back into the kitchen and walked over to point at a wall phone just above the gleaming black granite counters.

"And he didn't fire the weapon?"

"No."

"What did he look like?"

"He was wearing one of those balaclavas, you know, like you wear when you're skiing."

Or when you're robbing places. "He was alone, you think?" Mason said.

"He was all I saw and he looked about twelve feet tall when he came up those steps at me." She was breathing harshly now.

"Here, let's all sit down now. You mind if we take a seat at the table here? Now, he didn't say anything?"

"No, I told you. It all happened in thirty seconds, if it was that. I locked the door and turned out the kitchen light."

"But you tried to turn on the deck light and it wouldn't come on?"

"I think so. But I didn't think anything of it at the time. I just went to the top of the steps at the deck and then I saw this man in the shadows and then he pulled out a gun and ran at me…."

"Easy now, easy," Mason said. Tell me what the man looked like?"

"I can't remember." She shook her head. Light glinted on the diamonds in her ears. She was wearing a matching diamond tennis bracelet.

"Take a minute," Mason counseled, sitting back and taking up a pose that looked relaxed.

"You told me he was wearing a balaclava and had big shoulders," Robinson said standing behind Mason at the table.

Sorensen looked up at him. "That's right, but he was coming up the stairs at me in the dark. I was terrified."

Mason sighed. He made a few notes in his book, exchanged a look with Robinson, and then stood up.

"Where's your parrot?"

She frowned. "He's upstairs. I don't want him upset."

Mason nodded. "There's not much more I can do at this point."

"You mean you're leaving now?" Her voice rose.

"I can't do anything else, Dr. Sorensen."

"But what about Doris? What if he comes back and tries to kill me?"

"We'll put a watch on your house for the rest of the night, and as soon as the morning shift comes on, they'll be over here looking at the back of your house and the garage as though it's a crime scene. Officer Robinson and I will go out and check around. The guy's probably long gone."

"You hope," she said bitterly.

"How about spending the rest of the night somewhere else just in case? Just to be cautious."

"Oh, I will. I'm not staying here," she said with much heat. "Please just wait until I put a few things in a bag. I'm going to a hotel."

"Okay." Mason gestured with his chin toward Robinson at the back door. Sorensen stalked out of the room to the upstairs. They could hear her taking the steps three at a time, then cooing at the parrot.

"What do you think, sir?" Robinson said.

"Donno yet. I want to check for footprints by the garage, check the locks, print everything…" Mason said, stopping before stepping out the back door onto the deck shining his Maglite down and looking for footprints on the three risers that led to the back deck.

"We've had some break-ins over on Carlisle. Maybe it's that guy."

"Who knows? How's she strike you?"

"Thing is, she didn't seem all that scared until you got here," Robinson said. "She absolutely insisted we call you and I knew you were lead on that case over where she's the boss. She only seemed to get really worked up when you got here. Funny, huh?" he said, scratching his head.

"Yeah, funny," Mason said with a short, bitter laugh.

20

When Ginger showed up the next morning for a planning meeting with Sorensen, one of the parents, Stella Grainger, was sitting in Venetia's outer office holding a tiny white Shi Tzu. The Graingers had a difficult child and she spent a lot of time haunting the school as an unwanted volunteer.

"Have you heard?" Stella Grainger said, standing up and meeting Ginger just inside the door.

"Heard what?" Ginger set her purse and laptop down on a chair.

"Dr. Sorensen was attacked last night." Her eyes were big and round and her cheeks went pink with excitement. A soccer mom and Girl Scout organizer, Stella Grainger had a deep tan that told of many hours on the tennis court.

Ginger took a step back. She remembered all too well the occasion she'd been attacked, the occasion on which she'd met Dave Mason. Her hand flew up to her cheek where the knife scar had almost faded. "Was she hurt?"

"I don't think so. It's just so awful. She called the parent's group because she won't be in today and with what happened to Doris...We just don't know what to think. Do you think our children are safe here?" She leaned forward and touched Ginger's arm. "I'm thinking of pulling Chelsea out of here, except she likes her teachers so much."

Ginger turned as a hand rested on her shoulder. It was Rhys. She leaned back against him. Rhys, the Problem Solver.

"Hello, Ms. Grainger. Hello, Ginger. You're right. Dr. Sorensen has struggled on here far too long with a minimal staff. She and Doris did the work of five people. Poor Doris. We're all just sick about that." He kneaded the tense muscles in Ginger's shoulders. "The Board is meeting today and we're insisting Dr. Sorensen move more quickly on hiring assistants. And, of course, we're going to check into security coverage."

"Oh, thank you, thank you, Mr. Kensington," Stella Grainer bubbled. The parents loved Rhys. "I know that will make us feel better."

"My sister will be here soon to take over for you, Ms. Grainger. We all thank you for pitching in."

"Well, I could still make my Zumba class," she said. "If you're sure..." she said prettily.

"And Dr. Sorensen will be in later."

"So soon? We heard she was..." Grainger said.

"No, she wasn't hurt," Rhys said. He patted her shoulder. "She's more scared and upset than hurt."

"It's just so awful when something like this happens. You know, my sister and her friend were leaving one of the parking garages in downtown Santa Monica right in the middle of the day and one of those terrible homeless people..."

Rhys was urging Stella Grainger toward the door. He shut it behind her while she was still talking. He turned and held out his arms to Ginger. She came forward gratefully and leaned into him.

"What's going on here?" Ginger said, her voice strained.

Mason's mood was sour the next morning with too much coffee and not enough sleep. On the way to the bathroom he heard his name and turned back to Sgt. York's office, hanging in the doorway.

"What's this about the 415 you went out on last night? More on those Kensington Industries people and you don't have a solve on my desk yet? You realize the pressure the department is getting? You better get me something soon." He ran a rough hand over his scalp. He looked ready to blow then took the time to master himself, and when he spoke he was whispering, which made it worse. "The Chief isn't happy, and when she's not happy, I'm not happy."

"I know that, sir." Mason was determined not to sound defensive.

"You need more help, is that it? You're not up to it, Mason?"

"Absolutely not. No, sir."

The Sarge squinted at him. "I hear your old girl-friend works at the Windsor Academy. Is that getting in the way?"

"No," Mason said shortly. "Look, I've got forensics going over Sorensen's house, even though I think this guy attacking her is bogus. What I really need is a warrant to pull financials on her."

"In your dreams, Mason. You make a connection from Adler or Arnold to Sorensen and then a judge will give you a warrant."

"Yeah, I know. Far as we can see, nobody benefits from Arnold's death. We're checking alibis for the executives at KI. The bug guy dates Arnold's death to the last night she was seen. Plus we're waiting on the official autopsy report."

The Sarge waved him away. "Okay. Okay. Keep me updated."

Mason was still looking at Rhys Kensington who had attended the Silent Auction and said he'd gone home afterward. That is, to his penthouse home overlooking the ocean, not his home on 25th Street. Must be nice. He would love to nail Kensington to the wall and that's why Delgado would be handling it.

Ginger decided the effort of putting up her umbrella wasn't worth it. The day was grey and cloudy and it was drizzling. She was hurrying out to the parking lot to pick up some office supplies when a black Crown Vic pulled in and stopped next to her. Ginger saw Dave Mason in the driver's seat. The window slid down and the car stopped.

"Talk to you a minute, Ginger?"

Ginger stopped walking, her body angled away from the car. She hitched at the strap of her laptop.

"You know about Arnold. Did you hear about the attack on Sorensen?"

"Yes," she said nodding.

"You got any ideas for me? We're chasing our tails here."

Ginger looked up into the pewter-colored sky above and watched a private jet scream in for a landing at the Santa Monica Airport to the south. "You probably know more than I do. I don't know what I can add."

"Anything might help at this point," he said.

"It's scary here. Mr. Bricker being run over and Doris ending up dead. Now Venetia's been attacked. Nobody thinks that's all an accident." She twisted the toe of her high heel shoe into the pavement, as though crushing a cigarette butt, and chewed her lip.

"Look, could we sit down and talk," Mason said. "Wherever you like. Talk?"

She tried to read his face. He hadn't really made any effort to win her back. But then neither had she. His face was so locked in that she had no idea what was in his head. She'd ask him how he was and he'd answer fine. She'd ask him what was going on with him these days and he'd say not much. At least Rhys was aware he had an interior life.

"I could come into the station later," she said finally. She stopped herself from hoping this was anything other than business.

"That would be fine," he said tightly, turning the ignition in the powerful car. "About 2?"

"Fine, I'll be there."

On her return from the office supply store, Ginger grabbed a moment with Sorensen in her office. They were just making some progress when she looked up and saw Doug Paget in the doorway as the clock neared noon. The treasurer was bald as a light bulb. He had a big nose and jaw, and was narrow-chested and swelled to a thickened waistline.

"Oh, Doug, come in," Sorensen said. "You know Ginger McNair, don't you? Rhys's little girlfriend?"

Ginger stabbed Venetia with a look. His little girlfriend?

"Of course, I know Ginger. The board is very pleased with your progress." Paget seemed to have gained weight since he'd bought the brown suit he was wearing. The sleeves were too tight.

"Thank you. Venetia and I are just organizing a plan for the next year." Sorensen looked displeased to have anyone say anything positive to Ginger.

"Please excuse us, Ginger. I'm on the clock here for lunch, Venetia, shall we go?"

"Sure, sure." Sorenson gathered up one of her repertoire of Prada and Fendi bags and went to the door. "Ginger? I'd like to lock my office."

Ginger stayed where she was. "I'm just going to type up these notes before I forget things. We covered so much this morning. Okay?"

"Here?"

Ginger smiled as she said it. "The only place left now to work is the lunch room," she reminded Venetia. "It's very noisy right now."

"Yes, we're so crowded. It will be wonderful when we have our new campus. Don't put your fingers in Petrovich's cage. He bites people he doesn't like."

"Yes, I know. But he's never bitten me."

Venetia smiled grimly. She returned to her desk, took a set of keys from her purse, and locked her desk. "Set the lock on the door when you leave. Student confidentiality, you know."

"Certainly." You bitch, Ginger thought. She put a gracious smile on her face and waved good-bye.

21

The moment the door closed behind them, Ginger got up with every intention to snoop. "Petrovich, are you going to tell on me?" she grinned to the parrot who twisted his head and looked up at her from one shining eye. He ran up the side of his cage, bobbing. If Venetia came back, she'd tell her she was looking for the folder of old graduation programs that Venetia had gestured to on top of the row of cabinets. Guest lists could be used as the base of the school's first appeal letter.

Not exactly snooping, Ginger told herself as she moved folders on top of the filing cabinet. She tried each drawer. Locked. She finally found one open, just as she was going back to Venetia's desk to see if by chance, she'd left a drawer open with keys in it.

The third drawer down was open. She began flipping through the tabs on the hanging file folders, telling herself she had a good hour at least. She found a file of complaint letters from teachers about Sorensen's policy of never giving a student less than an A or a % grade less than 90. Reading them all carefully, she put them back and turned to another file and became absorbed in what she was reading. Very interesting.

Her heart stopped as Venetia sailed back into the room slinging her purse onto the back of the sofa. She glared at Ginger. "What are you doing?"

Ginger's heart spasmed. "Oh. Just looking for those graduation programs you mentioned...for the guest lists?"

At that moment Petrovich let out a scream that sounded accusing. "You won't find them in that drawer now, will you?"

"Yes, well." Ginger slid the drawer shut, and picked up the folder of graduation programs. "Gee, is it really this late? That was a quick lunch."

"We've had an incident here. We will need my office to consult with a student and his parents."

"Oh. Of course. Of course. I'm just leaving. I hope it's nothing bad," Ginger said, half way through the door.

"Incidents happen with students all the time. Now, if you don't mind...I need to make a phone call."

Caught dead to rights with her busy little fingers in the file drawers. There was no doubt in her mind that Venetia would report to Rhys that she'd been going through confidential records. She left the school and slung her laptop onto the seat of her car, catching sight of her face in the rear view mirror. Whew, red cheeks.

It was worth it. She'd found a file of paid up invoices for weekend stays at the W Hotel in downtown L.A., a very, very swank and expensive hotel. The same two signatures on each check request: Doris Arnold and Venetia Sorensen: or Venetia Sorensen and Doug Paget.

The name of the guest was Venetia Sorensen. A room for two. Nice. Another stress reliever like the spas, the gardener at her home, the masseuse that came to the school for Venetia, the airline tickets. Huge bills from an avian vet. Custom cages for Petrovich.

No wonder Venetia didn't want the school to close. And now to get ready to meet Mason.

"So you got nothing?" Mason's phone on his belt began to vibrate. He took it out and looked at it. Judy Klepper. Oh dear God in heaven, please, not now. He was half-listening to Palmer's long-winded explanation of how he was working the Bricker hit and run.

"I'm working the junkyards, the parts warehouses too at the same time. I'm also looking to see if they ever had this vehicle in storage. And I'm working DMV. Like I'm just looking for a name, right?"

"Yeah, I get it, Palmer. Move on."

"Just want to make sure you're following me, Mason. They say if you had a few more IQ points you'd be a Brussels sprout."

Mason turned to grin at him. "Yeah, yeah. Check out the big brain on Chuckee."

"Like I said, don't get your hopes up. I'm not there yet, but I'm close. Now get out of here. I'm meeting with Wilson and that loser Gomez from Auto Theft."

"I wouldn't trust Gomez to pick his own nose," Mason said.

"I look that stupid? He couldn't organize a farting contest."

"Catch you later then." He headed back to his desk. His eyes drifted toward the clock on the lower right of his screen, ticking towards 2 o'clock when Ginger would arrive. He leaned out of his cubicle and saw Fredericks coming down the aisle cradling a KFC bucket under her arm and about to take a bite on a drumstick she held in her hand. He jumped up and intercepted her.

"Hey, Fredericks, share-sies?" He reached to take the drumstick out of her hand.

She side-stepped him and gave him an elbow as she passed, then continued down the aisle chortling.

"Get your own, sir."

"Hey, assault on a superior officer."

"Yeah? Take me to court," she said, stepping into her own cubicle down the row.

Mason went back to his desk and took a call from the Chief's secretary. The Chief wanted to see him. Now. He took a look at the clock and winced.

❧

Ginger let herself into her one-bedroom, rent-controlled apartment on Third Street, north of the downtown shopping district, and slapped together a peanut butter and banana sandwich for lunch. Her heart thumped with anxiety at the thought of talking to Mason. As the time edged toward 2 o'clock and the meeting with Mason, she looked around her bedroom. Every potential outfit she owned was strewn over the bed and the desk chair. Nothing looked right.

"Why am I doing this?" she muttered to her marmalade cat, Raul. "He just wants to interview me about the case. I'm an idiot." Finally she hitched into a black skirt and flung a red tunic over it and rummaged through her store of costume jewelry.

"What about this one?" she said swinging a string of amber beads in front of the cat's face. "You like it?" Raul lifted a lazy paw, blinked once, then went back to sleep. "I can't believe I'm doing this," she said to him as she went out the door. "Does everybody ask their cat's fashion advice?"

She checked her mascara in the rear view mirror of her Audi, waiting for the light to change. Like every other major intersection, at rush hour you could sit through three light changes. Four cars felt entitled to make a left turn after the light had gone from orange to red. Where were cops when you need them?

When she got to the station, she gave her name and waited for Mason to come out from the secured area of the station and lead her back into the Major Crimes section. She planned to tell him her suspicions about Venetia, the money, the accounts, the way Venetia lived. Also mention the man who'd appeared in her office and whom she'd seen later bending her over a foreign car watched over by bodyguards. Instead, she looked up as she was reading one of the pamphlets on vehicle safety sitting on the bench in the airy lobby, and there was Delgado. Not Mason.

"Hey, Ginger," the big-bellied cop said, a smile of welcome on his cinnamon brown face. "What brings you here?" Delgado said in his scratchy growl of a voice.

"Dave asked me to meet him to talk about the Kensington case at 2 o'clock." She looked at her watch pointedly.

"Well, something's delayed him then. He didn't call?"

"No. I can't wait any longer."

"How about a coffee?"

"No, I need to get going."

"I'll tell him you were here. Great to see you, Ginger."

Ginger smiled and gave him a hug, disciplining her face not to show disappointment. She felt ridiculous knowing she'd made more of the occasion than it deserved. Dave Mason's whole thought process remained a mystery to her. He was attractive to a lot of women. He was probably snugged in tight in a new relationship by now anyway.

Mason did his best to curtail his impatience with the Chief. She didn't waste time usually, but today she was in a chatty mood. The hand on the clock swept closer and closer to 2. Just as he thought he'd be able to make the appointment with Ginger, the Deputy Chief appeared at the door. Both the chief and her deputy wanted Mason's opinion on a new database they thought might pay off over time. Next, one of the IT guys dropped in. Mason made an attempt to slide out the door saying he had a witness waiting. Neither the Chief nor the Deputy Chief seemed to care. When he got back to his cubicle, Delgado gave him a sigh and told him he'd tried to delay Ginger as long as he could.

"She knows it's your case and you'll probably get in touch with her again. Why didn't you call? Jesus, Mason, you're a fuckup sometimes."

"I was with the Chief."

"Oh."

"I can't just walk away. You know that." Mason rubbed his forehead, his heart sinking. He'd call and explain, but it was the same old story. The job. The job always came first.

"Shit, crap, and corruption," Mason said. "Okay, that's that then. Let's check in with the forensic techs at Sorensen's house."

22

In the daylight, Mason could see that major money had gone into Sorensen's flowerbeds surrounding the showy green lawns; yet he couldn't see Sorensen on her knees here, her ass up in the air, grubbing in the dirt. Fredericks was out in the street to greet them, waving her arms in the air as if he and Delgado were an incoming plane.

He got out of the car and said, "Yeah, yeah. You stick with the forensics people."

Fredericks pivoted on one foot and went out in back again. He couldn't deal with her energy right now. His mood was lower than snake shit in a wagon rut, but he pushed himself to pull out of it. Sorensen met him and Delgado at the front door, a large bandage over the scrape on her forehead, sipping coffee from a delicate china cup and saucer. Been a long time since Mason had seen a cup and saucer in everyday usage other than on *Downton Abbey.*

"How are you feeling today?" he said, as she welcomed him and Delgado.

"I'm okay." She shrugged, then winced, her hand going up to cradle the back of her neck as though it hurt. She led them through the house and then paused in the kitchen, setting the cup and saucer down on the black granite island next to a matching plate bearing half a pear and a piece of toast.

"Okay, okay," Mason said, "we'll check outside to see if they've found anything."

Two female forensics specialists were hunched over, peering at the scrap of lawn next to the garage. One of them looked up as Mason neared.

"Not sure if we've got anything or not. Ground's dry." She looked up, rolling her eyes.

"What?" he said, squatting beside her.

"Oh, nothing. That's the point, I guess. We haven't found anything. Guy could be in and out like smoke. And we've still got stuff to process from the Arnold car. Big backlog."

"Yeah, I know. We've had uniforms up and down the street doing knock and talks," Mason said, getting up to peer in the window of the garage at a gleaming black BMW. "We can hope, I suppose," Mason said, rubbing his face and yawning.

"Maybe there's nothing to find."

"You think?" Mason said, catching her tone. "There's always something," he said optimistically.

She gave him a look. "You've been watching too much TV."

"Little girl, I tell you when you need money. You want in. You want to play with big men like me. You need to give me money. I gave you date. You ignore me."

"But it's not that easy," Venetia protested, trying to pull him back into bed. He was already dressing, melting into another persona.

"Who says easy? You think my life easy?" He swung back to look at her, dark eyes narrowed. "I offer you big chance."

"But I'm going to have to abandon everything here I've worked for."

"Then you start over with me."

"What about your wife? The baby?"

"That is nothing to do with you."

She drew in a long breath and blew it out, pursing her lips, calculating.

"Okay."

Ginger stood at the window of the lunchroom across the quad, watching the scene unfold. A group of parents had been waiting for Sorensen, the conversation among them a hot, excited buzz. She knew the Peabodys and Stella Grainger. Venetia roared past the cottage into the parking lot in her BMW and the noise level rose. She watched Sorensen march toward them after parking the car. Sorensen looked up, her mouth a grim line, as she caught sight of the group, shifting the travel cage containing Petrovich to her other hand. He screeched in greeting.

The crowd of angry parents parted as Venetia mounted the three stairs to the deck that fronted the Administration cottage. Unsmiling, Venetia passed the armload of binders and files she had been carrying to a man who was hectoring her in a strident voice. The moment the group went inside, Ginger picked up a folder as though she was on official business, crossed the quad and came up on the deck as the delegation of parents followed Sorenson into her office and closed the door behind them.

Ginger parked herself in a chair on the deck outside Sorensen's office not caring who noticed that she was listening.

A man's cultured voice: "Can you shut that bird up so that we can hear ourselves think?"

"No, I can't."

"This is hardly ideal circumstances. Alright then. You should know that we've filed the petition to stay the closure of the school."

"Close the school?" Ginger heard Venetia say.

"Oh, come now. I'm sure you've been informed of our suit to stay the closure of the school."

"I have no intention of closing the school. I want the school to continue as much as you do. It's a legacy from my father that I honor. This is the first I've heard of this. And the first thing I want to do is check with my board."

Ginger's eyebrows rose in surprise. First she's heard? Really? The sheer gall of the woman amazed her.

He was interrupted by one of the women: "If you can't promise the school is going to stay open until the junior class graduates, then we'll be looking for somewhere else. And that's going to happen so fast your head is going to spin. And we want our year's tuition back."

"We need to have certainty here," another voice said. "So do our children..."

"Or else we'll see you in court. We know the board was served."

"We also want to know that our kids are safe here. There's too many terrible things happening. You have to know what the papers are saying."

The inner office door opened and Sorensen appeared with her hand on the doorknob, all business. "Threatening me or the board is not going to help keep the school open. These terrible incidents have nothing to do with your children's education. Or your children's safety. And that's the end of our discussion. Now if you will excuse me I have work to do. Please leave."

"You just can't make problems go away like this, Venetia," said Stella Grainger.

To let Venetia know she'd been a witness to this encounter, Ginger tapped her chin with a finger as the troop of parents filed past her, muttering among themselves. She stood up and walked into the outer office before the door closed. Sorensen's face was grim, and smug at the same time.

"We should talk, Dr. Sorensen…." she began.

Venetia closed the door firmly in her face. A moment later she heard Venetia shouting at someone, presumably on the telephone. Ginger knocked hard on the door, ready to have it out with her. She kept knocking. Sorensen jerked the door open, her face flaming red.

"What?" she snapped.

"What do you want? Why are you badgering me with your endless demands?"

"I overheard what was said. Is the school closing or not?"

"Don't be ridiculous. Don't you think I'd know?"

"What you know and what you don't know is a mystery to me, Venetia. You deliberately sabotage my job, which I might point out is only to help you."

"So what are you going to do then?" Sorensen said, her face twisting with nastiness. "Are you going to tattle to your boyfriend that I'm a bad girl and make him fix it for you again?"

Ginger took a step back. "Hey, your pathetic looking invitation was overruled on the grounds of bad taste, not anything I said. You want war? You can have war."

Cheeks hot, she turned on her heel, marched across the quad and flung her file folder on a table in the so-called café/lunch room. She was sick to death of being put off by the oh-so-very- superior Dr. Sorensen. Tired of being allowed five minutes of watching her peer into her laptop pondering her schedule, sighing about how she was so busy with endless high priority demands on her time. Everything Ginger tried to tell her she snapped that she already knew it. When she said she'd do something, she didn't do it, and when Ginger asked her about it, she got mad and told her to quit nagging. The last thing she wanted to do was involve Rhys or Caroline to help her do the job she'd been hired to do. Rhys had insisted the school was staying open. That was enough.

Then, giving herself two minutes to calm down, she pulled herself together.

Grow up. This is the way it is. Deal with it.

She marched back across the quad and into Sorensen's office without knocking. The headmistress stopped stabbing at numbers on her cellphone.

"Look, let's start over," Ginger said. "I know you don't like me and that's okay. You haven't given me much reason to like you."

Sorensen gave her a *yeah, so what* expression.

"There may be things here neither of us knows," Ginger said, sitting down on the couch without being asked. Petrovich was quiet, tearing apart one of the stuffed toys Sorensen supplied him with daily. Ginger looked over at him and swore he winked at her.

"Looks like your back is to the wall and I need this job. Do you want to work with me to save this school, or don't you? I can help you, if you help me. I don't know what your problem is, but you and I aren't getting anywhere as enemies. Seems to me with all that's going on around here you might need an ally."

Venetia said nothing for a long moment. She put down the desk phone and let her shoulders relax. "You have to realize I really resent having somebody forced on me."

"I can understand that," Ginger said. "But realize too that Rhys didn't just give me a job to be nice. I know how to raise money. I *can* help you."

The grim set of Sorensen's mouth loosened slightly. She laughed, a cold, bitter sound. "Okay."

Mason ran into Delgado in the men's room before lunch. "You get anything at Arnold's autopsy?"

"Long or short version?" Delgado said.

"Short."

Delgado pulled the report out of his jacket pocket and summarized. She'd been strangled by a thin cord. Fiber analysis had revealed it was a common type of twine available anywhere. Somebody strong got up behind her: the toes of her shoes were scuffed in the struggle indicating that her assailant was taller than her 5'1", which is most adults in the world. Her fingernails were broken off in a struggle, but there was no DNA material beneath them for analysis other than her own. The plastic sheet she'd been wrapped in bore no fingerprints. The padlock locking the gate to the chain link enclosure bore distinctive tool marks. But they had nothing to match it to.

"That's it?" Mason said. "C'mon, you're kidding."

"She was tased, then strangled. Bruises on her throat. Strong hands. Then stuffed into the back seat rolled up in the tarp."

"Maybe there were two of them?"

"Maybe. She didn't put up much of a fight. Looks like she went down fast."

"So she was either scared to death and froze..."

"...Or it's somebody she knew, and she didn't see it coming," Delgado finished.

"Probably a crime show watcher."

"Forensics are still all over her car." He shrugged. "They sell the tarps at Home Depot though and every other damn place." Delgado adjusted his belt under his gut. He gave himself a glance in the mirror, turned the faucet on, and dipped his tie in the stream. He yanked off a paper towel, and rubbed at a greasy spot until he'd made it wet and smeared it around.

He looked up at Mason who was watching this, "What?"

Mason shook his head. Delgado's shirt was hanging out at the back. "Nothing."

He held the door open for Delgado who followed him out into the hall.

Fredericks talked loud, racketed around from place to place, and filled every room with a burning excess of energy. A dog walker had seen something and thought nothing of it until Fredericks turned up at his door and nudged his memory.

"I got this guy," she said, triumph lighting her small, square face topped by frizzy red curls. "He's got a couple of mutts who are barking their heads off all the time I'm talking to him. I can't hear a thing. He's oblivious. Reminds me of that parrot Sorensen's got. Man, I'd strangle his neck so fast...he tells me he was passing by when he saw these guys wrassling a drunk out of an old Subaru over by Arnold's dump site on Euclid. Probably her."

"What time?"

"Just after the concert on the Pier got out. They get good bands. We should go sometime."

"Yeah, yeah," Mason said.

"He decided to walk over and back to the Pier because the traffic's so awful. He figures it maybe took him fifteen minutes to walk home to his place on Euclid."

Mason was all set to ask her to check with the concert people to get the time the concert let out. Fredericks put up a hand in a stop position.

"I already put in a call to them. I can read your mind. He piddles around first, then has something to eat." She waved a receipt in the air. "So it was around midnight."

Mason grinned. "Yeah, yeah. Okay. So did you get a description?"

"Two guys wrassling a drunk around. Big guys."

Mason leaned back, his size twelves on the edge of the conference room table, disappointed. He crashed his feet off the table, coming down on the floor with a smack.

"Two big guys. Oh, that's helpful. No cameras around there?"

"Nope. I hit every address on the streets surrounding there, and I mean every single address. We've showed her picture on every media outlet from Mexico to Canada." She teetered from foot to foot, bouncing.

"How can it be that nobody saw anything?"

"It's dark. Nobody's looking for a body dump in Santa Monica. They think bad things happen somewhere else."

Behind him, Mason heard Delgado snort with amusement.

"So they dumped the body and drove her car to the beach. See if we did a license scan sweep through the beach parking lot that night. The guy we saw on the tape didn't walk home. They had another car there to pick him up."

"It was a big night for patrol. Lotta calls. The last license scan of the beach lots was at 6:07 p.m.. Shit, huh?" Fredericks said.

"And where was her car from midnight to 2:20 when it was clocked in at the beach lot?"

"My witness said he also saw a school bus full of high school kids going through at the same time so I'm trying to nail that down too. They mighta seen something." Her eyes were bright.

23

Mason found an email from Jane Siegel in his email in-box, surprised he hadn't heard from the testy lawyer before now. There were about eight attachments, all of which bore legal-sounding names. He read the body of the email and skipped the attachments:

> The substance of our suit against the Kensington Foundation and Kensington Industries is that the trustees are acting in their own interest, and not the good of the students to honor the spirit in which Windsor Academy was founded. The trustees maintain that the Academy is on perilous financial footing and are planning closure. However, as executives employed by Kensington Industries, they are

officials of a separate, profit-making company. This is a clear conflict of interest—and we want them removed from oversight of the school. We want the current board replaced by parents and interested community members.

And we also want access to the financial records of the last three years.

You should know that a separate suit is being filed against the Academy by the University of Southern California. The suit alleges a breach of fiduciary duties on the part of Windsor School's trustees, claiming the construction of new buildings on the campus and continued operation of the Windsor Academy is financially unsustainable. USC stands to inherit a substantial portion of the trust assets should the operation of Windsor Academy be declared financially impractical.

"Ah, Jesus," Mason said. The smell of cleaning fluid was strong in the carpets this morning. Maybe it was making him stupid. "Here. I'm forwarding an email to you about the Kensington case." He hit send and leaned around the wall of his cubicle, looking at Delgado. "Is it there yet?"

"Yeah, yeah, gimme a minute to read it." Delgado absently scratched his chin while he read. He looked around. Wozinski was chatting up a pretty probation officer. Wozinski was their best white collar crime nerd.

"Hey, Wozinski," he shouted. "Come over here."

"Read this," Delgado said, pointing at his screen.

Wozinski thumbed his glasses up on his nose, and sank down into Delgado's chair. "Yeah? That's interesting. This is the Windsor Academy? Right? Let me read it again."

Woz thumbed his glasses up his nose two more times while he read the email and the attached documents. He had a sharp nose and narrow shoulders and invariably wore pale yellow shirts under a Sears brown suit.

"Wozinski, why don't you get your glasses fixed?" Mason said.

"I'm gonna. I'm gonna. When I get a minute…so look, what this means is the trust was set up to keep entire control within Kensington Industries. It looks like the foundation is invested heavily in KI stock. If they sell off stock to support the school, then Kensington Industries will no longer be in control of either KI or the school."

"Aren't you supposed to diversify?"

"Yes. Now why …." Mason waited impatiently for him to speak all the while studying the pits and scars in his head shaved down to a quarter inch of growth.

"Look," Wozinski said, standing up. "Let me check some sites here, look up the share price history, ROI, all that. I'll get back to you. Okay?"

"So when are we going to hear from you?"

"I've got other work, you know. Everybody's cheating everybody nowadays. Take it to the Sarge if you want it any faster than tomorrow or the next day. Maybe not then." He was gone.

"Hey, Wozinski's growing a backbone," Delgado commented, looking at Mason. "He used to cower if I even growled at him."

"Yeah, too bad, huh?"

Where the tradition referred to as "choir practice" had come from nobody remembered. On Fridays detectives, uniforms and a few unsworn personnel gathered in the parking lot to share a case of beer and bullshit. Hope and laughter kept the job alive. No insults were forbidden: hair loss, nationality, physique. Lots of fist-pumping-the-air woofing. Tonight it was mostly Palmer and the twelve traffic officers under his command. Big gusts of beery laughter as Mason got introduced to a new guy and took a Corona from the cooler filled with ice, tired after a long day of trying to unravel what happened to Doris Arnold. He leaned up against one of the unmarkeds and waited for Palmer to finish up the chat with his officers and come over. Palmer had his hands in his pants pockets and whistled to himself as he walked over to Mason.

"What's up, Mason?"

"Waiting on you, man. What have you got for me?"

"I think I might have narrowed down where that trim piece was bought."

Mason took a swig of Corona. "Yeah?"

"Out in Hemet."

"Hemet. What a godforsaken desert shit hole that is. They got lawns out there made of green painted stones, you know that?" Mason said.

"Water's expensive. Great place to pick up a used RV though," Palmer said, brushing at dirt on his pants. "One of the old people dies and the other one sells it off. And it's maybe got 10,000 miles on it. Happens all the time. They retire and the old guy dies."

"Jeez, you're a little ray of sunshine, Palmer. I'll remember that."

"Yeah, well, you're getting older, Mason."

"I'm only 37. How old did you think I was?"

"Actually I thought you were a lot older than that."

Mason cocked a play fist and brought it close to Palmer's chin. Everybody laughed.

"Maybe you're too busy to hear what else I got for you?" Palmer said.

"Tell me."

"Say pretty please with jam on it," Palmer taunted. He danced away as Mason took a jab at him. Fredericks jumped in to see if there would be any action. She loved to see people fight.

"Okay, okay. I traced the vehicle used in the Bricker fatality, at enormous personal cost, I might add."

"What enormous personal cost?" Mason scoffed. He pulled a chair close to the table that held the cooler, and sat back to front, his arms over the back of the chair.

"You want this or not?"

"Yeah, I do. C'mon. I'm busy."

"I traced the original owner to a guy in Lomita. He sells it on Craigslist, right? So how do I find him? I go to his place in Lomita. Nice neighborhood--not. Some of his neighbors are scarin' *me*. His place is empty, so I start knocking on doors. Nobody knew him. He was short term in the house but I finally get somebody who thinks he remembers the realtor's name. I find the realtor and he's in, which is the high point of my day. And the seller's got a forwarding address, but it's way the fuck out in Arizona, just across the border from Sonora. Place called Pirtleville. And he doesn't answer his phone. Of course."

"So now what?"

"Well, now what is me, and somebody else get ourselves out to Pirtleville and get a description of the buyer. See what we can shake loose."

"Hunh," Mason grunted. "So we're getting somewhere. Now if we could just tie Sorensen in somehow. She's burning a hole in my gut."

Sorenson took a pile of paper and smacked it down on a stack of files. She glared at Mason and Delgado who were sitting in her office looking relaxed. Mason glanced over at the parrot as it slid up and down the side of its cage using his talons and beak. Sorensen glanced at him with disdain, sensing his fear of the parrot.

"Why are you questioning me again?" she said loudly. "Of course, my hair might be in Doris' car. She picked me up at the car dealership when I left my car there not that long ago. I've been attacked. Why aren't you looking for the man who attacked me?" Her show of irritation didn't worry either Mason or Delgado who were used to dealing with pissy people.

"We can't find any evidence of your attacker despite the best efforts of our forensic specialists."

"Well then, try harder," she said. The bird screamed and flung pistachio shells on the floor.

"We're giving everybody hard looks again because of Doris Arnold's death. It's no coincidence that all these events point back here."

"What are you saying?" Sorenson crossed her arms in front of her chest, hard cords of muscle jumping on her thin arms. She rotated her hips at the waist so that her full gauzy skirt swirled around her, her expression one of outraged defiance.

Mason flipped through the pages of his notebook as though looking for something. "For example, we don't seem to be able to nail down any confirmation of your alibi on the night Ms. Arnold died. You say you were at home?"

Mason stood up, then pulled his chair and sat back to front on it, grinning at her.

"I was at home, probably up late working at my computer. I was tired after the Silent Auction. I went home as soon as I could get away." She breathed harshly through her nose.

"You make any phone calls? Anybody call you?" Without a warrant they'd have to take her word for it.

"I don't remember back that far." Sorenson stood up and began pacing around her office. She opened the door of the cage and flung in a stuffed toy which the parrot immediately began destroying, flinging cotton wads on the floor that was already covered with seeds and shells.

"People tell us you and Ms. Arnold had a lot of arguments," Delgado continued.

"What were these arguments about?" He swiveled in his chair to follow her throughout the office.

"Oh, for God's sake. Doris was impossible and I couldn't stand looking at her."

Mason quirked an eyebrow at that.

"So unfit. And her clothes!" She tossed her silvery hair. "Her sister demanded more and more time, and Doris just couldn't keep up. We were talking about hiring someone to do the basic bookkeeping. She kept making mistakes, and I'd have to go into the books after her and correct things and it was driving me crazy. The parents were complaining about mistakes all the time. But she needed the health insurance, God knows, and most of her salary went toward her sister's medical expenses. I'd have to be a monster to let her go. I just couldn't do it."

"You being such a generous person. She made a very good salary here, we noticed," Delgado said.

"Well, she was always available. I could call on her anytime and I need someone like her. You can't imagine the problems I'm going to have replacing Doris." She stopped and held a handkerchief to her face. "Did you search Doris' sister's apartment for the money?" she said suddenly. "Maybe it's there."

Mason wasn't even going to give that an acknowledgement. "Detective Wozinski from our office tells us that he was only able to get partial records from you–for the last year, was it?"

"Oh. I gave him everything I could find. Didn't he tell you that?"

"He did, but..."

She interrupted him, throwing her hands up in the air. "He couldn't make head nor tail of it either, could he? This was Doris' job. I didn't interfere unless I absolutely had to and then I could never understand what she was telling me. I've hired a CPA firm to help me figure things out. She's left me with a real mess and months of missing backup documentation, things like receipts, contracts, payroll, all that stuff. She told me she put things in a storage unit because we have so little space here, but I can't find any record of where the storage unit is." She sat down and put her face in her hands. "The last thing I need right now is somebody attacking me."

Delgado finally nodded and stood up to leave. Sorenson was on the phone as they went out the door.

They both leaned on the Crown Vic, not getting in, standing there in the open door of the vehicle in the parking lot. The sky was blue overhead and a faint scent of jasmine blew in the breeze. The jacaranda trees were nearly done, their blue flowers drifting onto the lawn. Mason looked up and saw Sorenson watching them from the deck of her cottage. She had come out holding the parrot cage to hang it from the railing.

"She's watching us," Mason said, jutting his chin slightly toward Sorensen's office window. "You buy her story?" Mason said.

Delgado scratched his nose, slapped the top of the vehicle and got in closing the door. Mason followed him, putting the keys in the ignition.

"Hardest alibi to disprove is I was at home alone."

Delgado poked his tongue around in his cheek while he settled his belt more comfortably under his gut. "You think she killed Arnold? She killed her because she made mistakes?"

"Maybe Arnold knew things she shouldn't," Mason observed. "Or was going to figure something out."

"Yeah, like what? Tell me what."

"You gotta admit it's suspicious her not being able to find the records and Arnold's computer missing," Mason said. "Maybe it's about one of the students. Maybe a teacher wanted to cover something up. Romancing up some kid's grades. We don't have cause to pull any paper on her."

"Yeah, but she says a CPA is looking things over, trying to put it back together. And so is Wozinski. Once Wozinski gets his nose down the rat hole, he won't quit."

"Yeah, I thought he'd already started, but the L.T. pulled him off to work on something else. He can't start till next week. And we only have her say-so she's got a CPA on it."

"Ah, you're fulla shit, Mason. Look at the victimology on Arnold. That picture of her? A born victim. Just one look at that moon pie face and the wolves would be sharpening their teeth."

24

Mason bobbed up like a groundhog to peer over the wall of his cubicle every few minutes to check the coffee pot. Somebody had brought in some homemade banana bread. Delgado would hit the banana bread if there was any left, and hang out there, bullshitting with the others. Phones rang. Keys clacked, and there were shouts of boisterous voices, laughter, and hard boots.

Today was his birthday. He had woken up to his daughter Haley's phone call singing him happy birthday. She giggled through a long story about how she'd chosen a present for him, which he would get when he picked her up next weekend. He hung up, smiling. His daughter: the light of his life. When he picked up his mail last night there was a generic birthday card from Ginger with a single ticket to a Dave Mason concert. Of course he liked the Dave Mason band. If she'd sent two, it might mean she wanted him to invite her. But one? He intended to call her and say thanks, but he put it off and put it off. It probably didn't mean anything anyway. He remembered the arguments. Her complicated life. A birthday card. Well, it was something. As soon as he had a minute, he'd call. But what if she said it was nothing? Or mentioned Kensington? Look how easily she'd blown off his apology for the botched meeting at the station. It meant nothing to her. She was just a nice person. She sent birthday cards to everybody.

Delgado's scratchy mess of a voice came over the wall of Mason's cubicle as he'd gone back to his email. "I made an appointment for us to interview Rhys Kensington to check his alibi," Delgado said.

"Yeah, well…" Mason replied. The last thing he wanted to do was see the guy Ginger was sleeping with. But if he said that aloud, Delgado would jump down his throat.

Delgado stuffed the last bite of banana bread in his mouth. "You're coming with me."

"Yeah. Yeah." Mason made a neat pile of carjacking reports in the middle of his desk, grabbed his brown leather jacket, and followed Delgado out. Kensington had agreed to meet them at his beach condo, which occupied the penthouse of one of Santa Monica's best addresses. Scowling all the way up to the penthouse in the elevator, Mason refused to be impressed. Delgado gave him a dark look but he ignored it.

"Behave yourself," Delgado growled as they knocked on the door.

"How can I behave myself when he's screwing my girlfriend?"

"She's not your girlfriend now, and whatever happened, you're probably the one who blew it, not her."

Before Mason could fire back, Kensington opened the door, holding a coffee cup in one hand and wearing a thick, long, black bathrobe with his initials on the breast pocket. He had small hands and shrewd eyes. "Come in. Come in. Thanks for meeting me here."

His mutt rushed up and sniffed them. Kensington reached down to pet her and made a big thing about introducing them. They talked dogs while Mason looked around apprehensively. Was Ginger going to come strolling out of the bedroom in a matching black bathrobe? Mason didn't think he could stand that.

He took in an expanse of honey-colored oak floors, floor-to-ceiling windows with a view of the Pacific Ocean and the smudge on the horizon that was Catalina Island. His eyes swept the uncluttered area dotted with Scandinavian furniture and book cases filled with hardback books against one wall. Kensington gestured them toward the grouping of red leather sofas and chairs with a triangular black glass coffee table at the center. The dog jumped up on the sofa beside him.

"I feel terrible about Doris Arnold, this stuff that's been going on at the school," Kensington began. "We've never had any adverse publicity before."

"Then you agree, these two deaths are connected in some way to the school?" Delgado said, taking the lead in the interview.

"None of us are stupid, Detective Delgado," Kensington said, directing himself towards Mason's stocky partner who today was wearing his blue suit with the mended right cuff.

"We need some help then," Delgado said. "Who stands to gain here? That's what murder is usually about. Domestic violence. Or jealousy. Revenge?"

"That's what's so hard to figure out for us, and believe me, we've tried," Kensington answered, spreading his palms wide. "Everybody's talking about this at KI. The operating budget of the school isn't worth killing Uncle Leonard for. Uncle Leonard had money, yes, but it was more in the line of savings and smart investments. That all goes to his daughter anyway. Doris? Well, yes, there's the $27,000 deposit that's missing. But you've probably been digging into her finances and I hate to think she was killed for that money."

"It was mostly credit card receipts, and we've been following those cards to see if they're being used….and the trail dead ends. Nobody's touched them," Delgado acknowledged.

"I wondered about that. You hear about identity theft."

"If anybody's using those cards, we'll know. There's the business of the school's recent financial records missing. The cancelled backup service."

"Yes, that was a great surprise to me. Venetia has always been more invested in the students and parents, and let Doris take care of the business side. I mentioned to Venetia on more than one occasion that wasn't good business practice. I blame myself as well. I've been writing death sentence appeals and I haven't been attentive to the school, I must admit."

That was all Mason needed to hear to start his day off right. Kensington was working to get some misunderstood, slime sucker murderer who'd raped and killed his grandmother off, so the felon could walk the streets and kill somebody else. He tried to keep the rage off his face. Oh, this guy and Ginger were just made for each other. Both bleeding heart liberals.

Delgado raised his voice and turned slightly to Mason with a keep-your-mouth-shut glare. "So who was most involved with the day-to-day operation of the school?"

"I guess Leonard since he retired six months ago. Doug Paget from KI has been the Treasurer for a while now. Have you talked to him?"

"Yes. We have."

"And of course to cover all the bases, we need to ask you for an alibi?" Delgado said.

"I figured you would so I asked the security company for a report of that night. And the next night too just in case. I've got this alarm system that clocks in any ins and outs on all the doors in my unit. I think you might find that my housekeeper who showed up at 7:00 a.m. will tell you I was here as well. And the roof door is alarmed too. I asked them to put that in as well." He handed the report to Delgado.

Mason wanted to hit him. He thought of everything. They'd check his phone records and the cameras too. Just in case.

Kensington pinched his forehead in a frown. "Do you think it could have anything to do with the students and drugs? I'd hate to think that, but you have to entertain all the possibilities."

"We just assume there's the usual amount of low level drugs you get when there's teenagers who have money. But word on the street is that there's nothing unusual, or nothing in any unusual amounts, going down at the moment," Mason said, entering the conversation for the first time.

Kensington looked at him without saying anything for a moment while he considered it. "I'm glad to hear that," he said, rising, pulling the robe tight around his compact frame. "I wish I could tell you more. I hate anything that casts a negative light on the Academy. My sister and I got a great education there and so did a lot of other kids. We went to school with scholarship kids from service worker families and we knew growing up that not everybody had our advantages. My grandfather made us do community service. That's how Caroline and I met Ginger."

Delgado tilted his head back and gave him a smile, "That's good. That's good, I guess."

Mason said nothing. There wasn't much more. When they got outside, they looked at each other and laughed.

"Quite the Democrat, isn't he? Do you hear that? He knows a few poor people," Mason said.

"Aw, c'mon, he wasn't that bad."

"No, I know he wasn't. It's me," Mason admitted.

Delgado stopped walking and turned to face Mason. "Well. How about that?"

"I know I'm an asshole. Being there and thinking she might turn up and go make coffee in his kitchen, whatever, made me realize I want to get her back. And then I think of all the fights we had over her politics. I just don't know if I'm up to it."

"Yeah, but she was good for you. It's about time you woke up, Mason."

Just to work every lead out to the end, Mason spent a couple of hours reviewing the backgrounders on the teachers at Kensington Academy, as well as the cleaning staff and subcontractors. The French teacher married to the man from Kazakhstan had called the department a couple of times to get him calmed down. He reviewed the 415 disturbance reports on the incidents. No charges filed. No physical stuff. The husband showed up drunk at the Academy once, and the teacher had called the station. Wonder how that went down with Sorenson? It was something he would follow up on.

It was a storybook sunny California day, and he soaked it in on the drive to the Academy to interview the

French teacher again. The whites of her eyes showed and her English seemed to desert her as Mason called her out of her classroom to talk to him. The little French woman was terrified of losing her job and her immigration status. She explained her husband had been through terrible things and he had PTSD. Everything she said had the ring of truth.

Mason dug a little harder when he got back, reviewing the immigration status of both of them and haunted the forensics lab looking for anything further on Arnold. Whoever had killed her was organized and planned ahead. They had the tool mark on the snipped padlock and Fredericks was pulling camera footage from all over the city looking for Arnold's car between 1:00 a.m. and 2:20 when it was driven onto the beach parking lot. She hadn't yet found the school bus driver. The driver had quit after a trip back and forth with the kids to Sacramento: the noise was bad for his heart. Mason went through the backgrounders on everybody else at the school as well and found a twenty-five-year-old felony conviction for the janitor, who was now 63. Nothing further turned up for the janitor. He'd been one of the few who'd kept his nose clean.

Mason hated waiting for something to happen and being at the mercy of circumstances and reports from other investigators. He tracked Palmer down while the traffic investigator was enjoying the sunshine in the new park that had been created on what had been a wide green lawn in front of City Hall. The lawn had been a favorite of all the troublemakers in the City to stage demonstrations. He stood a moment and watched big, white clouds skid across the sky and the branches of skinny, new trees toss in the breeze. Hard to believe sometimes there was a world outside the station and the pile of crime scene photos on his desk.

Palmer was eating a messy meatball sandwich and talking on the phone. Mason ambled over and sat down on the bench beside him, tilting his face up to the sunshine. Palmer was arguing with somebody on his phone, glanced over at Mason, and finally hung up.

"Mason, oh yeah, I was gonna call you," he said.

"Heard you went to Arizona to talk to the seller in the Bricker case. What happened?"

"First mistake was taking Gomez."

"Oh, yeah, Gomez is in love," Mason chuckled.

"Which I had to hear about the entire way to Arizona. He's like a high school girl."

Just then a trio of pretty City Hall office workers passed and both men paused to look.

"We get there and Pirtleville's like the ass end of nowhere, dry as dust desert. We drive out there in the biggest SUV the car rental's got. We're on this holy shit road in low gear going about five miles an hour trying to stay in the ruts. I'm driving and all of a sudden we hit a gully wash across the road with a big rock in the middle and the goddamn SUV busts an axle."

He turned to Mason with such a sense of outrage on his boyish face that Mason had to laugh. "Yeah? Then what?"

"We sit there on our asses and wait is what. Cochise County Sheriff finally turns up along with the tow truck. Sheriff agrees to drive us the rest of the way in. Good thing too because this guy's built himself a compound. Big fence with the dogs, the whole deal. Fortunately, our guy is some relation of his. We get in there and the seller's all smiles, which is not what I expected. Cops at your door in a place like that? I thought the guy would be militia and we'd have to shoot our way in."

"Yeah, big disappointment, so then what?"

"He's already pretty liquored up and it's 2 o'clock in the afternoon so we get him talking pretty easy. The white Corolla was his wife's and when she passed on, he let it sit for a couple years and then decided to sell it. So his granddaughter gets him to take a shot at selling it on Craigslist. She posts it for him."

"I love it, of course, it's the granddaughter" Mason said, slapping his hands down on his knees. "Sheriff's guy there with you all this time?"

"Yeah, and Gomez with his long face itching to get home. I've refused about fourteen invitations to have a beer with the old guy by now and I don't want any of the best goddam chili in Arizona. And I don't want to hear any more Vietnam stories. I just want to get something

249

and get the fuck out of there before it gets dark, so I work him around to talking about the buyer. Where's his paperwork on the sale? Surprises the ass off me again. He knows right where to find it."

"C'mon, Palmer, gimme a lead," Mason said impatiently. "Did you get a description of the buyer, this guy Evans or whatever his name is? An address?"

Palmer stood up. "You dreamer, Mason. Evans wants to pay him by Paypal. Course he doesn't know Paypal, but his granddaughter does. Seller pays him, tells him he's been out of the country and just needs a car for a while and then he's going back to wherever place he forgets to say. So the buyer doesn't know when he'll be able to pick it up that night, but he wants our guy to park it on the street and leave the keys and the pink slip in an envelope on the rear passenger tire. He'll pick it up when he can. Course my guy is curious, but he's got his money now and he's getting rid of the car. He's keepin' an eye on the car out in front of his house, but he can't stay awake all night. I'm figuring he passed out. But somewheres in the night, this John Evans picks up the car and leaves his copy of the pink slip in the guy's mailbox just like he said he would."

"Let me guess," Mason said, slapping his knee and standing up.

"Right. False address."

"And John Evans, whoever he is, is blowin' in the wind. And the Paypal account is anonymous."

"Yup."

25

Mason and Delgado sat in the office of their supervising sergeant. York looked up from a pile of paperwork and twirled his pen between two fingers. "I'm getting pressure. We're not the only department seeing more carjacking. It's happening all over L.A., everywhere I guess. The Captain's talking Task Force. The other teams are complaining they need help."

Delgado tried again. "Here's how I see it, but Mason and I aren't eye to eye on this. He's being pissy. Yeah, sure, it looks like they're connected. Bricker—the vehicle fatality—now it coulda been an accident. No witnesses. I know what Palmer says, but I'm not so sure."

"You're questioning Palmer's investigation? He has more training that *I* have!"

Delgado gave a huge shrug. "I donno. It just seems..."

"Coincidence, huh? Then why don't we see some action on the credit card slips?"

Sgt. York looked from Delgado to Mason, scratching the back of his head. Mason hitched forward in his chair, ignoring a sharp stab from his aching tooth.

"Maybe the son-in-law wanted to hurry along his daughter's inheritance? Weren't they in trouble with money?" Delgado said. "Maybe we should look at him for the hit and run."

Mason waved a hand in the air. "You're swinging wild now. Those people aren't the kind to murder anybody." His words sounded hollow even to him. Plenty of people weren't the kind of people to murder, and yet they went ahead and did it anyway.

"Not the daughter. I mean the son-in-law."

"They live in St. Louis." There was a lot of heat behind Delgado's words.

"You know for sure the son-in-law didn't come out here a few days before the old man's death?"

"No. But I'll find out," Mason said, making a note.

The sergeant's eyes went back and forth between them. It wasn't unusual to have disagreement between team members. Sometimes people disagreed just to spice things up. Sometimes team members fought like scorpions in a bottle.

"Maybe they didn't mean to kill Arnold. Something went wrong."

"Lotta maybes."

"Coulda though," Delgado insisted.

"Delgado, you're all wrong," Mason said, enjoying the debate. "My eye's on Arnold's boss, the headmistress at the Academy—Sorenson. The two of them made way too much money. At this point nobody knows where it all got spent, which makes me very suspicious. Sorensen's living like a rich woman. The teachers all say Sorenson is tight as a tick with money, paid them shit, and Arnold handled all the finances."

"So where's Arnold spending it? She isn't splashing it around," Delgado observed.

"What's Sorensen's alibi for both events?" the sergeant put in, scratching his crew cut.

"Both times she says she was home. Alone."

Sgt. York's mouth twitched. "So you've been canvassing the neighborhood, trying to catch her out. Right?"

Mason hesitated. "I just started thinking it was her," he admitted, "when she said she was attacked the other night. Man with a gun in her backyard rushed her when she went to check out a noise in the back yard. You saw the report?"

"Robinson?" York looked up. "At least he can spell." Grammar and spelling was a favorite rant for the Sarge. That and his divorce.

"One thing that stuck in my mind when we investigated her story was that Sorenson seemed to get a lot more upset when I arrived. Like she'd been saving up the waterworks for when it counted," Mason interrupted.

"...Maybe she was just realizing how close she'd come to really getting hurt," Delgado stepped over him. "There's been a rash of burglaries over in that neighborhood. What about those six break-ins at the stores on Montana? The North of Montana Neighborhood Association is all up in arms about the burgs. Accusations that we never patrol their neighborhood, all the resources go to the downtown."

Mason's voice rose. "Yeah, yeah, I know. Look, I want to dig deeper on this attack on her, go after the neighbors harder. The garage is in the back looking out on the alley. There's motion sensor lights all along there. Maybe somebody saw something..."

"Cameras?"

"Didn't see any."

Sgt. York looked over Mason's shoulder, and Mason turned around to look. Another team of detectives stood at the door waiting their turn with the Sarge. "Thing is, a lot of time has passed now. What's the date on Bricker? Three weeks or more now. You'll be lucky, Mason, to get anything. The Kensingtons are big news in this town. The media are all over this and we've got nothing to give them." He slapped a pile of dailies on his desk where the name Windsor Academy appeared in the headlines. "And one more thing," York stood up and stretched. "Don't get crosswise with Palmer. He knows what he's doing. If he says Bricker was a deliberate hit and run, it was."

Mason and Delgado worked the known associates of the carjacker who had died in the attempt to take the old lady's car at the mall. He got a lead on his one-time girlfriend and mother of his child, Sandra Stitt. She was living in a garage behind some tweaker's house in the not-so- nice Koreatown section of midtown Los Angeles. Stitt wasn't at the first address or even the next one. Mason remembered tweaker places from his own days on patrol when he worked LAPD. Uniforms knew what was going on working their beat. They stood on the sidewalk on a street of cheap apartment houses. Two patrol cars and his own Crown Vic. Mason could feel the vibration of the big engines under his feet. The patrol guys knew where the druggies lived and they dropped by every once in a while unannounced just to show the flag and have a look around for drugs or paraphernalia. Nobody on probation for drugs could object. They were probably used to it anyway.

One lead led to another like pulling on a tangled knot in a rope. He and Delgado went in behind the officers who knew these people, knew who was turning tricks, who was selling just enough--or ripping off businesses just enough--to keep their own buzz going. None of them worked at a job or knew anybody who did. After visiting five filthy, trashy drug apartments in a row, Mason's head was filled with stink and his hands smelled, even with gloves on. He'd sooner live in a landfill than one of these places.

Sandra Stitt hadn't remained faithful to the memory of her dead boyfriend for very long. They found her with her new guy rolled up in a quilt on a bare mattress still in bed in the late afternoon, the bedroom stinking of farts and cigarette smoke, and a chemical smell Mason's nose identified as meth. A lump of a girl, soft around the middle and sullen, with the brains of a sprinkler head.

Stitt gave up a name fast enough. The patrol guys looked at each other behind her and nodded. They had their carjacker who had run after breaking the old lady's arm and dragging her out of her car at Santa Monica Place mall. Harvey Laski.

Palmer leaned over the half wall of Mason's cubicle, his face dark. "I hear you're second guessing me on the Bricker hit-and-run."

"Who told you that?" Mason temporized. He pushed his chair back and stood because he was taller than Palmer. So was Delgado, the old bull cop with a double chin and a paunch.

"If you've got a beef with my work, you tell me, not the Sarge."

Mason felt his face color. He wanted to say that Delgado brought it up first, but that sounded juvenile. "Hey relax, Palmer."

The fury burned in Palmer. "I say it was a deliberate hit-and-run. Had to be. No skid marks. Nothing to show the driver tried to brake at the last minute. Nothing. And I still haven't found any witnesses and it's not for lack of trying."

"Then you don't think it's got something to do with the school? Both the victims are connected with the Kensington's school."

"Sure it's got something to do with them. Rhys Kensington and the CEO over there at that squirrelly place are chewing their fingernails down to the elbows about bad publicity. The media from here to Timbuktu is all speculating about what's going on there."

"If you're done ragging on me, you might like to hear some good news," Mason said, putting a tease into his voice.

"What?"

"We got the other carjacker from the mall. Harvey Laski? Remember, one died. His buddy, the other jacker. Got him tied up tight downstairs in a holding cell."

"Laski? Never heard of him."

"You gonna calm down?"

"Who me?" Palmer grinned suddenly. Homicide detectives were all actors. "Let's take him on."

As chummy as ever, the three of them clattered down the stairs together to get a jailor to bring Laski to an interview room on the first floor of the station. On the way they filled Palmer in on what they knew about the guy. Twenty years years old, medium, medium, brown and brown, your average car thief with one aggravated assault, and a sealed juvenile record. York and the Lt. of Operations were watching the video feed.

Laski cranked himself around in the chair he was shackled to when the three of them came in; Mason and

Delgado big and threatening, Palmer, smaller but fit and intense. Mason took his suit jacket off and flung it on the back of the chair facing Laski. Palmer stood by the door. Delgado leaned against the wall next to Palmer.

"So Mr. Laski. Mind if we call you Harvey?"

"Harvey's not my name," Laski objected. He was probably five foot eight, tweaker skinny, and already had the bad teeth. He had tattoos all up his neck and across the right part of his face, all seemingly unconnected, all of them different. Bad tat art. Bad.

Mason referred to the file he had on Laski. "Not Harvey. Yup, I see that here. One of your aka's is Skinny Pete. You like that better? Skinny Pete?"

Laski didn't answer. He examined his hands, which jittered on the table. He used one long fingernail to clean the thumbnail on the other hand. Nervous energy shimmered in the air around him.

"Bet you're a fan of *Breaking Bad*? Yeah? So was I. Skinny Pete's a great character. Too bad that went off the air. So here you are, Pete. You want a Coke, a smoke maybe? Some water? They gave you a chance to piss?"

"What do you care?"

"Hey, I want you to be comfortable. What do you think we are here? Barbarians? Everything okay?"

"Look, just fuck off, man."

Mason was going to take the early lead and they'd double team him until they wore him down. "I see by my file here you're driving a 69' Camaro? I had one of those back in the day. What color?"

Laski didn't answer. Mason went on. "Yeah, mine was British racing green. I loved that car. So much power it would go straight up a wall. Yup. Man, that was a great car." He let a little silence fall. "So what color's yours?"

Mason turned to Palmer. "You're a car guy, Palmer. What are you driving nowadays?"

"Not fair, Mason. I got kids."

"I saw you. You're driving a minivan."

"Shit, that's my wife's car. What I'd like is..." Palmer knew cars and that was all it took to get him going.

Slowly Mason drew Laski into the conversation. This sounded like time-wasting bullshit but he and Palmer and the watchers on the video feed were getting a bead on Laski, seeing how he reacted when the conversation was nonthreatening and he was comfortable. They bullshitted Camaros around for a while and good years for Mustangs. Finally Mason slapped at his phone in its belt holster as though it had vibrated. He drew his phone out and looked at it, "Gotta go. Sure I can't get you anything, Pete?"

"How about a Coke?"

"Great. I'll be right back." He grinned at Laski. "Don't go away."

Palmer worked Laski while Mason was gone. Mason watched him on the video feed. They talked good places to live in LA, Tito's Tacos and its imitators, and were getting down to the best beaches when Mason returned. The vibe in the room was relaxed now.

"I wasn't there when they picked you up," Mason said, sinking into a chair, "but here's what they tell me.

They could be wrong. There's this little problem of what happened that day at the mall, you and your buddy."

"I wasn't at no mall. When?"

Mason ignored that. "I don't see either of you guys as criminal masterminds, okay? I mean, you're a good guy, aren't you, Pete?" He had to admire himself, Mason thought, saying a line like this without gagging.

Pete nodded. "Yup. I do things," he thought, "like things…"

Real humanitarian. "Yeah, I can see that. Sure, you do a little thieving, you get caught just as much as you get away. Now, I can see that in your file here, and a couple of calls I made to guys I know over in your neck of the woods. We figure you've got your reasons. Maybe your old mama needs the money. Maybe you got little brothers and sisters. Right?"

"Yeah, that's right." Skinny Pete nodded, acknowledging his sense of family responsibility. Yeah, he was a good guy.

"You know your cars. You maybe like to joyride a little. No harm in that, huh? Nobody gets hurt. Now, what I figure happens is maybe somebody hears you're an okay guy, smart and all, and he makes big promises."

Skinny Pete was watching him carefully now.

"He tells you all's you gotta do is pick up a car here and there. Get me a white Honda Civic 2008. I need it for the parts. The owner's got insurance. What's the harm? You pick up a car, take it someplace. Easy money. Nobody gets hurt. That coulda happened, right?"

"Maybe." Laski was studying the floor.

"Now what went down at the mall, that was bad, but you never meant that to happen, did you?"

Laski was silent, looking up at Mason from under a unibrow over a thick, flaring nose in a narrow face.

"So we've got this problem here, Pete. Maybe you can help us with it. You want to tell us what happened there at the mall?"

"What mall? I wasn't at no mall! I told you."

"Pete, we got you at a carjacking where an old lady was hurt. You stole her Rolex right off her arm. You dragged her out of the car and broke her arm. Other injuries. You put her in the hospital."

"Not me. Not me."

Mason said carefully, tapping the table with one finger. "Cameras, Pete. Hear of them? Cameras?"

Skinny Pete bit at a fingernail, tearing a strip off down to the quick. A drop of blood pooled. He licked it off.

"C'mon, Pete. How many people got their face tatted up like you do?"

"Lots of people."

"Maybe where you live. Not in Santa Monica at the mall."

The shivery little tweaker in the dirty white T-shirt glanced over in the corner, then his gaze skidded up the wall to the height of the room, then back down. His gaze finally came back to Mason.

"What happened to Big Red?" Laski asked.

"Your buddy? Him? Oh, he died."

"I heard he was still in the hospital."

"Yeah. And then he died. He ran out in traffic and a bus hit him. That coulda been you, Pete. Think about it. He a good friend of yours?"

"Me? No, never saw him before."

"So you just happened to meet him there at the other side of that old lady's car and he talked you into jacking it? That's how it happened?"

"Pretty much…" Laski had to think about it and the thinking process was slow. Mason watched it happen, saying nothing, watching the pressure cook.

"So let me tell you what I think happened. Okay?" Mason said.

Laski looked up, hawked deep in his throat, jerked his chin up, looked around for a place to spit and then nodded. Palmer stepped forward to glare at him. He swallowed it.

Skinny Pete was watching Mason now, shrugging and rolling his shoulders.

"Now, what went down at the mall, that was bad, but you never meant that to happen, did you?"

"Hey, no, man. That was Big Red. Not me." The *togdi* defense. The other guy did it.

"Well, let's not focus on that now. I'm not interested in pinning your ears to the wall. I just want the people who give the orders. Maybe you're just the victim here."

Skinny Pete scratched an infected tattoo on his right cheek and made it bleed, thinking hard.

"Why should you take the big hit, Pete? Think about it. You want me to tell you what I could put you down for, how many years for hurting that old lady? Whoops, there goes my phone again. Say, you want another Coke? I'll be back."

Mason got up and closed the door behind him, joining Palmer and a few others watching the video feed.

The L.T. gave him a high five. "He's about ready."

Mason poured himself a cup of the good stuff coffee and broke off a piece of a cranberry scone, feeling good. There was no other rush like getting a confession. Well, maybe a high-speed car chase. Skinny Pete was bobbing his head, scratching, ass shifting in his chair, occasionally slapping his hands on the table. He was using the time to commune with his Inner Shithead, looking for ways to dig himself out of this hole. He looked around at Mason when he came back in. Mason put his hands on the back of the chair facing him, but didn't sit down. He loomed over him.

"I been thinking…"

"Yeah?" Mason said casually, "Thinking what?"

"Cameras there in the parking lot. We never seen them."

"No, you wouldn't nowadays."

"That old lady?" Skinny Pete looked up, worried.

"Yeah, she mighta had a heart attack. Heard she was pretty bad off." He shook his head sadly. He could tell any lie he liked in the interrogation of a suspect. "Yeah, if she dies. That would make it murder, wouldn't it?"

"Big Red was the one dragged her out of the car."

"Oh? Yeah, well, we haven't had time to watch the camera feeds yet," he lied. "But if that's what you say... now let's talk about the guys you're delivering cars to."

"Oh man, I couldn't. I'm more scared of them than I am of you."

"Aggravated assault. Murder?"

Mason sat down in the chair opposite and said nothing. He leaned back, linked his arms behind his head and watched Laski. The little tweaker looked up at him from under his eyebrows. The mad dog eyefuck wasn't a fair match. Laski broke the stare almost immediately.

"What? What? Whaddya want from me?"

"Names. Addresses. Let them take the heat. They're the bad guys. Not you."

Skinny Pete put his elbows on the table, rubbed his tattooed face, and made a whimpering sound.

"Like nobody tells you names. We just do the job and get paid."

"Address. Where did you drop the cars off?"

"The Costco parking lot over in Mar Vista. Put the keys on the right passenger wheel and then we take off."

"You never got curious enough to watch the pick up? Come on, Pete. Smart guy like you? You'd want some kind of insurance, man. I know I would if I was in your shoes. And it's just luck on my side I'm on this side of the table. I coulda been you, Pete. I did my walk on the wild side when I was a kid. I hate to see you in this mess right now, but there's ways you can make it easy on yourself."

The way to play this guy, all of them decided, was not to come on hard. He was young, scared, not yet battle-hardened. Mason leaned across the table. A long silence. Mason was better at silence than Skinny Pete, who had a lot of dark scenarios in his head.

Finally he looked up. "Maybe. Maybe I know something. So what can you give me? Amoninity?"

"Amoninity?"

"Yeah, like AA."

The confusion cleared. "Oh, immunity. You mean we drop charges if you give us names." Mason shook his head hard. "I can't promise you that, Pete. Now we could work on some kind of plea deal, but that old lady, Pete, I mean you hurt her bad."

"She's not gonna die, is she?"

"I can't say yes. I can't say no. She's in a convalescent hospital right now. But you need to help me out here first."

"Let me think about it."

"Sure, you do that. I got things to do." He forced himself to give Laski's shoulder a squeeze as he passed him on the way out the door. A buzz lit up the station, knowing they had a carjacker on ice. He went into the Watch Commander's office, always a busy place, just to look at the big board lit up, showing the position of every patrol unit in the city. Studying the jittering board that looked like some kind of video game showing the good guys out on the street calmed him. It reminded him there was still a system of law and order. Worms like Laski hadn't taken over yet.

Out in the hall, Sgt. York passed the Watch Commander's office, looked in and took a long step back, nodding at Mason, who came to the door. "Nice goin', Mason."

"Thanks, Sarge," Mason grinned at the compliment. That was nice, he thought. It took so little to lift his spirits. Was he more depressed than he thought he was? Don't think about it. Time to revisit Laski in the interview room down the long, white hall. This time Laski was biting his lip, and looked around when Mason came in.

"I'm getting worried about my dogs. I got two pit bulls and a Chihuahua, and my girlfriend's probably wasted and forgot to feed them."

Naturally this piece of shit would have pit bulls. He was probably trying to breed them thinking he was going to make money on the puppies. Or lining them up as bait dogs if he couldn't make them mean enough to fight.

"Sure, man. We'll look out for them, but in the meantime what are you going to do for me? We got your right address? You still over in Koreatown on Serrano?"

"Yeah, man. Knock hard. The bitch sleeps like the dead. Like you said, we wanted to know who we were dealing with. So Big Red and me followed them out of Costco one time. Like, I mean, all this was Big Red's idea, the whole thing."

He expected nothing else but that Laski would say he was the innocent victim in Big Red's scheme.

"Okay, so tell me."

"First time we lost them at the corner of Lincoln and Venice at the red light. But the next time after we dropped off a Honda Civic we made the green light and got around the corner with them. Their pick up guy turned into that new used car lot up there on Lincoln opposite the Whole Foods. We hung around for a while and they didn't come out…."

"Yeah, I know the place," Mason said, trying to seem casual. This was the new set up for Vlad Yurkov.

Yes!

∾

Now it was all plodding police work to start pulling the strings tight on Yurkov and his operation. Mason left the interview room, his spirits soaring. One lead would suggest another and another, and eventually the case would break—eventually. Palmer was waiting for him, big smile on his face. He felt like chinning himself and running around the station like a soccer player after a World Cup winning goal, slapping palms. It came to him again to call Ginger and thank her for the ticket to the concert. Maybe he'd ask her to go with him. His heart beat faster as he searched for Ginger's cell number, which he still had on fast dial. The phone rang. He hung up. He'd call later.

The high lasted until he read a memo from the Captain. Delgado must have been reading it at the same time. He stood up, put his hands in his pockets and said to Mason, "Jackings. Long Beach, Redondo and Manhattan Beach, the Marina, LAPD. We're looking at a Task Force. Everybody else can bitch, but when Rhys Kensington's vintage Porsche is jacked it's time for a Task Force. The rich homeowners are backing him because all these jackings means their property values are declining. The Captain will lead because of Arnold's murder. That means us, buddy."

Today Ginger was doing damage control, fielding calls from reporters. Siegel and Peabody had alerted the press to their lawsuit and were whipping the flames of media interest in the school. She closed her phone reluctantly to talk to one of her favorites on the fundraising committee she'd pulled together.

"I want to ask you something," Mrs. Patterson said, peering up at Ginger from behind thick macular degeneration glasses.

"I've been wanting to tell you, dear, that I donated a valuable silver and opal ring to the Silent Auction. You sent the fundraising committee an accounting of what items sold and for what. You remember?" she said in a whispery voice.

"Of course, sure," Ginger said, trying to pay attention and not be swept into the sound of rising voices coming from Venetia's office.

"Well, dear, it's just that I don't see the ring as one of the items sold. I gave it to Venetia the day before. I just couldn't decide whether or not to donate it until the last minute. And then I went on that cruise to the Bahamas and well, you know. The ring was my favorite aunt's and well, dear, if it didn't sell, I'd like it back."

"Oh my," Ginger sighed. "I promise you I'll look for your ring and make sure it gets back to you." She looked down into the old woman's cornflower blue eyes and thought, Ginger, you big fat liar. You're never going to get that ring back. If Sorensen took that ring, it's gone forever. She's found another way to steal. She decided to call Mason, even if she sounded foolish accusing Venetia. The only proof she had that the headmistress was pilfering from the school was this ring. She felt bad for Mrs. Patterson.

An hour or so later she slung her laptop back over her shoulder and left the café/lunchroom. She went back to the Admin Cottage and her one-time office in the kitchen to see if it was still being used. On the way she passed a door labeled *Do Not Enter. Electrical Panel.* The door was open and she looked in as she passed. Panels of circuitry lined both walls, but in the dim shadows at the end of the room she saw another door that was slightly ajar and a slice of daylight. What intrigued her was the sight of a stack of banker boxes that files were often stored in. Taking a quick look over her shoulder to see if anyone were around, she went in and closed the door of the electric panel room behind her.

In the dusty darkness, an old fear arose. What if there were spiders? What if a huge, movie-type tarantula fell on her shoulder? Heart pounding, she lurched toward the door at the end of the room and grabbed the handle.

Light flooded the room from the corridor. The outer hallways formed an interior square with the classrooms facing the street in front and the interior courtyard at the back. This narrow room was a passageway to the other side of the Administration cottage. She looked back over her shoulder. The neatly stacked moving boxes bore the labels 2009, 2010, 2012. The narrow passageway was too creepy to go back in and check. Wait until someone came with her.

"Spiders," Ginger said to herself. No spiders.

The Captain was able to pull together an Ad Hoc Task Force quickly, and he had the rank and the pay grade to deal with all the inter-departmental headaches. Mason and Delgado would have a major role on the Ops team once logistics and planning pulled it together. The debate among the partners was how to lasso the leaders all at once. Surveillance showed Vlad Yurkov, the guys Laski had tapped as the probable head of the carjacking operation hitting all the coastal cities down to the port of Long Beach. When intel was pooled other cities reported that they'd had an eye on Yurkov as well.

Among his other semi-legit businesses, Yurkov operated the cut and paste lot on Lincoln. From storage places and back alley deals, it was known his crews were disappearing the high-end vehicles. Yurkov spent a lot of time in Santa Monica, though he kept his wife and other family in Hollywood. His lot on Lincoln sold cars that had been in accidents, slapped together again and presented as new, all buffed up and shiny. No guarantees. The car you purchased could fall dead as you drove it off the lot, and that was your problem. Or you could buy a newer model Camry that gleamed under the lights. Or you could put in an order and one of his crews would pick up the model you wanted, new VIN #, and a legal-appearing pink slip that said it was all yours.

He had lots in other places, chop shops, and crews transporting parts to Mexico and Canada. Cars in container shipments went through the port of Long Beach to overseas buyers. Trouble was laying a finger on him. Other departments all over Los Angeles had tried. It was going to take an inter-agency Task Force to put him down.

26

Ginger was roughing out the dinner seating arrangement plan in the cafeteria at the Windsor Academy. Even though the status of the school was uncertain, Rhys and the Board members encouraged her to set the fundraising effort into motion. At 3 p.m. on the Friday of the Labor Day weekend, the headmistress breezed in like a dust devil, throwing styrofoam coffee cups and gum wrappers in the trash, and sweeping all the empty paper plates on the counter into a bin at the end of the counter. The students and the dietician and assistant had already left for the weekend. Ginger watched her flurry of needless activity. The school did employ a janitor.

Sorensen crossed her arms over her chest and eyed Ginger. "Everybody's gone. Either come now or lock up when you leave."

"I'll lock up."

"I'm off then," Sorenson said. "Soon as I leave here I'm headed out to Point Magu to meet my Sierra Club friends. We're hiking the Backbone Trail from Point Magu to Will Rogers in Santa Monica."

"That's a long hike." And hot. "How long will it take you?"

"Oh, we'll be back Sunday. We're not pushing ourselves too hard."

"Sounds hard to me."

"Well, not many people could do it that quickly."

"Good for you. I'm about done here."

"Okay. You've got your key? There's going to be nobody here until Monday afternoon. I gave Armando, our cleaner, time off over the holiday weekend to visit his people."

"Have fun." She gave Sorenson her best smile, dredged up from a place deep within where she found a tiny amount of good will for the thoroughly dislikable woman.

"Ta ta then," Sorenson called out. She breezed out the door dressed in cargo pants and brown hiking boots with a small pack over her shoulder, tanned and fit and healthy. Ginger returned to work on the dinner seating plan, making sure the alumni parents who had given the biggest checks were closest to the stage. Her personal networking was paying off. Caroline had also been making calls, pulling in favors, reminding parents what a good high school experience at the Windsor Academy their kid had enjoyed. So he was doing well at Yale? Great. And his friends had gone to Harvard. Well, well.

Satisfied with the day's work, Ginger slid her files into the One World cloth bag, humped her laptop carrier over her shoulder and headed to the bathroom for a last-minute visit. As she passed the Electrical Panel room, she noticed the door was still ajar. It was too enticing to pass up. The carefully labeled banker's boxes she'd glimpsed earlier just might be the financial records the Viper swore were missing. Ginger wouldn't put anything past her.

The thought blipped into her mind, fast as a camera flash, that if she did discover something it would be a chance to call Mason. She banished the thought quickly. She had put in a call to Mason to tell him about the ring and the man she'd seen. The call went to voice mail. He'd had a chance to see her at the station and blew it off, saying he was tied up with the chief. Yeah, yeah. Some excuse. And he'd never even acknowledged her birthday offering. Fredericks had probably swooped in the minute she heard Ginger had exited stage left.

She set her bag and laptop on the floor in the hall and pushed the door open. There was a light switch right outside the door. A quick flick and the lights went on. She looked both ways up and down the corridor. Nobody there. It was foolish to be scared of spiders. A few quick steps took her into the room where she squatted down to take the lid off the top of the first banker's box.

The door slammed shut behind her. Hard.
The lights went out.

Ginger pivoted, jumped up, and grabbed the door handle. It refused to turn. "Hey! Hey!" she said with a small laugh.

Silence.

"Hey, let me out of here." She pounded the door with a fist. "Hey, dammit. Let me out."

Silence.

The doorknob wouldn't turn. It was locked.

Classrooms lay on both sides of this narrow passageway. Somebody must still be around. In the sudden silence she heard soft quick steps outside the door where her purse and cell phone lay.

"Who's there?"

The steps retreated, the front door slammed.

The first step in nailing Yurkov would be surveillance and undercover infiltration. So many bodies in uniforms from multiple agencies appeared in the Task Force room in the Special Operations section that it would soon be too small. A new Task Force run from the station still created a buzz. Though Mason was at the heart of the operation, he still had to work other cases. The clock neared the end of shift on Friday. Before the empty Labor Day weekend began he and Fredericks got called out to a scene at the Medical Center of Santa Monica to investigate what looked like a suicide. A man walked off the third story roof. Somebody saw him leaning over the edge smoking a cigarette. Then he just stepped off the ledge and fell to the ground. It was long after quitting time when he and Fredericks got done with the sad business of death. Delgado had booked off for the weekend. He and Fredericks could put this one together easily, like most of the suicide/homicide/natural deaths they investigated. Unlike Doris Arnold, which still dogged them. The victim had lost his job. His wife left him and took the kids. Apparently he'd been more broken up by the fact that first she took an axe to his boat and poured sugar into the gas tank of the big outboard.

"Guess we're lucky he didn't take an axe to her," Fredericks said, whipping out a hairbrush to tame her bush of dense, red curls. "Feel like a beer?"

"Yeah, why not?" Mason said. "You doing anything this weekend?"

"Nah. I have no life. You?" Fredericks said, settling herself in the passenger seat of the department vehicle and buckling on the seat belt.

"Nah."

Spiders. Spiders. Spiders. Spiders. Spiders. Panic began to build and Ginger tamped it down. Stop that, she ordered herself.

Stop it. You'll make yourself crazy. You can't afford to go crazy. She banged on the door till her hand hurt, then used the other fist. She inched back past the stack of boxes to the door on the opposite side of the hallway in the cottage. This time she kicked at the door, then felt around the lock to determine if it was a solid deadbolt set in a steel plate. She palmed the edge of the door for a light switch or a key hanging on a nail, found none, then crowded past the stack of boxes to the other door, stubbing her toe painfully.

Sinking down, she clutched her foot, massaging her toe. "Oh, that hurt, that hurt. Damn you!" Furious now, she rose to her feet and pounded with the heel of her hand on the other door. She took off her sandal and pounded the door until she had exhausted herself.

Silent, listening hard for a giggle, she sank down with her back to the door. Kids thought scaring people was funny. She tried to hold her breath as long as she could and remain completely still to strain her ears to hear. She could only hear the sound of her heart beating fast, the blood rushing in her ears. The background hum of the heating system switched off. There were a few ticks of metal cooling and then silence. Outside the wind picked up.

"Damn you. Somebody. Damn you! Stop this! Open the door!"

Her fury abated with the realization she had screamed till her throat hurt.

"Oh, this is not good," she said aloud, hugging herself tightly. "This isn't good at all."

Two beers over a hamburger at Huston's led to a couple of games of pool at the billiards bar on Wilshire. And a few more beers. Fredericks went on a loud rant that the only men she met were felons and gays, and at least she had enough sense not to settle for a cop, much less a lawyer. There was something flirty in all this and Mason was feeling the vibe from her, but then he had another beer. Fredericks was certainly attractive enough, but she needed to tame down her mouth. He imagined waking up next to her in the morning and listening to that mouth. With all her martial arts stuff she could put him down in a heartbeat and she knew that he knew it.

At 9 o'clock that evening, Mason knew he was too drunk to deliver the Crown Vic back to the station. The Watch Commander would help him out without saying anything. He fell into a taxi with Fredericks who was having a giggling fit and had toppled over on her side. She gave her address to the cabbie, who gave them a dirty look.

"Don't you puke in my cab," the driver snarled, peeling out.

Crowded against the side door, Mason tried to shove Fredericks over in the seat and dig his wallet out of his pants pocket to pay the cabbie.

At Fredericks' apartment on 14th Street, she dragged him by an arm into her apartment. Everything was hilarious.

As soon as the door was shut behind him, Fredericks seemed to sober up. She grabbed his jacket and flung it on the back of the couch and shoved him up against the door.

"You're mine. I'm taking what's mine. I've waited long enough."

"Jesus, Fredericks, what're you doing?" Mason tried to fend her off with a little laugh, but not very hard.

She grabbed him and fell backward over the couch, twisting as she fell so that she was under him. He fell hard, his mouth striking her teeth in her open mouth, splitting his lip. He started laughing again.

"You're bleeding," she shrieked. "You're bleeding all over my new silk blouse."

Then he was the one giggling. Fredericks was still trying to twist his face around for a kiss.

"Wait, that hurts. My lip." Mason said, getting his hands around her shoulders. He pushed himself off her, off the couch, falling onto the floor between the couch and the coffee table. He brought his arm up to blot his mouth. The sleeve of his white shirt was stained with blood.

"Look what you did to me. I'll have you up on charges," he said, trying to keep the mood of hilarity going.

Fredericks wasn't laughing. He thought she was going to roll off the couch on top of him, but she didn't. Instead she sat up and ran her fingers through her hair.

Mason sat up with his back to the couch pushing the coffee table away from him. A napkin sat on a paper plate on the coffee table along with a dried-up pizza crust. He picked up the napkin and sopped at his bleeding lip.

"You're still hung up on her, aren't you?" Fredericks said, her mouth twisted.

"Who?"

"McNair. Ginger!" she shouted. "Miss Perfect McNair."

"Not so loud, Fredericks. No, I'm not."

She snorted and propelled herself over the back of the couch in a single leap and fell to her knees. She got up, kicked her shoes off and announced, "I'm going to bed. Maybe I'm gonna throw up first. I don't know. You can join me. Or not. I don't fuckin' care."

Mason got to his feet. "Um, I guess I won't. See you on Tuesday."

"Yeah." She stumbled off down the hall, reeling from one side to the other, and slammed the door of her bedroom. Nobody was laughing now.

Mason let himself out quietly, a lot less drunk than he'd been ten minutes ago. He stood outside her door, thinking about walking home to sober up. His place at San Vicente and Seventh Street was only fifteen minutes' walk away.

Near miss, he thought, fingering his split lip. He couldn't help it that his mind went in a different direction, running a scenario of what could have happened instead.

27

Next morning Mason examined himself in the bathroom mirror, hungover to the point of near death. He had a crusty scab on his lip he'd met with Fredericks' teeth. The lip was swollen and sore. He slathered on antibiotic ointment and hoped to hell his fat lip would heal by Tuesday. His phone began vibrating on the kitchen table as he picked up a piece of toast slathered with bitter orange marmalade, just the way he liked it. He thought the toast might stay down. Answering the call was programmed into him. He took a bite first while it was hot and perfect. Damn, he couldn't chew on the left side of his mouth because of the aching tooth. It was Palmer calling. "Yeah, Palmer. What's up?"

"You know I tracked back that headlight bezel to a parts store in Hemet. Then we chased our tails around a junkyard out there?"

"Yeah, okay," Mason said. He could barely keep track of his own cases, much less Palmer's.

"So one of my guys is out there in Hemet sniffin' around, and he's in the bullpen in the Sheriff's department calling his wife, waiting for the traffic to die down before he heads home. The I-10 is bad all the way to Vegas at 5 o'clock."

"Yeah, and..?" Mason said, chancing another bite of toast. Ow. The hard edge on the toast touched the cut on his upper lip.

"He hears the deputies talking. One of the guys is talking about his street people informers telling him a story about seeing a guy washing blood off a car, giving it a real good wash, running it through the self-serve car wash place a second time. His informant thinks it might be worth some money. So he's trying to sell his story to the deputy. This was the middle of the night a while ago. He thinks it's peculiar so he remembers it. My guy's sitting there and hears this and gets interested. Could mean anything but he's killing time anyway. So he and the deputy drive the streets awhile looking for the guy with the story."

"So...and..." Mason said, looking out the window at a dark day that threatened rain.

"He's talking about a 2003 white Corolla with a headlight missing."

That got Mason's attention. "You're thinking it's the Corolla that hit Leonard, way the hell out in Hemet?"

"Hey, you're sharp, Mason. I guess you didn't find that shiny, little detective badge in a box of Cracker Jacks after all."

"Hmmph," Mason said, carrying his plate to the sink for a swish before he put it in the dishwasher. He noticed the dishes were getting pretty dry and crusty in there. He didn't eat at home often enough to run the dishwasher.

"So, anyway, I'm going out there today to interview the guy. This Leonard Bricker thing is still hanging and I hate that."

"So you think this was the guy who bought it from the seller who moved from Lomita to Pirtleville? And you want me to come too?"

"Yeah, seeing as you're lead on the Kensington case."

Mason thought of the day ahead. He could run the dishwasher and go to a movie. He had to tidy the place up before the cleaning lady came anyway. He could call Fredericks to see whether her ass was up in the air about what happened last night. Or just chicken out and wait and see how she acted on Tuesday when they got back to work.

"Sure," he decided. "You drive. Pick me up. I'll be ready in half an hour."

"Two big-time dicks from the big city. We'll knock Hemet on its ear."

"Palmer, you don't know dick about dick," Mason said. He hung up laughing. The day seemed a lot brighter.

Palmer was curious about Mason's fat lip and he made up a story about tripping over something and falling with a glass in his hand. He said he'd turned his head at the last moment to avoid the breaking glass and hit his head on a book case. Palmer looked skeptical. Only on the rack would Mason admit this had anything to do with Fredericks.

Reaching Hemet, he and Palmer met up with the deputy whose street informant had a lead on the white Corolla. The deputy was supposed to have the guy on ice at McDonald's, the one on West Florida at Kirby.

Deputy Bailey had a florid face and about a quarter inch of blond hair sprouting from his head. His eyelashes were blond and his eyes the color of water. Rolls of fat bulged above the tight collar of his tan uniform shirt and body armor. Tan wasn't his color. "I gave him some money to go into Mickey's and wait there for me. I go back and he's not there."

Palmer was pissed and making no effort to disguise it. "Why didn't you bring him in? Any idea where he is now?" he barked.

"I couldn't find any reason to put a hold on him."

"You couldn't think up a reason?" Palmer complained. "Charge him with spitting on the sidewalk, fa'crissake. Stolen shopping cart. Do you know how long it took us to drive out here?"

"Yes, sir. Yes, sir. Sorry, sir." Bailey didn't look sorry.

"No point in sitting here. Put a call out for everybody to look for him," Mason suggested. "You know where he hangs?"

"I know his usual girlfriend," he shrugged. "Had them in for domestic violence before. Assault with a shopping cart."

"Well, c'mon, let's go," Palmer said, half-way out the door.

❧

Mason and Palmer followed Bailey to hit the streets. Hemet was a long, linear town flung out across the desert. It had been settled by old folk looking for cheap housing and brought in the service industries that kept them going. Lots of people thought the Joshua trees and yuccas and bare landscape of the desert had its own beauty. Mason couldn't see it. He liked green and blue himself, and except for the azure sky overhead there was only stubbly, low growing brown and tan clumps of vegetation in this landscape. The wind blew hard out here. Driving around reminded him of his years on patrol, driving around just looking for something, or somebody that looked wrong. He turned to Palmer who was twiddling the radio dial looking for something other than Jesus radio or Spanish language.

"How long you gonna give this?" Mason said.

"What? To find him?" Palmer said.

"Yeah. I got things to do."

"What have you got to do, Mason? Jesus, I'll give you a pacifier to suck on. Will that keep you quiet?"

"Why you got such a hair up your ass, Palmer?"

"I want this case to go down. That's why. I got a traffic fatality to clear, this Bricker thing, and I want it done."

"You think I don't? I know it's tied to the Arnold woman. She didn't deserve it any more than Bricker."

"You don't think she took off with the money?"

Mason turned away from watching two young girls saunter along the sidewalk to look at Palmer. "No, I don't. Somebody set her up. You know we never ID'd who parked Arnold's car over at the beach lot. Not for lack of trying either. Fredericks is trying to get a witness who might have seen something where they dumped Arnold."

"Heard the head of the school had a visitor?"

"How'd you hear that? I'm not even sure I believe it myself."

"Guys talk, you know that."

"No big secret. Something about Sorensen is off and I can't convince Delgado. You get that impression?"

Palmer screwed his mouth sideways. "Maybe. Don't think she's got much job security. They're gonna close the place; they're not going to close it. The papers and online buzz is playing this up as though it's the biggest thing in Santa Monica since the OJ trial. Everybody who ever went there has something to say about it. I saw your old honey on TV dancing on her tiptoes, spinning the story."

"Bricker's son-in-law told me Sorensen has been itching for a seat on the Coastal Commission. That's an appointment the governor makes. Big power. Hang on," Mason said, "maybe we got something going here."

The county sheriff's car they'd been following slewed off the main drive and hit the curb hard to drive between two big warehouse buildings. Deputy Bailey got out and began running. Palmer jerked the car to a stop behind him. Both detectives were out the door and running to catch up.

Bailey pounded hard across the paved parking lot in back of the warehouse that ended in the sandy soil of the desert. Mason saw him trip and fall to his knees. Mason put on a burst of speed and shot past Bailey to grab the runner by the collar, both of them panting hard and sweating. He march-walked a skinny transient back across the parking lot, tilting his head as far back as he could to avoid the stench off him. Bailey and Palmer were up and waiting for them.

"Here, stand in the shade," Bailey said. "Goddamn sun will kill you out here."

Mason took a look at the slight figure he had in tow. The guy was crying, snot running down his face.

"You hurt me. You hurt me."

"What? What?" Mason protested. "Why did you run? We just wanted to talk to you."

"My arms. My arms. Look."

Bailey had already cuffed his arms behind him. Mason could see blood on his runner's right arm staining the sleeve of his dirty white long-sleeved T-shirt. Pulling latex gloves on, he pulled up the sleeve carefully.

Infected track marks were bleeding. His arm was a mess of suppurating sores.

"You'll live." Bailey patted him down. His shopping cart had fallen over on its side halfway down the alley. "Sit. Sit down right here, back against the wall. Cross your legs." He walked up the alley and brought the shopping cart back to come to rest beside their informant.

"Your name's Donald Allen Murray. Right?"

"Hey, Officer Bailey, you know it is," he wheedled. "You and me are pals, aren't we? I mean you help me out sometimes ..."

"I wouldn't call us pals, Mr. Murray. These people here want to talk to your sorry ass."

Murray looked up at them into the sunshine behind Mason's head. "Can't see you right. Mind moving over? The sun's in my eyes. They ought to do something about that sun, doncha think?"

Mason had to laugh. "Yeah, they oughta do something about that sun. I'm Detective Mason and this is Detective Palmer. We're from Santa Monica. You must have a guilty conscience, Mr. Murray, that you run when you see us."

"No, no. I just felt bad Deputy Bailey gave me money for somethin' to eat and told me to stay there, but like I had to take a shit, and McDonald's won't let me in their bathroom...had a little accident in there once...so I went outside, around the back you know, and when I came back they wouldn't let me back in. And I still had some coffee in my cup. I knew Deputy Bailey'd be pissed off at me. You know how it is?" he said in one long whine to Mason. "He's a mean guy sometimes."

"Sure." Mason squatted down on his heels facing him. Palmer eased in beside him, down wind. Murray's hair was matted, his skin weathered, layers of Goodwill apparel covering his skinny bones. The sole of one shoe flapped.

"Deputy Murray said you might be able to help us out here with somebody we're looking for. The driver of a White Corolla."

Murray squinted up at Mason, his face gone cagey. "White Corolla?"

Bailey came over and kicked the sole of his sneaker. "You don't do this to me, Murray. You tell these men what you told me or I'll make your life real, real bad. I'll arrange with the guys from the psych hospital to pick you up again. You remember you didn't like that?"

"No, no. I remember. White Corolla. You think you might be able to help me out a little here? I'm awful hungry. Awful hungry. My stomach thinks my throat's cut."

"We'll see what we can do when you tell us about the white Corolla. Let's start there."

Big suck of air inward. Mason could hear his lungs rattle. Then a phlegmy cough and gob of spit. Mason looked away.

"What happened to your lip?" he said, peering up at Mason. "HepC? You got HepC? I know some people, they sell this…"

"Never mind me," Mason said as patiently as he could. "The white Corolla."

"Yeah, well. One night my girlfriend Wanda and me are bunked down for the night. Awful cold night. You don't know how cold it gets out here. There's a nice little place we sometimes go out behind the car wash. Out of the wind. Good little dumpster there. Quiet at night. We got a nice piece of cardboard. Oh, that ground gets cold and hard at night." Mason had met his share of transients in Santa Monica. Oh yes. Santa Monica was famous for its kindness to the homeless.

"The white Corolla?"

"I'm getting to it. Pretty thirsty too." He gave a dry cough.

"Deputy, could you get him some water," Mason asked nicely. Bailey went off pissed.

"Thing is hardly anybody washes their car at night, specially so late, so like you notice. Me and Wanda we're all settled down nice and cozy when this little white car drives up. Somebody gets out and starts up the car wash, makes a whole lotta noise, and wakes us up."

"Man or woman?"

"Guy wearing a parka, big dark sunglasses."

"Thought you said it was night."

Murray drew back, offended. "I did. You asked me what he was wearing. I'm telling you. He was wearing sunglasses. You can ask Wanda."

"We will."

"If you can find her. That bitch took my check. We got a bottle and she took all my money..."

"Maybe Deputy Bailey will help you with that."

Deputy Bailey gave him a dirty look and Mason grinned at him.

"So this guy was washing his car," Palmer said.

"Only reason I remembered it was that there was blood on the right side. I know what blood looks like because I got hit by a car once. Crossing the intersection on a green light," he shouted suddenly. "That's when things started going downhill for me."

"I can believe that," Mason said.

Deputy Bailey pulled Mason aside. "He's half-blind, sir. The VA got him some glasses but he claims somebody stole them. He's got a hate on for the VA because they replaced them and he lost them again."

"I heard that!" Murray screamed. "Cocksucker VA. Stealing my glasses."

"Was the guy white or what?"

"Yeah, white."

"And when was this?"

"First of the month when I got my check. That's when Wanda comes around. The bitch."

He and Palmer shared a look. Bricker's fatality happened on the first.

"You're sure about all this, are you?"

Tall white guy with a baseball cap and sunglasses. It wasn't much. Still it placed the Corolla in Hemet. He might be able to work this up into something. He and Palmer walked out of earshot in the shade. Eyewitness accounts were unreliable, but sometimes it was all you had.

"Let's go over to the car wash and take a look," Palmer said quietly. He beckoned Bailey over. Murray retrieved his shopping cart and began sorting through the plastic bags tied onto it, muttering to himself. Bailey and Palmer were discussing where the car wash was located and how to get there. Mason was half-listening to them, half-listening to Murray when something caught his attention in Murray's tirade.

"Right front quarter panel all busted in, headlight hanging...bastards...never even think about me..."

Mason walked over and hunkered down beside Murray, ignoring the ripe smell of rot that wafted off him in the hot desert breeze. Murray shot him a suspicious look.

"What's that about the right headlight? I'm listening, Mr. Murray."

Murray pulled his mouth in tight. No top teeth. "You get me some glasses?"

"I'll help you. Now what about the right headlight?"

"It fell out. I saw that. Blood."

"Fell out while he was washing the car?"

"No, no. It was gone."

"Anything else you remember?"

"Blood. When I got hit, the blood..."

"You mean when you got hit in the crosswalk or there was blood on the white Toyota?"

Murray went crafty. "You know I don't see so good."

"Yup, you told me. I'm gonna help you with that. Now what about Wanda. She saw any of this?"

"That ugly old woman. Lyin' bitch."

"I'm gonna want to talk to Wanda, Mr. Murray."

"You tell her I want my glasses back. Bitch probably sold them," he grunted, pulling a dirty T-shirt up over his nose to hide his face. His hair looked as though it hadn't been washed since water was invented.

"Any idea where we might find her?" Mason persisted.

The rest of it was gibberish. He poked and pawed among the plastic bags tied to his shopping cart and tried to sidle away. Deputy Bailey walked over and tramped a boot on the hem of Murray's pants, which were trailing six inches behind him, deliberately tripping him. Murray turned on him with a scream of fury. Bailey grinned at Mason and Palmer from behind his mirrored sunglasses. They gazed back at him without smiles.

"Hey, I was just funnin' with the guy. Gimme a break."

"Take him into the station. I want to get a statement from him," Mason said.

"Not in my car!" Bailey protested.

"Yeah. Yours," Mason said. "Suck it up, cowboy."

28

Ginger's neck hurt, straining her head forward with the effort of placing every noise in the creaking structure. She was still sitting on the floor her back pressed hard against the door, unwilling to move, as though if she were quiet and small she might melt into the safety of the door, which eventually must open. She hunted around in the dark, crawling on her knees searching with the palms of her hands on the floor to find some sort of weapon. Anything.

Sorensen was the obvious person to shut her in here. She had seen that streak of hatefulness in her. But a killer? No, she'd just do something ugly like this.

Surely to heaven Sorensen wouldn't kill her because she'd overruled her on a print campaign? But if it wasn't Sorensen, the real killer behind Arnold and Bricker's deaths was somebody who might open that door next. Maybe Venetia would come back early, which would be a godsend, unless it was Venetia who'd locked her in.

Her stomach growled. Rain spattered the roof overhead. She tried to pat down her mind into a small hard thing. Allowing her thoughts to wander made panic rise in her throat like a bubble. She'd told everybody she was on deadline to pull everything together for the fundraising dinner and please not call her this weekend. Stupid, stupid, stupid.

She was cold now and felt wet and damp hearing the rain fall outside. What could happen if she started throwing the breakers on the circuit board? She dredged around in her memory for some knowledge of electricity and circuit breakers. What if she threw all the switches to make the lights come on? If every light in the place was on, blazing in the night, maybe somebody would notice and call the police. Was that right? It seemed wrong. As far as she knew everything was switched to the on position. Well, what if all the lights went off? She set the breakers first one way, then the opposite way.

Nothing happened.

Maybe she could find something to dig at the lock on the door with. A screwdriver left behind by a maintenance worker would be ideal. She felt on top of the electrical panel on the wall to her right, and all around, running her fingers along the twisted coils of wire. Moving slowly and carefully, she mapped the room she was in. If this were a movie she would be able to do something clever with the electrical wires and a nail file so that a light flashed outside calling in help. This wasn't a movie and she didn't have a nail file.

She remembered the kid who hadn't liked Doris. This was a prank he might pull. She'd been watching him, and Chase Reynolds, Jr. was a nasty little shit with a cocky grin and too much money in his pocket.

There was nothing but the stack of banker boxes, filing cabinets, and the electrical panel. She took the tops off the boxes and felt around in them, but they only contained paper.

She went back to huddling by the door, concluding her purse and cell phone had been taken. Her phone would have rung many times by now if it were still there. Starting with a thumbnail, she chewed off her red nail polish. That was a small comfort. Her knees were drawn up to her chest, her fists curled against herself, pressing hard against her heart. A shudder, then a ray of hope lit her mind.

A heavy vehicle clattered into the parking lot behind the building. A dim bar of light illuminated a strip under the door, then blackness returned. She waited for a door to open, then slam closed, her mind sifting and interpreting. Waiting.

A screech of metal, hydraulic hoist, a burst of compressed air then a heavy thud.

It was a garbage truck emptying the dumpster at the back of the lot near the fence. The driver wouldn't even need to get out. Everything could be controlled from the cab.

Nevertheless she screamed. And screamed. She jumped to her feet and pounded on the door.

✷

After a Burger King lunch that turned Mason's stomach bilious, he and Palmer hit the streets again looking for Wanda. Or Merle or whatever the hell she called herself. Murray was left in an interview room at the station, happy to be inside where the air conditioning blew cold. Bailey's unit made a sharp right turn into a dollar store parking lot. Bailey got out, settling his Sam Browne belt under his gut. He jerked his head toward the entrance. Squatting behind a line of shopping carts was a small black woman wearing a wig with corkscrew curls. Her face had the weather-beaten, seamed look of the long-term homeless. She had a full set of teeth though, so things weren't that bad for her yet.

Bailey stood by his unit, his ear half-cocked toward the chatter of the police radio. "I might havta...all units reporting...give me a minute here till I see what's goin' on..."

Palmer said. "Take off if you need to. This is our girl here, is it?"

"In all her glory...."

"Yeah, take off. We're fine."

"Take your time," Palmer said. "Asshole," he muttered in an aside to Mason after Bailey had climbed into his unit and taken off. "C'mon."

Mason wore a white golf shirt with open neck and khakis, Palmer a pastel checked short-sleeved shirt with khakis. Both looked like cops and always would, no matter what they wore. Something about the haircut, the air of authority, big men who looked watchful.

Wanda saw them coming and butted her cigarette on the curb beside her. She rose, her mouth working

"Hey, Wanda, we just want to talk to you a minute. You mind? Just talk," Mason said, taking off his sunglasses. "My name's Dave. This here is Chuck."

"Whatchu want, cop? I'm busy here."

Doing what, Mason wondered. He sat down beside her. Wanda kept herself pretty clean, but she did emit the odor of some fruity alcohol gone sour on her breath.

"Nice place you got for yourself here in the shade." He looked around. "Breeze. My first time out here in Hemet in a long time. Place has got pretty built up, I'd say. Lotta new stores. Notice they got a whole new subdivision." He pointed out in the desert. "Cops treat you okay out here? I'm not from here myself."

"They're all assholes. You should know that."

"Yeah, maybe they are but me, I'm different," he said, giving her his best smile. "I'm from Santa Monica." The transients from every dinkshit place in America knew Santa Monica, the home of the homeless.

"I been there," Wanda growled.

"That so," Mason said.

"What happened to your lip? Somebody bust you?"

"You know how it is. Things get said."

She looked away and sniffed. "Pussy."

He felt Palmer perch beside him on the curb outside the dollar store. Saturday afternoon Shoppers gave them curious looks passing by. Palmer pitching in, between the two of them bullshitting around, they got Wanda talking, especially after they started calling her Merle, which she preferred. Palmer got up while Merle and Mason were talking and went inside the dollar store and brought Merle a cold Fanta.

"So, Merle, we've been talking to Mr. Murray and he told us a story about a night you two were sleeping over by the car wash."

"Oh, him. Whatever he told you about me is a goddamn fat big lie. I never took his goddamn glasses. What am I gonna do with his glasses? Crazy old fool."

"Was he wearing his glasses the night he was telling us about?'

"What night?" She pried the button out of her right ear, looked at it and shook it. She mashed it back in again, and said, "Something's wrong with it. Screeches at me sometimes."

Mason didn't want to give her any leads. He was silent.

"What?" she said eventually.

"He told us a story about something that happened one night over at the car wash."

Merle hunched into herself, considering, calculating. Finally. She reached out to grab Mason and he drew back. Then he saw she was pointing at his phone that he kept in a holder on his belt.

"I needa make a phone call. You lend me your phone there to call my daughter I might tell you what I know."

"Oh yeah? You tell me first. I'll see whether it's worth it to let you make a call."

Merle got up and Mason thought she was leaving. Instead she walked out to the street and looked both ways. Just as Mason was about to spring up and go after her she came back and sat down again.

The wind shifted and Mason began to get a strong scent of dried urine. Merle had seemed pretty together at first, but the more they talked to her the more inconsistencies and oddities began to creep in. She wasn't exactly wearing a tinfoil hat and receiving messages from Planet Altroid, but close to it. He and Palmer exchanged a look when she wanted Mason to look in her mouth and see what that dentist had done to her. He had enough problems with the dentist without seeing the damage left by some quack.

Then came a flood of tears, how bad the world had treated her. He couldn't count the number of times that tears had been used by some female hard-up hustler trying to pluck at his heartstrings. Life on the Street had ensured he had few heartstrings to pluck.

"First you," Mason bargained. "The car wash and then you can call your daughter. You can talk for ten minutes."

She was a wily old girl. "Fifteen."

"Okay, fifteen. See how nice I am."

She got herself settled down again. Then another homeless woman came into view, sauntering along. Wanda saw her and went tense as she approached the line of shopping carts, Wanda, and the two men sitting there on the curb. Wanda pulled her duffel bag and shopping cart closer and glared.

"Nobody touches my shit, Lulu," she said, getting to her feet. Mason pulled her back down.

"I shiiiiiiit on your shit, Wanda." The woman squatted over Wanda's duffel bag and rubbed her enormous buttocks back and forth over the top, challenging Wanda. Wanda was off the curb with an agility that Mason wouldn't have believed possible. He grabbed the challenger by the collar of her dirty T-shirt to avoid a punch up between the two women. Palmer had Merle/Wanda by the arm and was restraining her.

Mason got between them and addressed himself to the newcomer, steadily walking her backward away from Merle who was hissing and growling like a cat. Palmer had his hands full hanging on to her.

"Why don't you just go on about your business," he said. "We're talking to Merle here."

"Why don't you talk to me, handsome?" she said flirtatiously. "My name's Lulu."

"Because I'm talking to Merle."

"Her name's Wanda. She just calls herself Merle to be fancy," she yelled over Mason's shoulder, taunting Wanda. She struggled with Mason and he found he had hold of a real hellion street fighter. Teeth and claws and elbows and kicks.

"Put Wanda in the car," Mason suggested to Palmer. This put Merle/Wanda into a rage, screaming that Flappy Old Cunt Lips was going to steal her stuff.

"Put her stuff in the trunk," Mason barked at Palmer.

"There's no room in the trunk," he protested, wanting to keep his vehicle clean.

By now Mason was considering cuffing this squirming wildcat he'd got hold of but then what would he do with her? Shoppers were beginning to gather, hoping for a fight. Everybody liked to watch a fight. Palmer grabbed Wanda's ragged belongings and was stuffing them into the trunk, Wanda close on his tail screaming. Palmer pushed Wanda into the back seat and went around to the driver's seat and got in. Mason let go of Lulu, who stood with her arms akimbo hurling insults at Wanda who made faces at her from the back seat of the car, pounding at the window.

"What did I do to deserve this?" Mason growled as he got in the passenger seat, almost burning his hand on the door handle it was so hot in the sun. The car peeled away from the curb, the air conditioning roaring. "Take her back to the station and keep her away from Murray."

Ginger was wearing a short-sleeved white cotton blouse and a long, gauzy skirt and flimsy-soled sandals, not much protection against the dropping temperature that had come with evening.

"It's stupid to be scared of spiders. You know that you don't even die if a black widow bites you, even a brown recluse," she said aloud in a firm voice. "They're scared of you. Yes, but what if...there's no what if...forget what if." She clambered to her feet.

Could she die of thirst by Monday afternoon when the cleaner came back from his holiday? Was it true about dying without water in three days? One of the teachers might come in over the weekend. Maybe somebody had forgotten something and would just pop into the school to get it? Maybe kids would be meeting here for a field trip.

But what if the person returning was the one who had killed Leonard Bricker and Doris Arnold?

The thought kept her moving, first on her knees to slide careful fingers in the dust around the baseboards. Then crouching to move in circles across the walls around the room, feeling for something once again, anything to use to pry at the hinges of the door, jimmy around the lock.

A nail. A screw. Anything made of metal. Something she could poke in an eye. Rake down a cheek.

I won't die if a spider runs across my hand. I'll die if somebody comes in here and kills me.

To tamp down the fear she thought about Mason. It had probably been a stupid reason to break up. But things had been said between them. And then more things that built on weeks of strain. She had strong-armed him into learning the tango with her. He had always wanted to learn to dance, he said, and hadn't been all that resistant to the lessons. But then it got much, much harder, which he hadn't expected. Ginger was travelling California raising money for the Democratic Party, home the odd weekend, the odd night. Mason had a case that got under his skin. She was uptight because her job was ending, and her nest egg until she found a new job, was small. They saw each other on the fly, never enough to catch up, to settle into a routine. He'd been complaining about bills.

"You'd make a lot more money if you'd take the exam."

"But I like what I'm doing now," Mason objected.

"Then quit bitching about money," she hissed at him. "Go ahead and die in some shootout. I don't care."

They'd gone to a *milonga* together, stupid hard words simmering between them. Mason disliked Refugio, the willowy Argentinian tango instructor. The dislike was unreasonable, he admitted it. But he didn't like being corrected, and that was what learning to dance was all about, the guiding, suggesting. The touching, the words—straighten your back, Dave. No, start your turn with your left foot. Tango was all close up, touching, bodies pressed close, and Refugio held Ginger close to demonstrate. They were already bickering when they got there.

Ginger hadn't taken her eyes off Refugio and his succession of partners. He was so good it was pure pleasure to dance with him. Once he asked her to dance and she seemed to rise from the earth in his arms sweeping across the floor. At the end of the evening she and Mason happened to be leaving at the same time as Refugio. Ginger was rubbing a sore ankle and reached out to Refugio who gave her his arm to balance.

Refugio stood with his arm around Ginger and she put her arm around his waist, both of them laughing and chatting. Something made her defiant. She reached up and kissed Refugio on the cheek. Mason's face darkened with a primal jealousy. He grabbed her arm and whirled her away from him and went in close to Refugio, using all of his cop menace to intimidate the dance teacher.

Refugio pulled back, gone scared and babbling apologies. Ginger flared up, hating Mason.

Outside they'd gone at it again in the parking lot, shattering the memory of all the good times and what they'd built of a relationship of more than a year together. Ginger flung at Mason all the times she'd waited at home for him; he barked at her about how tired he was of her nagging him about going for promotion. It all burst out: he was tired of her pretentious culture-vulture stuff. Caroline Kensington had way too much influence over her. The more time she spent with Caroline the less he liked *her*.

"In fact, I'm not even sure I like you at all," he had said bitterly. "Much less love you."

"That makes two of us then, Mason. I don't like you either."

Ginger stamped off to her car and Mason got into his old Jeep. They drove in different directions and that had been six months ago.

It all seemed so foolish now.

29

Palmer and Mason got Wanda in an interview room at the station and Deputy Bailey joined them, bringing in the file they had on Wanda. She had no idea they had Murray down the hall where he was quite happy reading magazines and drinking coffee out of the blazing Saturday noon heat, his arms bandaged. They could take as long as they liked, even put his ass in jail. It crossed Mason's mind that he could hit up the Kensington Industries reward fund to see if they'd spring for a new pair of glasses for Murray.

Wanda wasn't as happy to be there. They allowed her to bring in her plastic bags and rolling duffel bag. That seemed to settle her down some. She wanted to be called Merle.

"So tell me about that night at the car wash."

"What night?"

"C'mon, Merle, I treat you nice. How about you be nice back? You know what I'm talking about."

"Yeah, yeah, I'm just playing with you."

"Well, I don't like it."

"Don't get mad at me." She actually cringed away from him.

"Merle, Merle, Merle, don't you play me. Detective Palmer and I want to hear your story but no more games, okay?"

She leaned across the table, now flirty, woman of a thousand faces. "Donny and me…"

"That's Donald Murray, right? Donny?"

"Well, yeah, who do ya think? He's my old man. Sometimes."

"Okay, go on," Palmer urged.

"So who's the boss here? You or him?" she said to Palmer and pointed at Mason.

"Doesn't matter, Merle. Either one of us. Who do you like best?" Palmer said, grinning.

"Him," she said, squaring herself at Mason who sat across the table from her in the interview room.

Palmer slapped the table and laughed. "You with the ladies, Mason. Okay, take it away."

"So you and Donny were having a party. And what did you see?" Mason smiled.

She leaned across the table again and whispered to Mason, pointing at Palmer. "I hope I didn't hurt his feelings."

"Never mind his feelings, Merle. He'll get over it. I get all the good-looking women. He's just jealous. Tell me your story. Forget him."

"This little white car pulls up. The lights come on when somebody pulls into the place where you wash your car. Right? Up to then it's real dark and quiet but the lights come on and wake us up."

She stopped. Mason wanted to strangle her. "And then..." he prompted.

"This woman gets out and walks all around her car looking at it."

"A woman?" He stopped himself from saying Murray had told them it was a man.

"Yeah. Wearing a hat and a big parka. And she washes her car. Me and Donny we both see the car's bloody on one side and a big dent on the front and on the roof. Donny goes crazy because it takes him back to the car that hit him in the crosswalk and I have to hear about that all over again. She's got all her own rags and stuff and... what? What'd I say?"

"You sure it was a woman?"

"Yes. Positive."

Mason put his head in his hands and groaned.

After they got her statement signed, Mason let her use his phone to call her daughter in Chicago, dialing the number himself. He tried not to listen while Merle whee-dled and pleaded for a bus ticket back home.

Finally it was over. He and Palmer followed Deputy Bailey to the car wash, busy on a Saturday afternoon. Leathery old geezers washed the Caddy here every Saturday whether it needed it or not while they waited for the wife who sat under the dryer in curlers at the beauty parlor.

Bailey got out of his unit and waited for them to walk over to him. He pointed. "See up there. That's where the bums usually hang out."

Mason paced it off. "Maybe 25 yards away," he said on his return.

Palmer stuck his hands in his pockets and rocked on his heels, squinting against the bright sun. "Murray's blind and the old girl's ready to tell Mason whatever he wants just to get in his pants."

Mason made a rude noise and punched Palmer's arm. "And both of them are drunk. Coulda been a troupe of monkeys out there washing a bus for all we know."

"They saw something," Palmer insisted.

"Yeah, what? You want to see either one of them on the witness stand holding our case together?"

Straining her ears to the utmost, Ginger could hear passing traffic on the streets outside. After the trash truck left no vehicle entered the parking lot. It didn't help that she could hear the rain throughout the night, which made the thirst and swollen tongue worse. Somewhere in the night she'd slept a little, leaning against the door.

The coming dawn lightened the strip at the bottom of the door, altering slowly from black to charcoal grey.

Morning meant she also had to urinate. Mad thoughts of drinking her own urine came to her, but she had nothing to catch it in. Her swollen tongue stuck to the roof of her mouth.

She took the lid off one of the filing boxes and peed into the lid. Then she emptied what felt like an entire manila file of loose paper and used it to soak up the urine.

"This isn't good," she said aloud to herself. "I don't like this at all." Her own voice felt small in the darkness. She fell silent not wanting to hear the whimper in her voice.

Spiders were the least of her problems. Thirst loomed larger and larger. And she was damned hungry, her stomach reminding her with gurgling plumbing noises.

Hours later Mason pulled himself out of a deep sleep and clawed towards the ringing phone on the night-stand, knocking the charger over. He had to get out of bed and stumble around to find the phone, which had fallen to the floor. The phone ringing in the middle of the night wasn't unusual. But Ginger's father had never before called him in the night. Ever.

"Hey, Dave, sorry. I've been calling everybody and then I thought of you. It's Bert McNair."

"What's up, sir?" He sat on the edge of the bed and turned on the bedside light.

"It's Ginger. Is she with you?"

"I wish. No. It's been months now. What's going on?" He went on hyper alert.

"Thing is I called her Friday afternoon because her Aunt Mabel had a heart attack and she'd want to know. Those two are really close since her Mom died. I keep calling her." Her father's voice went thick. "She doesn't answer her cellphone. That damn thing's stuck to her head and you know how she is about her aunt, the two of them thick as thieves."

"I do. Something's not right." Mason rubbed his eyes. He was fully awake. "You call her boyfriend, that Kensington guy? She might be with him."

"Yeah, I did. I told him to call her yesterday but she never called him back either. Or her brother. We've been at the hospital and it looks as though Mabel's going to be okay but I'm worried about Ginger. The boyfriend just blew me off. He actually told me to call him in the morning if she hadn't shown up. Apparently people flake out all the time in his life. He'd taken a sleeping pill and couldn't stay awake."

"Hmmmph," Mason said. "You call Caroline?"

"Sure. She can't get a return call either. I gotta give her credit. She was more worried than her brother."

"You checked her car with traffic, an accident and so forth?"

"Yeah, nothing."

"Tell you what. Let's meet over at Ginger's place and take a look around. You got a key?"

"I'm already there. I couldn't sit and do nothing. I tried to get the Watch Commander to start looking, just to get your guys interested, but you know how it is. I tried everything I could think of and you're sort of my last resort."

Adults who disappeared were seldom given much department time. Both he and Bert knew that. Kids? That was different.

"You know I'll do everything I can, Bert. I'll meet you over at her place." He remembered the day he'd slipped the key into Ginger's mail box with a curt note. He'd do anything to get that note back now. What did he write? Something short and hurtful probably. She dumped him after all. Well, it seemed like that.

Ginger's father was an L.A. County Sheriff's deputy and had the trim, taut body of an older cop who took care of himself. He wore a beige windbreaker, a ball cap, and khakis and swung around as Mason came up the walk. All the lights were on in her apartment. Mason recognized a reikki vase he'd given her in a position of honor on the coffee table. Papers, designs, brochures, everything she was currently working on were piled on the coffee table, the dining room table, and all over the counters. A smell of burnt food filled the air. Bert McNair was going around opening windows. Her cat was eating from the bowl next to the refrigerator.

"What's that smell?" Mason said, looking around, following McNair into the bedroom and out again. She had a new bedspread.

"Some Crockpot thing she was making burnt to a crisp." He led Mason back into the kitchen where a Crockpot was soaking in hot water and soap. He fussed around with some herbs in pots on the window, then put both hands on the counter and rocked back and forth on his heels.

"Ginger wouldn't leave the Crockpot to burn," Mason observed.

"Nope. The cat didn't have any food or water either," McNair said.

"Her car out back in her parking spot?"

"Yes, it's there. Everything looks okay to me. I know she's been taking the bus a lot when it's a short trip around town."

He and Mason shared a grin.

"The bus!" Mason said with a laugh. "She's still out to save the world. You called the boyfriend? Caroline? What did they say?"

"He said Ginger wanted the weekend to work on this Academy job and she would call them when she got finished, so neither of them had any reason to worry about her. She said she had a little shopping to do so she could be anywhere now. But she'd be there if she was getting my messages about Mabel. Her brother's working grave-yard right now or he'd be here too."

"So far as you can tell nobody's talked to her since Friday?" Mason asked, frowning.

"Around noon. And now it's early Sunday."

"Okay, let's start waking people up. Let me call that woman she's working with over at the Kensington Academy. I've got her number." He sat down at the coffee table and pushed away a pile of graduation photos and other Kensington Academy memorabilia.

No answer at Sorensen's place. Mason left a message on her cell as well. He stood up. Bert McNair was watching him.

"Let's do this systematically, sir. We should file a report, run the phone and credit card records. Locate her by her cellphone. Procedure…we can't just go crazy here, " Mason broke off at the look on Bert McNair's face.

"I know. She means a lot to me too. You want us to just jump in the car and drive around in circles looking for her."

Bert McNair ran his hands over the top of his crew cut and down his neck and then did it again. He paced in a small circle. The cat came in, looked at him, and skittered past him into the bedroom and under the bed.

30

Was the person who was first through the door going to kill her with a blaze of light blinding her and a bullet to the forehead? Nobody was going to be looking for her until Monday afternoon and already thirst had become a maddening lust.

She let Mason flood into her mind, the memories warming her. His solid strength, the tango, weekends with his daughter Haley, the good sex. Snuggling on Sunday mornings. His predictability, and the surprises. She'd never expected he would take to the tango lessons. The corny songs he crooned to her? He had a corny song for every occasion.

She'd let her fears of him being killed on the street get out of hand, fears amplified by the dread of her father and brother dead in some purposeless killing. The hours passed as she reconsidered the way that dread came out with Mason in shrewishness and nagging. Dammit, he could be so blockheaded, but then so was she. Fingering the scar on her cheek left by a psychopath not that long ago, the PTSD she was being treated for had spilled over on Mason. She and the therapist had talked about the fears, but she hadn't slowed down enough to realize they were eroding her relationship with Mason. But if he put in for promotion and sat behind a desk...if only ....if only she had...

She still had flashbacks from time to time and being shut in here wouldn't do her any good. But she'd learned techniques from Dr. Steiner, her therapist. She knew what to do now. Rhys understood PTSD in a way, but only on an intellectual level. He tried to reason with her when she'd come to a dead stop, panicked, in a narrow, darkened hallway of a restaurant with the buzz of people all around her.

Mason knew what to do. Grab and hold her. Let her shake with shuddering waves of panic until it subsided. Rhys would take her hands and try to talk her down, reason with her. Words didn't work. The static was too loud in her ears.

Then anger swept away the fears. All the work she'd done to get past the experience that had pitched her into panic and confusion was *not* going to go to waste. She stood up suddenly and crumpled with dizziness brought on by dehydration. It had to be Sorensen.

Maybe. Surely not. But what if? What if?

Doug Paget? Venetia was clearly tight with Paget – closure rumors, lawsuits...murder. In fact, two murders.

Was she going to be number three? Over and over she reviewed the list of alumni donors in her head. One of them? They were all people who had done something in the world, earned something, made a big life. Not all of them were the 1% rich, but the school had been critical to a phase in their lives. None of them seemed possible as killers… but then who? Sorensen? Had to be.

Her anger turned to Rhys. Something bigger than Sorensen had to be going on and it stood to reason he'd know what it was. Well, maybe.

Ginger had seen the hard, pushing will to dominate that made Venetia Sorensen grind away at her job and refuse help. She'd seen that kind of steel-edged competitiveness working for corporate clients. It wasn't pretty, but if a murder was involved every time there was backstabbing between two women, the corporate ranks would thin out pretty quickly. And besides, somebody had to get up real close to kill Doris. Could it be somebody who worked with her every day for years? That picture made her shudder.

Her mind ping-ponged back and forth between the possibilities. At one point when she had given into a panicky fear, she pulled a filing cabinet away from the wall in a feat of superhuman strength and squirmed in behind it. A little hidey-hole next to the wall. She piled a few banker boxes in front of her. Thirst grew maddening.

Something was fishy about the school's finances and Leonard Bricker had figured it out. Despite the thirst and her growing terror, Ginger forced herself to think logically. Bricker was murdered. Why? What did he know? Doris knew something that got her killed. Was there some key fact she knew as well, but hadn't figured out the significance? It seemed clear Venetia had been dipping out of the honey pot. Did Doris find out, or did she have her finger in it too? Who was the alpha male with the bodyguards she'd seen Venetia winding herself around out in the street? Was that connected?

The money couldn't be enough to tempt her to kill Doris. It was like the $872 in cash that everybody concluded Doris had run off with. But had she been killed for the $872? The school budget wasn't that great. Not enough to kill for. The whirling confusion of questions made no sense.

An endless amount of time passed. She tracked the passing hours by watching the shifting light in the space at the bottom of the doors. When it turned black again and the hiss of tires from passing cars on the street had dwindled, she knew it was night again. She dozed, her back against the cold wall, shivering.

By now thirst was a raging, roaring demon in her throat. Any moisture she could summon up felt as if razors were sliding down. Waves of cold, fear, adrenaline, and exhaustion shook her. Thirst and cold outweighed everything, even hunger. Panic surged through her, driving away all rational thought. Spiders were long forgotten.

The worst fear was that she'd miscalculated the time and it was only Saturday morning. What if Armando the cleaner didn't return until early Monday evening? How long did it take to die of thirst? Thanks to the enforced starvation she was probably losing weight. That was something.

※

"Vlad, something's happened. The Police are calling me." Venetia Sorensen stood atop a sandy bluff just off the Backbone trail looking towards Los Angeles sprawling in the distance. The day was hot, the breeze through the chaparral astringent on a hot Sunday morning.

"I tell you already. Be careful. They watch you."

"There's nothing to see. I *am* careful. I'm not stupid. What did you do?"

"Oh, always blame me. Blame somebody. What you do?"

"Nothing."

He laughed that hateful way he had. "You lie. Lie always. You I don't trust."

"How can you say that?"

"Where are you?"

"Don't worry. Nobody can hear me."

"You should be the one who worries. Nobody touches me. Sounds like is over for you."

"Don't you even care?" she howled into the wind, then looked around to see if any of the other hikers had caught up to her.

He laughed again. "Care? You think always you are smarter than me, that nobody touch you. You have money? Two days from now or no deal. Deal is off, you understand? I told you. For three months you know this."

The wind blew harder and pasted her shirt against her sweaty back. Behind her she heard the weary conversation of people who couldn't keep up to her. Then the panic passed and with perfect confidence she turned to them.

"Only another ten miles."

By 10 a.m. Sunday morning Mason was arguing with the brass about putting a missing person's procedure in place. No one had seen Ginger since Friday morning. The temp answering the phones at the Windsor Academy told them they'd cancelled classes Friday afternoon for the students to attend a city-wide sports meet. Sorenson was still not answering her phone. Mason's stomach was a mess worrying about her. He and Bert McNair were leaning against the breakfast counter in her apartment, talking. Mason was eating an uncooked Pop Tart.

He looked up as Rhys Kensington knocked on the door and hesitantly came into the room. He wore white shorts, tennies without socks, and a dark green La Costa golf shirt, sunglasses pushed up into his hair.

"I'm sorry about last night. I just barely remember you calling, sir," he said to McNair, ignoring Mason. "I'd taken the pill half an hour earlier and I just could not wake up. I've had insomnia problems since I was a kid. I hate taking pills, but after a few nights without sleep, I just have to."

"Sure, sure," Ginger's father said. "You know Dave Mason?"

"Yes, hello, Dave," Kensington said, extending his hand.

He had a good handshake. Mason kept his cop face on. Kensington knew something and he wanted to pick him up by the heels and shake it out of him and then pound him against the wall. He clenched his fists and kept his mouth shut.

"What do you think is going on?" Kensington said to Ginger's father. "I know how she feels about her aunt. Is Mabel going to be okay?"

"Far as we can tell, but dropping out of contact like this isn't like Ginger."

"No, it isn't," Kensington agreed.

"A lot of bad stuff has been connected to your school lately," Mason said, hearing the accusation in his voice. "First Leonard Bricker and Doris Arnold, and now Ginger. What have you got to tell me?"

"Beats me. The school's not that big an operation from Kensington Industries' point of view. KI takes an interest in it, of course, and likes to celebrate its successes, but Dr. Sorensen pretty much runs it on her own."

"You got any idea where Sorenson might be this morning? We can't get an answer on her landline or her cellphone."

"Lotta weekends she goes camping, backpacking, running a marathon, things like that. She's into physical fitness, extreme sports, that kind of thing."

Mason turned away to follow up on the details of the missing person procedure. Shutting down the phone, he asked Kensington, "You've got keys to the school?"

"Sure."

"Let's take a look. Apparently Ginger took the bus there sometimes, because her car's out back in her parking space. You didn't give her a lift on Friday, did you?"

"No. Actually I haven't seen her since Wednesday. We went to Disney Hall for a concert. I had things to do on Thursday and she was all excited about finishing the fundraiser dinner thing this weekend."

Please don't say anything more, Mason thought.

He didn't. "Let's meet over at the school," Mason said, taking charge. "Bert, you want to ride with me?"

Kensington's rental Lexus was parked out in front of Ginger's place on Third Street. Wouldn't you know a rich guy would get a parking spot like that, Mason thought to himself. Bert McNair got in Mason's old Jeep parked half a block away and didn't say anything.

"Wait. I want to ride with you," Rhys Kensington said, catching up with them.

"Shit," Bert McNair said quietly as Kensington hurried over to Mason's Jeep. Mason gave him a quick look. This was the first indication he'd had Rhys Kensington wasn't the man Bert McNair favored for his daughter.

He said nothing as Rhys scrambled into the seat behind them.

Mason took off heading south to Wilshire Boulevard, one of the main arteries through the city. They drove in silence to the Phoebe Windsor Academy. He tried not to think the worst, to hold himself together.

He yanked his phone off his belt when it began to vibrate, checking caller ID. It was Palmer. Reluctantly he answered, weaving around a car full of old ladies heading back from the big Baptist church on Washington.

"Where you at, Mason? I got something."

"I got something going on here."

"What? This is important."

"So's this? What?"

"You're afraid of breaking a nail? What?"

"This is personal. Make it fast, Palmer. What?"

Palmer laughed. "You're finally getting laid, you dog. How about that? Listen, I got a lead to the guy who did the work on the Toyota."

"You're gonna have to do this one yourself. Take Delgado. I'll check in with you later."

Ginger heard a car drive into the parking lot behind the Administration cottage. Her heart leaped up. Thirst was doing something to her heart. It was beating way too fast. Her tongue was so swollen that when she tried screaming it came out as a froggy croak. She squeezed back into her hiding spot behind the filing cabinet, listening, listening over the sound of her heart beating fast. Too fast. She was so thirsty she couldn't think straight. Car doors slammed.

If she heard a vehicle arrive and one car door slam, the probability was that it was someone with the intention of hurting her. But then again, it could be a teacher or Sorenson or somebody returning to the school with an innocent purpose. But what if it were someone who parked and headed into one of the other three cottages to pick up something from a classroom? No one would hear her even if she screamed her lungs out.

Her jailor would know exactly where she was.

She listened hard and heard another car door slam and then another.

A killer wouldn't bring witnesses. No rational scenario she'd come up with featured more than the one person who would shut her in here. But all the same, she wasn't sure she was being rational any longer. Strange, glittering half-second dreams danced in front of her eyes.

She felt feverish, hot, then cold. Her arms and legs felt heavy and she wasn't sure she had the strength to bat a spider away. The thought of another living creature there now was consoling. Even a spider.

31

Mason took the key out of the ignition and took a quick look at Bert McNair who was already stepping out of the Jeep. They had wasted time already stopping by Kensington's penthouse home, waiting outside his art deco building while he picked up his set of keys for the Academy.

Caroline Kensington called. He answered the phone gruffly. "Mason."

"Have you found Ginger yet?"

"No."

"What on earth could have happened to her?" Caroline's voice was tight, concerned. "I know how she feels about Mabel. You don't think it's anything to do with the Academy, do you? I just can't believe that, but so many crazy things have happened lately..."

"We're at the Academy now. Just ready to go in as a matter of fact."

"Oh. Let me know what happens, will you? I care about her too."

"I will," he lied. The fewer Kensingtons he had to deal with the better he liked it. Rhys Kensington and Bert McNair were on the steps of the Socrates Cottage opposite the Administration building, Kensington fiddling with a key ring. Ginger's father loomed over him impatiently. The Socrates Cottage housed the lunchroom. Kensington said she often worked there because they were so crowded.

Mason clipped his phone back on his belt and strode across the parking lot. From the outside, the four white clapboard cottages looked the same, slightly down at the heels, ready for demolition as soon as the money could be raised for the new building. This piece of property so close to the terminal of the new light rail track must be worth tens of millions.

Bert McNair was first through the door of the cottage that held the lunch room where Rhys said Ginger often worked.

Nothing there. Kensington walked behind them. His hands gripped behind his back like Prince Phillip on a tour of inspection. He knew better than to talk.

"Let's hit the Admin building now," Mason said. Ginger would not take off on a vacation without telling anybody. For one thing, the attack on her last year had knocked out some of the open-hearted trust she had for everyone. Bad people did exist and they didn't come with fangs and horns as a warning. He'd seen the effect the attack had on her, and whatever happened to her now was not through lack of caution.

His anxiety was rising. He moved through the steps of missing persons procedure in his head. They entered the Administration cottage.

Ginger strained, her shoulder hunched around her ears to concentrate better, squirmed in tight behind the filing cabinet.

Silence for a long time. Then she heard the front door open and something said. It was too far away to hear. Footsteps came closer.

A familiar voice.

She pushed the banker's boxes away and squirmed out from behind the filing cabinet, rising to her feet and hobbling in the dark toward the door, barking her shins painfully on one of the banker boxes.

The footsteps passed the door. She didn't have enough spit left in her throat to cry out. Instead she fell headlong onto the floor and by reaching out full length she was able to reach the door. With her last remaining strength she scratched at the door.

The footsteps continued down the hall. Her belongings must have been removed. Nobody knew she was there.

Kensington turned to Mason as they left the Administration cottage. Mason could see the toll this was taking on him. Kensington was the kind of guy who could usually pay somebody to make problems go away. Not this time.

"So what next?" Kensington said, jamming his hands in the pockets of his khaki shorts.

"We start backtracking from Friday afternoon." Mason looked around. "Where are the cameras you were putting in? The extra security?"

"They were supposed to work on them this week. Doesn't look like the crew came out on the holiday weekend. I doubt they're operational yet. Work is scheduled to start on the interior next week."

"Did you hire a service to patrol?"

"Yes."

"Well, call them."

Kensington was already scrolling down in his phone. "And get Sorensen in here."

They convened at the station. Mason pulled himself away from Ginger's Dad and her brother Art, who'd joined them when he got off graveyard shift. Her Dad was determined to stick with Mason and not let him out of their sight. As L.A. County Deputy Sheriff's Officers, they had no jurisdiction in Santa Monica and they both knew the realities and priorities of adult missing person cases.

Bert McNair threw an empty styrofoam cup in the wastebasket and approached him as he left the Special Operations unit. "Art wants to take another look himself. There might be something we missed. Would you mind taking us back to that school?"

Mason liked Ginger's brother. He saw the fear on his face. They'd talked hockey and had gone out for a beer once in a while. The only thing they couldn't talk about was Ginger after they broke up. Mason didn't have keys and had to call one of the Kensingtons to get back in. He couldn't bear to see Rhys Kensington again. He called Caroline. "We want to take another look at the school," Mason explained to Caroline. "Can you meet me there and let me in."

"You haven't found Ginger yet?" she said, her voice strained. "Where on earth could she possibly be?"

"I wish I knew, Caroline."

"I've been calling everybody I can think of."

"That's good. So I need to get into the school..."

"You don't need a key. Rhys called the people who are installing the security cameras. They're on their way there now. If you want, I could meet you there."

Mason smiled. Caroline Kensington wanting to see him? That was a first. They never thought Mason was good enough for Ginger.

Ginger's Dad and brother were slowly going crazy. Mason wanted to run around in circles himself and disciplined himself to stick to procedure. He could only do so much to drive the investigation. His first priority was the work of the Task Force investigating Yurkov. It had never been a secret that hot cars were shipped out in containers at the port of Long Beach. Too little inspection at the port made it an easy conduit to overseas buyers. That was where the focus of the Task Force was now going based on early reports. He knew for the sake of his career that should be his focus as well. Another team of detectives would take over Ginger's disappearance. He knew they would work it with the same diligence that he'd looked for Doris Arnold before she'd turned up dead. They'd do their best. But it was late Sunday afternoon now and Ginger hadn't been seen since Friday noon.

Rhys Kensington was talking to two guys with toolboxes standing outside one of the cottages when Mason arrived with Ginger's father and brother. Kensington walked toward them, his smile hesitant.

Greetings were cool on the McNair side. "Maybe you could talk to these guys from the security company, suggest some things," Kensington said. "There's no news, is there?"

Mason shook his head. "You mind if we just take another look around?"

"I'll come with you. Is there anything I can do?"

"Find Sorensen. That would be good."

Palmer called again as they walked up the stairs of the Socrates cottage. Mason paused to answer.

"I'm still out here in the ugly-ass end of the world in Hemet sniffing around while you're enjoying yourself at the beach."

"Yeah, I'm having a great time back here," Mason said. He filled him in on what had happened to Ginger.

"That's bad," Palmer said. "Bad."

"I know." There was a short silence.

"Well, I got a lead on a guy out here does a little chop shopping, little of this, little of that, you know," Palmer said, changing the subject. "He's grinding off VIN numbers, cutting and pasting cars. Making shaved keys. Here's a surprise. What happened is I hear a lot of stories linking him to one of Yurkov's crew out here, which I'm trying to chase down. So I'm drivin' around looking for people. You know that old story?"

Yeah, Mason knew about drivin' around lookin' for people.

Mason was impatient, his mind on Ginger. Despite his efforts to keep calm, dark scenarios nagged at him.

"Yeah, so, you telling me you linked it up to Bricker?"

"Mason, you dreamer. My guy is giving me the dance. We're doin' the cha cha salsa here."

"Look, I gotta go, Palmer. McNair, you know, gotta take care of that."

"Captain says to keep working' it. You'll hear from me."

Ginger came to awareness from an empty place in her mind hearing a door open and men talking. I am going to die here unless I do something. Her mouth was too dry to scream. She was still lying prone on the floor where she'd fallen headlong. From out of her chest came a roar that sounded puny even to herself. She tried again and the rumble of sound was louder.

Somebody get me out of here! Dammit. She used her last bit of strength and coherent thought to slap her sandal at the bottom of the door.

The footsteps stopped. Someone was down the hall, listening.

She slapped at the door again.

The footsteps returned. Stopped. Voices muttered, then came the distinct sound of keys jingling and fitting into the lock, a sound more beautiful than any soaring music ever written.

Light blazed, stinging her eyes. The door opened. A matted hank of hair fell over her face. She knew she smelled, hadn't brushed her teeth in days, and the fresh air flowing into the room did nothing to dispel the stink of urine and fear. It didn't matter now. There was Mason. Then her father was there too. Her brother. And Rhys.

"I thought you'd never come," she said in her head but no words came out. Mason was kneeling beside her, lifting her against his chest.

"We've been looking all over for you, babe. Scared me half to death."

"Water," she croaked out, trying to struggle out of Mason's arms and stand, wanting only to get out of this hated room. It was no good. She fell back and reached out for her father.

"Dad….."

Her father half-carrying her, Ginger stumbled out into the brightly lit hall and fell to her knees. The effort to talk, with her tongue so thick and throat so desiccated, set her coughing so hard that she vomited a weak stream of bile.

Mason barked at Rhys to bring her some water. Kensington scrambled down the hall. "You're alright, Ginger?"

She shook her head. Sinking back against the wall, she slid onto her bottom. Her father sank down next to her and put an arm around her, pulling her close.

"You worry me half to death," he said. "I don't know, girl."

Kensington returned with a bottle of water. Ginger reached out to grab it from him, half mad from thirst. Her brother hunkered down facing her and brushed a hank of hair off her face.

"Careful, careful," Rhys said, twisting off the cap. "Ginger, I've been so scared."

She grabbed the bottle of water from him and held it to her mouth, prepared to drink the whole bottle in one long gulp. She got in one swig that moistened her mouth like a dry sponge. Mason snatched the bottle away from her.

"Wait. You haven't had any water in there with you? Aw, Jesus, Ginger."

She reached to get the precious bottle of water back.

"Little sips," he said, holding the bottle. "You'll just vomit it up. Little sips."

"I hate you," she wailed, reaching for the bottle.

"I know," he said.

Ginger watched from what felt like a long way away as Rhys Kensington and Dave Mason battled for control of her, two woolly mammoths huffing and snorting and pawing the ground. Mason was bigger, taller, and had a badge, but this was Kensington's property. Her Dad allowed her tiny sips of water from the bottle. Her throat, which felt as though it had closed to the size of a keyhole, slowly relaxed, her voice returning.

"This is a crime scene. Wait outside, Mr. Kensington. You guys can stay," he said to Ginger's father and brother.

Ginger made a protesting noise and waved her hand in the air as though to chase them all away. The room spun. Kensington argued, then took another look at Ginger. Was he going to push this into a schoolyard fistfight?

"Okay, I'll be outside," he vowed, challenging Mason with a hard look but not going anywhere.

"Okay, then," Mason said. "Go."

Rhys pushed by Mason to Ginger who was sitting on the floor and kissed the top of her head. She didn't raise her face for his kiss. She didn't want anybody to see her like this and she didn't have the strength to deal with either one of them.

Bert McNair whispered to Mason when he was gone, "Don't mention anything about her aunt. I'll tell her later."

By then the paramedics had arrived and were checking Ginger's vitals.

"Pretty dehydrated," the one who looked about thirteen years old said over her head to Mason. "It's up to you, ma'am, but somebody ought to check you over."

"No hospital," she swore, her voice strained, whispering. "I'm so cold." The paramedic wrapped a blanket around her.

"Come to my place," Rhys pleaded. "I'll get a nurse. We'll bring in everything you need."

"No, no. Home." It hurt to talk. The room swam in confusion.

"Out, Mr. Kensington. Out," Mason shouted.

Rhys would fuss and never leave her alone and she couldn't stand that. The paramedics took another call and left her sitting in a chair at a table in the classroom next door.

"Purse?" she croaked. "Where's my stuff," she said, letting her hair sweep forward to cover her face.

Mason took a seat at the table facing her. "We didn't find anything. Where did you leave it?"

She gestured over her shoulder. "There." She remembered the hurried footsteps just after she'd been shut in.

Mason looked tired, purple shadows under his brown eyes.

"What happened to your lip?"

"Forget about my lip," he said gruffly. "What happened to you?"

"I went in that room and somebody shut the door behind me and turned the lights out."

"This was when?"

"Friday afternoon about three?"

"So let's see," he consulted his watch. "You've been in there about 52 hours. That's a long time to go without water."

"And nothing to eat..." she pointed out, sounding grouchy.

"You could lose a few pounds," he said grinning.
"Yeah, yeah. Not funny. I don't think it was any accident."

She looked up at him. "This really pisses me off!"

"You wouldn't have been in very good shape if we hadn't got here."

"I realize that," she croaked out. She looked down at her hands. They were filthy, streaks of dirt up her arms from exploring her prison looking for something to help herself. She felt utterly wretched, tired beyond endurance and confused. There was Delgado now. He gave her shoulder a squeeze and skidded out a chair to sit down beside her.

"I heard," was all he said.

"Where's my dad? He's coming back, isn't he?" From the corner of her eye Ginger saw the forensic specialists who were pushing their little wheeled carts down the hallway. Mason gave her another sip from the bottle, which strengthened her voice.

"He's outside making a phone call to your aunt Mabel. Your brother had to go back to work," Mason answered. "Why were you in there?"

"Looking for something. I work here in this awful place. You know that."

"So who else was around that could have shut you in there?"

"Please, no more now. Later?" She just wanted this to be over, get her Dad to take her home, have a shower and sleep. Just sleep. The fear of that dark prison was wearing off.

"Ginger, somebody shut you in there intentionally. Your purse is gone and somebody destroyed your phone too because we couldn't locate you by triangulating the signal. So it wasn't an accident, was it?"

"Sorensen. Ask her. Last one I saw."

"That room is marked Electrical Panel. Why would you go in there?" Mason said, leaning toward her from his chair.

"Sorensen. Ask her." She felt color wash out of her cheeks and a long wave of weariness approaching like a tsunami. The story about the record boxes took too much energy to make coherent. She put her face down on the table. Art Delgado put his hand on her shoulder.

"What's going on here, Ginger?" Mason persisted. "Do you know?"

She shook her head wildly. All she could think of was a shower and her own bed with its cool, clean sheets.

"Don't you want to get the guy who did this to you?" Mason said. "You could have died, Ginger. This isn't a safe place. The Kensingtons are going to protect their own interests here. You're expendable. Something's in play here and you could get hurt."

"Rhys?" Her eyes narrowed and she flipped dirty blond hair out of her face.

"I wasn't being personal. There's money tied up in this place. Somebody thinks you know something, or you're onto something. You're in danger here from somebody."

"Rhys?" she said again, shaking her head, which made logic swim in confusion.

"I didn't say that. This is a warning. Can't you see that?"

"Can I be curious later?" she said through her hands over her face.

She heard Mason's chair skid out from the table and saw him stand up. "Bert," he said to her father, "Make her go to the hospital to get checked out."

"No," Ginger said.

"You should be on IV hydration. That's what the paramedic said."

Ginger was shaking her head but by then she was strong enough to push herself to her feet though she wobbled.

"Okay. We'll give you a call later, set up a time to come into the station and get a statement."

It was over.

For now.

32

Sunday wasn't over for Mason. He gave orders for a search of the school and put out a BOLO for Sorenson. She had leaped from person of interest to suspect, being the last person Ginger had seen. It still wasn't enough to pull paper on her. No other staff member seemed to be available as a backup if she couldn't be reached. What a way to run a place. He went back to the Electrical Panel room to look at the boxes since the forensic people were finished documenting the scene. He gloved up and went through a couple of boxes. Nothing but student records. He'd do a real search later. He heard Kensington trying to force his way past the uniform Mason had left at the door with a sign in sheet. Guess he hadn't gone home with Ginger then, Mason thought. Interesting.

"C'mon, Mason. I want to know what's going on here," Kensington called out down the hall.

"Let him in." He watched Kensington walk toward them.

"What's going on here?" Mason said. "That's what we're trying to find out, sir."

"You don't have to call me sir, Dave. For God's sake. C'mon, Mason, don't be such a hard ass."

He could tell Kensington was going to say something else, but he bit whatever it was back with an effort. If it was about Ginger, then Mason didn't want to hear it.

"We should close the school or find temporary quarters until you figure out what's going on," Kensington said. "It's my responsibility to make sure the students and staff are safe. And this thing with Ginger has really shaken me."

"That's a damn good idea. I'd say somebody's got it in for you."

"My sister tells me Facebook and the chat rooms are just going crazy with rumors. See the media people outside? A lot more talk about removing their kids from the school. And then there's the other faction that's determined to keep the school open. The press are badgering me. Somebody tipped them. I suppose we can't ask Ginger to handle media right now... "

Mason looked at him as if he'd lost his mind at the thought of asking Ginger to do anything right now. However, if he could sit in the same room with the fuckweasels he brought in every day, he could deal with Kensington. He pulled out a chair and sat down. Kensington sank into a chair opposite him.

"It's occurred to you what would have happened to Ginger if we hadn't turned up?

Kensington sank forward, put his head in his hands, and said, "You think I've thought of anything else? You'd be wrong. You know I've asked her to marry me."

Mason did his best to keep his face impassive. "No. I didn't. And what did she say?" His heart raced.

He looked up to meet Mason's gaze. "She hasn't made up her mind yet, but I'm very hopeful."

"Well, congratulations," Mason said, standing up. The conversation was over for him. For now. If Kensington knew anything, he wasn't telling. Suddenly his whole body hurt and he realized how tired he was.

"What happened to your lip?" Kensington said curiously.

"Nothing," Mason barked. "We'll be pulling out in a few hours. Keep me posted on any changes in contact information in case I need to get hold of you in a hurry. The security cameras will have to wait until we're done."

Kensington and Mason walked out to the porch of the Administration cottage together in the last shadows of the afternoon. With a sudden hard gust of wind the tree boughs bent and swayed with a rattle of palm fronds. By morning the streets would be littered with fallen leaves and the withered skeletons of dead palm branches. Both stood there, checking their phones for messages. A wave of sadness and lost opportunities flooded him. Ginger could do a lot worse than this guy, he supposed. Even though Kensington seemed to have no motivation to do her harm, he still didn't trust him.

Both Mason and Kensington looked up as a black BMW raced down the lane beside the cottage and screeched to a halt in the parking lot behind the cottages. A door slammed and Mason heard running feet. Moments later Venetia Sorensen stomped across the quad toward them.

"Detective Mason, I got your messages and now I get here and see police all over the campus. What's going on here?" Sorensen wore hiking clothes that looked sweaty and dusty. Her tanned face was pink with outrage.

Mason took his time. "Ginger McNair was locked in the electric panel room and left there for the weekend without food or water. We just found her."

"That's terrible," Sorensen said, loud and in a hurry. "Is she still here? My heavens, I don't know what to say. Is she okay?"

"She's very dehydrated and shaky, but she'll probably be okay. As far as we know."

"That's just terrible." Sorensen sat down hard on the bottom step of the deck stairs. Then she swung around to look at Mason. "How did she get herself locked in there? Why would she even go in there?"

"Somebody locked the door behind her and shut off the light. Seems you were the last person to see her."

He came down the three stairs and faced her, watching carefully for a tell. She wore sunglasses and a floppy hat that shaded her face.

"I was? Really? There must have been someone else, because when I left on Friday afternoon there was a car in the parking lot."

"What kind of car?"

She dismissed the question with a little wave. "One of those small grey cars. They all look the same to me."

Every instinct bred by experience told Mason she was lying. "New? Old? Anything on the dashboard?" Mason said. "Any dents or marks on it? Help us out here."

"I only gave it a glance. I was in a hurry to beat the holiday traffic. Let me think about it. Maybe I'll remember more."

"Think about it now, would you?" Mason said with an edge in his voice.

Rhys Kensington stood listening at the top of the steps. "Venetia, we should find temporary quarters until the police figure out what's going on here. I worry about the staff, the students."

"We can't do that," Sorensen said firmly, standing up to face him. "Do you know how much that would cost?"

"Venetia," Kensington said with a snap. Mason watched him intently as well. His concern seemed genuine. But …

"Come inside, Rhys. We need to talk." She turned her back to Mason.

Mason tapped her on the shoulder. "This is a crime scene. There is a search in progress. I want you down at the station to make a statement. Right now."

"I have things to do here, Detective Mason," she protested. "We can't have the press getting hold of this." She was preparing to push him out of the way and get into her office.

"It looks as though you're way too late," Mason said, pointing to a reporter edging up on them. The reporter looked like an elementary school teacher and was followed by a gorilla loaded down with sixty pounds of camera equipment. The camera guy was already aiming at them with a long lens. Where was the department's Public Information Officer? He'd called him half an hour ago to run interference.

"Oh, God. They're here already. This is a disaster."

He didn't want Sorensen trading stories with Kensington. "I won't have this investigation depending on your convenience, Ms. Sorensen." He used the "Ms." deliberately.

"You can surely give me five minutes before you begin the interrogation," she said, going from blustery to flirty in a nanosecond. "Let me comb my hair, change my clothes."

"No. I can't. I'll follow you to the station, or you can ride in the back of my vehicle."

"You don't understand. I have to please fifty-five students and their parents and many, many important alumni."

"That will wait."

She went back to being nasty. "You're a real Nazi."

Mason had been called worse. Sorensen didn't like it but Mason got her skinny ass twitching in a chair in an interview room at the station. Delgado took a chair across from her. They had ratcheted things way up past the small talk stage. But so far she hadn't asked for a lawyer.

"You want to know where I was at this weekend?" she said looking around the room. "I was with 26 other people on a Sierra Club hike from Point Magu to Will Rogers Park."

"And when did you leave here on Friday afternoon?'

"Around 3 o'clock, I guess," she said pinching her mouth in displeasure at being questioned.

"You were the last person to see Ms. McNair then," Mason said. "She said you told her that as you were leaving."

"That would only be important if you thought I was the person to lock her in," she said, leaning across the table aggressively. "And I wasn't."

"She didn't say you were."

"Well, why are you questioning me then?"

"Because we question everybody." Mason made his face wooden. "Somebody is trying to make trouble for the Academy..."

"And succeeding," Delgado added.

Sorensen swung around to give him a dirty look.

"Slowly, methodically, we're going to take this place apart," Mason said, grinding the words out. "Tell us again about when you left on Friday."

She gave a big sigh and gritted her teeth in annoyance. "As I told you..." she said pointedly, "I hit the freeway at 4th Street along with everybody else hoping to beat the holiday weekend traffic. It took me two hours to make it past Malibu. Can you believe that?"

"Yeah, I can." Traffic in L.A. always made a good alibi.

"We camped out Friday night and hit the trail at 7 a.m. the next morning." She was scribbling names and numbers on a yellow pad. "It's called the Backbone Trail."

Mason nodded.

She swung her head back and forth in annoyance. "I don't see why you're looking at me like that. I had nothing to do with what happened to her."

"See, we've been doing a neighbor canvass looking for the guy who was at your house..."

"I've been wondering if you cared enough to look into that," she said, interrupting him. "I've been worried sick he'd come back when I'm alone at night."

"You don't seem the worried-sick type, tell you the truth," Mason said.

"Now, how would you know that?"

"Extreme sports, ultra marathons, things you mentioned. Background check," he lied.

"I don't seem to need a man to protect me. Is that what you're saying?"

Mason grunted in surprise. "I didn't mean that at all."

"Tell me what you did mean," she snarled.

"You're at the center of everything that's going on. Chair of the Board of the School is killed, then your assistant turns up murdered, and now this with Ms. McNair. I gotta look at you pretty closely."

"Look all you want. You're not going to find anything. Are you going to arrest me or not?"

Mason and Delgado looked back and forth between each other.

"That's what I thought. I'm leaving."

"Where are you?" Another message. "Call me!"

Venetia fought to keep her spirits from soaring into manic territory as she reached the sanctuary of her home. She slammed the door of her BMW and locked the garage, wishing now she had the old Corolla. Vlad had walked her through how to buy it, then store it in a rented garage in Venice, use it to kill Bricker, and then sell it. Everything had gone right. She was untraceable. The stupid incompetents had nothing on her.

This was her third call to him that hadn't been picked up.

Time to move. Now.

She needed one more day. No, tomorrow was the holiday. First thing Tuesday.

Mason was anxious to see Ginger but when he and Delgado got to her place to take her statement, there was a note on the door from her Dad. He'd taken her to St. John's Hospital ER. Delgado leaned over and put his hand against the window next to the door trying to peer in. Mason turned on his heel and ran down the walk.

"C'mon. Let's go." Anything could have happened. Dehydration. She could have been running a fever, had difficulty breathing. She could have fainted. His mind ran the worst-case scenario. Brain damage.

He hit lights and siren. Delgado frowned at him. "Hey, man. Take it easy."

Mason's mind was racing, recalling everything he'd heard the EMT guys say about dehydration. Ginger was sleeping when they arrived, a big girl with long limbs who filled the bed in a curtained-off section of the busy ER. Her father beckoned the detectives into the hall. They stood in a quiet huddle.

"What happened?" Mason asked.

"She insisted on making a cup of tea in the kitchen. I just heard her go down. She was only out a minute or two, but I didn't like her color and she wasn't making any sense, so I dragged her here just as a precaution. All kinds of bad stuff can happen to your liver and heart with dehydration."

The scene recalled another occasion when Ginger had been hospitalized. Mason remembered the beginning of their relationship with sadness. All that freshness and optimism and love had come to this.

"When she wakes up, she's confused. Doesn't make sense. Don't worry though," McNair said. "The doc says she'll be fine."

They heard Ginger calling. Mason stuck his head around the curtain. She was trying to sit up in bed, struggling.

"I feel better now. Pull the curtain back. All the way. I want to see the whole room. Open the door. I don't want to feel shut in." Her hands danced on the cover, fidgeting, touching palm to palm, wringing the edge of the sheets. Mason saw tears well in her eyes. He'd seen Ginger, who seemed so strong and positive, buckle once before and it had taken time to recover her jaunty progress through life.

Mason sat down in a chair by the bedside. She smiled at Delgado and let the smile trail off when she turned to look at Mason. Delgado and her father stood at the other side of the bed, big men whose presence sent a message that the worst was over.

"Take a guess then. Who did this?" Mason said.

"I think it was Sorensen but I have absolutely no proof other than that she's a Grade A BitchViper. You go after her, Mason, you pin her ears to the wall."

"Oh, I will. It would be a pleasure actually."

"I want to know everything you do. You promise me?"

He laughed. "You want me to hold her while you take a punch at her?"

"Absolutely, I do. Yes."

When she grinned back at him, he knew she was going to be all right.

"At first I thought it might be one of the kids who thought he was being cute?" she said. "You know, some kid who planned to come back later and let me out and he forgot. Or maybe the door to the cottage was locked and he couldn't get back in. Something like that."

"We've backgrounded any of the students who've been pointed out already and nothing's turned up. Can you tag anybody?"

Ginger shook her head. Her hair hadn't been washed in days and her fine complexion was splotchy. He knew she'd hate being seen like this.

"Venetia's poisonous to everybody and she's cheap and greedy. I don't feel singled out, but she resents me because I'm supposed to be helping her. Did you get anything from forensics? Is it too early to know? I've completely lost track of time." She turned to her father. "Dad, see if you can get the doctor. There's no reason to keep me. If you want, I'll go home with you, but I need to get out of here and go and see Aunt Mabel." Hampered by the IV line, she tossed the covers aside, to reveal long, bare legs beneath her hospital gown and her feet in white socks.

Mason met Bert McNair's eyes across the bed.

"Your electrolytes are all out of whack. Aunt Mabel knows where you are and she's going to be okay. You need to keep that thing in your arm there overnight at least," Bert McNair said, weary patience in his voice.

33

Sgt. York glared at Mason as he entered the spartan office a little late for the case update meeting. Chuck Palmer was already there. York looked up at them from under bushy eyebrow, using a staple remover to clean the grime from under his fingernails. The Sarge leaned against the wall, watching.

"What have you got, Palmer?"

Palmer said. "I've got a tie to the Bricker hit-and-run."

He explained about the homeless couple out in Hemet. The Captain's eyebrows went higher and higher, and he leaned further back in his chair. When Palmer was done, he looked back and forth between Mason and Palmer and started to laugh. "They're both drunks. He's blind and she's nuts, and you call them eye witnesses?" He lurched forward in his chair. "Plus one said it was a female, the other said it was a male?"

"They gave us a good tip and I'm working it," Palmer said defensively. "They confirmed the right headlight was out. It's gotta be repaired somewhere. I'm looking under every rock out there. And this brings in the head-mistress, Sorensen, at the school. It makes sense that she'd be involved somehow with the Arnold murder."

"How?" the Lieutenant said.

"I'm looking for the link. Me and Mason are real skeptical about this so-called attack on her."

"If she was involved, why would she want to draw attention to herself then?"

Mason scratched an ear and said, "I don't know yet. But everything about this whole deal makes me suspicious of her." Palmer nodded agreement. "Everything points a finger at that school."

He then jerked his head toward Mason who related McNair's brush with death in the electrical panel closet over the weekend. York looked down and shuffled through paper. "You believe her?"

"Absolutely. Being shut in there was no accident."

"You're out of it completely with her then, I hear."

"Yeah, she's probably going to marry Kensington, the heir to the fortune."

"You looking hard at him?"

Mason shook his head. "I'd love to peg him. But I can't make it work."

"Let's take it to the Captain."

Capt. Maggio who was in charge of the Task Force wasn't in a good mood having to work on Labor Day, but reports were accelerating on the Yurkov operation that needed to be evaluated, the action plan coming together. The Task Force room down the hall buzzed with officers wearing tan, navy blue, and black uniforms and scruffy-looking characters working undercover at the port. Lt. Ross and Capt. Maggio bent over a pile of reports in tense, low-voiced conversation, ignoring Mason and Sgt. York. Mason went through it all again. He was tired and charged up on coffee, on adrenaline overload, and probably not making the best case he was capable of, and he knew it. The Sarge shrugged his shoulders, looking to the L.T.

Maggio pushed Mason. "And how are we supposed to keep the city running? We've got this Task Force going. Remember that? I took you off that to run down this lead and now you bring me some other convoluted deal at this Kensington place. No proof. What's the crime? What would we charge Sorensen on, even if we could prove it was her?"

He seemed angry and Mason didn't figure it was his fault. Before he could open his mouth, Maggio went on. "Why do you think Sorensen's gonna rabbit? This school's a big deal to her." His bushy eyebrows came together and his face reddened.

"A hunch based on experience," Mason said. "She's on overdrive. Something's ready to pop."

"Hunch. Okay, I don't discount hunches, Mason, but you still gotta bring me more than that. All's I can spare is some extra drive-bys. Get it done and fast because there's Task Force logistics I need you for. LAPD and the guys at the port think there's a shipment of stolen cars from the Yurkov operation going through soon. We've got an undercover source in place. They've put tags on a couple of containers that should move in a couple of days."

"Whenever the bust is planned," Sgt. York put in, "Auto Theft goes with you."

Mason shuddered at the thought of Gomez and his long face. Delgado knocked on the door frame, came in and sat down.

The Captain turned away to pull Sgt. York into another conversation. That was their cue for dismissal. "Delgado and I plan to get Sorensen back in here today and take her apart," Mason got one more thing in, "that is if she's still talking to us. It won't go happy if any of the Kensington executives are behind all this."

"The chief plays golf with the CEO," the Captain acknowledged. "I got a call this morning telling me to do it easy. Kensington's sponsoring a big golf tournament and the chief wants to look good. Kensington Industries can always pull out of town, you know, and run their business where labor's cheaper."

Ginger was sitting on the edge of her hospital bed, feeling woozy if she leaned forward too far, but better overall.

Bert McNair stuck his head in. "You ready to go?"

"Just about. What am I going to do with all these flowers?" She looked around the room. Rhys was drowning her in a sticky, cloying kind of love. She couldn't bear to have him fussing over her and wanted to get out of there before he showed up to claim her.

"Leave 'em for the nurses. C'mon. I'm on a meter out front and you know these parking devils in Santa Monica."

"They're evil. That's why I take the bus sometimes." She tottered into the bathroom and struggled into her clothes. Just as they were leaving, Rhys turned up with more flowers. Ginger tried to smile at him.

Rhys looked confused. "You're leaving? The doctor is releasing you? I just talked to him and..."

"Nope, I'm leaving and I don't want to talk about it," she said firmly. "I want to go see Aunt Mabel. Then I'm just as well off at home as I am here."

Rhys looked at her father quickly. "Don't you think she..."

"Hey, I'm the one deciding here, Rhys," Ginger said, throwing on a sweater. The effort overbalanced her and she caught herself by hanging onto a chair. She sank back onto the bed. "I can't sleep here and I've got a lot of work and..."

"You're not thinking of working at the Academy, are you?" Kensington looked alarmed. He sat down hard in one of the chairs with the bouquet of flowers across his lap.

"Yes, Rhys. There are deadlines for the dinner. Things I need to follow up on…"

"Whatever you want, darling. But maybe we should cancel the dinner."

"Maybe you should keep the school and get rid of the director. The school is great. Sorensen is toxic. I think she's the one who slammed that door behind me, Rhys.'

He drew in a breath. "Oh surely not. I know she's hard to get along with, but she wouldn't…."

"Oh no? You've got a lot of funny ideas about her. I keep thinking about those kids, Rhys. That guy I saw her with. Maybe it's crazy, but all this stuff at the school, maybe it's about you? You're the heir."

Rhys looked gut shot. "Me? You can't imagine the legalese that ties everything up. It's not like I inherit everything. It's just not that simple, Ginger."

"Well, that's my best shot at it then. I think it was her and I'm going home. I can work from there."

"Ginger, you need time off. I hate to tell you this but the board has hired a team of people." He mentioned one of Los Angeles' most prestigious PR firms. "You can see this has become far more than one person can handle. We have to have people handling media, the parents, the teachers. So much. We're releasing you from your contract, but of course, once this crisis has passed…" He talked on and on—what a good job she'd done, how much everyone liked and respected her, how she'd increased the donor base, given them a real footing for the first time. On and on.

Ginger gazed at him, half listening and sorting through her emotions. She was angry at being replaced, and at the same time relieved. To give herself time to think she took the envelope he handed her and ripped it open. The severance check made her eyes widen. She tilted off the bed, slowly getting her feet under her.

"I'll get a wheelchair," he said, jumping to his feet.

"Rhys, I've already signed myself out. They don't care anymore. Please. Just let me go." She pushed him back into the chair with a firm hand on his shoulder. "I'll call you."

He handed her the bouquet of peonies. "Please, don't be angry."

She smiled. "I'm not. Really, I'm not. Thanks for the flowers."

Mason had noticed Ginger was low on cat food and had gone over early the Monday of Labor Day weekend and tapped on her door. Her father answered and Mason handed him a case of the good cat food. On the top was the new J.A. Jance novel. Ginger was sleeping. They had a low-voiced conversation at the door. She was better and that was all he needed to hear.

First in priority was to pick up Sorensen but that took paperwork, which took time. The Task Force was meeting this morning to coordinate the bust on Yurkov. The Yurkov operation had been under surveillance by GPS, undercover officers, phones and trackers.

Mason took a place in the largest conference room where everybody on the Task Force could spread out. The Feds were there, trying to look smarter than everybody else, along with LAPD and Long Beach port police, a few customs guys, and a show of uniforms from all the coastal cities where the carjackers had hit hardest. Fredericks took a seat next to Mason, sliding a memo over for him to read. He read it, looked at her, and grinned.

The Chief was there, conferring with the Captain, her eyes gleaming with interest.

"Can you give me a status on Yurkov's whereabouts?" Capt. Maggio pointed to the side of the table where Palmer and the Auto Theft team of Gomez and Wilson were sitting. Palmer spoke up.

"He was seen yesterday. No eyes on him today."

The Chief frowned. Growls of disappointment were heard around the room. "We got something though," Mason said. He gestured to Fredericks and the memo he'd just read. "Fredericks' got a solid tie-in linking Sorensen and Yurkov. We got a tip to check the W Hotel for Sorensen's name on the register. The staff recognized her regular visitor, one Vlad Yurkov. He spread around the big tips. Venetia was nasty to the staff. They remembered her too."

"So pull her in," an LAPD guy said to Mason. "Get her talking."

"We're pulling the paper to do just that."

Mason's phone vibrated. It was Rhys Kensington. What now? He shook his head in annoyance, then forced politeness into his voice. What now?

"I'm in a meeting," he said curtly, turning aside.

"Well, Ginger's fine. That's a big relief."

Mason said shortly," Yes, it is. So what's up?" he repeated.

"I got this call," Kensington began. "At first I didn't take the guy seriously. Just some goofball. It's about the reward the company offered for news on Leonard Bricker's death. And Doris Arnold, I suppose too."

"Yeah?" Mason said.

"Yeah, well, the caller says he can tell me who killed Leonard Bricker. He knew things about the car that hit Bricker that I never saw in the papers. I probably made a mistake. I said he should call the police. He gets all excited and starts yelling no police, no police. And he hangs up."

There was a silence. "So you got his number right? On your phone? Where are you?"

"At my office at KI."

"I need that phone," Mason said. He wanted to see how easily Kensington would surrender his phone. He was still suspicious of him. Most people's lives were lived out on their phones nowadays. Maybe he could pick up something on Kensington from his call history.

"Wait right there. I'm coming over to pick up your phone. Just leave it alone, okay?"

"I'm getting important calls. I can't just…"

"You must have people who can redirect your calls. Put it in an envelope and don't answer it. I'm asking you nice. Okay? I'll be there in ten minutes."

"We have an emergency board meeting. I can only give you a few minutes."

Mason held up a hand and the captain gave him a look. "I've got something. I'll be back in 20 minutes."

Today Kensington was wearing a good-looking suit, the first time Mason had seen him so formally attired. So Kensington Industries was working on the holiday weekend as well. Mason gloved up and took the phone from a manila envelope. Kensington sat down behind his desk, taking control of the room.

"So what did he say?" Mason said.

"He said he didn't want any dealings with the police. He wanted to meet me on his own. I told him I had nothing to do with the reward money. The police were handling everything."

"Then what?"

"I told him he was crazy if he thought I would meet him somewhere on my own. He hung up. The conversation was maybe 30 seconds." Mason was already punching through the menu with gloved hands.

"Thanks a lot. I'll be in touch." Mason got up and headed for the door without saying goodbye. Kensington didn't want to talk about Ginger, and neither did he.

Mason stood a moment outside in the fresh sunshine, thinking. He got back to the station and the conference room as quickly as he could. The meeting had broken up and Delgado was back at his desk. He told Delgado what was going on. "The number connects to a pay phone in front of Target out in Hemet."

"Hemet? That pretty much bites the moose. Good luck getting anything off a phone booth."

"What if he made more than the one call to Kensington though? Maybe if he used a public phone he might have called somebody else next to let them know how it had gone. Or maybe beforehand, you know, like working up his courage?"

"Well, maybe. Sounds like a long shot," Delgado said dubiously.

"It worked for me once before." Mason's face brightened with optimism. "You remember that case where somebody threw an axe in the window of Callahan's restaurant?" Mason shrugged, hearing himself talk. "I know. I know. We're not going to get much in the way of eyewitnesses at a Target pay phone. Give it a try though," Mason said. He went about his business, trying to keep his mind away from thoughts of Ginger.

A stack of Santa Monica dailies piled in front of the mailboxes in the Special Operations office screeched loud headlines. "Prominent Private High School Center of Controversy."

A lightning strike of pain arced through Mason's jaw, causing him to slap a hand against his cheek and groan. He put his finger to his jaw and pressed hard to hold the toothache in.

34

Rhys showed up at her door mid-morning on Labor Day, surprising Ginger. Her Dad had gone back home, and she was doing her best to put the bad experience behind her. Today her plan was to reconnect with the victim's support group, and practice the PTSD techniques the counselor had taught her. She had worked too hard to tip back into the fears and black despair of acute PTSD. Without much enthusiasm, she let Rhys in, her arms crossed, preventing him from hugging her. He looked haggard and worn.

"Quiet. There's a teaser coming up on KTLA." She turned the sound up on the TV as Jason Peabody and his lawyer wife flashed on screen. They were representing the school's parents, and demanding to speak to the headmistress, who could not be found. A PR representative Ginger vaguely recognized was standing in front of the doors of the school trying to smooth everything over. When the clip ended, Ginger turned the sound down.

"So you already know that Venetia's gone?" she said, pointing to her open laptop. "It's all over social media and the school's Facebook page."

"Now what?" Rhys said, his face white. "That looks like a press encampment outside the school."

"You better get over there then." Ginger didn't want him there. Not now. He just required too much and she had nothing right now to give.

"You're not worried something's happened to Venetia?" he said, following her into the bedroom.

"That woman is venomous. She'll take care of herself, Rhys."

"There's no money to run off with if that's what you're thinking," he said.

"Hey, Doris and the $872? What if Venetia's dead too? What about that?" Ginger turned to face him.

"Well, if she's such a dangerous person, who killed her? This is terrible for the Kensington image," Rhys said, leaning forward and then back to stretch his back, which was a long-term problem. "It will take the school years to recover from this."

"It might be real terrible for Venetia too, though I don't really care. Rhys, your PR people need you there to put a good face on things. You want to be available for the cops too, or they'll come and get you and I don't think you'd like that."

"And I keep calling Caroline. I wish she'd step up. I need her to be there too." His voice took on a complaining note that irritated her.

"Caroline's got her strengths, but putting lipstick on this particular pig still isn't going to make it fly."

Rhys followed her into the bedroom, watching as she threw off her robe and drew a skirt and blouse from the closet. The room was small; the window looked out into the parking lot of the building next door. From the apartment overhead footsteps went back and forth, then came a blast of music. They both looked at the ceiling. The metalhead music went on.

Rhys seemed vague and distracted. "Those are new," he commented, pointing to a set of bedside lamps. "Where did you get them?"

"Salvation Army," she said, tucking in her blouse. The waistband of her skirt was as loose as it ever got. "It's the best thrift shop in the city."

"You don't have to buy things at the Salvation Army," he said, smiling. "You know that. Let me take you shopping."

"I like buying my own stuff, Rhys, even if it's with your paycheck," Ginger said over her shoulder. "It's amazing what the rich people of Santa Monica throw out."

He sat down heavily on the unmade bed and leaned back on his elbows. "I told Mason about a phone call I got from somebody who swore he knew something about Leonard's death. I couldn't tell if it was important or not. He doesn't give much away, does he?"

Ginger grinned at him. "Nope."

"He was very unforthcoming."

"Unforthcoming. That certainly describes Mason."

Rhys got up and followed her out to the kitchen. She poured him a cup of coffee and sat down opposite him at her small kitchen table.

"I think everything's going to work out in the end," he said hopefully. He played with the paper napkin next to his cup.

"What are you going to do about the school if Venetia has really and truly taken off? Would you send your kid there at this point?" she said, eyebrows raised.

"What about our kids, Ginger? Are we going to have kids?"

Ginger jumped up and touched him on the shoulder. "I wouldn't worry about Venetia. She'll land on her feet. People like Venetia always do." Ginger couldn't help herself.

Before Rhys could return to the subject of *their* children, Ginger walked him to the door. He was still talking when she grabbed up her stuff and walked out with him. He followed her to her parking space in back, talking.

"When am I going to see you again?" he said, as she slid into her old Audi and hoped it would start.

"Hey, I'm gonna be late to see my therapist," she lied. She did have a therapy appointment but first there was a networking lunch with a group of event planners and fundraisers. Like lots of people in this economy, she had no savings to speak of and the Audi had a burning smell when she shut it off. Her father said it was too soon for her to go out, but she argued she had to find another job and the walls of her apartment were closing in.

The temptation was to just abandon the struggle to hop from one contract job to the next. The ultimate goal was to get a permanent job that paid benefits. There must be a job like that somewhere.

She could marry Rhys instead, and never have to think about money ever again.

Ever again.

Venetia held her breath and kept the smile on her face breezy and confident. She knew this guy at the bank and had once offered him a roll in the hay to keep him happy. Then she'd had to console him because he couldn't get it up. What a waste of time that was.

However, he did keep her happy in other ways from time to time when she needed a banker who would look the other way.

Like now.

Mason presented himself to the dentist at the end of the day. He'd sooner make a felony pick up alone on a crack house at midnight than go to the dentist but the pain was becoming unbearable. Until he'd walked in the door his mind had buzzed with the high-octane fizz of all the incoming reports from the Task Force and his team's search for Sorensen. The instant he caught a whiff of the smell and heard a high-speed drill, his tooth immediately stopped aching. The receptionist greeted him as if his visit were some ordinary occasion. Mason perched on the edge of a chair in an agony of dread, waiting to be called in. The lights went out and all the machines in the office went silent. The receptionist looked up from her barrier behind the counter and smiled at him.

"That's funny," she said.

Nothing looked funny to Mason at this moment. She came out from behind the counter to check offices down the hall. No electricity anywhere in the building. Another patient came in and took a seat opposite Mason, who was sitting on his hands, trying not to rub his jaw.

"Lights out all over the city apparently," the man said. There was just enough light from the windows. He picked up a magazine and began to read.

The receptionist returned, made a call and consulted with the dentists. She came back to announce to the waiting room that the power would be out for some hours. Wearing a look of concern, a dental assistant in a white coat emerged from the back office to tell him that appointments were cancelled for the rest of the day. Immediately Mason's tooth amped up the pain quotient, and he couldn't decide if he was grateful for some power company fuck up, or worried that the tooth was going to explode. The scab on his lip had finally dried up and fallen off. Squad room know-it-alls had kept it going with sly remarks and innuendos that soon became fact. Fredericks had said nothing. The dentist gave him a prescription that he filled on the way home. He had to get some sleep or he'd go stupid. He wondered if he could ask the dentist for general anesthetic while he worked on the tooth.

Delgado called just as Mason was walking in his door, ready to zone out in front of ESPN with his friend Jack Daniels.

"Let's go. I got our auto body guy out in Hemet. Pick you up in ten minutes. Captain says follow this lead while it's hot. We need to establish all the links we can get to Yurkov."

Mason was suddenly awake. Delgado pulled up in front of his condo on San Vicente and honked. Mason got in the vehicle.

"Do you know I sat in the goddamn dentist's waiting room for three-quarters of an hour and then the lights go out and his appointments are cancelled the rest of the day. Can you believe that?"

"Yeah. I hear you. You want to know what I got, or you want to bitch about the dentist?"

"Gimme a minute to decide." That got a smile from Delgado. "Okay, tell me."

"I'll spare you every step of my brilliant detective mind then."

"Yeah, yeah. Watch that guy on the bicycle."

"Settle down, Mason. I'm checking the phone records on the pay phone in front of Target, right? Call before the one our reward seeker makes is to a beauty shop. But the next call is the one we want. Turns out our caller gets somebody on the line who has an illegal body shop, which makes me real interested. I got Deputy Bailey, remember him?" Delgado took his eyes off the road to grin at Mason. "He does a drive by for me and sees the call went to a little auto body repair shop going in this guy's back yard. Bailey knows him already. I told him to leave it alone and we'd be out there. I figure the drive's worth it."

"You figure it's worth it at 5:30, everybody in the world driving home to the Inland Empire?" Mason said.

"Why don't you just get yourself some sleep on the way out there? You wore yourself out at the dentist's office."

"And I still gotta go back," Mason said miserably.

"This is our big break in the case. I just gotta whiff of it. This is it."

"This might also be a waste of time," Mason complained. Maybe his tooth was infected. He felt plain sick as well as tired, but the dentist had given him good painkillers, so he slept the entire way to Hemet.

35

The Riverside County Sheriff's database put the phone number in the name of Raymundo Gallego, with an address in one of the older, poorer parts of Hemet.

Deputy Bailey snorted. "Gallego. I can give you very good intel on Gallego because he's on a short leash with me and he can't afford to jack me around. If he pisses me off, I'll have his probation officer violate him on a burglary beef. He'll go straight to the slammer and pull a dime." He pounded a fist into his other hand and yanked his Kevlar vest down over his gut. He was ready to go. "Man, I love these pickups when I've had my eye on a guy for a while."

In the low-rent area of the city, small stucco homes were surrounded by fences. The Gallego house needed a paint job and had a weathered board fence and an alley in the back. Teenagers slouched along the alley, exchanging gang signs. A few little kids chased each other. Bailey was going to let them play this because if they got Gallego as an accomplice in a murder rap, that would take priority.

Mason knocked on the front door, hearing a television blaring inside. A dog that sounded like he had big teeth was snarling and barking from behind the door.

They knocked again, giving the rap of authority. "Police. Open up."

"Don't hurt him. Don't hurt him." A kid's voice came from inside over the barking.

"I'm gonna kill that fucker if he doesn't quit the goddamn barking."

The dog yelped and went quiet. The door opened on a short, business-like chain. If this was Gallego, he was wearing the longest mullet Mason had seen since the 1980s. Buzz cut on top and long on the sides and at the back. Greasy too. Just the way women liked it. Alcohol fumes rose off him like heat shimmers off a burner on the stove.

"What?"

Mason introduced himself and Delgado. Gallego looked at Delgado.

"Habla español?"

"We both do." This was a lie. Mason could catch every ninth word—maybe. And he didn't catch all the negatives, so sometimes he had the meaning completely reversed. But he didn't want Gallego thinking Delgado was the only one he had to play.

"Hi, there, asswipe," Bailey snarled at him from behind Mason and Delgado.

Mason stepped in front of him. "We'd like to come in and talk. Just talk."

"You got a warrant?" A kid about ten years old, already with the banger look, stood at his side holding back the pit bull by its pinch collar. The dog wanted to eat somebody.

"Now, what would we need a warrant for? We just wanna talk to you, man. Santa Monica cops. You jaywalked in Santa Monica? Maybe it's about that."

Delgado stepped forward and he and Gallego did the dance for a while. Finally the door was opened enough to let them in. Gallego snarled at Bailey and Bailey snarled back.

The dog gave a strangled growl and lunged at Mason as he passed. The kid hung onto him, but barely. Mason turned uneasily to watch the dog over his shoulder.

They went into a living room that smelled of nicotine and bacon grease and had a huge bath towel with the image of the *Virgen de Guadalupe* hanging on the wall. They weren't invited to sit down. Bailey made a move to go strolling through the house. Anything in plain view was fair game. Gallego started screaming at him in Spanish. Bailey dropped his jaw and made as if he didn't understand.

"Hey, Bailey. Why don't you wait outside?" Delgado said.

Bailey slouched past Gallego, both of them eyefucking each other. They waited until Bailey had gone. Then Delgado began. "You made a call today at the pay phone in front of Target to Mr. Kensington in Santa Monica," Delgado said in English.

He looked astonished. "Well, fuck me." Then he launched into a spirited defense in Spanish and Delgado answered back with just as much animation. The kid grinned. Mason got bored trying to figure out what was going on. Gallego sank back into the purple velour couch. The kid rested his butt on the sofa's arm. The dog continued to strain forward rumbling with a growl now and then. Mason kept his eye on the dog.

Delgado finally translated for Mason. "He admits, yeah, he did some work on a white Toyota Corolla 2003, right front headlight, and when does he get his reward."

"Ask him for his records."

"Records? He don't keep no records he says."

Gallego tapped his forehead. "It's all in here."

Gallego's sudden mastery of English was amazing.

Delgado gave him a long look and said in English, "So how you expect to collect the reward if you can't prove you worked on the car?"

This made a big difference. Suddenly they were up and Gallego was marching them past a 60-inch flat screen TV showing Honey Boo Boo into a back bedroom. The mechanic pawed through some boxes and came up with a yellow invoice form that he shoved at Delgado who put on his glasses and pored over it.

"So what did the owner look like?" Mason said.

Gallego suddenly didn't speak English again. More in Spanish followed which Delgado translated for Mason.

"He says this broad woke him up after he'd been party-ing all night. She was wearing a hoodie with a ball cap and had long brown hair. Not young. Not old."

Sounded like Sorensen, except for the long brown hair. Yatter yatter in Spanish. Mason was furrowing his brow trying to follow it. Delgado turned to him.

"He says she comes in with this story that she hit her neighbor's dog and she feels real bad but there you go. She's not in a big hurry to get it fixed so he takes $500 cash from her and tells her to come back."

"When did this happen?" They watched as Gallego went to a little fridge on the floor and brought out one Dos XX for himself.

"He was hung over. His wife left him. If she was here she'd remember."

The kid butted in at that point. He remembered the date his mother left and it squared with the night Bricker was killed. The old man grabbed the kid around the neck and gave him a hard noogie on his shaved head. The kid yelped. The dog growled. The guy smiled.

"Just like his old man," he said to Mason in perfect unaccented English. "She gets me to call her a taxi and she's gone. Tells me she's moving so she don't got a phone number but she'll call me. I say okay and..."

"What's she look like?"

"She's a tall one, skinny, bossy."

Mason and Delgado looked at each other. Delgado whipped out a set of photos taken from the Windsor

Academy website and several other women who looked like her.

Gallego pointed straight at Sorensen.

Mason grinned in triumph. They had the link between Sorensen and the car that killed Bricker. Now to prove she was driving it. He knew the devious logic of defense attorneys.

Just then the dog got loose and attacked Mason who leaped back behind a chair. There was now a Chihuahua's yapping to add to the din.

The kid flung himself over the dog, pleading with Mason. "Don't shoot her. Don't shoot her. She's got puppies. Thass' why she scared."

In the melee Gallego ran. Mason chased. He ran him down in the backyard as he tried to scale the fence, hampered by his T-shirt that caught on the top boards. Mason fell on him, panting, cuffed him up and dragged him back in the house. Delgado said, "Thanks, man. I can't run like I use to."

"No kidding. Not with that belly hanging over your belt."

"Yeah, yeah. You and the wife."

He hauled Gallego in and flung him down in a kitchen chair while he caught his breath.

Using all his strength, the kid dragged the dog back into the TV room where Honey Boo Boo's mama grinned her shrewd, toothless grin.

"Why'd you run, man? Just makes it harder for you. We just want to talk," Delgado said. It went on for a while.

The guy would only speak to Delgado in Spanish, who translated for Mason. He thought we were here on an old drug warrant, Delgado explained.

"He saw the story about the Bricker hit-and-run by a white Corolla on local news, even way out there, and the announcement of the reward. So he was already looking forward to getting an address on her when she picked up the car. Then he was going to track her down and put the bite on her too. Like threaten her. He figured he couldn't lose. Either way."

"Yeah, and..."

"She never show up again. This time it was a kid, some *gabacho* who gave him the other $600 in cash and drove the car off."

"And you just let this guy go along with the chance of collecting the reward. I don't think so." Mason addressed this directly to Gallego who gave a shrug.

"Thass' the way it happen, man."

"I don't get something better than that out of you and you and me are gonna take it down to the station."

"Hey, I can't leave my kid here alone. He's justa kid. This is a bad neighborhood."

"You helped make it that way. So what really happened here? Siddown. The kid came back with the money. Then what?"

"He's got a certified check but I don't want to take. A check. You think I crazy, man? I don't take no checks."

Delgado didn't want to go into it. "So what happens then?"

"The kid, he goes, he don't know nothing. I'm not gonna give him the car. I scare him with the dog a little, but I can tell he don't know nothing. So I tell him to go back to the lady. Tell her I had problems and need to do more work. She needs to pay me more. In cash. I tell him to get her in touch with me."

He eased back onto a purple velour couch that had bald spots where the plush had worn thin. "Sit down, why doncha? C'mon."

Reluctantly Mason took a seat across from him on a chair covered with dog hair. The kid leaned up against the sofa arm next to his father and picked his nose. The dog held his eyes on Mason. Whenever Mason looked at her, she drew back her lips over two-inch-long teeth and menace rumbled deep in her chest. Fuck you, dog. I win. I got a gun. It had become personal between them.

"I never did nothing wrong. That's all that happened."

The dog made a move toward Mason. Mason jumped. "You get hold of that dog. I'm telling you." He didn't like to admit to anybody he had become scared of dogs after one of them bit him on the calf.

Delgado regarded Mason, shook his head and said, "Sorry about my partner here. He gets crazy. One brutality charge after another. He goes off all of a sudden, you know."

The guy gave Mason a look of increased respect and Mason got up, crossing his arms, giving Gallego the wide-legged authoritarian stance.

"Yeah, so where's the car?" he said.

"Maybe I sold it," Gallego said, his eyes crinkling shut.

"So which is it? You got it, or you don't got it?"

"Hey, where's my reward? I know where I sold it. That's just as good, and I'm keeping an eye on it."

"I don't know. You've been doing a lot of illegal stuff here." Delgado had spotted the roaches in the ash tray. That might be enough to bring him in on a drug violation.

"You wanna see the car? I still got it. Anyway, I got my sources too, ways to get paper. I got a cousin works at DMV. I got the lady's number off the VIN thru a contact at DMV and called her up to have a little talk with her. She's smart enough to give a false name and address when she buys the car, but not so smart that my cousin doesn't find her. She's got other cars registered too. If she just had the one car under her name I wouldn't find her, but she's not as smart as my *prima*. I got her name. Venetia Sorensen."

Mason's heart leaped. The aha moment. "So you call her up. Then what?"

"She freak. That's what she does. She freak."

Delgado and Bailey looked at each other. They'd almost forgotten Bailey who had come in the back door. He'd been quietly ambling around the house. He brought back a crack pipe he'd found and wiggled it in front of Gallego.

"Hey, man. Plain sight. I gotta use the toilet. It's right there. Plain sight."

After the screaming died down, Gallego was ready to talk again, but this time it was going to be on video at the station. Gallego's sister lived next door, so they had a place to leave the kid. They got the rest of the story standing in the driveway. Delgado translated.

"She told him she'd match the reward but it would take time. So he calls Kensington to find out how much the reward is. It says $100,000 but this lady, she says she'll give him $150,000. But he doesn't trust her."

"So maybe somebody actually did go by her house and scare her. It was this guy."

"He swears he didn't though." Delgado insisted.

"Ah, you believe him?"

"Some of it. Maybe. Who knows? We can get phone records on Sorensen now."

"Let's book him for the weekend. Just so we can keep an eye on him."

"On what?"

Mason was impatient now. "Fixing cars without a license. Not cleaning up his house. Scary dog. C'mon. Let's go."

"There's always attempted blackmail," Delgado said, checking his email.

Bailey was still running his mouth, making everything worse. Mason snapped cuffs on Gallego and patted him down. Gallego's baggies hung down his ass. Mason yanked them up.

Gallego refused to get in Bailey's vehicle. "I'm not getting in his car, man. That guy, Bailey, he…"

The shouting had drawn the whole neighborhood to watch Bailey and Gallego sling shit at each other. Bailey's pals on patrol had filled the street with vehicles strobing red and blue lights like a carnival. The kid came out on his aunt's porch with the dog, who began barking his head off, dragging the kid almost the length of the drive way to bare his teeth at Mason.

Gallego warned them he was going to puke but nobody believed him until he threw up beery chimichanga vomit all over Mason's shoes and pant legs. Before he could stop himself, Mason cuffed him on the shoulder for ruining his new Balas. You could never get vomit out of leather.

"Ah, Jesus, Mason," Delgado barked, seeing this. "Why'd you do that?"

"You see my shoes?" Some neighbor was sure to have caught that move on his cellphone. Mason could already hear the screaming. Police abuse.

"Don't put him in my car," Bailey objected. "He's a puker."

Gallego's sister from next door rushed out to throw a towel at her brother to wipe off his T-shirt and pants. Bailey thought she was attacking him and wheeled on her with a shout of alarm. Mason grabbed the towel and wiped vomit off his pants legs and shoes before wiping the mess off Gallego. Now what to do with the little fucker?

"We don't want him in our vehicle," both Delgado and Mason protested. They stood there arguing in front of the whole jeering neighborhood until Bailey got a roll of black plastic garbage bags out of his trunk and made a poncho over Gallego with his head sticking through. Gallego was grinning and by now Mason knew they were on camera somewhere.

"If you guys want this bust, you take him in your car." Bailey drove off laughing. "Meet you at the station."

Delgado covered the back seat with plastic and shoved Gallego in. Both he and Mason got in the car. The kid released the pit bull who charged the car, ready to bite the windshield wipers and mirrors off.

Mason drove. Delgado was on his cell phone back to the Sarge. Gallego stunk. The whole car stunk.

"We're going to have to drive all the way back to Santa Monica smelling this," Delgado growled.

"I'm gonna throw up again," Gallego warned. He was squirming around in the back seat making gagging noise. Mason and Delgado exchanged a look. Several other sheriff's units pulled in behind.

"What's wrong with you, man?" Delgado bellowed at Gallego, trying to get a garbage bag unrolled and fashion a makeshift basin in front of him.

"I got a nervous stomach."

Mason jammed on the brakes. "Get him out of here."

Bailey screeched to a stop behind them. The whole convoy of sheriff's vehicles stopped in a row, lights strobing overhead.

Delgado jumped out of the car, opened the back door and dragged Gallego out onto the sidewalk down the street under a streetlight. Little kids had followed them on bicycles. Mason half expected Gallego to make a run for it, hands cuffed behind his back, his baggies around his ankles.

But he didn't. Instead he grinned at them, "Gotchu, man. Gotchu good."

Bailey had already called his Sarge to make sure his department got in on the bust. He wanted to see his name in the reports, his collar. They overheard him bragging about his role swaggering around in the squad room as they brought Gallego in. The pissing contest had begun. It was time to haul out their heavy artillery, get him back to Santa Monica and catch up with what was going on with the carjacking Task Force.

Delgado made notes while Mason drove, Gallego sleeping in the back of the car, waves of stink rising off him, the windows open. Mason relished what the arrest of the headmistress of Windsor Academy would mean to Rhys Kensington, and grinned.

The tasks lay lined up in Mason's head. Pull Sorensen in: get hold of the Corolla that hit Bricker and link her to his death; make sure Gallego's ID would stick. Run forensics out to Hemet to go over Gallego's work area to match trace to Sorensen's vehicle, if they could find any. And they might find something to link her to Arnold's death. He wanted to arrest her arrogant sneer and parade her through town all cuffed up in the back of a police car.

The Sarge finally seemed pleased with Mason. "What's Gallego got on his sheet? What kind of witness is he going to make?"

Not a good one, Mason admitted. "But better than the two eye witnesses."

Sgt. York snorted when he heard that one. "Pick her up tomorrow morning."

36

It was 3 a.m. before they got the paperwork done on Gallego. By 7 a.m. Mason and Delgado were knocking on the front door of Sorensen's house. No answer.

Mason walked around the house and looked in the window of the garage. He came back to tell Delgado, "Her car's gone."

Delgado pounded his fist on the door. He checked the paperwork first, then popped the locks and they made a search of the place. From the turmoil in her bedroom it looked as if Sorensen had packed in a hurry and blown.

The parrot had been left outside on the back deck to scream at the neighbors.

"What are we going to do with this thing?" Delgado muttered, looking at the bird who regarded them with a fierce, daring scowl. He kept well away from its long beak.

"Call Animal Control. Thought she loved this thing. And she just left it? Whew, that's cold."

Mason tried to explain to Sgt. York, knowing he and Delgado looked inept at losing Sorensen.

"Why didn't you put a watch on her?" he demanded.

He couldn't say I tried and you said you didn't want to put resources on her. Don't you remember that? You turned me down. He shrugged and gazed up at the ceiling. York just gave him a disgusted look, turned on his heel and left. The L.T. wouldn't even look at Mason. The captain was handing out assignments at the end of the Task Force meeting.

"Mason? You and Delgado see if you can bring in Sorensen this time." Mason sat back, ignoring the others as they filed out.

Palmer looked triumphant as he got up from across the table. Ever the competitor. "Sorry you're missing the action, Mason?"

Mason shrugged and Palmer breezed out, whistling. He couldn't decide if he was sorry not to be in on the Yurkov bust or not. He thought of the hugely pregnant woman he'd seen at the bar standing beside Vlad Yurkov. What would happen to her and her baby? Was she in it up to her belly too?

He'd miss the takedown though. That kind of excitement didn't come around all that often. Their tie-in to Sorensen was probably marginal to the Task Force in the long run anyway. But he had personal reasons—Ginger—to enjoy pulling Sorensen in. They proceeded with the search of the Windsor Academy, starting with Sorensen's computer, looking for her and nailing the case down tight against her. Delgado began going through her files, his big body filling her executive chair. Uniforms were removing hanging files from the cabinets that lined the back of her office. They couldn't get rid of Rhys Kensington, who insisted on being there. He leaned back against Sorensen's trophy case, taking one low-voiced call after another on his phone.

"When was the last time anybody saw her?" Mason asked Kensington in a rough voice. Kensington finished the call.

"The last I saw of her was Sunday when you and your partner hauled her down to the station," Rhys said, taking off his jacket and flinging it on the black leather couch.

"Where do you think she's gone?"

"I don't know that much about her personal life," he said, ignoring Delgado hunched over Sorensen's computer. He yanked the cord on the wooden blinds to check the street for media vans.

"I thought she was somebody important to you. You've told me before her father was a central figure in your life and your sister's."

"Yes, he was, but we weren't friends with Venetia," Rhys shrugged. "We don't get together socially. She wasn't so likeable you wanted to spend time with her."

Mason turned on his heel and headed into the bathroom in the Administration. Armando, the cleaner, was already in there with his pail and mop, and Mason was about to back out and use the bathroom in another cottage when the old man reached out to grab him by the arm.

Mason reacted automatically in the way that had been drilled into him in the hundreds of hours he'd spent training with krav maga.

"Wait, wait," the cleaner whispered. "I just want to tell you something."

Mason took a close look at the old man's face. "Oh, sorry, sorry, you caught me by surprise."

"I've wanted to tell you something. The Missus she was good to me when I got out of prison. She gave me this job. So I keep my mouth shut about things. But then so many bad things started happening here. I don't like that. I just want things quiet. No trouble. Right? No trouble."

"Right. I got it." Mason skidded the pail over by the door and went back to lean against the sink. "I've got no reason to think you're involved in any of this. What have you got to tell me?"

"She goes to this place up there by the Grapevine."

"Yeah?"

"I put up some shelves for her a couple of Saturdays and she never paid me. It was all part of my job, she said. That woman, she was mean, had a mean mouth on her with people that didn't matter to her. She thinks I'm deaf or something the way she talks. Oh, nothin' that's gonna help you. Things about people that don't need repeatin'. Things about the students and the teachers."

"Anything in particular?" Mason just wanted to pee and get out of there because things were happening fast. He was waiting for Fredericks to report back from Homeland Security to see if Sorensen had been able to break past all the barriers there were nowadays and board a plane out of the country.

"She's not coming back, is she? I heard talk about those boxes in the Electrical Panel room where that nice Ms. McNair got locked in. You know where I mean?"

"I sure do." Mason was suddenly riveted.

"Dr. Sorensen told me to take those boxes out and put them in her car. Boxes and boxes of stuff. Said she'd take care of them."

"When was that?"

"Last week?" He thought. "Wednesday maybe. The whole electrical room was full of them. I could only get half of them. She yelled at me for not moving them all out but I can only do so much, can I?"

"So you're telling me they're gone?"

"The ones she was so concerned to get moved I put over in the storage bin that Doris had on 26th Street near the freeway. I figure knowing her, she was up to something. I thought you should know. Here's the key."

Mason grinned and clapped him on the shoulder. "You have made my day!"

Ginger had discovered as she was driving to the networking lunch at Lulu's that she wasn't as together as she thought she was. She froze at a stop light, with horns honking behind her. A wave of panic made her breath catch in her throat. Sudden heart beat acceleration. The windshield glass shimmered, waving in and out. She couldn't breathe. Seeing some guy get out of his Hummer behind her and marching toward her car in a rage, she jerked the wheel right on Ocean Avenue instead of left to drive to Ocean Park. She drove on autopilot to the end of Ocean Avenue, white noise sound swooping around her. Making an illegal turn, she parked in the red in front of a stone wall at the end of Palisades Park. Hands clenched on the steering wheel, she was finally able to breathe. Breathe. Just breathe. Knowing that it will pass.

And it did. She pulled the car forward into a parking place, locked it, and got out of the car to walk over and perch on the stone wall looking up San Vicente Boulevard. Joggers pounded up and down the grassy median lined with coral trees. Slowly she gathered strength in the sunshine and birdsong of the park, resting in the smell of cut grass and quiet. For the moment, the future and all its responsibilities did not exist.

Then her phone rang. She looked down and thought about not answering. It was the third message from Mason. What now?

"I need your written statement, Ginger, and I've got a few more questions. Some new developments. Where are you?"

"Um, can we talk later?"

"Your voice sounds funny. You okay?"

"I'm trying to be." She tried a laugh. "I'm just sitting here trying to pull myself together. This is as good a time to talk as any, I suppose." She told him where to find her. He must have been close by because in minutes he was there. She watched him park and walk towards her.

Trustworthy. Married to the job.

A good father. Wanted more kids.

Dangerous job. His addiction to adrenaline. His mission.

All the old problems flooded back. The problems that never seemed to have any solutions.

And there was Rhys. Any woman who said money didn't matter was either a fool or very, very young.

"What's happened?" she said. "I'm not working at the Academy any longer, you know."

"Hunh. You okay with that?" He studied her.

"I'll find something else. I always do." The prospect of job hunting made her pleasure in the moment darken a little.

"I heard that job in Community Relations with the City has opened up again."

"They've danced me around once before. I can coast for a while."

"Sorensen's taken off. You know anything about that?"

She couldn't look at him. "You know up at the top of the Grapevine? You know the turn off there to go to Mt. Pinos? All the astronomers go up there. You know?"

"Sure, I know the area." The Grapevine was the narrow pass on Interstate-5 that cut through the mountains connecting Central to Southern California. The mountains ringed California's flat Central Valley, the breadbasket and vineyard of the nation. Santa Monica PD had a previous case that took them there to liaise with the sheriff's substation.

"Venetia did a lot of hiking in the mountains," she said. "Are you looking for her there? I don't see her hiding out in a tent somewhere in the wilderness, hardly. She'd have to have some sort of comfortable hidey-hole with electricity and running water and Internet. Maybe you should try through her ISP account."

"We've got people on that, Ginger. We're pros at this, remember?"

"I know. I know. But you asked if there was anything." She looked away again.

"You think she had some friends she could hide out with?" he said.

"Friends? Venetia? I think she cultivated people who could be useful to her. Caroline told me once she liked bad boys. And once I saw her all over some guy, and I saw her with the same guy once before in her office."

"Yeah, we know him."

"Oh. Good. Venetia needs big stimulation to feel alive. Big risks. Drama all the time. Real sociopath stuff. So are you looking for her up in the mountains?"

"You know I can't tell you something like that," he said smiling and leaning closer to her.

"Oh, for God's sake, Mason. If she's gone, she's probably gone for good." She explained about the ring that had never made it onto the table to be bid on in the Silent Auction, even though it wasn't much in the way of proof of anything. She told him about the copies of checks she'd found paid to a landscaping service to pay for all that lush, well-watered beauty around her house. "She's not coming back."

Mason's gaze was far-off down the street. He nodded, but she didn't feel she'd added anything he didn't know. "Looks like Kensington Industries are getting ready to sell the property the school is on," he said, to test her reaction. "One of our guys picked it up digging on a commercial real estate site. The Kensingtons will be sitting pretty if that goes through. Did you know that?

"Really?" Ginger said, sitting back. "What about the school?"

"Lotta property around there changing hands with the light rail stop coming so close. The subway…"

"Nobody told me anything about that."

"The Kensingtons are going to take care of themselves first, Ginger."

"What do you mean?"

"There's too much money changing hands to ignore. It's not just the school."

"Then what?"

He shrugged. "I think there's a lot Kensington's not telling you. I heard on the radio that the school is closed until further notice. I gotta get back."

She'd already concluded Rhys knew more than he was telling. She tilted her head and looked up at him. "Venetia wanted things so badly it was a sickness in her. She was pea-green jealous of anybody who had money. Everything she did she had to swank around and get a lot of attention. You ever notice her jewelry? I certainly did."

"Yeah, I did, but I'm fooled by anything that glitters." He grinned. "We're going to get her," he said confidently. He put a hand on her shoulder and fluffed her hair, drawing the blond curls through his fingers. "I miss you, Ginger."

"Even at my worst? I was pretty hard on you."

"Even then. I'm no prize either. I get crazy sometimes."

He stood a foot away from her, radiating heat. He looked tired, his face tight with fatigue. She ran her hands hard over her cheeks into her hair and scratched her forehead hard, squinching up her entire face to harden herself against him.

"I can't, Dave. I just can't. I just can't think about that."

"Oh, well." He hummed something that almost sounded like the old Beatles song, *You Say Goodbye. I say Hello.* Mason was a terrible, terrible singer.

He walked away to his vehicle, waving at her over his shoulder, feeling as though a switch had been flicked releasing a flood of endorphins. There might be hope. Ginger sat back, thinking. Then she called Rhys to check out the rumor that the land was up for sale, feeling only a dull curiosity at this point. This was the reason why closing the school didn't matter? Rhys was in an emergency Kensington Industries board meeting. She sat awhile longer until the sun got too hot. Then she went home and turned her phone off.

37

"Why haven't you found that woman? I want her found so we can file charges and see her punished." Craig Knight was no longer the cool CEO of Kensington Industries when they got him pinned in his office, the treadmill desk forgotten. He started off full of brash anger, then all of a sudden the air leaked out of him. He slumped in a chair, looking grey and ashy. His face was tense, prepared.

"I've got too much going on to deal with this."

"What?" Mason said. "You called me here. Why?"

The place was buzzing with lawyers and accountants. With two lawyers in attendance and the meeting recorded, Knight informed them that in the process of preparations to dismantle the Academy, they'd discovered the capital reserve account had been emptied. Three and a half million dollars was gone, along with the account that held the year's fully paid up tuition. He paced around the office, slamming his hand on the furniture.

"Apparently Doug Paget and Sorensen transferred the funds from the capital reserve to an anonymous account in the Caymans. It's all gone," he said bleakly.

"You're just finding out now?" Mason said. *So that was why she ran.*

"This is one of many problems we're dealing with," he admitted.

Seeing no sympathy from either Mason or Delgado, Knight stumbled on, telling them about a hidden account.

"She and Paget set up a foundation called the Kensington Family Foundation over which she and Doug had signature authority. Looks like they siphoned off the capital reserve account to the foundation account then wire transferred it on to a numbered account in the Caymans."

"I thought that old dodge had been stopped," Delgado said.

"Some of the banks have just gotten smarter. Look, there's some people here who explain it better than I do." He brought in two pretty accountants to explain the way they had covered their tracks, while he paced the office, jiggling the change in his pockets and flossing his teeth. Some tension displacement.

Knight pleaded, "Can you keep the lid on this? Just for a day or so. Our PR people have their hands full. They're just asking us for a day to get organized. I mean, we have investors. We want to disclose this in our own way."

Delgado snorted. "Mr. Knight, you got more to worry about than investors. Everybody who ever went to this school is going to be pissed at you and demanding answers. Our white- collar guys will definitely be in touch. My job's to find Sorensen and nail her to the wall. Which I'll do with great pleasure."

"I thought you had financial controls over this sort of thing," Mason said, closing his notebook and getting up to leave.

"We do, of course we do." Knight said. "Certain negotiations are proceeding, and we don't want to upset the balance of those negotiations."

"What negotiations?"

"I'm not at liberty to say."

"Then I can't help you."

"Did you ever find the night deposit bag with the $27,000?" Knight asked.

"Not yet."

There was a short silence and Knight leapt to his feet and began pacing the office, tearing off a new strip of dental floss. "What she did was crude, no real finesse to it. She got away with it because no one was watching her. I have to admit some responsibility here."

"Yeah, I'm sure somebody's head is gonna roll on this one. Maybe yours," Mason said unsympathetically. Knight's assistant handed Delgado a list of forged checks. There were $200,000 in expenses with no documented Academy purpose, including a personal chef, non-business travel for Sorensen, personal parties, food, wine, and gifts. A memo stated Sorensen had fabricated board meeting minutes to give herself raises, and took charitable deductions on her taxes for donations made using Academy funds.

Mason just shook his head. And nobody noticed?

He knew from Wozinski that things like this happened, mostly in nonprofits associated with a good cause; organizations that operated under a high level of trust and good will. Good people simply never imagined this could happen to them. Knight followed them to the door, still pleading for delay of any public announcement.

Doug Paget had disappeared. No sign of him. Mason put out an APB. They called at his home to see if he was hiding under the covers.

On hearing the news he was going to be arrested, Paget's wife had to be sedated. They left Fredericks and another team to chase Paget down and continued the search for Sorensen.

The Task Force bust on the Yurkov operation was suiting up, big grins on all of them. Palmer waved at Mason and Delgado who were passing by the conference room on the way to check in with Sgt. York. The table was piled high with reports, coffee cups, and equipment, the air charged with excitement.

"See you girls later," Palmer called out. "Play nice while we're out having fun." Everybody laughed and they streamed past, gear creaking.

Delgado grunted, next to Mason.

The plodding work of locating Sorensen had to be done. It wasn't a felony bust and pick up of an international criminal operation though, and they both felt sidelined.

Property record checks on Sorensen showed nothing other than the place on 23rd Street she'd inherited from her parents. She could be anywhere now. Wozinski was working with the bank to unravel the wire transfer that went through a series of financial institutions to the bank in the Caymans. They'd left a local banker who admitted he knew Sorensen personally. Wild with anxiety, huddled in his office gobbling tranquilizers.

Mason and Wozinski hit the storage place the janitor had directed them to and found the financial records. On the way over Wozinski clicked his pen and groaned, his own tension displacement tic, and now it didn't even bother Mason. Wozinski chortled with glee as he turned up bills for furnishings, club memberships, golf lessons, fine china, and restaurant and bar tabs.

Paget might have been smart enough to engineer a fraud in collusion with Sorensen, but instead of bolting down a hole somewhere planned in advance and staying gone, he called his wife. That was all it took. The Mercedes pulled out of the garage with a distraught woman at the wheel. A surveillance team on Paget's house followed his wife to a room at the Viceroy, a smart hotel overlooking the beach. Mason and Delgado got the call and prepared the warrant. Fredericks was already there, storming the general manager who just wanted to keep the apprehension quiet. Fredericks turned to greet them.

"Fourth floor, Room 437." Her face was flushed with excitement at a chance to draw her gun. They had prepared for Paget being desperate enough to come out shooting.

Mason knocked on the door. "Room service," he called out.

Paget opened the door and crumpled to his knees when he saw them, guns drawn. His wife sobbed, sitting on the edge of the bed as they read him his rights. Paget wasn't savvy enough to lawyer up. He was scared and sweating, ready to sell out his grandmother to keep the his and her Mercedes and the new swimming pool. Perched on the bed beside his shell-shocked wife, his eyes kept darting around the room as he gulped water. His face twitched spasmodically, moustache bouncing above his lip, the corners of his mouth tightening and releasing.

"Venetia made me sign things. She said none of this would ever come to light."

"She made you sign things." Paget the victim. "And you believed her? A smart man like you?" Mason let his skepticism show. "I would think a guy like you had to be smart."

"No, I was stupid. I admit it. It just started out with so little here and there, and then she had me on the hook. Me and Doris Arnold. They were already sucking money out of the accounts and as long as it wasn't that much—comparatively—I didn't object. I know. I know."

He mopped his face with a handkerchief. "Then Leonard came on as Chair of the Foundation and he started asking questions. He insisted on a new audit firm. I knew if we were audited that would be the end. My life has been horrible for months now. You can't image what I've been through. And then wondering what happened to Leonard, and then Doris." Paget's sweaty face pleaded for understanding.

"Did you kill them?" Mason asked.

"No, no, how can you think that? Surely you can't think I'd do something like that." His denial was feverish.

"Venetia says she had nothing to do with it, but you don't know her. No, no, I don't know anything about that. Honestly." He looked shaky and sweaty, jiggling his leg, the tic under his eye bouncing.

Mason almost smiled. "Why did you do it? I mean you're a guy who had everything." Mason asked.

"Was it sex?" Delgado interrupted. He seemed genuinely curious.

"With Venetia?" A look of horror flew across Paget's face. "God, no."

"Um, it was about our son and the free tuition. He's a junior at the Academy and Venetia made sure he got the grades to get him into the Ivy Leagues." This made his wife cry even harder. He looked over at her and continued, "See, as CFO of Kensington Industries, I could alter the financial reports that Kensington's legal staff and accountants saw. We figured it would take the IRS years to catch us, if they ever did. Just like the FDA, the IRS has had so many budget cuts there's nobody left to sit at a desk and do any work. And there were severance checks and a golden parachute if the school ever did close."

The usual strategy was to separate the conspirators and tell each of them that they would be offered a sweet deal if they'd roll over on the others. Paget had no one to point the finger at other than Venetia. They got him down to the station and made his hysterical wife wait outside the interview room.

"How did Doris Arnold fit in?" Mason yanked his tie off and stuffed it in his pocket. He and Delgado were sitting in the interview room close to Paget with no table between them to interrupt the rapport.

"She and Venetia were in it up to their necks. As long as Doris had two signatures on a check that made it look legit, we could be buying land on the moon. We raked off a share for her and that kept her quiet." His confessional mood changed. "Do you think we could work out some sort of deal?" Paget said. He actually seemed to believe there was still a way out of this.

"Deal? What have you got to trade?" Mason said.

"I can break it all open for you, lead you places you wouldn't think of looking..."

"You think we're dumb cops, do you, sir," Mason said, rising, and giving Paget a grin. "See, that's what keeps us in business and gives me a job and a nice pension. I may not be all that smart about embezzlement, but we've got these guys in the Economic Crimes unit that love people like you."

Wozinski had seen it all before. "See, smart people are often the ones who are victims, like investors who go for get-rich-quick schemes." He had repaired his glasses with a paper clip. "They think the only hustlers they know stand on street corners selling drugs or pimping women. It's called gaming the system. People do it all the time."

The prospect of the job, the cars, the prestige, all sliding away, had pushed Paget to places he couldn't have imagined. Law abiding citizens would hit the crumbling edge where there was no way out. The edge slid under a lifetime of mild, peaceful decency until all that was left for Doug Paget was teeth and claws and panic. Venetia Sorensen was another matter entirely. Mason doubted she'd sob and plead.

"Okay, it's done. I wired you the money. I did it," Venetia said into the throwaway phone. "Where are you? I'm waiting."

She said again, her perfect confidence and self-regard slipping.

"Vlad, where are you?"

38

Mason went to the dentist because he couldn't stand the pain any longer. He shrank low in the chair, eyeing the sharp, pointy steel instruments on a tray next to him. Dr. Ellis looked in Mason's mouth, studied the X-Rays, turned away and sighed. He yanked off his latex gloves, revealing hairy hands. His assistant left the room. Mason interpreted her look as pity, which charged up his anxiety twenty more notches.

"What? What?" Mason said. He sat bolt upright in the reclining chair, clutching the arms. "Is it bad?"

"This has got to be hurting you. Why did you leave it so long? It's too late in the day for me to make a start on this. Let's set up an appointment for you to come in tomorrow."

"How long do you think it will take?"

The dentist studied the X-rays on a computer screen, his back to Mason. "I'm not even sure I want to tackle this," Dr. Ellis said, turning back to look at him. "I'm going to send you over to a friend of mine, a specialist, who'll take care of you. My girl will give you a call when she sets it up."

"It's that bad?" Mason's heart sank even lower. What? He was going to die? He was about to take a sharp stone to his tooth as Tom Hanks had done in *Castaway*.

"Oh, don't worry. It's just a little tricky. I'll give you something for the pain to get you through the night. This has to be taken care of right way. You understand? Don't let this go on. I'll make an emergency appointment for you with him first thing tomorrow morning."

The pain pills worked, but left Mason feeling stupid and slow. He drove back to the station. The pressure was on and the rest of the team was putting in long hours. He thought of calling Ginger who would commiserate with him. She shared his dental phobia. Their last meeting had given him a warm glow of hope. Delgado gave him a look when he came into the station. Fredericks ignored him. She didn't do compassion.

"You get that tooth taken care of?" Delgado barked.

"No, it was too bad. I have to see a specialist in the morning."

"I don't know what you're so scared of. Dentistry doesn't hurt nowadays. Don't give me that glum face. You look like a kicked dog. We still got work to do. Here, you start on Venetia's Sierra Club buddies. Check her alibi for the weekend. See if they can add anything to her whereabouts."

Mason sat down in his chair, probing his sore tooth with his tongue, hating Delgado.

"Get going, Mason," Delgado said over the cubicle wall.

Mason pulled himself together and looked up some phone numbers on the Internet, hike leaders for the Southern California Sierra Club.

One was Maura Josephsen. "Santa Monica Police Department? Yes, of course, I know Venetia," she said in a waspish voice. "What is this about? Why are you calling me?"

"I'm calling you because Ms. Sorensen has not been seen in several days," he lied. "We are trying to locate her."

"It must be more than that. What has she done?"

"We don't know that she's done anything. We just want to talk to her."

"Why on earth would you call me? I wouldn't have her here." Strident Brooklyn accent.

"We were told that she led a lot of Sierra Club hikes and I'm starting with you because you're listed first on the website," Mason explained none too patiently. "She also gave your name as someone who was on the Backbone Trail hike last weekend. Is that correct?"

"She could be anywhere is what you're saying. Is that right?"

"Yes, but we need to start somewhere and she has not been found in the usual places."

"And you won't tell me what's she's done?" she said impatiently.

"We just want to talk to her. Can you confirm she was on the hike that left the Point Magu trailhead at 7:00 a.m. last weekend?"

"Well, I don't like the police and I don't like Venetia either. But yes, she was there. She's a pushy, grabby liar. I'm busy, and I know I don't have to talk to you, so good-bye."

Mason stared at the phone, shaking his head. He thought of calling back and decided to go on to the next number on the list. Apparently Venetia hadn't spread much charm around even in her private life. Whatever charm she had must have been saved for parents and the board of directors.

"Where are all the places you've looked for her?" the co-chair of the hiking committee said in Mason's next call. Butch Runyan was an old retired guy who had worked for the County and liked talking to cops.

"You ever heard she had a man friend?"

"Venetia? No, I always thought she was queer." This was followed by big gusts of male laughter along with a confirmation she had been on the hike. Among guys you could still get away with saying things like that. Mason thought of Fredericks and that drunken night. Ah, Fredericks. She acted as though she'd completely forgotten it. He heard her shouting at somebody on the phone in a cubicle near his.

They reported to Sgt. York, who made it clear that the main action was with the Captain and the Task Force. Mason and his team focused their search on the little towns that led up to Sorensen's favorite hiking trails in the Frazier Mountain Recreation area. Fredericks was dogging any route leading out of the country. She had turned up the school bus driver who remembered dimly that he'd driven by the place where Arnold was found and seen some pushing and shoving around a car parked near the embankment. She was hoping some of the kids on the bus had sharper eyes and a better memory.

Delgado called property managers, working the line that Venetia had a rental. He got hold of a bad-tempered property manager who worked the Frazier Mountain area. Bingo. The rental agreement had been finalized with a certified check and she'd never met Sorensen, but she also took care of a property next door to Sorensen's place. Once she'd gone there to show the place and seen Sorensen getting into a black BMW with a tall, good-looking man. The agent recognized a photo Delgado emailed her. She'd taken a look and identified Yurkov.

Best bet was Venetia would make that her hideaway. Just as Ginger had suggested. Mason and Delgado went after her. They left the city scorching under high temperatures and hit the area late in the evening under a sliver of moon. Lightning flashed across the sky at the summit of the Grapevine before they dropped down several hundred feet to the swerving turn off the interstate.

"Ah, shit," Delgado muttered. He was driving. He hunched down to peer up into the sky. "This feels like rain."

They stopped in at Denny's to kill time while the Sergeant directing the Sheriff's Department substation got his people together. They were in Kern County jurisdiction now. Delgado ploughed into a piggy feast that would leave him in a chemical stupor with enough additives and preservatives to extend life by a decade. Mason couldn't chew anything and mechanically worked his way through a bowl of tomato soup. Around them exhausted-looking truckers waited for a turn at the shower. Family groups bickered over who would take the next turn driving. The waitress who held a coffee pot aloft passed them with a smile.

Mason gazed across the table at Delgado who was still forking up rice and beans and scraps of chimichanga left on the plate.

"I feel sorry for Arnold's sister now. Do you want to be the one to tell her that her sister was a criminal embezzler?" Mason shoved the soup away.

"No, I don't. The church'll probably help her out though," Delgado said. He slouched back in the booth. "I figure Sorensen asks Doris to meet her somewhere nice and dark, no cameras, nobody around, and she takes her down. Fredericks will find witnesses on that school bus yet. So Doris doesn't see it coming. She wraps her in the tarp and stuffs her into the car. Then she waits somewhere dark and drives the car into the beach lot where we pick her up on the cameras."

"What if Yurkov helped her out. All in a day's work for that guy?" Mason took a look at his watch.

"Yeah, right. Prove that." Delgado's face went dark. "Frederick's guy said it was a man."

"Yurkov keeps his hands clean though," Mason said.

"So one of his crew did it as a favor to the boss. Doris may be harder to prove, but we'll get Sorensen on Bricker. We'll squeeze that out of the puker in Hemet."

Mason grinned. "I'm looking forward to that. Wozinski always says it's easy to defraud a nonprofit," Mason observed. "Happens all the time, according to him. The good-hearted civilians who sit on a volunteer board are just grateful to turn the money over to somebody else to manage. And besides, nice people don't think like we do."

"Good thing," Delgado said, grinning and reaching for a toothpick.

"Yeah, but thing is, the board members were executives of Kensington Industries. They weren't good-hearted civilians. How did they get fooled?"

"Take another look," Delgado said, patting his belly. "They're chemists, engineers, things like that."

"Yeah, but…"

"Yeah, but what?"

"It shouldn't be that easy."

"You're telling me it wasn't fair. Is that what you're saying, Mason?" Delgado gave a laugh and grabbed the check.

As they left Denny's, a storm was gathering, a mist of rain in the air. The team assembled a few miles away up the mountain at the sheriff's substation, which was full of noise and talk and uniforms. A Chippie from Highway Patrol was also there. The Sarge running the station only had two guys on patrol at night and he was there himself as a backup. Drinking styrofoam cups of coffee, reading bulletins, everybody was charged up and ready to head out for the bust. A little excitement for these guys who spent a lot of time driving around looking for bears attacking garbage on a usual night. Still, they had their meth and heroin problems too, like every other rural community.

39

M ason made one last call to find out what was happening with the Task Force bust on Yurkov's operation at the port. He could hear the charge in the whispered conversation he had with Wilson, Gomez's partner, and was disappointed again by what he was missing, stuck up here in the ass end of Kern County.

As soon as the cabin had been located, they had a patrol unit on watch parked down the road. The Sarge had pulled the officer off at the end of his shift. He just didn't have the resources to do a stakeout. Curtains were closed. Nothing was going on. She must be alone. Hadn't poked her nose out of the place all day. Her BMW was parked in the dirt driveway. With that intel they drove through a tight corridor of trees, black in the night on each side of the road, a channel of sky above like a river ferrying fallen stars. Pulsating white light suddenly arced across the night sky. Thunder grumbled above, rolling deeply from east to west. A few heavy drops plopped on the dusty roadway.

A stealthy little convoy of vehicles parked down the road, out of sight of the property.

Venetia prowled the one big room of the rental cabin, sneering at the cheap furnishings, picking dog hair off the sofa. Vlad arrived with Yuri Koslov late in the afternoon when she was frantic, the two of them all business. She remembered Koslov's body, the night she watched him administer a beating, then unpeeling his blood-soaked clothes afterward and learning that he dyed his blonde hair black. She wanted to be part of their violent, exciting, thrilling, short life. Koslov grinned at her as he came in. Yurkov's men liked the crazy wildness in Venetia, her insistence on satisfaction, her way.

"What's this?" she said to Vlad, moving away from the back door as they carried in an arsenal of heavy weapons. "You know I hate guns."

Vlad grabbed her face in his heavy hand and twisted it hard, hurting her neck. "Shut up. Make some coffee."

Astonished, she saw the hardness in him, the yellow flare of the wolf flicker in his eyes. She wouldn't give him the pleasure of hitting her in front of Koslov, treating her as if she was a woman like his wife. Her breath came fast as she turned to the kitchen, defiance barely under control. They were speaking Russian when she returned and she stood, arms crossed in the doorway.

Interrupting, she asked, "What happened? I know something happened."

They went on talking to each other. "There is raid tonight happening on my cars at the port," Vlad snapped at her finally. "We are here to pick up what I left here."

"What? What did you leave?"

He snapped a command at Koslov, who looked up, unzipped a duffel bag, and pulled out a pry bar. Yurkov knelt in a corner of the cabin, pulled up the carpet, and yanked up a floorboard. He reached inside and pulled out a metal box and stood, opening it for Vlad so the contents were hidden from Venetia. Koslov brought over an empty duffel bag. He reached in and stuffed more materials into it.

"You got my money? I know it went through." A terrible thought occurred to Venetia. "Do you mean they got the shipment? What about my money?" she said, narrow-eyed and unconvinced.

Venetia grabbed Vlad by the arm. Without a second of hesitation he backhanded her. Hard. She reeled in surprise and fell against the wall.

Koslov hefted the heavy duffel bag and hit the door.

"What about me?" Venetia insisted, pulling herself up.

"I call you."

"No, you won't. I'm coming with you."

"You stay here."

"I won't stay here. You're not leaving me here. I want my money."

※

"Here we go," Delgado mumbled as he heaved his bulky body from under the seat belt and slid out of the car. Crickets chirping and the skitter of small creatures in the roadside chaparral accompanied their careful crunching down the unlighted road. No streetlights up here. A line of junipers along the property line was lit by solar lights, which cast a pale glow.

The cabin was lit up, a shadow passing in front of the curtains.

The door opened onto a narrow front deck, showing Sorensen's narrow silhouette. Two men in dark clothes pushed past her. A muttered expletive.

Mason whispered to Delgado. "What's this? She was supposed to be alone."

It started raining in earnest. The lights went out in the cabin.

Too late they heard running steps, Sorensen screaming. Then gunfire. Heavy automatic fire, a hammering metallic chatter.

Confusion. More automatic gun fire heading west on the road from the cabin, away from them. Scuffles and muffled shouts. A car engine started. The car roared toward them. No lights.

The rain turned hard and cold.

Mason took cover in the shadow of trees at the roadside. He couldn't see the white flame of muzzle flash in the driving rain.

Vehicle coming at him blazing and fast. He leaped off the roadway.

"Wait a minute. This is a movie. I'm in a fucking movie," Mason stuttered to himself as Sorensen's BMW sped past him, lights out. He heard gunfire from behind the cabin. The deputies? Who were they firing at? Who else had been there they didn't know about? Dammit.

Across the road from him a running deputy tripped and fell headlong. Mason raced to his vehicle in pursuit of the car.

"That's her," he shouted. Delgado leaped in, cranking it up to follow the car. Was Sorensen the one shooting? They raced onto the main road. The speedometer read 67 and they were taking the curves on two wheels. Behind them came the wail of sirens, pursuing another vehicle, whoever had been in the cabin with Sorensen.

A Prius suddenly ahead of Mason had the back window wipers and brake lights on. Mason hit the siren hard, screaming down on it, and the Prius pulled over so quickly it ploughed into the ditch.

Just past a curve he came up on a truck and passed it on the narrow two-lane road, swerving back into his lane as spray from an oncoming car hit the windshield almost blinding him. He was going too fast; he saw a curtain of spray ahead, spatter turning into heavy drops..

He braked and the rain hit in sheets, gusts, drops hard and stinging, her car ahead of him throwing up plumes of mist. He couldn't see, and had to slow. The red brake lights flared.

Sorensen's BMW swerved and ended up slewing across the road. Mason tapped the brakes, steering into the skid, hoping it would take him around her.

She had hit a deer. Its front legs shattered the windshield, bouncing the rest of the animal on the roof. The deer landed hard on the highway, Mason veered back into his lane and slid to a stop. Large buck mule deer, over 300 pounds. Its injuries were fatal, blood streaming onto the highway. It tried to get up and the effort made it convulse.

Venetia ground the engine hard to keep going and she was able to get the car out again on the roadway going the opposite direction. The hood and roof of her BMW was caved in, the right front fender chewed up, pressing against the right passenger tire. High, singing noise of metal screeching, shredding the tire right down to the rim. She slewed to a skidding stop.

The driver door swung open and Sorensen ran off the road into the underbrush. Mason went after her. He could hear Delgado stumbling along behind him and more swift-footed deputies crashing through the sage brush and scrub oak on his left and right.

He plowed through the chaparral, thorny branches of scrub oak slashing back at him, showering him with rain off the leaves. He blinked the rain out of his eyes, light-headed, realizing he was breathing too fast and shallow.

The ground was muddy and every step he took the deeper he sank. Mud clumped up on his boots until he felt as though he was trying to run with concrete blocks on his feet. Every step pounded the abscessed tooth.

She was there right in front of him and then she was gone. Had she gone over a cliff? Fallen in a hole? Gone, just gone.

Behind him, Mason heard Delgado huffing, a radio crackling, someone far away yelling. The whole world went still except for the falling rain. Then he smelled her. A faint whiff of perfume drifted through the rain. A deputy put a hand on his arm.

Mason wheeled around, adrenaline flooding his reactions. Time jerked to a stop. Then, in an instant, it jolted forward. The deputy pointed. There was Venetia twenty feet away crouched, a feral creature looking as though she'd just come down from the trees. Blood ran down her face and her arm hung wrong.

Mason took a run at her, slipping and falling, and brought her down. She fought him with all the strength of an alligator, screaming, twisting and buckling out of his grasp. She got her fingers dug in his face, trying to get him to loosen his grip.

He shouldered her down, getting her cuffed up, both of them panting. Blood pumped from his nose.

He gave her head a good twist and ground her face into the mud, snarling. "That's for Ginger."

She screeched, choking on it, "Bastards. You were just lucky."

Mason yanked her to her feet. Her shoulder poked out in a wrong direction. He hoped she was suffering.

Behind him Mason heard a shot from a service weapon. Shouts, flashlights, radios. A deputy had put the deer out of its misery. He wished he could shoot Sorensen and save the city the costs of a trial. Behind him he heard shouting and gunshots and then a silence. Then a cheer went up. Mason stumbled back to the road dragging Sorensen. He saw tan sheriff department uniforms, two prisoners in cuffs, testosterone and adrenaline scenting the air through the pelting rain.

40

Mason was on the phone with Palmer who was still down at the port, winding things up. "Yeah, we got the shipment. Got some of his crew, lot of his records. Missed Yurkov though. LAPD's blaming everybody else. It's a real clusterfuck. He musta got inside warning from one of the customs guys. I gotta run."

"Never mind, Palmer. We got Yurkov up here all nice and cuffed up. Put me on with the Captain." He grinned at Delgado as he said it.

"What? You got Yurkov?" Palmer shouted. "What the fuck?"

"Yeah, you heard me." Mason suddenly felt good enough to do a little jig.

"The Sarge and his deputies up here brought him down. We got Sorensen too. Plus enough weaponry to start a little war."

He heard Palmer shouting the news. The high of the chase and capture was worth all the bullshit. Delgado ambled by, stirring his coffee. Mason couldn't wait to begin taking Venetia Sorensen apart.

The Sarge with Kern County gloated over and over that he and his boys had been the ones to pull Yurkov in. Eight law enforcement departments and the Feds had failed to get Yurkov and Koslov, and his deputies now had bragging rights for the collar of an internationally sought criminal operation. Mason grinned as the Sarge flipped through the first pages of Yurkov's file, slapping the side of his head. And this was just the scum on top of the septic tank.

He thought of Santa Monica's money scene, the new Silicon Beach. Just the place for an extremist sports figure like Sorensen to meet a guy like Yurkov with spare money. What motivated women to like bad boys? He didn't get it.

By then Fredericks had arrived. She greeted them at the substation, pissed, arms akimbo.

"You didn't call me, you bastards," she complained.

"You were hot to go on the bust. Remember? We thought this was going to be a routine pick up on Sorensen," Mason said, heading off the worst of her mouth.

Sorensen had lawyered up immediately and sat mutinously silent all the way back to Santa Monica. She wasn't even hurt badly in the run-in with the deer. Her lawyer was already working up a charge of police brutality against Mason for the struggle in which he'd taken her down. She claimed she was suffering internal injuries, every scrape and bruise a major complaint.

Mason got her in an interview room with her lawyer early the next morning. Sorensen was now a woman stripped down to the bone, all her titles and degrees and prestige meaningless in the damp-concrete smell of the Santa Monica jail. She'd tried to bribe a jailer to find out what had happened to the parrot. The parrot might be the only creature she'd ever loved. Her eyes were filled with rage—not remorse, not self-pity— primal rage. She glared at him, teeth bared, seeing the future without the security of money, the weekends at the W, the house, the prestige wardrobe. She hadn't yet acknowledged to herself that she might spend a long time in prison. Mason hoped he'd be there when it finally hit her.

At Mason's first question, she jumped at him across the table, handcuffs and shackles rattling, which brought her up sharply. She tried to spit at him and the spittle landed on the table between them. He handed her a tissue.

"Wipe that up. I just want to know one thing. How did you expect not to get caught?"

One thing that kept Mason smiling was that he finally had good news to tell Judy Klepper. One guy on Yurkov's carjacker crew had led to another. Somebody was willing to roll over for a deal. He gave up his buddy, the one who had pulled Andy Klepper out of the car and cracked his head on the pavement. Claimed the guy had kept a souvenir from Klepper's car. He burned to get his hands on him. He called Loretta Swinson next to update her on Sorensen's role in her sister's death. She didn't seem surprised. In fact, he was the one who was surprised that she sounded so upbeat.

Mason and Delgado got major credit for pulling in Yurkov at the debriefing for last night's operation. Mason tried for modesty and probably failed. As the meeting broke up, Mason saw Gomez talking to a thin LAPD officer who'd been part of the bust. They stood in a corner outside the conference room, away from all the others. Gomez loomed over her like a gorilla. This must be his heartthrob. She was obviously giving him the brushoff and he wasn't having it. One of the guys went over and put his hand on Gomez' arm. Gomez turned with a look of menace and saw all the faces turned in his direction. His fist went down. He turned on his heel and marched away, leaving her white-faced and shaking. Palmer went over to talk to her. Wilson went after Gomez.

Gomez had just crossed the line.

Later that day Mason sat down amid the paper clutter of Wozinski's office, flicking a finger through a pile of Excel spreadsheets on his desk, his tooth gone quiet for the moment.

"We're thinking it was easy for Sorensen because everybody over at Kensington Industries was focused on the negotiations for the big property sale and cashing in. She cut out the real people who could look at a financial and know what they were seeing. Like somehow the accounting department never got copies. Hunh? I don't know much about money, but how could that be?"

Wozinski jammed his glasses up on his nose. "Smart people like Knight and all the other MBAs over there think they're too smart to get cheated. It makes me laugh."

Ginger and Rhys stood outside the front doors of Kensington Industries early the next day, a light drizzle falling. He'd hustled her outside away from the chaos, fearing she might make a scene.

"Oh, Ginger," he sighed. "Please, don't be like that. It's a financial decision." He looked tired, his eyes ringed with fatigue.

"I didn't even hear it from you. I had to read it in the paper." She thrust a local newspaper in his face and he stepped backward. "That is so chickenshit not to tell me."

"I was going to tell you today."

Ginger felt like hitting him. "Why? I don't get it. Is it because Venetia got away with the capital reserve account? I had to read that in the paper too. Dammit, Rhys. I bet you even have insurance for things like that?"

"We had insurance on her, of course. The reserve account can be recovered."

Ginger's face blazed with heat, "So you didn't even lose any money and you're still going to close the school? You could afford to fund it yourself until the seniors graduate, couldn't you? You could find another location, somebody else to run it. You'd just let it die, everything your grandfather wanted?"

She heard herself wail, drawing the attention of a group of secretaries who were returning from lunch. "The rest of them can find other schools, but it matters to the juniors and seniors. You know that. And what will the kids on scholarship do? Don't you think you owe it to some of those kids who've been there since freshmen year?"

"We have a buyer for KI so we'll be headquartering somewhere other than Santa Monica. The land package was one of the selling points of the deal."

"What? It's not a school anymore. It's a land package now." She sank down on a low stone wall and pulled the head off a flower. "So this will make you a lot richer?"

"If you want to look at it that way..." he shrugged. "You know the money doesn't matter to me."

"You say! That's what you say. That's because you have all the money in the world. What do you need more money for, Rhys? What else can you possibly buy? What else do you need?"

He said urgently, sitting down next to her. "I need you, Ginger. Please. Let's get married."

She threw off the hand he'd put on her arm. "What about all the teachers?"

"We'll give the teachers a handsome severance package," he said soothingly.

"It's not going to be that easy for some of them to find another job. You know that."

"We'll give them excellent recommendations."

"I know, but there just aren't that many jobs around." She was out of a job as well. One more time. "And the kids?"

"We'll help them find other schools. Not so loud. Please, Ginger."

"That Raymond kid, he's fragile." She named some others she'd come to know and care about as she paced around. "Some of them are real misfits. They just can't walk into another school."

Rhys jammed his hands in his pockets and paced on the sidewalk. "I can't right every wrong in the world, Ginger."

"But you must have known. I was set up to fail. You must have known! These kinds of deals take months, years even." She couldn't even look at him and spoke with her eyes shut.

"We were in negotiations, Ginger."

"For how long? And who was doing the negotiating? You? You knew," she guessed. "You and Knight. That woman almost killed me, Rhys. You know Venetia was the one who shut me in there. No matter whether they can prove it or not. How could you do this, Rhys? All for money."

"Not just for myself, Ginger. Please understand. It's for Caroline too. And for the company. For the good of a lot of people who have jobs and a stake in Kensington Industries."

"You mean the investors." Ginger couldn't stand looking at him any longer. Mason had hinted the Kensingtons would look out for themselves. And Mason had been right.

41

A hard lump had formed on Mason's jaw and his face was swollen. He hadn't slept because there was too much work tying up all the loose ends but it was worth the fatigue to finally have Sorensen pinned. He was at the door of the dentist's office at 8:00 a.m. the next day, waiting for him to open. He called in and explained why he wasn't at the station doing his part to wind the case up.

"Thought you might like to know," Delgado said, a note of glee in his rough voice. "Sorensen's been singing like a little tweety bird once she figured out that Yurkov was going to roll over on her. She saying Doris was the one who set everything up. She says she has proof. When she took over the school, she figured out Doris was pilfering and caught her at it. So Doris talked her into going into business with her."

Mason gave a hoot of disbelief. "And you believe her?"

"She says she has proof. She kept it just in case. Wozinski's talking to her now."

"I'll believe it when I see it."

"Something else. You remember ordering whatever security tapes we could get for the night of Arnold's murder? We got a good shot of Yurkov going into the 7-11 on Wilshire at 12:28. His buddy Koslov is waiting for him in Arnold's car."

"Good," Mason said. "That nails it, along with the kids on the school bus."

The news brought a smile and prolonged the high of the chase and capture. First was the dentist. He couldn't avoid it any longer.

Delgado made a call when Mason hung up.

It only took Ginger ten minutes to drive over to the address in Ocean Park. Both she and Mason went to Dr. Ellis because he was liberal with the laughing gas. She found Mason just as he was being called in by the nurse. He turned to look at her, his expression of misery that of a sick dog at the vet's. His face lifted in surprise as he rose to his feet.

"Delgado told me you were here," she said smiling. "Mason, I was so stupid. You remember what you said, the Beatles song?"

He took her outstretched hand and held it to his swollen face. His tooth suddenly felt better. The problems between them that never seemed to have any solution fell away. He would make it work. It had to work. The certainty came to him that he could do it.

"I was stupid too. Will you be here when they're done with me?" he said hopefully. "Please."

"I'll be here."

This was not the first time Loretta Swinson and her good friend Billie had gone through the shoeboxes filled with plastic cards. Doris had stored them with Billie some time ago and neither of them had thought about them until Billie was cleaning out closets and came across the letter from Doris with all the instructions. The letter gave both of them a good cry. There had been a lot of tears and whispered conversations since in Loretta's overheated box of an apartment. Billie got out to the stores more than Loretta did and recognized the prepaid gift cards you could buy, some of them MasterCard and Visa. They were surprised you could buy them in such huge denominations. There were also bundles of cash, twenties and fifties that Doris had taken every time a cashier had asked her if she wanted cash back with her purchases. It had mounted up over the years.

"I knew she'd never leave you in the lurch," Billie said, a marshmallow moustache of hot chocolate decorating her upper lip.

"I'm so pleased there's enough for both of us," Loretta said, shifting in her chair to ease the pain in her shoulders. "We can buy into that over-55 place that Doris always talked about, the one with the nursing home right there, if I ever needed it. They'll take care of us the rest of our lives! Oh, Billie, Doris thought of everything, didn't she? She was so good to me—to both of us. It's so sad she couldn't be here to share it. You know what the police said. That Doris was an embezzler? That can't be true, can it?" Loretta said. Her white boucle sweater slipped off her shoulder and Billie jumped up to adjust it.

"No, no, of course not," Billie assured her.

"She was just careful with money and didn't trust banks, don't you think? Doris never spent money on things like jewels and cars and foolish things like Dr. Sorensen did. That Dr. Sorensen was horrible to Doris, all that screaming and yelling at her, and not paying her what she was worth. I'm glad they're going to put her in prison. Still, I feel bad not telling the Monsignor about these cards," Loretta whispered.

"No, no, remember Doris warned us about that," Billie said sternly. "We can't tell anybody. Especially those nice policemen. She told us how careful we had to be. They'll be watching us if we spend any big money."

"Isn't it fun, all these little trips we're taking to cash in the cards?" Loretta said, her face glowing. "I just love it."

"I always wanted to see the rest of California," Billie said, helping herself to another cookie.

"Doris was so good to us," Loretta repeated with a small smile. "And so good with money. God wouldn't want me to suffer and not have the things I need. You too, Billie. We know God wouldn't want that."

The End

Thank you for reading *A Very Private High School*

Read previous Dave Mason mystery novels in either eBook format or paperback version at:

(2013) *On Behalf of the Family*: http://www.amazon.com/ ebook/dp/B00I82BFVK/
(2012) *Rip-Off*: http://www.amazon.com/ ebook/dp/ B007WTYGI4/
(2011) *No Dice*: http://www.amazon.com/ ebook/dp/ B00BYDMNN4/

℘

Payback, the debut of a second series featuring Dex Stafford, Kern County Sheriff's Homicide Detective is also available at:
http://www.amazon.com/ ebook/dp/B00BS8F5OY/

Website: http://marpreston.com
Facebook Author Page: https://www.facebook.com/ pages/Mar-Preston/136299239777273
Twitter: Author Mar Preston

I invite you to email me at marpreston@frazmtn.com

Made in the USA
San Bernardino, CA
03 July 2015